His Fourth Date

HAMMOND FAMILY FARM ROMANCE, BOOK 4

LIZ ISAACSON

# One

Travis Thatcher walked into the house where Chris Hammond lived, the scent of bacon and basil meeting his nose. "Just me," he said.

The older gentleman came out of the kitchen, which sat off to the left of the front door, near the back of the house. Chris smiled, his bright eyes showing Travis that even brown eyes could shine like stars. "There you are," he said, hobbling slightly toward him. He wore a black apron tied around his waist, with a blue golf shirt and a pair of shorts.

Travis couldn't help smiling at the man. "You look like one of your mutual funds had a very good night."

Chris laughed as Travis took off his cowboy hat and hung it on the rack beside the door. The blessed air conditioning reminded him that some people worked without sweating all day. He honestly didn't mind the weather he had to put up with here in Colorado, because anything was better than living in the city.

"Come see," Chris said, turning to go back into the kitchen. Travis followed him, noting the man's desk in the living room still overflowed with papers. Gray, his son, had told Travis that his father had run their family company for decades, and even after he'd retired, he couldn't get rid of some things.

He loved investing, any talk of stocks, bonds, holdings, accounts. He took risks because he was almost eighty-seven years old, and why shouldn't he? He'd been a billionaire since birth, and Travis loved the old man as if he were his own father.

"It's HMC," Chris said, indicating the laptop on the kitchen table. "Didn't I tell you to buy up our stock? I knew they were going to split it. I just knew it."

Travis glanced at Chris and then the laptop. He'd made the text bigger, so Travis didn't even have to get that close to see it. "So now I own twice as much as I used to."

Chris laughed again. "I almost have the sandwiches ready." He bustled back into the kitchen, where the sizzling sound of something frying met Travis's ears. He sat at the table while Chris talked. "Hunter didn't tell me. I know you're thinking that."

"It's a valid thought," Travis said, peering closer at the screen. "It's already going up." Investing in HMC had been a good thing, and while Travis was good with numbers, he couldn't math that fast.

"Boone and Matt are coming," Chris said. "Can you put that on the desk? I don't have room otherwise."

"Sure." Travis watched the decimals tick up, then down, then fly up for another few seconds. "So what next?" He stood and closed the laptop. After picking it up, he started toward the desk. "Are you going to sell?"

"Not yet," he said, flipping over a grilled cheese sandwich. This wouldn't be just any grilled cheese though. Chris always doctored them up with things Travis had never thought to pair together. "I think the stock will go higher as soon as Hunter announces the new shrink foam." Chris grinned like it was the money he cared about.

Travis knew it wasn't. The man hadn't had to live a day of his life without what he wanted and needed. Chris's joy came from experiencing his children and grandchildren achieving great things, and it touched Travis's heart in a way that reminded him of his own single status.

No children, and no girlfriend since moving to Colorado. From there, his thoughts immediately moved to Poppy Harris, the woman who lived on and ran the farm next door. She had an eleven-year-old son named Steele, and Travis had done his darnedest to help her over the past several months. She didn't seem to want his help, and he could admit he hadn't told her much about himself or why it was so dang easy to help her.

The only people who truly knew that he also had over a billion dollars in the bank was Chris and Gray Hammond. Elise too, of course, and Travis wanted to keep that number as small as possible.

The front door opened as Chris said, "These are apple-bacon grilled cheese sandwiches." He put one on a plate and picked up a big chef's knife to cut it into triangles. "With basil dipping aioli."

"...I'm just saying, it would be fun," Boone said, his voice always full of laughter and joy. Travis liked the man a whole lot, because while he worked hard and did amazing things with their therapy horses, he was always the life of the party too.

In many ways, Travis wished he could be more like Boone. The man said whatever was on his mind, to anyone. He didn't hold back in showing his happiness—or his heartache. He felt things, and he felt them deeply.

"A motorcycle is a death trap," Cosette, his fiancé of only eight days, said. "Not fun."

The darker version of Boone came inside and closed the door too. Matt Whettstein, his brother, chuckled and said, "I kind of agree with Cosette."

"Traitor," Boone boomed. He grinned at Travis and clapped him on the shoulder. "Howdy, Trav."

"Hey, Boone." Travis smiled, because no one could look at Boone while he was smiling and not feel the pure radiance from him. Travis was a bit surprised he'd gotten the formal, polished, precise Cosette Brian to even go out with him, and he wondered—not for the first time—if he should ask Boone for some tips when it came to Poppy.

"If you get a motorcycle," Matt said, also arriving at the island in the kitchen where everyone else stood. "Then Keith will want to ride it. And Britt. Then I'm going to be the bad guy who won't let her."

"It's *such* a great deal," Boone said.

Cosette looked up from her phone, and as usual, she wore a pretty flowery dress, perfect makeup, and this time, a smile. "Too bad," she said in a voice that didn't indicate she thought anything was bad. "Raven said the bike sold already." She smacked her lips and shook her head in mock disappointment.

Matt and Chris chuckled while Boone blinked at his fiancé. "You think this is so funny," he said, teasing her. He swooped his arms around her, the two of them laughing, and Travis couldn't help basking in their love.

He couldn't remember the last time he'd been in love with a woman. Maybe he never had been, though he'd been married briefly and then had dated Jenni for a long, long time. She'd been so focused on her career, and truth be told, so had he. The relationship was so they didn't have to eat alone at night, and he could watch her cat while she traveled for work.

"Where's Gloria?" Travis asked Matt, who nodded a silent hello while Boone and Cosette settled down.

"The sandwiches are done," Chris said. "Someone take this one and eat it."

"Don't have to ask me twice," Boone said, claiming the already-cut sandwich before anyone else could even reach for it.

Chris turned back to the stove to get more out of the pan, and Matt said, "She's tired today, so I made her go home to take a nap."

"When is she due again?" Travis asked, picking up a plate and handing it to Matt. He stood around the island, closer to the stove, and he got the next sandwich.

"Uh, let's see," Matt said. "August twenty-fourth." He smiled at Travis, who took the next sandwich and handed the plate to Cosette. The two of them joined Boone at the kitchen table, and Travis waited for Chris to dish up the last two sandwiches. Then they joined everyone at the table too.

"Molly should be having her baby next week," Chris said, his voice once again filled with pride and joy.

"I can't believe they didn't find out what they're having," Cosette said.

"It's a baby, baby," Boone said with a grin. "I know it won't be a chicken." He laughed, and Travis couldn't help joining him. Cosette just rolled her eyes, though she did smile.

"Did you find out with Gerty?" Cosette said. Travis dipped the corner of his sandwich in the basil sauce and took a bite. Salty bacon, sweet apple, and gooey cheese. With the basil, this sandwich was perfection.

"Yes," Boone said. "Nikki wanted to decorate the nursery. We had so much pink stuff, it was unbelievable." He spoke easily of his deceased wife, his smile only growing fonder and wider.

Sitting there with the four of them, and thinking of Molly and Hunter Hammond starting their family in just a few short days, Travis determined he needed to do something more than try to discover himself. He'd left his big-wig finance job in the city and come west, where he'd found this farm and this job to be a safe haven for him.

He'd learned who he was beneath the shadows of the huge Rocky Mountains, and he knew his place with the Lord.

Now, he needed to find someone to share his life with. Someone who could tease him the way Cosette did Boone, and someone who could help him continue to try to improve every single day the way Molly did for Hunter.

"So," he said in a lull in the conversation. "Has anyone ever gone to the Lazy Summer Days in town?" He put the last bite of his sandwich in his mouth and looked up. Boone and Cosette shook their heads, but Matt and Chris had sort of frozen.

"What?" Travis asked.

Matt cleared his throat. "You know what the Lazy Summer Days is, right?"

"Clearly not," Travis said, already reaching for his phone. "I saw a poster in the window at the grocery store a couple of days ago. It said there were activities and movies in the park."

"Yeah," Matt said. "For couples. It's a dating event."

Travis looked up from his phone, his search forgotten. "Dating event?"

Matt shifted and cleared his throat again. "It's for like, you know, a summer girlfriend. You sign up, and the first event is speed-dating. Hopefully, you find someone, and then you...spend the summer with them, doing all these 'activities' and going to movies in the park." He exchanged a glance with his brother.

Travis wasn't sure how that was bad. "Don't people keep going out after summer ends?"

"Sure," Matt said easily. "I just—well, usually the people who do it are in their twenties. I went the first summer I got hired on here with Gray, while he went up to Coral Canyon. I was one of the older men there."

"You went to that?" Boone asked, chortling.

Travis knew then that should he choose to go, he would not be telling Boone. Cosette whacked him in the chest and said, "Stop it." She looked at Travis, her deep, green eyes partly worried and partly compassionate. She'd always been kind to him, if professional, and Travis did like her.

"That was a long time ago, Matt," she said, dropping her eyes to her phone. "It says here that there are age ranges. Twenty-one to twenty-nine. Thirty to thirty-four.

Thirty-five to thirty-nine." She paused and looked at Travis.

"Keep goin'," he said, his voice almost a growl.

"Forty to forty-four, forty-five to fifty." She read out ages all the way to sixty-five, and then said, "And sixty-six-plus." She looked at Matt and Boone and Chris. "So even Chris could sign up should he want to see about finding someone special again."

Chris looked horrified at the thought, and everyone at the table chuckled. Cosette said, "So it's for everyone." She cut a look at Travis again. "Love can be found at any age, anywhere."

Travis gave her a nod and stood up. He picked up his plate and then gathered everyone else's, taking them all into the kitchen. "Well," he said. "I best be gettin' back to work."

"The sign-up date ends tomorrow," Cosette said. "The speed-dating event is this weekend." She had to be talking to him, and Travis's face heated.

"All right," he said, neither committing to signing up nor saying he wasn't going to.

———

THE FOLLOWING EVENING, Travis sighed as he sat in front of his computer. The sign-up form for the Lazy Summer Days already open. It had been open since he'd returned home last night, and he'd been stewing about signing up for over twenty-four hours now.

He looked at the screen, his fingers acting almost of their own accord. His name got entered, then his phone number, and email. Before he knew it, his mouse hovered over the submit button, and then he clicked on it.

A breath of air whooshed out of his lungs, and Travis jumped to his feet. He backed up a couple of steps, staring at the computer screen like he'd just committed a heinous crime. He turned away and took a breath.

"No," he said. "It's time, Trav. Time to take the next step in your life." He felt like he'd been on quite the journey in the past few years, and finding a girlfriend who could become a wife was simply the next, natural thing for him.

So it was that Travis showed up at the high school gymnasium the following evening. He'd arrived early, but he wasn't the first person there. After he'd watched the fifth or sixth man walk through the doors, he gathered his courage close and unbuckled his seat belt. No one had been much younger than him, because he'd signed up for the forty-to-forty-four age group of men.

He'd been emailed a time for his speed-dating event, and he still had ten minutes to spare. He walked the short distance to the steps, up them, and through the door without panicking or turning back.

Inside, lines of men waited to be checked-in, but everything ran smoothly. Voices filled the air, but Travis didn't talk to anyone. Nerves ran through him, and he wasn't the only one. It felt like someone had electrified the oxygen in the high school, and then Travis gave a younger man his name.

His got checked off, and he took a number from the guy. "That's your table number," he explained. "In the gym, you'll find a matching one. The ladies are moving tonight." He smiled like this speed-dating event was something Travis should be thrilled to attend.

He managed to smile back, looked at his twenty-eight, and tucked it into his front jeans pocket. Yes, he'd worn jeans, but he'd paired those with a really great blue and yellow shirt. Well, really great according to Vivian, his sister. He'd called her about tonight's activity, and with the help of the camera on his phone, she'd gone through his closet with him an hour ago.

He found his table easily and sat down. Glancing left and right, he saw men his own age stretching in both directions. He barely had time to wonder how there could be so many singles his age in this area before a man stepped over to the microphone up on the stage and started speaking.

"All right, gentlemen," he said. "Our ladies are getting debriefed right now, and then we'll open the doors and let them in." He beamed out his happiness at all of them, and Travis couldn't help searching for a wedding ring on his hand. Sure enough, this guy was already married.

Travis cleared his throat as someone put a bottle of

water on his table. He practically lunged for it while the guy on the stage went over the rules. Six-minute rounds. Bells ringing. Women moving.

Travis was the one who suddenly needed to move, and move now. Before he could get up and admit he'd made a terrible mistake, the first bell rang, and the doors in front of him opened.

# Two

POPPY HARRIS LOITERED NEAR THE BACK OF THE group of women now entering the gymnasium. She had an assigned seat, and she didn't need six minutes to know if she liked a man or not. In fact, that was about five minutes too long, and she was fine to let the other, more eager, women get into position first.

She'd opted into the male thirty-five to thirty-nine age range, as well as the forty to forty-four. She'd already been doing this speed dating thing for an hour, and she'd struck out spectacularly.

Ten dates, and not a single man in her age range had asked for her number. Even if they had, Poppy wouldn't have given it to them. One of her dates had looked to be the same age as Steele, and Poppy didn't need two eleven-year-olds to mother, thank you very much.

These were men five to nine years older than her,

which was still an acceptable range in her book. Other than Eli, her ex-boyfriend, her dating playbook was quite empty, and Poppy had decided she needed to do something about that.

Elora had told her about this Lazy Summer Days event, not that Poppy hadn't known about it. The town of Ivory Peaks had been running it for a lot longer than just this year. She'd never attended, though her sister swore by the event. Elora had met her husband a few summers ago, and she'd managed to get the man to marry her and do things the right way.

Of course. Elora was the younger sister, but she was the far superior daughter.

Poppy pushed her perfect sibling from her mind, reminding herself that she had a brother who seemed to need to move home every other year. No one was perfect, and she didn't have time right now to dwell on all the ways she needed to improve.

She would meet ten more men, and hopefully one of them would become the love of her life, the way Briggs had for Elora.

She went to her left, because she knew where station twenty-five sat. She'd rotated through it an hour ago. Now, she'd start there. She drew in a deep breath and smoothed down her errant curls as the woman in front of her veered toward table twenty-six, leaving her view clear of table twenty-five.

A man she didn't recognize sat there, looking anxious.

Poppy knew the feeling, as her stomach tried to vacate her body while her feet kept moving toward him. "Hello," she said just as the bell rang.

"Six minutes," the man up on the stage said. The man at the table didn't stand, not like Twenty-Six had to meet the blonde who'd gone his way. Poppy gave her guy a strike, but kept her smile stitched in place. "Your first date starts now!"

She had no idea how the caller could sound so excited, but he had. With several more age ranges to go, she hoped he had plenty of coffee or a whole case of energy drinks nearby. She'd consumed four slices of turkey from the deli and a Red Bull before making the drive to this high school gym a couple of hours ago, and as she sat down, she cleared her throat nervously.

"I'm Poppy Harris."

"Dwayne Rush." He smiled at her and extended his hand. He wore a cowboy hat, but he clearly didn't work outside. His hands looked like he'd just gotten a manicure, and his skin felt softer than hers. "It's great to meet you."

"You too." She pulled her hand away from his. "So, Dwayne, what do you do?" She could really use a chef or a veterinarian, but Poppy had told herself to be open-minded. She couldn't afford to be picky about who she went out with, and Dwayne was good-looking in a non-cowboy kind of way.

It really was a shame her attraction to true cowboys

was so strong, because she'd never met one who could be tamed enough to settle down. At least not by her.

*What about Travis?* she asked herself as Dwayne said, "I run the cellphone store in town," like he'd single-handedly delivered Christmas gifts to all needy people in the state of Colorado. "What about you?"

"I run a farm," Poppy said as pleasantly as she could. *Two strikes* ran through her mind, though she wasn't sure why. If she ended up marrying Dwayne, she could eliminate a very expensive bill from her long list of them.

The conversation stalled, and Poppy struck Dwayne right on out. She made it through the six minutes, and with seconds to spare, Dwayne asked, "Do you think I could get your number?" He wore hope in his bright blue eyes, and Poppy could admit that pleasure and satisfaction filled her.

"Sure," she said, and she filled out the paper with her name on it and handed it to him. He gazed at it, truly seeming surprised, and he did stand to shake her hand this time.

"Move to the next station," the caller on the stage bellowed into the mic. "You have thirty seconds until your second date begins."

Poppy offered another smile to Dwayne before she turned her attention to Twenty-Six. He was still talking to the blonde. Neither of them seemed to have heard the man on the stage, and Blondie tipped her head back and sent gut-laughter toward the ceiling. The man across from her laughed too, and Poppy stood there awkwardly.

She couldn't go back to her seat, because someone else had already taken it. In the three-foot space between tables, she barely fit, and she towered over both people *still* talking.

"You're supposed to switch," she said. Only a moment later, the microphone squealed, and Blondie finally looked toward the stage.

"Oh," she said, giggling as she got to her feet. "Looks like we're supposed to change."

"Your second date starts now."

She wrote her number on the slip of paper with her name printed on it, tucked it in the man's pocket and moved over to the next station. Poppy rolled her eyes as the guy watched her, completely oblivious to his next date.

Poppy sat in the now-vacated chair and pulled out her phone. She'd taken three breaths before the man across from her sat down. He cleared his throat. "Sorry about that."

"Yeah," Poppy said without looking up. "You know, for future reference." She did raise her head from her mobile social media. "If you're that interested, you can ask the woman to leave with you right then. Then the whole station is taken out of play, and I would've just moved down to that guy."

She hooked her thumb to the right, but she didn't look away from Mister Smitten.

"Really?" He looked over to the next table, where Blondie let loose with another hysterical round of laughter. *Of all the luck*, Poppy thought. Of course she'd get behind the perkiest, funniest woman at the speed dating event.

She already battled a demon who told her she was dull and drab, and following Blondie around for the next hour wasn't going to help one bit.

"Yeah," she said. "But you have to do it in that thirty seconds. Because if you go now, then the whole rotation is off."

"Maybe I could ask her after this round," he said, looking at Poppy with extreme hope. "Then, this station would be gone."

"And then the one past her won't have anyone. Because I haven't gone out with that guy yet." She shook her head. "Nope. You had to ask her and leave before I sat down here and she sat down there." She went back to her phone. "It's fine with me. I have a couple of comments to leave anyway."

He hadn't introduced himself, and Poppy wasn't about to give him her name. The six minutes passed fast enough, and the bell rang. "Great to meet you," she said as pleasantly as she could, getting to her feet and reminding herself that Dwayne had asked for her number.

*Thirty seconds. Third date beginning...now!*

"Hello, Sal," she said, smiling at the man who'd once sold her some...overripe fish. She'd driven right back to the butcher shop and told him so, and thankfully, he did think the customer was right. She'd gotten something else for dinner, but of course Steele didn't eat it. The boy only ate dino nuggets and tater tots, boxed macaroni and cheese, and cold cereal.

Poppy supposed that could've been a commentary on her parenting skills—and her lack of cooking skills—but her son hadn't died yet.

"Poppy," he said, smiling at her. "How were those pork chops?" And date three would be six minutes of meat talk.

Ivory Peaks wasn't that big of a place, and Poppy understood she'd likely run into some men she knew at this event. She never looked down the line to see who came next, because that was half the fun of speed dating.

"Thirty seconds to switch."

"Good luck tonight, Sal," she said as she stood up.

"You too," he said, glancing to Poppy's next station and then toward his next date. "And come get that beef roast on Monday. I'll have it wrapped for you."

"I will." She smiled and turned toward station twenty-eight. The man there met her eyes, shock immediately entering his.

Then Travis Thatcher jumped to his feet, knocking the table in front of him a foot or two forward. "Poppy," he said, his voice low and sexy.

"No," she said out loud, but it wasn't to him. It was for herself. His voice was *not* sexy.

Except that it one-hundred percent was.

"I'm sorry?" he asked.

"Nothing," she said, shaking away her surprise. She wanted to say something else, but nothing came to mind.

Travis gave a nervous chuckle, and she realized a flush had worked its way into his face. "I, uh, haven't ever done this before."

"The speed dating?" she asked.

"Yeah."

"Me either." She moved toward the chair and pulled it out a little further. "How's it going?"

"Not great," he said as he retook his seat. He smiled at her from across the table, his big, rough hands clasping together. "You?"

"Not as bad as last time," she said.

His smile faded slightly. "I thought you said you hadn't done this."

"Before this year," she said, clarifying. "I signed up for two age groups. This one, and the one before it. The younger guys."

"Ah, I see."

"How old are you?" she asked, realizing how blunt she sounded. "I mean, that was rude. Sorry." She gave a light laugh. "I actually belong in the younger group, but I figured someone who was forty-four was still only nine years older than me." She shrugged, another horrible giggle coming from her mouth.

Travis's smile brightened again. "I'm forty-two," he

said. "And I'm not from here—or any cowboy-dominated region—but my mother did teach me some manners. I won't ask how old you are."

Poppy grinned at him, surprised at how easy he was to talk to. He'd always been fun to be around, and she was the one who'd put up bars and barriers between them. He'd taken her displeasure at him paying her mortgage, and she swallowed just thinking about it.

"Listen," she said, leaning her elbows onto the table and inching closer to him. She told herself it wasn't because his cologne did strange things to her pulse. "I want to apologize for making a big deal about...." She cleared her throat. "My mortgage payment."

"I did say I was sorry for paying it," he said. "I was just trying to help."

"It did help," she said. She wasn't sure why the two words she needed to say always stuck in her throat. "Thank you."

Travis tilted his head to the side, his dark brown cowboy hat perched so deliciously on his head. He wore a full beard, the darkness of it showing some gray and making his white teeth shine in the bright overhead lights.

"That seemed hard for you to say," he said.

"It is," she admitted, feeling one of her walls crumble to the ground. "I...can I tell you something?"

"I wish you would." He grinned at her, and Poppy realized he was flirting with her. Travis Thatcher. Flirting.

She blinked out of the surprise—this cowboy had

plenty of them to throw at her—and said, "It's hard for me to thank people. I'm working on it."

"Why is it hard to tell someone thank you?"

"It just is," she said. "See, I've had to do everything myself for so long, and I hate feeling like I can't do something. I hate requiring help."

"Everyone needs help sometimes," he said.

"True," she said. "My sister says I need to swallow my pride and just let people in."

He leaned closer, a glint in those gorgeous eyes that reminded her of the color of chocolate mousse. "You've let me come help you. I heard you tell Gray and Elise thank you. I listened as he gushed over how helpful Cody was up in the hay loft."

Poppy swallowed, because he wasn't wrong. "Maybe it's just you then."

"Why me?"

"You make me nervous," she admitted.

His eyebrows went up. "I do?"

"Yes." She pulled her arms back and folded her arms as she leaned against the back of the uncomfortable chair. "Happy?"

"Not at all, Miss Harris," he drawled.

"If you're not a cowboy, where are you from?" she asked, the question a clear challenge.

"Raleigh," he said. "You?"

"What makes you think I'm not from right here in Colorado?"

"I didn't say you were from somewhere else. I just asked where you were from." He could hold his own with her, and that made him so much more attractive to Poppy than he already was.

Her pulse pumped out an extra beat, and a certain sense of instability flowed through her. "I'm from Laramie," she said.

He nodded. "Why'd you move here?"

"I came with my boyfriend," she said. "We were to live and work on the farm where I still am."

Travis simply blinked, no judgment filled his face. "I moved here from New York City. I worked in investment banking there."

"No wonder you could find out my private financial information so easily."

He chuckled and shook his head. "It wasn't like that."

"You still haven't told me how you figured out where I bank and how to pay your money onto my past-due mortgage." She raised her eyebrows, wondering if he found her even slightly attractive. She'd been thinking about him for weeks and months, and she really wanted to go out with him again.

"Time's up!" the man screeched into the microphone, and Poppy flinched.

Travis got to his feet while the guy said they had thirty seconds to move. "Hey," he said "What do you think about us getting out of here and continuing to talk somewhere else?" He swallowed visibly, his expression filled with anxiety and hope at the same time.

Numbness flooded Poppy, and she couldn't make sense of his words or her thoughts.

"We could go to dinner somewhere. I'll tell you how I figured out where your mortgage was." Travis glanced to the woman who would be his next date, but Poppy couldn't look away from him. "I guess this is something we can do, but the clock is ticking."

Yes, it was. Every tick seemed to take a very long time, and Poppy couldn't get her voice to work.

Another chuckle, and Travis's eyes bored into hers. "Poppy?" he asked. "What do you think?"

# Three

TRAVIS HAD NO IDEA HOW LONG A SECOND could be until that moment. He knew he didn't want to sit down with the woman waiting to slide into the seat where Poppy still sat. He wanted to make an executive decision and opt out of the next date whether Poppy said yes or not. He couldn't really do that, as then his table would be empty. There'd be too many women and not enough men.

His stomach rolled as Poppy got to her feet. She shook off the shroud she'd disappeared behind, and when her eyes met Travis's again, she said, "I'd love to go to dinner with you."

Relief like he'd never known cascaded over him, and Travis let it all come out in an exhale and a laugh. "Great." He patted his back pocket for his wallet and swept his phone off the table in front of him. "I think I have to check out with someone...." He looked at the woman standing there, waiting for her date with him.

She pointed toward the stage. "You sign out with Veronica," she said. She faced him and Poppy again, looking between them. Travis didn't like that, but he didn't know the woman. "Hello, Poppy."

"Evening, Bonnie." Poppy didn't seem as enthused to be leaving with Travis now, but he put his hand on the small of her back and guided her around the still-staring Bonnie. The man on the mic yelled that it was time to start the next date, and Travis relaxed even more when he saw he and Poppy weren't the only couple leaving early.

"Who is that?" he asked in a low voice once they'd left Bonnie far behind.

"Bonnie Mason," Poppy said. "She's only been divorced for five or six months." She looked behind her, but Travis kept his eyes on the check-out table. "I'm surprised she's here, and she aged down. She's almost fifty if she's a day."

Travis chuckled for some reason, and Poppy's gaze landed on the side of his face. "You don't like her much?" He looked at Poppy too, those dark blue eyes making his stomach tap dance this time. His attraction to this woman had always been off-the-charts, and he couldn't quite believe she'd said yes to dinner.

"I like her fine," she said. "She's the postmaster, so she sees everyone every single day. She'll have told the entire population of Ivory Peaks about us by noon tomorrow."

Travis grinned and ducked his head, cutting off his view of the pretty Poppy Harris as he did. "Surely some people get their mail after work."

She giggled, and Travis reached for her hand. He slipped his fingers between hers, and she silenced. "Is this okay?" He didn't want to release her, but he would if he had to. Current ran from her body into his, and Travis warmed from head to toe from it.

"It's fine," Poppy said, but her voice sounded strangled.

He stepped up to the table and said, "I'm Travis Thatcher, and we're leaving," indicating Poppy at his side.

"Sign here," the woman at the table said, and Travis had to release Poppy's hand to do so. "Number?" The woman held out her hand, and Poppy put the number twenty-eight in her palm. A couple of check marks later, Veronica smiled at them both and said, "Have a great evening, you two." It sounded fairly suggestive to Travis, who experienced a nearly crippling bout of panic as he faced the exit.

What in the world were him and Poppy going to talk about? Their conversations over the past nine months had not gone well. Not a single one of them. He thought about her day and night. He'd only wanted to help her, not buy his way into her heart.

He swallowed as they passed through the gym doors and out into the summer evening. "Have you done this event before?" he asked.

"Nope."

"Matt says it runs all summer," Travis said. "There are concerts, events, dinners, activities." He cleared his throat. "It's part of the summer program, if you meet someone at the speed dating."

"We didn't meet at the speed dating," she said.

He hadn't taken her hand again, and he stuffed his in his pockets. They felt cold and empty without hers to hold, and Travis looked up into the settling twilight. A sigh escaped his mouth, and he said, "I love a summer evening."

Poppy linked her arm through his, and surprise darted through Travis. Could she honestly like him? Feel anything for him besides irritation and loathing? He looked at her out of the corner of his eye, but it was impossible to decipher the many facets of Poppy Harris without fully looking at her. That felt like the most dangerous move he could make at the moment, so he looked back toward the mountains, the soft glow of sunset lighting up the tops of them.

"So do I," Poppy said.

Travis led her toward his truck, and when they reached it, he opened her door for her. "Where do you want to go eat?"

Her gaze came to his again and locked. All of the thoughts inside Travis's head fell out, save one. The only which had been obsessing over kissing her for months and months now. His pulse sped, and his throat turned to sand. Her mouth moved, but his ears had gone on vacation.

Finally, his brain caught up to the situation, and it screamed at him to *back up. Do not kiss her. Don't you dare.*

Travis listened to himself and backed up. Poppy got in the truck, and he closed her door. With the slam of it, his senses returned. He shook himself as he went around the tailgate, and by the time he sat behind the wheel, his brain had conjured up what she'd said.

*I don't care, but since you're going to be telling me how you paid my mortgage, maybe we better go somewhere with a good dessert menu.*

"The best dessert menu around here is actually a bit further north," he said, reaching for his seat belt. "How adventurous do you feel?" He looked at her, his mouth tipping upward. What he'd just said was about as flirtatious as Travis ever got, and Poppy grinned back at him.

Could his dry sense of humor and mostly silent tongue be what she liked?

"I feel great about that," she said. "Where are you thinking?"

"There's this great Italian place outside of Golden," he said. "I used to work a ranch up there, and when we finished the cattle drive, the boss would take us there." He grinned, his mouth already watering. "Pasta for days, and the tiramisu is to die for."

Poppy laughed, and Travis joined in with her. "Funny," she said once she'd calmed. "You don't strike me as a tiramisu type of guy."

"No?" He backed out of the spot and drove for the exit. "What kind of dessert would you give me?"

"Cobbler," she said. "Something rustic. Something that doesn't have to be pretty to be enjoyable."

"I do love a good peach cobbler," he said. "My mama makes a killer one, and she serves it with homemade vanilla ice cream." He tossed her a smile as he turned right.

"Sounds amazing," she said. "I never did feed you for fixing my leaking barn."

A wind blew through Travis, making his smile dim. "You don't need to. I was hopin' you'd forgotten about that."

"Please, Mister Thatcher," she said, her voice high on the flirtiness too. "I'm a single mom. We don't forget *anything*." She laughed again, and Travis joined her this time too. She wasn't joking, and he was glad he hadn't said too many things he regretted.

She cleared her throat, and Travis's windpipe narrowed. "Listen," she said at the same time he said, "I want to ask you something."

A pause filled the truck. A beat of time where he wasn't sure if he should tell her to speak or if he should forge ahead with the concern in his heart.

"Go on," she said.

"You go first," he said.

"You won't forget?" she asked, peering at him. He

shook his head, smiling. "I don't want to distract you from what you want to say."

"I'll remember." The way she'd called him a *good friend* and a *neighbor* followed him into his nightmares. He wasn't going to forget.

"I know I've apologized before," she said. "But I feel like I need to again. I was just embarrassed about you paying the mortgage. And fixing the barn. And that you caught me crying in the barn." She sighed. "Honestly, I'm a bit of a mess, and I didn't want you to see that."

"Just me?" he asked quietly.

"Anyone," she whispered back. "But it was especially bad that it was you, yeah."

Travis's chest expanded, his lungs finding more room for the air they needed. "I've been thinking about you since that rainstorm in September." He swallowed. "I appreciate the apology, Poppy. You have said it several times, and you don't need to keep repeating it." He looked at her, his eyebrows up, waiting for her to acknowledge him.

She nodded, and Travis did too. He breathed in and then out. "All right. I have a lot of contacts in finance, as you now know. Plus, the banking arena here in this pocket of Colorado is quite small." He cleared his throat. "And you tack your bills to that board beside the back door."

The truck rumbled along the highway, the night around them becoming darker and darker with every mile.

"You stole my bills?"

"No." He squirmed in his seat. "I'm real good with numbers."

She scoffed. "Like a photographic memory?"

"Not quite photographic," he said. "But I remembered enough of the numbers, and I took a picture of the bill so I had the others."

"When?" she asked.

"When we came to help with the hay," he admitted. "Then all I did was call the automated system. I didn't even talk to a person. No one knows it was me but you."

"And Gray and Elise," she murmured.

"Gray and Elise?" Travis flinched, the wheel getting jerked as he did. The truck swung, and he focused on driving. "Why would they know?"

It was Poppy's turn to squirm, and she did quite spectacularly in the passenger seat. "Poppy," he said. "You told them?"

"I thought Gray might've paid the mortgage," she said, her voice taking on that haughty quality he didn't like. She'd spoken to him many times in this voice, and he realized now that it was her first line of defense against people and situations she didn't like. "So I went next door to ask him about it. He said he didn't."

She had chewed him out in front of everyone at Thanksgiving last year too. Travis hadn't breathed a word about why to anyone, not even Cord, the cowboy he lived with. They'd asked too, and he'd said nothing. He frowned and gripped the wheel tightly.

"That was it," she said. "But they probably know it was you."

"Because you reamed me at Thanksgiving." He'd been embarrassed, sure. Mostly because of the very public way she'd forced him onto the back deck. But standing in front of her while she threw her displeasure at him? Travis hadn't minded that so much, and he didn't know what that made him.

Pathetically lonely? Desperate? Something else which was worse?

"I'm really sorry about that," she said.

"Again, something you've already apologized for," he said. "I was just putting pieces together out loud." He gave her a smile and offered his hand to her. She slid her fingers through his, and he squeezed.

Silence accompanied them, and lights started to twinkle up ahead, marking Golden. He'd just put on his blinker when Poppy asked, "What were you going to say?"

A familiar bolt of nerves went straight down his throat, but Travis managed to tame them. He pulled into the lot and found a spot, needing both hands and all his wits about him. Once parked, he twisted slightly to look at her. She was so beautiful, and when she wasn't yelling, she had a soft edge in her eyes he really liked.

"Uh, I can't remember."

"Liar," she said, that edge becoming harder. "Say it."

"I don't want to ruin anything." He dropped his head, showing her the top of his cowboy hat.

Poppy reached out and put her hand on his chest, then under his chin. He looked up, her hand coming with his jaw. Her expression broadcast hope toward him, as well as a hint of wariness. "We're too old to keep secrets," she said firmly. "If there's something you need to say or you need to ask me, then it's okay. You can."

He nodded, because she was right. He was too old to tiptoe around. "I didn't like it when you said I was your good friend and neighbor."

She squinted at him, her expression going blank. "What? When did I say that?"

"Just after the New Year," he said quickly. "When I came to ask if you needed anything now that you had to start paying the mortgage." He swallowed and shook his head, his gaze moving out the windshield. "I don't want to be friends. Or—I mean, I do." He took a breath, trying to center his thoughts.

"Of course I want to be friends. I just don't want to be *only* friends." His chest went tight again, and he couldn't believe he'd said so much in such a short amount of time. His head went back down, and he wished she'd say something. Poppy had never been one to hold back her thoughts.

She kept quiet now, however. Travis's stomach growled loud enough to wake the dead, and that got her to giggle. "Come on," she said. "Let's go get you something to eat."

He looked up as she opened her door, and then he

hastened to unbuckle and get out of the truck too. She had a head start, and she met him at the back bumper of the truck on his side.

He very nearly crashed into her as he swept his hands down the front of his shirt to make sure it wasn't wrinkled. She grabbed onto his arms at the elbow, and they steadied right in front of one another.

Their eyes met as he murmured, "Sorry," and the whole world went still.

Poppy slid her hands up to his shoulders, really leaning into him. Travis sure did like that, and he couldn't help putting another smile on his face.

"I'm a little surprised," she murmured. "That you like me after how mean I was to you." Her eyes shot questions at him now—questions Travis couldn't answer.

"You're a strong, capable woman," he said. "I wouldn't expect anything less."

She melted then, and he thought he heard her sniffle as she laid her head against his chest. He wrapped her in his arms and held her tightly the way he had in that leaky barn all those months ago.

His heart budded with tiny little blooms, and he told himself not to get too excited too fast. Poppy may have said yes to this date, and she may have forgiven him for his intrusion into her life. But he'd also spoken true. She was a strong, capable woman, and before they'd left the gym, she'd admitted she didn't like accepting help from anyone.

*Wear her down*, he thought, but the words didn't enter his mind in his own voice.

*Help me*, he prayed, because he felt certain the Lord had just given him some directions. Perhaps a direction Travis didn't know how to follow without divine help, and he really didn't want to put any more wedges between him and Poppy.

*Four*

POPPY COULD STAND IN TRAVIS'S ARMS ALL
night long. The spark, fizz, and crackle that had first
entered her blood last fall while they'd stood in the barn
during a thunderstorm had not lessened. She almost
couldn't believe that she felt such amazing things for
Travis, but just like nine months ago, they couldn't be
denied.

He was tall and strong, without an extra ounce of
body fat on him. He wore a nice pair of jeans with a blue
and yellow shirt that drew her attention to the width of
his chest and right up to his handsome face. He was dark
everywhere, with nearly black hair in his beard and
mustache that extended all the way onto his head.

He ducked his cowboy hat too much, but she figured
there was a story or two behind the action. Heaven knew
she had plenty of reasons for doing what she did.

She stepped back and looked at Travis. He'd said some significant things to her in the past few minutes, and she wanted him to know she appreciated it. "I like you too," she said, falling to his side and taking his hand in hers. "By the way."

He chuckled, that head down again. "Do you?"

"Yes."

"I don't irritate you?"

"You do that too," she admitted as they took the first slow steps toward the restaurant. She'd never been here before, but she'd been sold with a single word: Italian. She adored pasta and garlic bread, and her feminine curves testified of it. "But...I don't know. There's something about you that...does something to me."

"Does something to you?" He laughed now, no husky, sexy chuckle within earshot. "Wow. That almost sounds like an infectious disease."

She scoffed and swatted at his chest playfully. "No, it doesn't. It's just...you're kind. Even though I didn't want you to fix the barn or help with the hay, you did. And you did it because you're a good man." She glanced over to him, her words starting to choke in her throat. "You paid my mortgage, and that was a huge deal for me."

She'd felt so stupid, so weak, and so grateful, she hadn't known how to react. Even now, a flicker of embarrassment filled her body and soul. She pushed against it, because what he'd done was done. It was over. She didn't have to live in torment forever because he'd helped her of his own free will for a few months.

She paused only a few paces from the entrance. Travis looked at her, his eyebrows up. "I mean it, Trav," she whispered. "You kept me and Steele in our house, and I appreciate it. I'm not sure I've told you that strongly enough."

"You've thanked me plenty," he said, his expression turning to stone. He did that sometimes, and if he started speaking without any inflection in his voice, she'd know he'd retreated from her completely. "No more apologies, and no more gratitude." He squeezed her hand. "Okay?"

She nodded. "As long as you know."

"I know."

The mood lightened, almost like a weight had been physically lifted from Poppy's shoulders. "All right," she said. "Let's go see how amazing this food is." She grinned at him and tugged on his hand to get him to come with her. He did, chuckling again, and it was the sexiest sound Poppy had heard in easily a decade. Maybe longer.

She couldn't believe Travis had been thinking about her since last fall. And not just in a charitable way, but in a more romantic way. Had she been blind to him living right next door to her all this time because he'd done something kind for her? And if so, how could she possibly make up for that?

*You don't need to,* she told herself. *No more apologies and no more gratitude.*

She did find herself praying for guidance all through

dinner and then as Travis drove her back to the speed dating venue. He then followed her back to the farm, all while Poppy kneaded her steering wheel, his headlights in her rearview mirror.

He walked her all the way to the door before he removed his hand from hers and tucked both of his in his pockets. "I had a great time tonight," he said. "Would you like to go out again?"

Poppy grinned at him, at his boyish charm, at the pure hope in his eyes. He was so...*good*, and Poppy sincerely hoped she was good enough for him. Her porch light had come on with their movement, and it illuminated the pair of them. She suddenly wanted it to be still and dark out here. Then maybe she'd be brave enough to kiss him and whisper that she couldn't wait to see him again. She was so eager, she might just let her goats out, so he'd bring them back in the morning.

He shifted his feet and leaned against one of the pillars at the top of the steps. "Boy, you sure do know how to make a man sweat while he waits for an answer." He kicked a smile in her direction too. "It's far past my bedtime, Poppy. How about you text me if you want to go out again?"

"No," she blurted out, realizing she'd fallen into a dream where she lured Travis to her farm just to kiss him.

"No?"

"No, I don't want to text you," she said, her heartbeat

suddenly like a jackhammer against her ribs. "Yes, I want to go out again."

He pushed away from the pillar and came toward her one slow step at a time. It only took three before he reached her and drew her into another embrace. "You do owe me a dinner," he murmured, that sexy, throaty voice making a reappearance.

"Tomorrow night?" she asked, almost afraid he'd say no.

"It's the Sabbath," he said. "With Steele or without him?" He pulled away. "Who watches him while you're out?"

"Tonight, I got a sitter," she said. "Tomorrow...maybe we could both come to your place." She looked up at him, pure hope filling her. "What do you think of that?"

Travis didn't smile or respond instantly. His face clouded slightly, and then he asked, "What will you tell him? That we're seein' each other?"

"That I owe you dinner," she said.

Travis clearly didn't like that. He stepped away from her again, but he didn't lower his head this time. "So you're going to bring dinner to a friend."

Poppy knew the label wasn't right. "Yes," she said anyway. "And no. To Steele, yes. To us, no. He's eleven, Travis. He doesn't have to know everything right now."

The turmoil cleared from Travis's face. "All right."

Poppy feared she might lose him any moment, and she quickly put one palm against his chest to steady herself.

She swept a kiss across his cheek and said, "I had an amazing time tonight. Thank you, Travis."

"See you tomorrow," he said, one hand on her hip as he leaned into her touch. Then they parted, and he turned and went down her steps. Poppy followed him to the top of them and watched him go back to his truck.

A sigh filled her whole body, and she waved as he backed out of the driveway. Inside, she closed the door as quietly as she could and pressed her back against the solid wood. "Wow," she whispered to herself, another smile—this one huge and taking over her entire being—filling her face. "Just...wow."

———

"STEELE!" she called up the steps. "I'm leaving for church in thirty-five minutes!" Poppy hadn't seen hide nor hair of her son that morning, but he knew better than to keep her waiting. Especially on the Sabbath.

She and her son went to services every single week. Poppy had fed the animals that morning, patched up the gate separating her garden from the chicken coop, showered, dressed, and made breakfast. The plate of scrambled eggs, one of bacon, and one of fried potatoes sat on the counter.

"Well, I'm not eating a cold breakfast," she said loudly. "All these eggs? They're not good cold." She walked away from the base of the stairs and toward the counter. Upstairs, she heard the drop of her son's feet to the floor, and she smiled to herself as she pulled out a barstool.

She'd laid out plates and silverware already, and she picked up what she needed to get eating. She put a scoop of eggs, a few pieces of bacon, and had just touched the spatula for the potatoes when Steele came barreling toward her.

"Mom," he said. "I'm up."

"You've been up for a while," she said, twisting toward him. She smiled, but her expression stayed serious. At least inside her head, she kept it that way. She turned back to the food and dished up some potatoes. She set down the plate beside her and held out her hand.

Steele put his game machine in her hand, a hint of sadness entering his expression. "Sorry, Mom."

"You need to eat, shower, and get dressed in a half-hour," she said, leaving no room for arguing in her tone.

"I will," he said.

She wanted to challenge him. He never did anything fast—but come down for breakfast when there was scrambled eggs and bacon—but she held her tongue. "I want the white shirt today," she said, thinking of Travis. She hadn't seen him at church over the past several months, and she wondered if he had too much work on the farm next door to attend services.

She fantasized about what sitting beside him on a narrow pew would be like. He'd hold her hand, and she'd be so distracted by his cologne and the warmth in his skin that she wouldn't hear a thing Pastor Benson said.

"Okay," Steele said. "Can I wear the blue pants?"

"Not the ones with a hole in them," she said. "You threw those away, right?" One look at her boy, and she knew he hadn't. "They go in the garbage," she reminded him. "And pick a tie with some blue in it if you're going with the blue pants."

"Okay." Steele smiled at her, and Poppy couldn't help returning the gesture. Her son looked more and more like Eli every day. He had her blue eyes, but nothing else had really transferred over from her. His hair was light, the color of sunlight shining through clouds. Almost white it was so blond. He had Eli's rounder nose and Eli's angled jaw. He was already as tall as Poppy, but that didn't mean she couldn't keep Steele in line.

He ran free out here a lot of the time, actually, and that was one of the things she loved most about living out here on this lane—right at the very end of it, actually. No one came this way unless they meant to come to her farm, and hardly anyone did that.

"We're goin' to dinner at a friend's house tonight," she said, taking a quick look at her phone. Travis had texted last night for a few minutes after he'd gotten back to his cabin, but she didn't have any new messages from him this morning.

"All right," Steele said. "What time?"

"I don't know yet," she said almost absently. Her

mind wandered as she contemplated sending Travis a message. Steele finished breakfast, and Poppy realized she'd wasted the last several minutes thinking about her date last night.

"I'll be fast," he said, leaving his plate on the counter.

"Dishes," she said, and he huffed as he came back to get them. She ate while he rinsed and practically threw his plate into the dishwasher. Then he raced for the stairs again, and Poppy shook her head.

She'd tried to keep everything negative out of Steele's life. She'd never breathed a word about their financial woes to him. They weren't his anyway. They were hers. She wanted to provide a steady, stable life for him, and carpooling with Gray and Elise provided that. Staying in the same home for years and years did too. Giving him chores around the farm and house had helped him learn the value of hard work.

Cotton, her blue heeler, huffed and flopped on the floor at her feet, his way of saying he wanted some eggs too, please. She giggled at him and then put another scoop of scrambled eggs on her plate.

She put it on the floor for Cotton, then smiled as he started wolfing down the food. She kept busy by cleaning up breakfast, and when Steele had five minutes left, she went to the bottom of the stairs again. "Steele," she yelled up them.

"I can't find my shoes!" he yelled back.

A sigh pulled through Poppy's whole soul. Every

morning mirrored this one. Every morning where they had somewhere to be at a certain time, at least. Monday through Friday for school. Every Sunday.

Poppy had never been happier that school was out for the summer, and joy lifted her heart as she climbed the steps. She'd just located Steele's second black dress shoe when her phone rang.

*Iris* sat there, and Poppy smiled. "It's Grandma." Sort of. Iris was Poppy's step-mother, but she'd practically been raised by the woman after a few years of being looked after by her single dad. Her mother had died when Poppy was only ten, and Iris had been on the scene since the age of thirteen.

"Hey," she answered as Steele sat on the bed to pull on his shoe. "What's up? We're just leaving for church."

"Oh, of course," she said. "I forgot you live so much further away than we do."

Poppy nodded, though Iris couldn't see her.

"Are you going to the potluck tonight?" Iris asked.

"Of course she is," Dad yelled from somewhere on his end of the line. "She goes every month, and I saw her signed up with her famous scalloped potatoes."

Poppy's stomach dropped to her feet, her heart not far behind it. "The potluck," she said to herself. She'd forgotten all about it. The church hosted a potluck dinner on the first Sunday of every month, and that was tonight. Poppy did attend every month, and she always brought something that everyone complimented.

Iris and Dad bickered for a few more seconds, and then Iris said, "I didn't call about the potluck."

"Okay," Poppy said, gesturing for Steele to get going. He did, and she got up and followed him. "What's going on?"

"Your dad and I would like to take Steele on a trip this summer," Iris said. Poppy envisioned her lifting her chin high, her dark brown eyes blazing with determined energy. "He's almost twelve, Poppy, and we take all the grandkids on a trip the year they turn twelve."

"New York City," Poppy said, because she was aware of the traditions Iris had started with her own children. She had three, and they'd all been older than Poppy and Elora. Elora had just gotten married and didn't have children yet. Poppy had Steele, but Iris's other children had five or six grandchildren, a couple of whom had turned twelve in recent years.

"We can handle him," Iris said. "He'll have a lot of fun."

"When?" Poppy asked.

Iris gave a little squeal. "The last week of this month. He'll be home right before the Fourth of July."

"No," Dad said. "We're keeping him past the Fourth."

"No, we're not." They started back and forth again, and Poppy honestly didn't have the energy for it.

"Let me know the exact dates," she said, though she didn't really need to know to give her permission. Steele loved being outside riding his bike, hiking, or with the animals. But he wasn't inclined to sports at all, so she wouldn't have to pull him from baseball or soccer camps. He didn't take lessons of any kind—horseback, piano, art. She didn't have extra money for those, and Steele had never asked. Thankfully.

Poppy picked up her Bible as Steele ran down the hall that led to the front door, her heart full of gratitude to the Lord for what He'd given her. A son who didn't ask for things Poppy couldn't provide was a huge blessing, and she acknowledged it as Iris said, "I'll text you when I have the final dates. Your daddy is looking at airfare right now."

"Okay," Poppy said. "Thanks, Iris."

She would barely know what to do with herself without Steele, but as her job with Elise Hammond's landscaping company was really picking up now that summer had arrived, perhaps she wouldn't have to always be on the lookout for a babysitter. She wouldn't have to bring him with her. She wouldn't have to ask if he could hang around Pony Power and help out while she was gone mowing, weeding, or designing someone's new backyard fountain.

In the car, she handed Steele his game machine and said, "Only on the drive there and back."

He nodded and then buried himself in the game. She sighed and got her nearly dead minivan to start up and start chugging down the road that led toward the suburbs closer to Denver.

The potluck.

She tapped to dial Travis, the line blipping as it started to ring. She picked up her phone and turned off the Bluetooth, knowing she shouldn't be driving with a phone in one hand. There wasn't anyone on the highway right now, so she reasoned she was safe enough.

His phone rang. And rang. And rang. He didn't pick up, and she thought, *Who's making who wait for an answer now, Mister Thatcher?*

She grinned to herself, suddenly wanting to hear his voice so badly. She also wondered if he'd be able to get away from the farm for just a couple of hours tonight. She couldn't imagine the gossip that would fly when she showed up to the potluck with the handsome cowboy on her arm.

All of those thoughts flew through her mind, and each one made her smile bigger and bigger and bigger. He might just be the man to rescue her from her drab life of single motherhood, mucking stalls, and praying for the type of weather she needed to grow alfalfa.

If only he would answer.

# Five

"HOLD 'IM," CORD SAID, HIS VOICE STRAINED.

Travis couldn't hold the cow any tighter, and Matt pulled on its legs too. They both grunted as they dug in their heels, and Matt said, "Hurry up."

"I'm hurryin'," Cord said, and then *snip, snip, snip,* and he cut the bovine free. "Got 'im."

The cow bleated, clearly upset by getting rescued from this fence, and Travis and Matt stumbled backward. The animal limped away, but it wouldn't get far. Travis had roped it so they could get as close as they had, and they'd need to get it back to the barn so the vet could check it out.

Matt groaned and stretched his back. "This is too much work for this early in the morning." He grinned at Travis, who just shook his head as they all chuckled. "At least Chris is having pizza after church."

"What time's that?" Cord asked, though Travis had told him that morning. He didn't go to the same church as most of the cowboys here at the Hammond Family Farm, and to his knowledge, Cord didn't go at all. At least he hadn't since he'd moved in with Travis last December.

"Church?" Matt asked. "Or lunch?" He reseated his cowboy hat and threw a playful grin toward Cord.

He rolled his eyes and turned his back on Matt.

"Church is in about a half-hour," Travis said, bending to pick up a pair of gloves that had fallen to the ground. "Lunch will be about twelve-thirty, at Chris's." He looked at Matt for confirmation, and his boss nodded. He pulled his phone from his pocket, his heartbeat shooting through his body at the missed call notification. Not just any missed call, but one from Poppy.

He cleared his throat as his body stopped telling his brain he was free-falling through space. "I missed a call," he said, glancing up. They'd come out to the northwest side of the ranch to rescue the cow, and he frowned back at his device.

"There's not a lot of service up here," Matt said. "Let's get back in." He didn't like being out of communication with his wife, as Gloria was six months pregnant now and getting bigger by the hour it seemed.

Travis helped clean up the supplies they'd brought, and then he swung into his saddle. "I'll take the cow."

"You sure?" Matt was already passing over the rope though.

"Yeah, then you can get to church. I'm goin' with my momma, so I've got more time." His mother had been attending the same church for almost five decades, and she saw no reason to change now. Travis loved seeing his mother every week, and not only because she sent him home with freshly baked bread every Sunday. Their services didn't start until eleven, which was an hour later than where Matt and almost everyone else went.

Matt smiled at him and said, "Thanks, Travis," before he reached for the reins on his horse too. "I'll head in with Cord then." He gave Travis the reins for his horse, and Travis would take care of all of it.

As he and Cord motored off on the ATV, Travis started the slow walk back to the farm, where he'd take care of the two horses, pass off the cow, and then head to his momma's house in his jeans and long-sleeved shirt. He had a white one with a tie in his truck, and he wouldn't stand out in the congregation that way.

His phone beeped several times when he was about halfway back to the farm, and he tugged it out of his pocket. Poppy had texted a couple of times, as had his mother.

He decided he wanted to figure out what had her calling him that morning, so he dialed her back. Her messages had simply asked him to do that, and she'd said what time church started.

"Hey," she said. "There you are."

"Sorry," he said. "We had a cow stuck in a fence pretty far out. No service."

"Hmm." She took a breath. "So there's a problem with tonight's dinner."

Travis grinned for some reason. "Oh, yeah? What's that?"

"It's the potluck at church," she said with a sigh. "I always go. I signed up to take scalloped potatoes."

"Oh, well, we wouldn't want anyone to miss out on those." He chuckled, hoping she'd know that was his lame attempt at flirting.

She giggled too, so he thought he'd gotten the point across. "Right. Uh, would you want to come with me and Steele? The potluck is usually pretty good, and I asked the pastor what the main dish would be. Scott Hamilton is bringing a roast pig. So."

Travis's eyes widened. "Wow. Scott Hamilton as in Hamilton bacon?"

"The one and the same." Her voice held plenty of teasing now too. "I knew that pig would get you." She trilled out a laugh, and Travis could listen to it for hours.

"All right," he said. "What time do I need to be off the farm?"

"Do you work every Sunday?"

"Yeah," he said. "I'm headed to my momma's for church with her. I usually eat lunch there, and she loads me up with baked goods before I come back here and finish up the evening chores." If he went to the potluck, he wouldn't be able to do any of that. His stomach twisted. He'd have to talk to Matt, and that meant he'd have to tell him about Poppy.

*So what?* he asked himself. He could tell Matt he was dating. It wasn't a secret, and Travis wasn't embarrassed about it.

"Oh, so you go to church with your momma every week." She didn't phrase it as a question.

"That's right," he said. "She's about a half-hour from here, up in Edgewood."

"That's a lovely town," she said.

"It is," he said. "They have an ice cream tasting this next weekend I was thinkin' we should hit up."

"Is that so?" Poppy's flirting skills were far sharper than Travis's, that was for sure.

"That's so," he said, smiling. "All day Saturday, at the Myer Creamery, so it's legit ice cream."

"All I eat is Myer's," she said, a touch of haughtiness in her tone.

Travis laughed, because that tickled his funny bone for some reason. She joined him, and Travis relaxed so much he nearly fell out of his saddle. His horse, a beautiful gray gelding named Captain, kept moving, so Travis didn't have to do much.

"I miss you," he said at the end of his chuckle. When he realized what he'd said, and that she hadn't responded, he added, "What time do I need to be at your place to get you and Steele to the potluck?"

"It starts at five-thirty," she said. "So five?"

"Five," he repeated. He'd have to move the mountains and high water to be able to do that, but he wanted to. So he'd move the mountains and high water—and show up on her doorstep by five o'clock. "I've got to talk to Matt. I'll text you, okay?"

"Okay," she said, and once the call ended, Travis instantly dialed his boss.

"Yep," Matt said.

"I want to go to a church potluck tonight," Travis said, swallowing. "At five. What are the chances of that?"

"The church potluck?" Matt asked. "You're going to go to that?"

"Maybe."

Matt let several seconds of silence come through the phone. "Cord says it's fine. He'll do the evening feeding."

"There's nothing else?" Travis pressed. "I can get out early in the morning too."

"It's summer," Matt said. "The horses graze and the fields grow."

"Ask him," Cord said.

"We want to know why you're goin' to the potluck," Matt said. "You don't have to say."

Travis scanned the landscape in front of him. Everything here had grown in green, and this land reminded him so much of tranquility and peace. "Poppy Harris asked me to go with her," he said, his voice frayed and rough around the edges. "I went to the speed-dating last night, and we met up. Went out. She was gonna bring dinner to my house tonight, but well, she forgot about the potluck."

He took a long breath, because he didn't normally string together so many words. Matt chuckled, which only made Travis's frown deeper.

"Don't tease him," Cord said, and Travis's heart expanded for his cabinmate. He hadn't said anything to Cord about his date last night, but he had been floating when he'd gotten home. Right up in the sky. "He likes her."

"Does he?" Matt asked.

"Yes," Travis said with Cord. "I'd be grateful, Cord, and I'll cover for you another time."

"No problem," Cord said.

"Yeah," Matt said. "No problem. And Travis? Good for you. Poppy's a nice woman."

Travis nodded without saying anything. He'd thought it might be nice to have the activities and planned dates built in from the Lazy Days of Summer event, but Poppy said they didn't have to do those. They could if they wanted to, but she didn't think any of them sounded all that fun.

Travis honestly didn't know what sounded fun and what didn't. Simply seeing her again was on his agenda, and he managed to gruff out, "Thanks, Matt," before he ended the call. Now he just had to figure out how to be less boring, less predictable, and less...himself before Poppy grew tired of him.

———

"WELL." Travis groaned as he stood from his mother's couch. "I have to get goin', Momma." He smiled at her, but he really wished she'd buy some new couches. The bright blue one he'd been sitting on was far too short, as it was least fifty years old.

"You have to go already?" She reached out for him, and Travis took her hand to help her stand.

He'd stayed too long already. "Yeah," he said. "I'm meeting—someone—a friend—for a church potluck at five, and I've got to get back to the farm first."

Momma frowned, the permanent lines between her eyes only deepening. "Our church isn't having a potluck tonight."

"No, I know," he said, his chest vibrating with the need to get out of there. "I'm going with someone else. To their church potluck."

Momma shuffled into the kitchen, her empty coffee mug in her hand. "Who?"

Travis watched her start to rinse out the mug. She did dishes after every meal, as it was just her, and she didn't like the dishes piling up.

*Tell her*, he told himself, and he committed to go into the kitchen, though he wanted to head for the front door.

She'd never given him grief about dating, living in the city, getting divorced, none of it.

"A woman named Poppy Harris," he said as he joined her at the sink. He put his mug in the stream of water too, immediately pulling his hand back. "Momma, that's like liquid fire." He looked at her as his skin burned. "How do you have your hands in that?"

"Tsk, tsk," she said, nudging him with her hip. "Who's Poppy Harris?"

Travis just wanted to go, and he didn't know how to answer his momma anyway. "She's...I went out with her last night." He took a long breath in, and by the end of it, he realized Momma hadn't gone back to washing the mugs. He met her eyes, and he found pure shock there. "What?"

"You're dating?"

"It was one date," he said quickly.

"And another one tonight."

Travis tilted his head. "Is a church potluck a date?" With Poppy's son? And all of her friends from church? No wonder Travis's stomach felt like he'd eaten a hive of ants for lunch instead of his mother's delicious breakfast sausage casserole.

"Yes, it is, young man," she said, poking him in the chest. "If you're going *with* her."

Travis grinned and let himself fall back a couple of steps as if Momma had the strength to move him. "I'll be back this week to help you with that fertilizer." He cocked his right eyebrow. "Promise me you won't try to lift those big bags by yourself."

"I won't," she said, giving him a dry look. She looked down into the sink but lifted her chin. "I'll call Norman next door."

Travis blinked and then burst out laughing. "Momma," he said, the word barely audible between his laughter. He quieted before he said, "Norman is a decade older than you for sure. You ask him to help, and he'll throw out his back." He continued smiling at her, but he pointed one finger in her direction. "I don't want to be payin' his medical bills so you can lure him over here for a date."

"*Lure* him over here?" Momma looked like Travis had just suggested she was involved in the scandal of the century. "I'll have you know that he's bringing lunch tomorrow, no luring necessary." She held her head high as she put the mugs in the dish drainer.

Travis took a moment and fell back another step. "So *you're* dating?"

"No," Momma snapped, though she hadn't quite turned seventy yet. She could easily be dating the man next door.

"Momma," he said.

She sighed and flipped off the water. "No, we're not dating. We just like spending time together." She smiled as she faced Travis again. "We eat lunch together, and sometimes we walk down the block to the ice cream shop."

Travis didn't like the sound of that. "Does he hold your hand?"

"No," she said. "Do you hold Poppy's?"

"Yes," Travis said, becoming quite confused. "So you're...friends." He lifted both eyebrows this time, and Momma nodded.

"Yeah," she said. "Friends." She turned to the counter and picked up the oversized brown grocery bag. "Don't forget your bread."

"Momma, I would never forget the bread." He smiled at her as he took it, then he leaned into her to give her a one-armed hug. He stood about a foot taller than her, with a much wider wingspan, so he could embrace her easily with only one arm. "I love you," he said.

"I love you too, my son." She smiled as she stepped back. "You'll tell me more about this Poppy when you come this week." No question mark there, and Travis simply nodded.

"I'll let you know when," he said. "The farm is—"

"Unpredictable," they said together, and Travis swept a kiss along his momma's forehead. She followed him to the door, and Travis waved once he was behind the wheel of his truck.

He'd really let time get away from him, because he only had twenty-five minutes before he needed to be at Poppy's, and that meant he'd have to speed and he couldn't go home to freshen up.

Travis had vowed he'd be on time, but perhaps even he

couldn't move the mountains and high water, no matter how badly he wanted to. Torn between calling Poppy and saying he'd meet her there and going straight to her house with coffee on his breath, he kneaded the steering wheel for a mile or two.

"Bless me that there won't be any cops," he muttered, and then he pressed on the gas pedal so he wouldn't be late.

# Six

POPPY PERKED UP WHEN COTTON DID, THE BLUE heeler looking toward the front door. She'd changed out of her church dress and into another one. This one was bright blue and hugged her body along the upper half, tightened almost uncomfortably at the waist, and then flared into a full party skirt. She wore a pair of matte white heels with the dress, and she'd clipped her hair back on the sides. The curling iron had come out this afternoon, and Poppy currently wore about twice as much makeup as she did normally.

Who was she kidding? "Normally," Poppy didn't wear much makeup at all. Only pink lip gloss when she went grocery shopping. To church, she paired that with a hint of mascara and nothing else.

Her face felt caked in foundation, blush, concealer,

then this finishing powder that made her shine like a star. She hoped.

The doorbell rang, and Cotton flew into a barking frenzy. Poppy got to her feet and set aside the book she'd been pretending to read. "Steele," she called. "He's here. We need to get going."

She'd taken the scalloped potatoes out of the oven about ten minutes ago, and since they needed to sit to firm up anyway, it wasn't a problem. They'd hold their heat in the aluminum tray, and she'd covered that with more foil. She didn't want to try to lift it again, so she followed Cotton to the front door, intending to ask Travis to load the food in the back of his truck.

She opened the door, and cowboy perfection stood there. This wasn't the first time Travis Thatcher had come to her house. He'd come in January too, asking about her finances and if she and Steele were okay. He'd made her blood boil then too—for an entirely different reason than why it bubbled now.

"Howdy." He reached up and touched the brim of his hat. "Don't you look festive?" His smile lit up the porch the way the motion-sensor light had last night, and Poppy ducked her head.

"I maybe forgot to tell you this was a dinner-dance."

"Oh, boy," Travis said with a chuckle. "I'm not much for dancin'."

She looked him in the eye again. "You're not?"

"If you don't mind getting stepped on a time or two,

I'd dance with you." He looked over her shoulder, and she hadn't realized he'd inched closer to her until he remade the distance that had once been there.

"Ready," Steele announced as he arrived at Poppy's side, and she blinked her gaze from Travis's to her son's.

"Good boy," she said. "Steele, this is Travis Thatcher. He works next door."

"Yeah, I know him." Steele smiled at Travis. "Are we taking your truck?"

"Yes, sir," Travis said, glancing at Poppy. "Do you need to get the food?"

"Could you?" she asked, stepping back and out of the way so he could enter. "It's really heavy."

"Sure thing." Travis swept between her and Steele, his hand landing on her hip for a beat of time. A breath. Barely a moment. Still, an electric current shot through her, and Poppy pulled in a breath.

Travis was gone by then, and Poppy nodded to the porch. "Go get in."

Steele whooped as he ran outside. "We need a truck like this, Mom," he yelled over his shoulder.

Poppy eyed Travis's truck. That thing probably cost as much as her farm, and she didn't answer her son. She turned back to the house as Travis's footsteps approached.

"I can see you and my mother are cut from the same cloth." He gave her a smile, his steps quick and small. His biceps bulged in the black shirt he wore, and my, Poppy didn't mind that. "This is enough scalloped potatoes to feed the whole town." He chuckled as he bustled by her and went right down the steps.

She pulled the front door closed and followed him, appreciating the sight of him here on her farm. She wasn't sure what that meant, and a bolt of confusion wound through her. She was so used to doing things on her own. She didn't need help carrying a pan of potatoes from the house to her van. She did it every month. For lots of events.

Still, it was nice to have someone else do it for her. Poppy frowned, because she'd often had thoughts about how nice it would be to have a husband. A partner. A support system built right into her life, waiting for her right there in the farmhouse. She'd never had that, and after a while of fantasizing about it, Poppy had put the thoughts to bed.

It hadn't done her any good to wish on stars, wonder about what-ifs, or cry when she needed help to put the leaf in the dining room table and she didn't have it.

Travis put the potatoes in the back seat with Steele, closed the door, and turned toward her. The joviality slid from his face. "Are you all right?" he asked, his cowboy twang impressive for someone who'd once lived in the Big Apple.

"Yes." The word came out rusty, so Poppy cleared her throat and said, "Yes," again. She put a smile on her perfectly painted lips. "Thank you, Travis."

He didn't smile back, and he paused a good pace or two away from her. "You want me to come, right?"

"Yes," she said again. "Why wouldn't I?"

"You looked a little like...miffed," he said. "Like, I've seen that look on your face before, right before you marched over to me at Thanksgiving." He didn't duck his head this time, and Poppy supposed that was some improvement.

He looked over his shoulder, and she wasn't sure what he was checking for. Steele to be watching, maybe? He turned back to her. "I'll dance with you tonight, my pretty Poppy," he said, moving right into her personal space. "If you think it wouldn't be scandalous at your church potluck." He chuckled in her ear, easily swaying her left and right, and then spinning her away from him.

Surprise coursed through her again. "You said you couldn't dance," she said.

"I didn't say I couldn't," he said. "I said I wasn't much for it." He dropped her hand and stepped to open her door for her. "I'm sure you don't want to be late for the potluck. By the looks of it, you'll be feeding the whole congregation, and there'll be a riot if those potatoes aren't in the right spot by precisely five-thirty."

He grinned at her, a dark sparkle in his eyes that made her heartbeat thump and bump and spin out of control. Oh, he was dangerous to her health, and he didn't even know it. She knew it, but she boosted herself up into his truck, arranged her skirt so it was covering her legs properly, and beamed at him.

"Better get us there quick, cowboy," she said, enjoying this flirtatious game with him.

"Yes, ma'am," he said, and she liked those manners too —even if she wasn't quite old enough to be called "ma'am."

———

TRAVIS CARRIED IN THE POTATOES. Poppy accepted all the gushing praise about her dress from her friends at church. Steele ran off to find his friends.

"Who is that?" Melinda Perry asked, eyeing Travis. He'd just set down the pan of potatoes, and Margaret Benson had him pick it up again to move it. Poppy loved the pastor's wife, and she currently wore a pink dress with a white apron tied around it.

"Travis Thatcher," Poppy said, lifting one hand to her mouth so she could chew on her nail. She had friends here at church. She had friends in Elise's landscaping company. She simply lived so far away from everyone and everything that she didn't meet her girlfriends for lunch or to go walking in the morning. "He works next door to my farm."

"He's gorgeous," Dolly Jolley said. "You're seeing him?"

"Yes," Poppy said, otherwise all available women

within a ten-mile radius would know the name Travis Thatcher by nightfall. Probably all the married women too, as Dolly had said I-do over a decade ago.

"Good for you," Reggie Nelson said. "Come on, ladies. We're mingling tonight, remember? We need to find a cowboy like that for Wendy." The women dispersed, leaving Poppy with the opportunity to cross the gym to Travis's side.

She did, lacing her arm through his elbow just as he turned toward her. "Here she is," he said, smiling at her with a wariness in his eyes that told her not to leave him alone like that again. "Miss Poppy Harris."

"Oh, everyone knows Poppy." Margaret beamed at her. "How are you, dear?" She came around the end of the table and drew Poppy into a hug.

"Good." Poppy took a long breath of the woman's powdery, feminine scent. She'd always loved the Bensons, and Maggie was a huge reason why. "Where's your husband?"

"Make way for the pig!" a man yelled, and they both turned in the direction the voice had come from.

"Right there," Maggie said dryly as the pastor led the way through the gathering crowd, Scott Hamilton right behind him. He carried the front end of a spit—yes, a legit spit, complete with the crispy-skinned pig still hanging from it—while his son carried the back pole.

"My word," Poppy said, sliding out of the way and

barely grabbing Travis's hand to tow him with her. "Look at that."

"This is the best thing I've ever seen," he said. His voice carried wonder and awe, and Poppy couldn't look away from the spit-roasted pig to look at his face.

"Me too," she murmured.

Scott and his son set up the protein on the far end of the table, and then Pastor Benson clapped his hand three loud, booming times. "Everyone!" He could bellow like no one else. She'd always enjoyed seeing the more human side of him outside of church, out from behind the pulpit. "Dinner is here. Let's eat first, and then we'll get our DJ to start spinning the tunes."

Poppy groaned, but Pastor Benson sure looked proud of himself for trying to be hip and young and cool. Travis laughed, as did several others in the crowd, and then the pastor called on Hunter Hammond, his son-in-law, to say the prayer over that night's food and activities.

Poppy bowed her head, but her thoughts were too scattered to focus on the prayer. Her nerves buzzed around her body, making a noise in her ears that made it hard to think about anything but the very solid, warm, kind, handsome form of Travis beside her.

"Amen," he said loudly, and that startled Poppy out of her mind.

She added, "Amen," far too late, drawing Travis's attention. Thankfully, she had food to distract him. "If you want to eat in the next half-hour." She nodded toward the table, which they stood only a few paces from. "I suggest we get in line immediately."

One had already started to form, and Travis wasted no time grabbing her hand—claiming her as his—and joining the fray. She giggled with him and suddenly remembered she had a child who needed feeding. She glanced around for Steele, but she didn't see him.

She kept one arm in Travis's as she continued to look, and then her phone vibrated in her dress pocket. She pulled it out and found a message from Maya, one of the moms of a boy named Peter, whom Steele knew quite well. *Steele's with us. Do you want me to send him up to you?*

Poppy looked up and back down the line, finally finding Maya and Cameron, along with their boys—and Steele. He bent over Peter's arm, watching him do something on his phone. She shrugged, her way of saying, *If you want to.*

Maya went back to her phone, and a moment later, Poppy's buzzed again. *We'll keep him.* She'd sent a smiley face with that. *Enjoy your cowboy.*

She smiled at her device and sent Maya a quick, *Thank you, Maya. I appreciate it,* before she repocketed her phone. She looked over to Travis, who now had a blush creeping up his neck. She trained her grin on him. "What?" she asked, enjoying this fun, easy flirting with him.

He shifted his feet and turned the movement into a step when the line inched forward. "Am I—is what she said true? I'm yours? I'm your cowboy?" He cleared his throat and actually reached up and pulled at his collar. He wore a black-on-black plaid shirt, the sleeves short, and the collar open. With his jeans, cowboy boots, and the big black hat, he truly personified perfection.

"I mean...." Poppy weighed the words flying through her mind. She had to be careful what she said here. "I told the other women that we were dating. I didn't want them thinking they could catch your eye and steal a dance tonight."

He nodded, his jaw working as it tightened and then released. Tightened. Released.

"Does that bother you?" she asked coolly.

"No," he said. "Not at all." He looked forward though, not at her.

"Was I wrong?"

"No."

Poppy wasn't sure why he'd turned the color of a ripe tomato then. She also wasn't sure she should press the issue. At the same time, she wanted to know what he was thinking. "Why don't you tell me why you blushed when you saw her text?"

She focused forward this time, refusing to look at him even when his gaze burned into the side of her face.

"I don't know," he said as he leaned closer. His voice lowered as he added, "It felt intimate. To be called yours."

She nodded, his breath sliding across her bare skin and

making her shiver in delight. "Did you like it?" she whispered.

"Yes."

A thrill moved through Poppy, and the night was only beginning. "So it was okay."

"It's okay," he said. "And I guess I'd like to call you mine if someone asks. Should I?"

Poppy didn't hesitate, and she didn't get too lost inside her thoughts. She did that a lot, especially once she started making up situations that hadn't happened yet. "Yes," she said, her voice just as rusty and froggy as it had been back at her house, when he'd picked her up. She cleared the nerves and emotion from it. "I think that would be okay."

"Great," he said, his smile evident in the tone of his voice. "I can't wait to dance with you." He said the last words in a whisper and then straightened as they reached the corner of the table, the glorious pig in front of them.

"Travis," Scott said, pleasant surprise in the man's name.

"Scott." They both laughed, and Travis clapped the older man on the back in a man-hug. "It's great to see you again."

"I wish I couldn't say the same," Scott said, still chuckling. "You don't want to quit at the Hammond's, do you? We'd love to have you back at Hamilton Farms." He wore a look of resigned hope, and Travis shook his head instantly.

"It smells better at the Hammond's," he said with a grin. "But I will take plenty of pig." He lifted his paper plate for Scott to serve him, and Poppy marveled that Travis knew him. Why, she wasn't sure. For some reason, the man in her mind wasn't outgoing. He worked the farm, and he went home. Alone. He didn't talk to people. He didn't have friends.

Of course, none of that could really be true, and she pasted a smile on her face for Scott too, thanked him for the pig, and continued to wonder about the cowboy Travis Thatcher as she loaded her plate with the food the church members had brought.

Travis reached the end of the serving tables before her, and he waited. "Where should we sit?" he asked, looking around at the round tables that had set up. Poppy was notoriously bad for choosing a spot to eat, as she always got stuck talking to someone about their garden or their lawn. That, or they wanted to tell her all about their family issues, health problems, or other insanity. Once, she'd sat with a group of people she didn't know, and not one person had spoken to her.

Thankfully, Melinda lifted her hand and gestured that she had two seats at her table.

Poppy nodded to her and muttered, "I hope I don't regret this," as Travis started in Melinda's direction.

# Seven

TRAVIS LOOKED OVER HIS SHOULDER AS THE music started. "Sounds like it's time for dancing." He smiled at Poppy, who immediately got to her feet and started picking up their plates.

"We'll have to clear the floor," she said.

Around them, everyone started doing exactly that, and Travis joined the commotion of men, women, and children clearing dishes, folding chairs, and putting tables away.

"All right," a man said into a microphone, but Travis couldn't locate him past the now-standing crowd. He'd also lost sight of Poppy, but happiness filled his soul at the first strains of the song piping into the gym. "We're gonna start off easy with a line dance."

Several men whistled and whooped, and Travis

laughed. He could line dance, and he actually really liked it. The rhythm in his body got his toe tapping, and he situated himself into a line beside a couple of people he didn't know.

He glanced around for Poppy and found her standing against the wall. Their eyes met, and she looked like she'd glossed hers with sparkle and shine. She clapped along with the beat, and in the next moment, the caller said, "And we're off!"

Travis moved forward the three steps, tapped his toe, and shuffled backward. "Yeehaw!" and other whoops continued to fill the air, but Travis just did the movement. He did tuck his thumbs into his front pockets, and his heartrate increased as he continued to dance and dance.

This was a long song—but it was easy. *The Electric Slide* set to country music. A fun beat, a lively crowd, and Travis had a great time.

He lifted his voice into the air once the song ended, adding a hearty round of applause to it. Poppy stepped into his arms in the next moment, her palms flat against his chest, branding him.

"Wow," she yelled above the noise in the gym. "You're incredible."

He laughed, because that wasn't true. "It was a line dance, sweetheart." The music slowed now, and the caller said something into the mic. Travis wasn't sure what, because his pulse still sprinted like it had fifty meters to go in a race it did not want to lose.

He sucked down air, trying to catch his breath. Poppy didn't seem to mind as she folded herself into his arms and they started to sway together. She was definitely the biggest reason he couldn't compose himself, but he didn't mind how close she stood to him, how she'd laid her cheek against his chest, and how sweet she smelled.

He eventually calmed as the slow dance continued, and he didn't step on her feet at all. Her heels brought her closer to his height, but she still had to look up at him as the song ended. "That was nice," she said.

"Mm." He wasn't sure what else to say. He slid his hand across her hip to hers and said, "I need something to drink."

She led him off the dance floor, and he noticed several people watching them. He didn't come to this church, so he simply kept his smile in place and let Poppy take him over to the refreshment table.

Gray stood nearby, chatting with Matt. The owner of the Hammond Family Farm usually took his family north to Wyoming for the summer, but Gray and Elise had stayed this year in anticipation of their first grandchild being born.

"Mighty fine dancing," Matt said, and Travis ducked his head.

"I'm all right," he said, accepting the cup of water Poppy handed him. "Thank you." He nodded to Gray and took a drink. "I didn't know you guys would be here."

"When Elise heard it was a dance, she insisted we

come." Gray smiled and looked around, supposedly to find his wife. "She's off doing something with the boys, though." He finished his own drink and tossed the cup in the trash can. "Howdy, Poppy."

"Hey, Gray."

He looked between the two of them, and while Travis wasn't holding her hand anymore, he really felt under a microscope. "How's the farm?" Gray asked.

"Good," she said. "Really good."

"Elise wanted to talk to you," he said. "Something about our yard. She said you'd have a magic tree anti-fungal or something." He grinned, and Travis watched Poppy. She'd been alive before, but she really became animated now.

"It's your maple trees," she said. "They need some TLC, and I told her I'd come treat them."

"That sounds right," Gray said. "Well." He sighed. "I'm going to try to get my family out of here."

"I'm leaving too," Matt said. "Gloria's home alone with Britt, and we've all got an early morning tomorrow."

"We do?" Travis asked. He drained the last of his water. "I can cover for you, boss."

"You're covering tonight," Matt said. "After this."

"Mm hm." Travis was, and he still had a few hours of work in front of him. He'd be doing some of it with a headlamp on if he didn't leave soon too. Even then, it would be past nightfall by the time he returned to his cabin. So much for the Sabbath being a day of rest.

He had an extremely busy week ahead of him too, what with having to get out to his mother's to help her with her garden. He thought she was planting a couple of things too early, but he'd never tell her. Momma would do what she wanted anyway.

"We can go too," Poppy said. "Steele won't care. I just have to find him...." She started looking for her son, and Travis tossed his cup in the trash.

He spotted the boy first, and as another woman stole Poppy's attention, Travis went to get Steele. "Hey," he said as he arrived in front of the eleven-year-old. Everything suddenly shifted, the child looking up at him. He wasn't this boy's father. Would he even listen to him?

Travis liked children. Plenty of them came to the farm for riding lessons or their appointments at Pony Power. Travis didn't work with them directly, but he'd always gotten along fine with kids.

"Your mom says it's time to go," Travis said, his gaze skating away from Steele's and to the other boys he sat with.

"Okay," the boy said without an issue. He handed the device in his hand to another kid and stood up.

"Just like that?" Travis asked, his eyebrows up.

"Yeah," Steele said. "That game is boring anyway, and I'm honestly surprised Mom stayed this long. She doesn't usually dance."

"She doesn't?"

Steele shook his head. "She says she hurt her ankle once when she was younger, and she doesn't like it."

"Huh." Travis didn't know that, and Steele's statement only served to remind him that there were a lot of things about Poppy he didn't know. "She did just do the slow dance with me."

Steele didn't respond, and Travis didn't know what else to say. They made it back to Poppy, who wore a look of relief at their arrival. She deftly excused herself, and the three of them started for the exit. "Thank goodness," she murmured once they'd reached the lobby. "I wasn't sure how to get away from Hailey."

"You always tell me to say you texted," Steele said.

"I don't have that excuse, do I?" Poppy grinned at her son and flung her arm around his shoulders. "How's Peter? Did you listen to his mom and dad?"

"He's good," Steele said, not answering the second question. Travis felt like a tagalong with the two of them, even when he told himself not to be stupid. Of course he was always going to be the odd man out when it came to Poppy and her son. He barely knew the boy, and they'd shared their whole lives together.

They all remained quiet on the drive back out to the farm, but Travis didn't mind the silence. He kept the radio on low, and that provided the perfect background for him to relive holding Poppy in his arms as they swayed to the music.

It had been magical, and he could only hope and pray

that he could be the cowboy prince she wanted and needed.

———

TRAVIS APPROACHED the door he needed to go through, but it sat closed. Cosette Brian ran a lot of the administrative tasks around the farm, including payroll. He'd been donating his check to Pony Power since Molly had opened the children's equine therapy unit a couple of years ago, but the money had been deposited into his account this month.

Cosette didn't normally keep her door closed either, and Travis's step slowed until he stopped just outside the office. A chuckle came from the other side of it, and he knew instantly that Boone Whettstein was in there with her.

His face heated, though he could just knock and interrupt them. Boone and Cosette had gotten engaged last week when he'd taken her and his daughter to Montana to sell the property he owned up there. Travis had asked him about it, but to his knowledge, it hadn't sold yet.

*Knock*, he told himself as silence met his ears. Silence meant kissing for an engaged couple, and Travis wanted to simply come back later. *You have no time later.*

And he didn't, so he raised his hand and knocked briskly on the door a few times. Something banged and then crashed inside the office, and Travis backed up a step.

The wall behind him wouldn't let him go any further, and Boone's voice filled the air as he swung in the door.

"...fine, baby." He looked at Travis. "See? It's just Travis. Howdy, brother." Everything about Boone screamed casual and confident. He was fun-loving and loud, and Travis had never met a man who could talk to horses the way Boone did.

"Howdy," he said. "Sorry to interrupt." He cleared his throat. He'd dropped off Poppy last night after the church potluck and dance, but there had been no kissing. Not even a quick sweep of her lips across his cheek. It still burned from when she'd done it on Saturday night, though, and Travis almost reached up to cover the spot. Like Boone would be able to see it.

"I just had an issue with my paycheck," he said. "I needed to talk to Cosette for a minute."

"Come on in, Travis," she said from behind Boone. "Boone was just leaving anyway."

Boone grinned at Travis, all indicators pointing to *I wasn't just leaving, but it's fine.* He clapped Travis on the shoulder as they squeezed by one another and continued down the hall. "Hey," he called right as Travis entered Cosette's office.

Travis stuck his head back out into the hall. "Yep?"

"We're goin' riding this afternoon, right? You said you'd come watch Zelda's gait."

"Planning on it," Travis said. He was tired and hungry,

but he'd be there. "Are you going to lunch at Chris's today?"

"He stayed downtown with Hunter," Boone said. "So nope."

Travis hadn't known that, and his lunch plans at the elderly man's house dried right up. Great. That meant he'd have to find something boxed or bagged to eat, and his first thought was to text Cord and find out what he was doing. Travis could feed himself just fine, but Cord actually cooked.

"Travis," Cosette said, her tone all business now.

He ducked back into the office as Boone disappeared around the corner. Cosette wore her usual attire—a pretty dress with sensible shoes. Not a hair sat out of place, and neither did a stitch of makeup. So maybe she and Boone hadn't been kissing.

"Something with your paycheck?" She sat in front of her computer and started clicking. "This says it went through just fine."

"Yeah." Travis took off his hat and gripped the brim. "It's not that. It's that I usually donate it to Pony Power, but this time the money came to me."

Cosette looked up at him, blinking. Her long eyelashes seemed to move in slow motion, and Travis wasn't sure what was so surprising about what he'd said. "You donate your paycheck to Pony Power?" she asked.

"Yes," he said.

"Since when?" She opened a drawer in her desk and started rummaging for something.

Travis frowned now too. "Since they opened," he said. "A couple of years now. You didn't know?"

"Your check is auto-deposited," she said, finally selecting a folder and lifting it from the drawer. "I don't know where it goes."

"But you know the financials for Pony Power." Travis took a seat, because he might as well rest during the conversation. Then he'd head down the hall and see if any of the doughnuts Molly had brought that morning were still there. He'd already had one, but he could definitely use something to eat before lunchtime, which still sat a couple of hours in the future.

"Sort of," Cosette said. "Molly does the financials for Pony Power." She tugged a paper out of the folder, which Travis could only assume was his file. "It looks like she could only do your direct deposit from the farm account to Pony Power for a year at a time." She looked up, her eyebrows punctuating her statement with a question mark. "Does that sound right?"

"I have no idea," he said.

"Pony Power started in June," she said. "Your donation contract with them is up, and it looks like she didn't renew it."

Travis's fingers kept gripping his hat. "I can talk to her."

"I will too," Cosette said. "I can make it a permanent direct deposit, from one account here to the other."

"Could you?" he asked. "That would be great."

"I can't do anything about June," she said. She got clicking on her computer again. "But I can find the forms we need moving forward. Get it all taken care of for next month." The printer behind her started to whir, and Travis wouldn't put it past her to have found the right form already. And she'd printed it.

Their eyes met, and he nodded. "Thank you, Cosette."

"You don't need to earn a living from the farm?" She folded her arms on the desk in front of her, open curiosity on her face.

"Uh...."

"Not my business," she said, lifting one hand. "I'm sorry."

"I have an offer on Saffron Lake!" Boone bellowed, startling both Travis and Cosette. She yelped, and Travis spun around, his pulse bobbing in every vein in his body.

Boone held up his phone, triumphantly standing in the doorway. "James just called, and someone has put in an offer on Saffron Lake." He laughed, the sound boisterous and full of joy.

Cosette jumped to her feet and rounded the desk. "That's great, Boone," she said sincerely, and he wrapped her in a hug and spun her around. She squealed, and

Travis once again felt like an unwanted third wheel. It was starting to become annoying.

"Congrats, Boone," he said, shaking the man's hand. "I'll get out of your hair."

"Is it good?" Cosette asked. "Are you going to take it?"

Travis left the office as Boone started to tell her about the offer, the happiness and harmony between them something Travis desperately wanted in his life.

He hadn't planned on seeing Poppy that day. He hadn't spoken to her yet, via text or a phone call. She had a job to do that day, and so did he.

But he thought he better move her up his list of priorities if he wanted to have the kind of relationship Boone and Cosette did.

He did, so once he'd ducked around the corner from Cosette's office and into the front lobby, he pulled his phone out of his pocket to text Poppy. *I had a great time last night. What are you doing this evening? Maybe I could stop by with a soda or a treat and we can just—*

He looked up, wondering what to put after that last word.

*Talk,* he typed out, and he quickly re-read the message as someone came in the front door. He'd just tapped *SEND* to get the message off when Cord said, "Yes, there's one left."

Travis looked up in time to watch his cabinmate snag the last doughnut, and his stomach growled at him. He should've taken it before texting. He should've been faster about knowing what to say. Something.

Disappointment at losing the doughnut shot through him, but he still smiled at the ridiculously wide smile on Cord's face as he bit into the glazed pastry. His phone buzzed, and Travis looked at it.

*Anytime after six*, Poppy had said. *I'll be home.*

Travis's own smile solidified and filled with more radiance and happiness. He'd lose any doughnut if the tradeoff was a date—even a simple one—with Poppy.

# Eight

FAVORITE TREAT IS A RICE CRISPY TREAT, POPPY
said, her fingers flying fast. She could text at work, but it
still felt a little dangerous. Like Elise would pop her head
outside and yell at Poppy for flirting with Travis.

He'd already asked her if she wanted a soda or a treat,
and she'd chosen treat. Then he wanted to know what her
favorite kind was.

*And say you'd chosen soda*, he said next. *What would a
cowboy bring to you then?*

She grinned, because the idea of someone wanting to
bring her something she really liked was a bit foreign to
her. No one had done that in years. A decade. Longer. Her
needs always came last, and even Steele didn't care if her
favorite place to eat was the complete opposite of his. Of
course, they hadn't been out to eat in many months, as she
couldn't afford such luxuries.

*I like Fresca with cranberry and grapefruit*, she said. *There's a soda shop on the outskirts of the city where you can get drinks like that.*

*Noted*, Travis said.

*What about you?* she sent back to him. *If I wanted to show up at your cabin with something you'd really enjoy, what would it be?*

*Pizza* came his response in record time. *Pizza and root beer together. Mmm.*

She was surprised he had time to text in the middle of the morning, but she wasn't complaining. She got up at six to be to work by six-thirty in the summer. A chill still rode in the air at that time, because it was still very early in June. But by July, Poppy would love getting the bulk of her work done before the day got too hot.

The early start time also meant she got off work by two o'clock, and that left her the entire afternoon to work around her own farm, run errands, go to appointments, or spend time with Steele.

The thought of her son reminded her that she hadn't answered Iris and her dad about taking him to the city. She'd sent the real dates, and Poppy tapped on her step-mom's text to see them. She wouldn't have anything on her calendar, and sure enough, when Poppy checked, there wasn't anything preventing Steele from going on the trip.

Only Poppy herself.

It was a ten-day trip, from the end of June all the way

through July fifth. She wouldn't even know what to do with herself for ten days without Steele. Now, she had to perform a delicate balancing and juggling act for where he would be while she worked. Today, she'd dropped him off at her sister's house, because Elora didn't work Mondays, and the yard Poppy was working on today was only ten minutes away.

Tomorrow, she'd made arrangements for Steele to be home alone in the morning, and then go over to Pony Power to help out from nine to two. He could clean out stalls and pick up buckets. He could take kids to their appointments or hold a horse's reins while they got shod. Something, and Boone, Molly, and Mission always found something to keep him busy and occupied.

If, for some strange reason, they didn't have anything, Poppy would find him at the farmhouse with Deacon and Tucker, Gray and Elise's children. They were all about the same age, and they got along well. At least according to Poppy's knowledge.

She sighed, the mental load of caring for her son in the summer almost more than she could handle. Adding Travis to the mix had only made things heavier, though she didn't want to admit that. When he came over tonight, where would Steele be? What would she say to him?

"He's eleven," she muttered to herself, still looking at her step-mom's text. "You can tell him you're dating. Talk to him about it." She talked about everything with Steele, and she couldn't keep her relationship with Travis a secret for very long. He'd walked her to the door last night instead of just dropping her and Steele off and going.

Steele hadn't said anything, but Poppy had been hyper-aware of the situation.

*Steele can go to New York City*, she told her step-mom, and then she really did shove her phone in her back pocket and get back to work. After all, these flowerbeds weren't going to weed and then plant themselves, and she had to finish this job today.

She got back down on her hands and knees, the water she'd left running while she'd been texting still going strong. She tugged her gloves back on and attacked the weeds with new vengeance. Because the ground was softer and wetter now, they came up in big clumps, giving her a supreme sense of satisfaction that nothing but weeding ever did.

Poppy loved pulling out the bad and replacing it with something good. There was nothing as amazing as taking a before picture of a garden or bed full of weeds, then tearing through it, cleaning it up, and taking an after picture of the fresh, dark dirt.

She did that with the sun high overhead, her fingers aching. She'd just rinsed off her gloves and hands when the sound of a truck pulling up to the curb met her ears. She turned to find Elise jumping from the passenger seat, a smile on her face.

She beamed at the wheelbarrow full of weeds, as well

as the newly cleared beds. "Poppy, you're incredible," she said.

"It looks good, right?" Poppy asked, so proud of herself. She'd always known how to work hard, but nothing showed the progress quite like gardening. "I just finished and was going to eat lunch. Then I can get planting."

The deafening sound of the back of the truck lifting kept Elise from responding instantly. They both watched as Gray got it all the way up and then started pulling out the ramp that led up to the interior of the big truck.

"Go eat in the air conditioning," Elise said. "I'll help Gray get everything unloaded, and then we'll get planting."

Poppy wasn't going to argue about that plan. She smiled at Elise and headed for her car, where she kept her cooler with her lunch, snacks, and plenty of water. The sun had barely started to touch it, so everything should be plenty cool still.

She climbed into the cab of the truck and started eating, and she spent a most enjoyable half-hour flirt-texting with Travis too. He kept detailing all of his favorite kinds of pizza—*there's nothing better than the deep dish in New York City*, he'd said—until an idea percolated in Poppy's brain and wouldn't let go.

————

"Knead it gently," she said. "It's pizza dough, baby, not the hard rolls we made a couple of months ago." She smiled at Steele, who had flour smeared across his face. Poppy loved cooking and baking with everything inside her, and doing it with her son as she taught him had only helped her love it more. In a different way.

"Like this, Mom?" He barely pushed the dough away from him and then looked at her. Bright hope sat in those eyes, and she loved him so very much.

"Yes," she said. "Like that. We don't want it to be as tough, and we didn't put in as much yeast, so we can't overwork it."

"Overworked dough isn't good," Steele said.

"Nope." Poppy finished up with her dough and plopped it in the prepared bowl. "I'm done. I bet you are too. In the bowl it goes."

He started to shape his ball while Poppy covered hers with a clean tea towel. "We'll let them rise while we work on the toppings." She'd stopped by the grocery store after picking up Steele from her sister's, and she currently had an array of toppings sitting on her counter. Some needed to be cooked before going on the pizza—the green and red peppers, as well as the ground beef—but some could be taken straight from the package or can and placed on the sauced dough.

"First," she said. "The sauce."

"I can still have my own pizza, right?" Steele asked.

"Yes," Poppy said as kindly as she could. Her son had a

way of asking her questions she'd already answered. Multiple times. "Marinara sauce and pepperoni for you." She smiled at him, her plans for the pizza she wanted to surprise Travis with much different than that.

He'd said he liked "all the meats" and pizza was one of the only times he didn't complain that there were veggies present too. He'd said he liked olives and peppers the best, but he could tolerate onions and mushrooms.

Poppy adored mushrooms, pepperoni, olives, and bacon on her pizza, and she had enough dough to make all three varieties. A quick glance at the clock told her that would be the limiting factor. Travis had said he'd drop by about six with her rice crispy treat, but she wanted to be sitting on his porch with two homemade deep dish pizzas and a bowl of salad by five-thirty.

"Your sauce is done," she said to Steele. "So is your pepperoni, but I need you to brown the ground beef and the sausage together. Can you do that?"

"Yep," he said, reaching for the pans they had hanging above the island where they'd kneaded their dough. Poppy cleaned up that mess and then she started putting together the Alfredo sauce while Steele worked on the meats.

With the two of them standing shoulder-to-shoulder at the stove, she said, "Steele, do you know what dating is?"

Her son looked at her, and Poppy gazed on back. "Yes," he said. "I'm almost in sixth grade, Mom. Jordan was dating this girl last month."

She smiled, but Poppy also shook her head. "You can't really date when you're eleven or twelve," she said. She nudged him with her hip. "I mean, you guys might call it dating, but what do you do? Hold hands on the bus?"

"Yeah," he said. "He texted her all the time, I know that. Sometimes he'd go over to her house."

"Mm." Poppy was extremely glad she hadn't had to deal with any of that yet. She had a lecture about dating too young poised on the tip of her tongue, but she swallowed it back. This wasn't about Steele and girls. "I'm dating Travis," she said, watching the cream and butter as it came to a simmer. She turned to grab the shredded parmesan cheese. "And we're old enough to go out together."

"Travis from next door?" Steele asked.

"Yes," she said.

"Is that why he came to the potluck with us?"

"Yes."

Steele stirred his browning meat too, and he'd gotten a nice, brown crust on some pieces. "Good job on the meats," she said. "That looks great."

"Thanks," he murmured.

"Are you upset that I'm dating him?" Poppy asked. She hadn't dated anyone since Eli had left. Not a single person. It had always been her and Steele. Fine, her, Steele, and all the naughty goats. She did make it a point to get outside and spend at least a half-hour with Dorothy too, her donkey best friend. She hadn't done that yet today, and it might be dark before she could.

"No," Steele said. "I just...." He didn't continue, and Poppy gave him some time. Steele was a bright boy, but he liked video games more than books, and running and biking outside more than anything indoors.

"Our first date was on Saturday," she said into the silence as it stretched. "It's not like I've been sneaking around for weeks or months."

"You're taking him a pizza," Steele said, obviously putting together all the pieces.

"He fixed the leaky roof in the barn last fall," she said. "I promised him dinner then. So yes."

"But you just said your first date was Saturday." Steele frowned, his confusion obvious.

"We were friends before," she said. "Sometimes that's how couples start out. They're friends for a while, and then there's these...deeper feelings that grow." She couldn't believe she was describing Travis as a friend. Until she'd sat down in front of him on her fourth date of the hour on Saturday night, she wouldn't have categorized him that way.

She knew him, sure. He'd paid her mortgage and annoyed her because of it. He'd stopped by a few times to check on her. He'd sent food over the holidays. She knew why now—the man had more money than he knew what to do with, and he just wanted to do something good with it—but she hadn't before Saturday.

"So if I like a girl," Steele said. "It's okay to be friends with her first?"

"Absolutely," Poppy said. "You want to be friends with the people you date and marry too, Steele. You have to have something to talk about, and friends talk to each other."

He nodded, and Poppy lifted the complete sauce off the burner. "This is good. Let's get these going, or we're going to be late."

"Am I going over to Travis's with you?" Steele asked.

"No." Poppy faced him, nerves streaming through her. "Unless you want to. Do you want to? Or will you be okay here for an hour or so while I go?"

"I'll be fine here." He reached to flip off the flame under his pan. "Can I watch the new Batman episodes while you're gone?"

She looked at him and swept her fingers across his forehead, moving some of his long hair. "You need a haircut."

"Mom, all the boys wear it long now." He shied away from her, and Poppy only smiled.

"All right," she said. "You can watch the new Batman episodes while I'm gone."

Steele grinned and then said, "All right, I'll get the doughs out and flattened. Is the oven ready?"

It was, and they once again worked side-by-side to put together the three pizzas Poppy had envisioned in her mind. Only one of them was a deep dish, and that was for

Travis. She slid it into the oven first, as it needed more time to bake, and then she ran a dirty hand through her hair.

Panic shot to the soles of her feet. "Can you get the others in?" she asked. "I need to go change."

"Yeah," Steele said. He sprinkled mozzarella cheese over the last pizza and twisted to look at the oven. "I'll put them in when that one has twenty minutes left."

Poppy pressed a kiss to her son's temple and said, "Thanks for cooking with me this afternoon. I have to run out and feed the animals really quick too." She glanced at the clock again. Alarms wailed in her head.

She wasn't going to make it to Travis's by five-thirty. She'd be lucky if she made it back inside by then. She'd need to freshen up after that, and a new war started in her head. Maybe she could wait for Travis to come and ask for his help on the farm. Together, they could feed the goats, chickens, and horses twice as fast.

*He's coming for a date*, she told herself. *Not to work on your farm after he's spent all day working on his.* The Hammond Family Farm wasn't Travis's, but Poppy didn't argue with herself on that point.

She darted for the back door, already praying that God could slow down time, just this once.

# Nine

TRAVIS CLIMBED THE STEPS TO POPPY'S FRONT door, his legs barely able to propel him forward. He hoped they could relax on a couch or comfortable chair some-where—and that he wouldn't fall asleep—while they talked.

He carried a plastic sack from Grover's Corner Store, where he'd rushed to get her the biggest rice crispy treat he'd ever seen. The marshmallow had been dyed pink for some unknown reason to him, but they'd only had one left, so he figured it was a popular treat.

He pushed the doorbell, and Cotton answered with a howling bark. No one came to the door for several long seconds, and Travis wondered if he should try again. Just when he'd lifted his hand to knock, the front door swung in.

Steele stood there, and he wore a denim apron that

went from his shoulder and fell to his knee. Travis smiled at him and said, "Evening, Steele."

"Mom," the boy yelled. "Your date is here."

Surprise darted through Travis, and he looked past the boy to see Poppy. She wasn't there, but her voice called from somewhere inside the house.

"Come on in," Steele said. "We're just about to eat, if my mom will ever come out of her bedroom." He didn't sound super happy about the happenings here at the farmhouse, but Travis's nose had detected something far better than he'd anticipated.

"What were you cooking?" He stepped into the house as Steele turned and went down the hall toward the back of it.

"We made pizza," Steele said. His voice grew a touch more animated. "Mom says you've been to New York and like the deep dish there."

"She's right," he said, pausing when he caught sight of a trio of beautiful pizzas sitting on the island in Poppy's kitchen. "You made these?"

"Yes, sir, we did," Poppy said from his left, and Travis turned toward her. She wore a pair of jeans that could've been painted on her body, and a dusty pink sweater with tan roses on it. She made him smile with the simple sight of her, and his first instinct was to reach toward her and draw her into an embrace.

His fingers flinched in her direction, and his hand lifted from his side before he reminded himself they weren't alone. She smiled at him and touched his hand with hers. "You clean up nice, cowboy."

"You told your son we're dating?"

"Yes," she said, her smile dimming.

Travis wanted to talk more about that, but he figured they'd have time. "You look fantastic," he said. "How was work today?"

"Good," she said. "Hot in the afternoon, but Gray and Elise were there to help with the planting, and we had the map, so it went really quickly."

He indicated the pizza sitting on the counter. "Then you came home and made three pizzas."

"Just one sauce though," she said, her voice set on high-flirt. "Steele likes the marinara on his pizza, and to make a really good marinara sauce, you need more than a couple of hours." She went over to the counter and pulled plates from the cupboard beside the fridge. "Steele, did you put napkins on the table?"

"Yep," he said, looking up from a big bowl of salad. Travis honestly didn't know what to think. This felt so homey. So domestic. So...exactly like what he wanted to come home to after a long day of working on the farm.

A beautiful wife, a fun-loving son, and good food. His mouth watered as he approached the pizzas, and he found one purely pepperoni, one deep dish with a lot of meat and veggies on it, and one with plenty of mushrooms, pepperoni, olives, and not much else on it.

"I know which of these is for me," he said.

"You think you get a whole pizza?" Poppy teased.

Travis grinned at her and then the food again. "Yeah, I think that deep dish is for me."

"Steele's going to New York at the end of the month." Poppy threw her son a look. "Tell him, baby."

"My grandparents are taking me," Steele said. "The salad is done, Mom."

"Do you guys cook every night?" Travis asked.

"Yes," Poppy said while Steele said, "No."

Travis volleyed his gaze between the two of them. Poppy scoffed, her eyes wide. "Yes," she said again, more emphasis on the word this time. "Maybe not gourmet pizza with handmade Alfredo sauce, but yes."

"Does microwaving hot dogs count as cooking?" Steele asked, his smile spreading wider by the second.

"You get out of the kitchen," Poppy said, swatting at him with a towel. "Just for that, you can have your pizza last."

Steele laughed, and Travis saw him as a real person in that moment. Of course he knew Steele Harris was a real person, but it was easy to put children to the side sometimes. But Steele wasn't a tiny toddler or even a little boy. He was eleven years old, with thoughts and feelings and opinions.

"I made brownies the night I microwaved hot dogs," Poppy said, still plenty of haughtiness in her voice. Travis couldn't stop smiling either. "So if you're unhappy with the main dish, then I guess there's no dessert for you." She shook her head when Steele didn't respond and looked back at Travis. "Can you believe him?"

"I always microwave my hot dogs," he said. "I don't even know how else to cook them."

Poppy blinked at him for a moment, once again showing surprise. "You grill hot dogs for maximum flavor," she said. "Can I get you a piece of this fine Alfredo combination pizza?" She picked up a plate, her lips highly glossed in that pink shiny stuff she liked. Travis really liked it too, and his hormones fired at him.

"Yes, please," he said. "More than one."

She handed him a plate with two oversized square pieces of pizza, and he stood from the barstool to add some salad to his plate. "I brought dessert," he said. "For later."

He wasn't sure how long he'd thought this date would be. An hour or so, sitting on her front porch or maybe the patio furniture she kept on the back deck, while they talked and ate dessert bars he'd bought at the corner store. This was so much better, and his heart grew and grew when he thought of Poppy cooking for him.

And not just cooking for him, but making the exact pizza he said he liked best.

"Does Steele cook with you a lot?"

"Yes," she said. "I try to teach him whatever I can, microwaving hot dogs included." She put two pieces of the mushroom and olive pizza on her plate and tonged on some salad. Steele followed her, and to Travis's surprise, he also took salad.

"Can I go, Mom?" He looked at Poppy with soulful puppy dog eyes, and she nodded.

"Take the paper towels, please," she said. "If you spill, clean it up."

"I will." The boy grabbed the paper towels and headed back toward the front door.

"He's going to watch Batman," Poppy explained. "I was hoping to surprise you with the pizza on your porch tonight, but I ran out of time." She looked at him with a measure of apprehension in her gaze. It fled quickly and she added, "I had to do the chores on the farm, and then get ready, and it just wasn't in the cards to get over to you before you came here."

"It's okay," he said. "I'm fine to come over here. At my place, we'd have to share with Cord, and he has nowhere else to go to watch Batman." He smiled at Poppy, who reached up and tucked her pretty strawberry blonde hair behind her ear.

"How is living with Cord?" she asked.

"Good," Travis said. "I don't mind it at all." He headed for the table, which had a vase of fresh flowers sitting on it, and two places set, one across from the other. He sat facing the sliding glass door, but Poppy gasped.

"I forgot the root beer," she said. She yanked open the fridge and pulled out two bottles of it. Her smile could've made the sun look dim, and Travis laughed as she practically pranced over to him with the soda pop. "For you, my cowboy prince."

After she'd set the bottle on the table, their eyes met. Time stopped, and Travis wondered if she could feel that crackle between them. Was she thinking about kissing him the way he was her? Could he lift up just a little and see what she did?

Before he could get himself to move, Poppy stepped back and cleared her throat. She put the other bottle of root beer in front of her spot and returned to the island to get her food. Travis tracked her every move, wondering how he could be so attracted to a person he didn't know very well.

She sat across from him and lifted her fork. "So," she said. "What do you want to talk about?"

Travis blinked, completely unsure now that he'd arrived. He had said they could just talk, so he shouldn't be thinking about kissing at all. "Tell me about Steele's dad," he said, hoping that wasn't too sensitive of a subject.

Poppy's mouth dropped open, and Travis wished he'd made a list of easier dinner conversations. He hadn't been expecting dinner at all. "I mean, you don't have to. It's—"

"No," she said. "It's okay." She put a bite of salad in her mouth and chewed, watching him. After she swallowed, she nodded. "His name was Eli. We were together for a few years. We came here to Ivory Peaks together. Bought this place." She swallowed, and Travis looked at his pizza so he could lift one piece to his mouth.

Everything about it made him sigh and moan. The creamy Alfredo sauce. The salty sausage and ground beef. And bacon too. Holy cow, this was amazing. Poppy had put on red and green peppers, and he loved the pop of sweetness he got from them. Sauteed onions, as well as olives adorned the pie too, and he got the spice of pepperoni and the calmness of Canadian bacon to round it all out.

"This is awesome," he said around the mouthful of food.

Poppy watched him, her smile permanently stuck to her face. "You like it."

He nodded emphatically, as he couldn't speak with all that goodness in his mouth. After he'd finally gotten it down, he said, "That was the best thing I've ever eaten."

"Better than your pizza in New York?"

"Ten times better." He wiped his face with his napkin and went in for another bite. He'd opened the door for their conversation, but Poppy focused on eating for a minute too.

"I was married once," Travis said after he'd finished his first piece of pizza. He told himself he didn't need to inhale it. Not in front of Poppy, anyway. "It ended about fifteen years ago. I dated a little in the city, but nothing too serious. Then I came here."

"How long have you been in Colorado?"

"Ten years," he said.

"You haven't dated here?"

"Here and there," he said. "Again, nothing serious." He looked at her, the unspoken question sitting on the table between them.

"I haven't dated since Eli left," she said. "He was spooked by being a father." She looked over his shoulder, past him, in the direction Steele had gone. "He didn't want the baby." She swallowed and brought her eyes back to Travis's. Pain lived there, and she couldn't wipe it away fast enough. "We weren't married, and he just...left. I haven't seen him or heard from him since."

Travis's eyebrows shot toward the ceiling. "He left you while you were pregnant?"

She nodded. "I think he tried to stay, but in the end, he couldn't. I had Steele by myself, and I named him Steele, because I wanted him to grow up to be as strong as steel. As a single mom, I knew I wouldn't be able to do everything he needed me to do, and he'd have to be strong from a young age. He'd have to help me almost immediately."

Her smile wavered between happiness and sadness now, and Travis wanted to erase all the difficult trials of her life.

"I'm sorry." He reached across the table and squeezed her hand.

"It's been okay," she said. "Well, until last year, when nothing seemed to go right. I had a ton of machinery issues, and I only brought in half as much alfalfa, and I couldn't pay my bills." She looked away, and Travis ducked his chin toward his chest too.

He picked up his second piece of pizza. "Do you ever think that'll be okay between us?" he asked. He held his pizza up, but he didn't take a bite. "I'd really like me helping you to just be...normal. Not this thing that makes everything awkward between us."

"I think...maybe," she said. "I'm working on having it just be normal."

"People help each other," he said.

"They do."

"You just don't like getting help."

"No," she said, lifting her chin. "I don't."

Travis nodded, though he didn't like the answer. He wasn't going to debate with Poppy about it, and while he had plenty of personal stories to share where he'd been the recipient of help, she didn't seem open to them right now.

"I have to go help my momma tomorrow," he said.

"Has she lived here long?" Poppy asked.

Travis nodded and quickly finished his bite of pizza. "She moved here after my daddy died. I was born and raised in Raleigh, but my mom got remarried and moved here. My step-dad died about oh." He blew out his breath. "Four or five years ago, and my half-sisters were here, so Momma stayed."

"Are they still here?"

"Funnily enough, no," he said. "Roberta moved to Albuquerque last summer, and Vivian's husband started dental school in Pennsylvania." He smiled at her. "Do you have siblings?"

"Just one sister," she said. "Elora just got married a couple of years ago. She lives on the northwest side of the city. She watched Steele for me today while I was at work."

Travis liked small families, though the Hammonds were huge, and they had a certain vibe he liked too. "And your parents are taking Steele to New York City."

"It's my step-mom, but yes," Poppy said. "I can't believe both of your mother's husbands died."

Travis let a bit of remorse flow through him. "She's a tough lady," he said. "She's seen a thing or two in her life." He brightened and added, "She taught me to always look for the silver lining in everything, and to always thank God for the good things He's given me, as well as the hard times that might come my way."

"Is that right?" Poppy warmed to him, and Travis realized her faith meant a great deal to her.

"Yeah," he said. "Momma used to preach to us kids that trials were hard yes, but that the Lord must've thought we could endure them, so we better do our best." He chuckled. "I can still hear her ranting as she chopped chocolate for our Thanksgiving Day pies." He pointed toward the kitchen with his salad fork. "You teach Steele how to make pizza. My momma lectured me about everything under the sun while she cooked."

Poppy laughed lightly too, just a few giggles before she sobered again. "Have you had many trials, Travis?"

"A fair few," he said, clearing his throat. "Momma told us that the Lord gave us trials so we could learn something. I've tried to find the lesson in all the things I've endured."

She smiled at him, the gesture filled with light and encouragement. "Name one."

Travis shifted in his seat. "Uh, let's see."

"If you want," she said. "If it's too personal, it's okay."

Travis thought about all she'd shared with him that night. She'd gotten pregnant with Steele when she wasn't married. He wasn't going to judge her for that, and she hadn't had to tell him that. He appreciated that she did, however, and he wanted to trust her. He wanted her to trust him.

"We had a hard time getting pregnant," he said. "I was working a lot in the city, and we didn't—I don't know. We didn't come together when we should've. We suffered on our own, and we didn't need each other. It was easy to split up then." His voice hurt, because he'd pushed the words through such a small opening. He hadn't quite ever put into words why his marriage hadn't worked out, but he'd said the truth.

"Jenni—the last woman I dated in the city—was the same. Our relationship was more about convenience than anything else. She didn't need me, and I knew it."

Poppy simply looked at him, an energy pouring from her gaze he couldn't decipher. Travis couldn't hold the weight of it and he returned to his plate of food. He finished in silence, and Poppy got up to clear the plates.

She put everything in the sink, and he knew she'd have a ton of dishes to deal with eventually. "Do you want to come meet Dorothy?" she asked, pressing one hip into the counter beside her.

"Is she a goat?" Travis asked, getting to his feet. "Because if so, I'm fairly sure I've met her."

"She's not a goat. She's my only donkey."

He smiled at her and caught her around the waist as he started to go past. "We're okay, right? You're not freaked out by anything I said?"

Her pretty blue eyes focused on him, and he could get burned by this woman. In fact, he was fairly sure his skin was singeing right now. "No," she said. "I'm not freaked out. I hear you saying it's important to you to feel needed."

"Sure," he said. "Everyone wants to feel that way."

"You want a partner who'll lean on you, and you can lean on them."

"Accurate," he said, swallowing. He may blow open everything with what he wanted to say next. "I'm tired of living alone. Coming home alone. Relying only on myself. If I have a bad day, I want to tell someone about it. I want that no-judgment zone I see Gray has with Elise, and Matt with Gloria, and Hunter with Molly. Their wives love them, even if they're not perfect, and I don't know."

Travis couldn't keep talking. "That sounds nice to me, I guess."

He released Poppy and stacked his dishes in the sink too. "I'll help you with these when we get back."

She hadn't moved, and when he faced her again, she said, "I want that too, Trav. It does sound really nice." Then she ducked her head and added, "Grab the crispy treats, cowboy. We can wander the farm and keep talking, but only if there's the promise of sugar." She gave him a sugary smile that said the harder part of their conversation had ended, and relief rushed through Travis.

Then he grabbed the bag with the rice crispy treats and followed her onto the back deck.

# *Ten*

POPPY LOVED A SUMMER EVENING, EVEN IF THE breeze was a bit brusque tonight. The sun had gone behind the majestic Rocky Mountains in the west, but there was still plenty of light and heat leftover from its time in the sky that day. She sighed as she went down the steps from her deck to her back yard, and she glanced over to Travis when he took her hand in his.

He wore a smile to go with his rugged good looks and the cologne that literally made Poppy's mouth turn dry. "I brought the treats," he said, lifting the bag.

"I think you'll like Dorothy," she said, returning his smile.

"You seem to," he said.

"I love her," Poppy said. "I rescued her about a month after Steele was born, and honestly...I think she rescued me." She went through the gate and out onto the farm,

Cotton right at her heels. He darted ahead of her on the path, already doing his canine thing. She smiled at him too. "He needs a proper herd of sheep. He'd be so happy corralling them around."

Travis chuckled and said, "I could get you those sheep."

"Oh, please," Poppy said with a laugh. "What am I going to do with sheep? I don't have time to take care of them right now." She thought about working the farm full-time, as she had in the past. She could see the emerald green fields in her mind, and they extended all the way to the mountains. Little white dots of sheep populated them, and her smile grew. "It is a nice thought, though."

Poppy looked up to him. "Why don't you have a farm of your own?" He obviously had enough money. Heck, he could buy her place, and then she wouldn't have any room to get upset if he did show up with a few dozen sheep, paid all the bills, and fixed leaky rooftops.

"I don't know," he said with a sigh. "When I first moved here, I didn't want one. There was too much I didn't know and didn't want to learn."

"You've been here a while now."

"Yeah," he said. "I love the community on a family farm like the Hammonds. It's not huge, but there's several of us there. It feels safe and comfortable. I'm not sure I know how to build that."

Poppy took a moment to consider what he'd said. "You think that comes from Gray and Elise?"

"Absolutely," he said. "And Chris and Hunter, Molly and Matt. They all play a part in making everyone feel welcome."

"You don't think you're welcoming?"

"No," he said, ducking his head. "I don't."

Truth be told, Travis could be intimidating. He was tall, and that didn't help for Poppy, who wasn't quite so blessed in the height department. He had dark features all around, which she found sexy and strong, but that she could see perhaps warning others to stay away. He was talented, rich, and kind.

"You're a really nice person," she said quietly. "I think you're more welcoming than you think you are."

"That's a kind thing to say," he whispered.

The braying of a donkey met her ears, and Poppy turned toward the pasture. She released Travis's hand and got up on the bottom rung of the fence. "Dorothy!" she called. "Come meet Travis. You're going to love him."

Dorothy's voice got closer, and she rounded the thicket of trees out in her pasture only a moment later. She brayed and brayed and brayed as she ran toward Poppy, whose whole heart opened to the animal.

"Wow," Travis said, chuckling. "She loves you."

Poppy loved her too, and she wrapped her arms around Dorothy's big head and hugged her. The donkey embraced her back, her voice still a bit of a moan in the back of her throat. "Hey, girl," Poppy said to her, her voice tender. "Did you miss me today? Did you eat all your dinner?" She'd been out here only an hour or so ago, so Dorothy couldn't be that lonely. Not only that, but Poppy had put all the goats and horses in the pasture with her once summer had hit. She had some repairs and improvements to make on the stables, paddocks, and pens those animals otherwise lived in, and they could all use good grazing this summer.

"This is Travis," she said to Dorothy. She dropped from the fence and indicated him. "Say hello now."

Dorothy opened her mouth and brayed in a "Hee-haw hello!" and Travis burst out laughing. He tousled Dorothy's mane right between her ears, and the donkey tried to get closer to him too.

"Oh, she likes you," Poppy said, plenty of teasing in her voice. "She's particular about who she likes, so you must be something special."

He looked at her, and Poppy could only widen her smile. She hoped she met his standards for a girlfriend, though homemade pizza in a messy kitchen, on a farm that barely operated, surely didn't tick any boxes for him. She had changed into a pair of skinny jeans and paired them with a cute pink sweater with tan roses on it. It was short-sleeved and hugged her curves, and Elora said she looked beautiful in it.

She wore makeup—but not as much as last night—and if she'd put on her work boots and hat, she'd be the cowgirl complement to Travis's hot cowboy vibe.

Travis took her hand again, pulling her closer to him.

He pushed his cowboy hat up with his free hand and lowered his head as if he'd kiss her. Poppy's pulse boomed through her body, because she hadn't kissed a man in a very, very long time.

Her muscles tensed, and her progress toward Travis slowed. Cotton chose that moment to bark, startling her and Travis alike. He exhaled and looked to his left. "He scared me."

He'd also broken the moment, and Poppy wasn't sure if she was relieved or completely disappointed. Surely she'd remember how to kiss a man, but right now, she didn't even know where to put her hands. One sat limply in Travis's and the other hung loosely at her side.

Cotton continued to yip and bark, and Poppy frowned. "That doesn't sound right." She turned and went through the slats in the fence to enter the pasture. Dorothy brayed at her, and she ran one hand along the donkey's neck as she went past her.

She reached the trees and went around them, Travis on her heels. Out in the field, Cotton had laid down flat in the grass, just like a border collie did when herding sheep. He'd gotten all the goats together with the horses, but he wasn't trying to keep them in a pack.

Instead, he had his back to them as he faced out toward the open pasture. Poppy looked that way too, her pulse picking up speed again for an entirely new reason. "What is it?" she called to the dog, but Cotton didn't look at her.

She strode through the grass toward her animals, and the couple of horses she'd managed to keep were definitely nervous. "Travis," she said. "Do you see anything?" Maybe a coyote or a wolf or something had wandered out of the hills.

Goats bleated, and her big horse, Valentine, neighed nervously.

"Right there," Travis said, pointing in the same direction Cotton was looking. "Something moved out there."

Poppy strained to see through the twilight, but she did see something twitch and move a moment later. "It's gray," she said. Sudden understanding bloomed in her mind. "It's a lynx."

"Could be a cougar," he said.

"It has spots," she said, finding the animal fully now. She tracked it as it took a single step and then paused again. Cats could hold so still, even the big variety. As far as big cats went, the lynx was one of the smaller ones, and Poppy exhaled slowly. "Will you help me get the animals in the barn for tonight?"

"Of course." Travis started toward them. She wanted to call to him that she'd get some ropes for the horses, but he simply led them to the gate, all of them following him willingly. They didn't scatter out on the path, and once Poppy had gone through the gate too, she whistled to Cotton.

The dog jumped to his feet and turned toward her before breaking into a run to meet her. Dorothy cried, but

Poppy just patted her neck and said, "Keep going, honey. We're almost there. You'll be safe in the barn."

She and Travis got all the animals in stalls, with fresh straw and food and water, and then she let him leave first, and she secured the door behind her. "I'm not going to be able to let Steele come out alone in the morning."

"Oh, that thing'll be long gone by morning," Travis said, peering into the distance again. He faced her, took her hand, and said, "We're always going to have a canine chaperone out here, aren't we?" He grinned, and Poppy couldn't help giggling.

"Probably," she said. They fell into step as they started back toward the house. "Do you not kiss in front of dogs?"

"Sure, I do," he said as he laughed. "You seemed a bit nervous about it though."

"Just the kissing," she admitted.

"Why's that?"

"Remember the part of my history where I haven't dated in twelve years? Heck, longer than that." She'd met Eli when she was twenty-one. "Eli and I were together for three years, so you're my first new boyfriend in fourteen years, Travis."

"I see your point," he said.

She wasn't sure what else to say, and he didn't try to kiss her again. He'd looped the rice crispy treats over the post closest to the fence, and once they'd returned to the back deck, he handed her one. She sank into the rocking loveseat on her deck, glad when Travis chose to sit directly beside her.

She kicked off her shoes and tucked her feet under her, then leaned into him, easily putting herself into his arms. His heart beat steadily and with power against her ear, and she simply held her dessert and listened to his body talking to her for a few seconds.

"I sure do like you," she whispered. "I know it may not have seemed like it for a while there, but I do."

"I'm glad," he said. "Because I sure do like you too." He filled the silent sky with the crinkling of his wrapper then, and Poppy smiled to herself. "I've never had one of these before."

"Never?" she asked. She pushed herself up so she could watch him. "You've lived here for ten years and have never had one of these. Unbelievable."

He grinned at her and then studied his pink rice crispy treat. "Is it really that good?"

"It's life-changing," she said. "Go on then. Take your first bite."

He grinned and did exactly that, and Poppy watched as those dark eyes filled with surprise and delight. Then they rolled back in his head, and he closed them, a moan coming out of his mouth. "Yeah," he said with the treat still in his mouth. "That's good."

She laughed and started unwrapping hers too. She sure hoped she could elicit such a sound of pleasure from him when they finally did kiss. But for now, she too took a bite of her rice crispy treat and let the delicious sugar, marshmallow, and cereal fill her soul with joy.

After she swallowed, she said, "Okay, this or that: apple pie or pumpkin pie?"

"Uh, neither," he said. "If I'm eating pie, it better be chocolate."

Poppy grinned. "Okay. Hot breakfast or cold breakfast?"

"Hot, if someone else is making it. Cold, if I am."

She took another bite of her treat and looked at him.

"Uh, morning person or night owl?" he asked.

"Morning person," she said. "You?"

"I love staying up late," he admitted. "Especially if I have ice cream to keep me company."

That tickled Poppy's funny bone, and she laughed. Travis joined his lower voice to hers, and she adored the music they made together. She felt whisked away from her hard, dry life on this farm. Travis infused new life into it—into her—and she couldn't wait to see what would next transform right before her eyes.

# Eleven

HUNTER HAMMOND LEANED DOWN AND SWEPT his lips across his wife's forehead. "I'm headed out, hon," he said.

Molly still lay in bed, though the summer sun had started to lighten the day. That happened earlier and earlier lately, but she wouldn't get out of bed for a while. Hunter didn't want her to. She was nine months pregnant, and now overdue with their first baby by a whole day.

She'd cried last night when she didn't go into labor, and he'd never felt more powerless than he had in that moment.

"I know the baby's going to come today," he added as she stirred. She rolled over and wrapped her arms around the back of his neck. "I'll have my phone all day, and I've made sure everything I'm doing today is cancel-able. Call me the moment you feel anything."

"I will," she murmured. "I love you, Hunt."

"Love you too, sweetheart." He kissed her then, one hand easily sliding to her belly and their baby. He loved the life inside her with everything he had, and Hunter hadn't known he could feel so much for so many people. He'd come a long way in his life, and he experienced a powerful wave of gratitude for good therapists, good parents, good family members, and the love of a good woman—all of which had helped him get to this point.

He straightened, and Molly kept her eyes closed. He adjusted his tie and practically tiptoed out of their bedroom. They lived in a high-rise building in downtown Denver, and Hunter only had to collect his briefcase from the dining room table where he'd left it last night, head down the elevator, and walk to the building next door to get to work.

By the time he went through security and rode another elevator up to his office on the top floor at HMC, he'd been away from home for about nine minutes. Getting home took less time, because he didn't have to wait in line to get into the building.

He sighed as he sat, his briefcase having been tossed into the chair on the other side of his desk. He immediately turned and looked out the wall of windows, wondering why he'd come today at all. He'd been prepping everyone at HMC for his absence for the past month.

The company could run without him for a while, and besides, he had a phone.

He wasn't going to miss the important things in his child's life, no matter what. He did some important things here at HMC, but being a father—and a good one—was Hunter's number one priority.

His phone hadn't chirped or buzzed, but still, he checked it. Nothing from Molly yet, and a vein of foolishness opened up. Of course there wasn't anything from her yet. He'd only been gone for ten minutes.

"Please, dear Lord," he prayed. "She has to have that baby today." He wasn't sure what he could do about it if she didn't, and he didn't want to listen to his wife quietly weep as she fell asleep for a second night in a row. "I'd take this from her if I could. Please let the baby come today."

They had a couple of male names on their short list, as well as a few female names, as Hunter and Molly hadn't learned the gender of their baby. He looked out over the city, letting his feelings ebb and flow, come and go. He honestly didn't care if he became a father to a baby boy or a baby girl. He just wanted the baby to come so his sweet Molly could be spared another night of swollen feet, tightness in her back and shoulders, discomfort, and pain.

At the same time, Hunter was pretty sure no one should allow him and Molly to take an infant home and be the sole caretakers of it. He smiled just thinking that. He'd been ill-prepared for a lot of things in his life—including marriage and becoming the CEO of his family company at the age of twenty-five. Sometimes, in quiet moments like this, he could see his accomplishments and growth, but he pressed against the pride that tried to creep into his heart.

He was ready to be a father, while at the same time, he had no idea how to be a father.

His phone rang, and Hunter jumped for it. The word *Dad* sat there, and Hunter's pulse went down a notch. The adrenaline still flowed through him, and that would take longer to dissipate. "Hey, Dad," he said after he'd answered the call.

"No baby overnight?" his father asked.

"Unfortunately, no," he said, his frown deepening. "We walked around the block a few times. She ate some spicy Mexican food. She's ready to start drinking the castor oil."

"Don't do that," Elise called from somewhere. "It doesn't work. Old wives tale."

Hunter chuckled. "That's what I read her online. She's not going to do it."

"He'll come today," Dad said with confidence, but Hunter wasn't so sure.

"You guys can go to Coral Canyon," Hunter said. "It's fine. The baby will be around for a while, and you don't need to be here the moment he's born."

"You're out of your mind," Dad said with a chuckle. "Not only do I want to be there as soon as you and Molly will let me, but your mother would grill me and serve me to the children if she was a thousand miles away when that baby is born."

Hunter laughed with his dad, but it felt good to have so much love and support surrounding him. "How's Jane?"

"Oh, she's thrilled we're still here," Dad said dryly. "She's making plans to try to get us to let her stay here."

"Is that going to work?" Hunter asked. "She could be my nanny for the summer." He knew it was hard on his teenage sister to leave for the summer, every summer. She basically lost all of her friends and had to start over every year. He'd been lucky enough to step back into his relationships when he returned from Coral Canyon, but Jane hadn't had the same fortune.

"It's not a bad idea," his mother said, and Hunter perked up.

"It would help me and Molly," he said. "She wants to keep working at Pony Power, and I've already arranged to be gone a lot this summer. So I can stay out at the farm with Jane." There were plenty of adults out on the farm, including Hunter's grandfather. The foreman lived nearby, and several cowboys out in the cabins. "Just a thought."

"I'm so tired thinking about it," Dad said wearily.

"She's fourteen," Hunter said. "And finally has some good friends."

"Let's see when the baby comes."

Hunter nodded, his jaw tightening. He knew why his

father didn't want to leave Jane behind. Magical things happened in Coral Canyon, and Hunter did love going up north, to the cooler summers in the Teton Mountains. He also understood why Jane didn't want to go. He felt torn, the way he often did when it came to his parents and then his siblings.

"Well, do let us know when she has the baby," his mom said. "We can't wait."

"I'll let you know," Hunter said. The call ended, and he reached out and put his phone on the windowsill.

It didn't beep, chime, ring, or buzz for hours.

———

HUNTER FINALLY COULDN'T TAKE SITTING in his silent office anymore. He picked up his phone and went downstairs to Lab Six, where he'd first worked when he'd come to Hammond Manufacturing Company. He still had friends there, and he stepped off the elevator at the same time a huge cheer went up further in the lab, where the men and women sat at desks.

Beyond that, they had spectacular equipment here to run their tests, improve their predictions, and perfect their science. Hunter loved math and science, and numbers had always spoken to his soul. He did crossword puzzles on the daily as well, simply because he liked it when things lined up neatly and nicely.

He entered the desk area to see a man named George

standing on a desk, his phone lifted up in one hand. Hunter smiled, because the joy on George's face couldn't be denied.

"What's going on here?" he asked the nearest person. The woman—Kellie—glanced at him without even looking at him.

"George just got notified that he's a finalist for the Fields Medal."

"That's fantastic," Hunter said, and he joined his hands together in the applause still happening. George saw him, and the smile slid right off his face. He hastened to jump down from the desk, and more heads turned Hunter's way.

"You don't have to stop celebrating," he said in a quiet voice. He hated this part of the job. Because he'd moved upstairs to the big office—and now signed their checks—everyone in Lab Six looked at him differently. He supposed they should, but he wished they wouldn't.

"Did anyone get a cake?" he asked.

"Hunt," Cassie said, his former co-worker in the lab coming toward him. "Did you hear the good news about George?"

"Yeah," he said, receiving her into a hug. She'd just had her third child last year, and Hunter suddenly wanted to ask her for all kinds of advice. "Kellie just told me."

"Mister Hammond," Kellie said, one hand pressed to her heart. "I didn't know it was you."

"It's fine," he assured her. He gave her a smile and looked back to Cassie. "Did anyone get him a cake?"

"We didn't know they'd be calling today." She smiled at him. "You're still here, so no baby, I'm assuming."

"No baby," he confirmed, leaning closer. "Molly's dying. How do I get this baby to come already?"

Cassie laughed. "Oh, Hunt, they have minds of their own. It's best to learn that now, actually."

He sighed and plucked his phone from his pocket. "I'm ordering lunch for Lab Six," he said, his voice much louder now. No one had really gone back to work, but George wasn't standing on the desk anymore. "From Poultry and Porridge. I'm sending the menu to Cassie right now, and she'll distribute it. I want orders on my phone in ten minutes." He held up his device as he turned in a full circle.

He faced George again and went to tell him congratulations. He shook the man's hand and said, "Good for you, George. I mean, amazing." He grinned as his phone started pinging and pinging. "I want you to come upstairs and tell me all about it one day, okay?"

"Yes, sir," George said, and Hunter had gotten used to men twice his age calling him "sir." He didn't like it, but at least he didn't flinch.

He kept his eyes on his phone then, because Molly's message could get lost in the fray of lunch for Lab Six. He stood among them, not really one of them, and Hunter hated feeling like an island. He caught Joel's eye, and the two of them moved toward a small conference room they'd used several times. They'd been working with crystals and x-ray machines when Hunter had moved out of Lab Six, and he missed the work with a fierceness only Lab Six could remind him of.

"I printed a roster of everyone here in Lab Six," Joel said, putting the paper on the table. "You say the names of the orders you have, and then we'll know if we have everyone."

Hunter started reading them off, and by the end, he was only missing two. He started the online order at Poultry and Porridge, and while he did that, the last two orders came in. He'd no sooner hit ORDER and gotten a confirmation when his phone rang.

His wife's name sat there.

His heart leapt into the back of his throat. "It says it'll be ready in ninety minutes," he said. "I might not be here." He showed Joel his phone and swiped on the call. "Mols, tell me you're having the baby."

"Hunter," she said, her voice mostly made of air. "I'm having the baby."

"I'm five minutes out." He strode from the conference room, his goal singular now.

"My water broke, I think," she said. "I've had a couple of contractions." She sniffled through the line, and Hunter wished he'd gone home instead of coming down to Lab Six. He dismissed that thought, because he loved going to Lab Six.

"I'm going into the elevator," he said. "I'm probably going to lose you."

"Okay." Molly gasped. "Another contraction is starting, Hunt. Hurry-oh—?" The call ended as the elevator doors slid closed, and Hunter looked up at the ceiling. He wished he could teleport to her, but he couldn't.

When he dashed inside his penthouse apartment only a few minutes later, Molly sat at the dining room table, the baby bag she'd packed weeks ago sitting in front of her. "Hey, sweetheart," he said, nearly ripping his tie from around his throat. "Let's go."

"Did you call a car?"

"Yes," he said. "They're already downstairs." He owned a truck, but it would take too long to get it out of the parking garage, as it was oversized and had to be parked in a special spot. They could take Molly's sedan, but Hunter knew there'd be no shortage of people to give them a ride home later. Or, he could come back here and get one of their cars before Molly and the baby were discharged.

Molly got to her feet gingerly, and Hunter didn't remove his hands from her once as they made their way downstairs. The driver waited at the car, opened the door, and said, "I've called the hospital. They're waiting for you."

Hunter didn't know what to say. Foolishness filled him. Who had a driver of a shiny black car call the hospital for them? He shook the thoughts from his head as he slid onto the backseat beside Molly. "Thank you," he finally said to the driver as he pulled away from the curb.

Ten minutes later, two nurses met them at the entrance to the hospital, and one said, "Mister Hammond, we've called your doctor."

Molly hissed, and every eye flew to her. She stumbled, and Hunter yelped as he grabbed onto her. His heart had never beat so hard as it did in that moment, everything moving so slowly and yet so fast at the same time.

His wife ended up on her knees, Hunter keeping her from going down any more. "Mols," he said, desperate to get her up and into a room. "Are you okay?" Tears pressed behind his eyes, but he would not let them out.

Not right now.

Molly's leaked down her face. "Yes," she said. "I... contraction." She pressed her eyes closed as a nurse knelt beside her.

"Breathe, Molly." she said kindly. "You need to breathe."

She did, and Hunter did, and the two nurses, him, and the driver managed to get her into a wheelchair. "I'm okay," she said once, then twice. Then again. She squeezed Hunter's hand as they moved inside the hospital. Before they'd reached the elevator, she moaned, her grip tightening to the point of pain.

"Another contraction," the nurse said, and Hunter caught the look she threw to the other woman. "That's fast."

"When did they first start?" the second woman asked.

Hunter blinked, his mind blank. "Uh, she called me about twenty minutes ago."

"Only a few minutes before that," Molly said through gritted teeth. "My water broke, and I had a contraction. Then another one, and I called Hunt."

They went up to the fourth floor, and Molly finally relaxed back in her seat as the door opened. Two more nurses stood there, and Hunter realized something was happening.

"What's going on?" he asked.

"We need to get her in a room, stat," one of them said, and he got separated from his wife. He followed at a brisk clip, and he tossed his jacket over the back of the chair while they got Molly in bed.

"She's dilated to a nine," a nurse said. "Page her doctor right now."

"A nine?" Hunter asked. He'd taken the birthing classes with Molly. He knew what that meant. "She's going to have the baby right now."

"Yes," a nurse said, and he looked around at all the bustling activity. Warmers being set up. Tools and instruments set out.

"Doctor Gillmore is ten minutes out."

"She might not have ten minutes."

He looked at Molly, who wore pure fear on her face. "Hunt," she whimpered. "I can't have the baby without an epidural."

He looked at the nurse, but she shook her head, her eyes wide. He moved in front of his wife, bending over the side of the bed to do so. "Hon," he said. "You're going to have the baby without an epidural. Maybe without Doctor Gillmore. It's fine." He cradled her face in his hand and smiled at her gently. "It's going to be okay. All these fine women are here with us, and they're not going to let anything bad happen to you or the baby. Okay?"

She nodded, and Hunter once again found his Molly to be the strongest woman he knew. Her face tensed up again, and she laid back in the bed, groaning already.

"She's at a ten," a nurse said. "She needs to push."

"Now?" Hunter asked.

"Now." She looked over her shoulder. "Do we have any doctors on the floor?"

Someone ducked out into the hall, where a red light flashed. A woman Hunter had never seen before hurried into the room, taking gloves from a nurse and pulling them on. "She's at a ten?"

"Yes, ma'am," the nurse said. She vacated the stool in front of Molly, and the doctor took it.

She smiled at Hunter and then Molly. "Hello, I'm Doctor Streamer. You're going to have a baby, so let's see what we've got." She peered at Molly. "Boy or girl?"

"We don't know," Hunter said.

"Oh, I love a surprise," she said, smiling as she looked up. "You're ready, Momma. On the next contraction, you push, okay?"

Molly nodded in short little bursts of her head, and Hunter moved to stand behind her. Her next contraction came quickly, and Hunter held her up while she pushed. Only a few minutes later—hardly any pushing at all—and the tiny, tinny, beautiful cries of an infant filled the room.

Hunter couldn't look away from the angry red human as the doctor lifted him up. "It's a boy," she yelled, and Hunter's happiness knew no bounds. He kissed Molly's forehead and repeated what the doctor had said.

"It's a boy, Mols."

She smiled too, tears in her eyes, and Hunter once again let his emotions run cage-free through him. "What do you want to name him?" she asked.

Hunter took a couple of steps down the bed, and Dr. Streamer looked at him. "Do you want to cut the cord?"

He nodded and went to do what she'd said. The boy wailed with a healthy set of lungs, and Hunter loved him so very much. One look, and he'd do anything for that child. Anything at all.

Once the baby had been separated from Molly, a nurse whisked him away to be bathed and wrapped, and Hunter could only watch. "Hunt," Molly said, and he turned back to her.

"Ryder," he said. "I think we should name him Ryder."

"Ryder Christopher," she said, and Hunter nodded, his own tears slipping down his face now, no restraints in sight.

# Twelve

GRAY HAMMOND PRESSED A KISS TO HIS grandson's cheek, the infant the most perfect thing he'd ever laid eyes on. "I love him so much," he murmured. He'd thought his heart had been full when he'd had Hunter all those years ago.

This was so very different, and yet so much the same. The boy didn't have his eyes open, and all anyone could talk about was how much of a Hammond he was. The nose, the chin, the forehead. Gray had texted his brothers up in Coral Canyon that Hunter and Molly had had the baby, and they were all waiting for news of the name and gender, as well as pictures.

He cradled the slumbering baby in his arms and took his phone back from his wife. The picture she'd just taken of him and baby Ryder made him smile, a joyful sigh pulling through his whole body.

*This is Ryder Christopher Hammond*, he typed out. He attached the picture and sent the message flying from here to Wyoming.

Elise's best friends lived there, and they were as excited as she was about the birth of this new baby. Some of his brothers still had very small children of their own—Ames had a three-year-old, which only served to make Gray feel all of his sixty-two years. He was old enough to be a grandfather. It was the fact that he had little kids at home still that tripped him up.

*He's gorgeous*, Bree said.

*Definitely a Hammond*, her husband Wes texted.

*He looks like Wade*, Cy said, speaking of his youngest. *He looked just like that when he was born.*

*I love him already*, Sophia said.

*I can't wait to meet him*, Patsy said.

More love came from Gray's family, and he was glad he was the one fielding the texts and not Hunter. His son looked a bit shell-shocked, to be honest, and Gray would actually be worried if he didn't.

He looked up from his phone and found his fourteen-year-old daughter standing there. "Do you want to hold him?" he asked Jane. She'd inherited her features from her mother, and she was light and airy from forehead to big toe. She had pretty blonde hair that spilled down her back in long, straight strands, and a gorgeous pair of blue eyes.

Jane nodded, and Gray got to his feet. He'd take any

opportunity he could to connect with Jane. Especially right now, when she seemed to be angry with him at every turn. He'd never parented a teenage girl, and he had no clue what he was doing. Elise assured him he was doing a good job, and that if Jane wasn't mad at him, Gray was doing something wrong.

He turned as Jane took his place, and he gently lowered the newborn into her arms. "Watch his head." He stepped back after he'd transferred the baby to his daughter, his heart filling with so much love for her. He leaned down and touched his lips to the top of her head. "I love you, bug."

"Love you too, Daddy."

He stayed nearby, wishing he knew how to talk to her. He didn't, so he simply let the silence say all the things he couldn't. Elise had taken Hunter to get something to eat, and Molly slept in the bed. They'd left their little boys with Cosette, Boone, and Gerty at the farmhouse, and Gray would bring his father to see the baby tomorrow, when things weren't so chaotic.

"Daddy?" Jane asked, and Gray looked up from his phone.

"Hmm?"

"I wanted to ask you if I could bring Paisley to Coral Canyon with us. Just for a couple of weeks, not the whole summer or anything. I've already talked to Ava and Ella, and they won't feel bad. They said they wouldn't. The other cousins aren't really my age anyway, and they're boys." Her eyes were so wide, and Gray hated the fear in them. "Her mom said she can come for a couple of weeks, and Uncle Wes said he's going to be coming down to check on Mikey about then, and he can bring us home and take me back."

She rocked the baby, giving him a healthy pat and shake. Gray didn't know what to say or do. She'd clearly thought this through. She had solutions for all of the questions he would've had.

"Have you talked to your mother about this?" He knew she had, because this conversation screamed of Elise.

"Yes, she helped me brainstorm ways to get there and back without bothering you."

"Jane." He hung his head and shook it. "You don't bother me."

"I don't want to lose her as a friend, Daddy. She's the best friend I've had, and she's already asked her mom." Jane's voice pitched up, and Gray couldn't stand it when she cried. When she was angry, he had a much easier time putting on his Dad-mask and saying no.

But when she was calm and quiet and really trying to have a conversation with him, he couldn't stand the tears. It hurt his heart too much.

"Jane," he said. "It sounds like you have it worked out." He smiled at her; her bottom lip trembled.

"Really?"

"Yes," he said. "Really."

"I can't believe this worked," she said, shifting the baby to reach up and wipe her face. "Can I get one of those new phones like Hunter's?"

Gray burst out laughing and shook his head. "No, baby, let's start with this friend in Wyoming, okay?"

"Everyone has a new phone," she said, and Gray felt the moment slipping away from him.

"I know they do." He straightened and glanced over to Molly. She slept still, and he was glad she could get the rest she needed while they were there to hold her baby. He still couldn't quite believe he was now a grandfather, and his heart swelled with love again.

"When will we go?" Jane asked, and Gray switched his attention back to her.

"Probably the day after Hunt and Molly take Ryder home," he said. "Momma will want to stay until then, make sure they have a fridge full of food. All of that." He knew his wife, and Elise would not leave a moment before that baby went home. "So a few more days."

"Okay." Jane looked back at her nephew, a softness entering her face that only a newborn could bring. Gray wanted to take a snapshot of that moment, when his daughter was so soft and so angelic —just the way she'd been when he'd held her for the first time in the hospital—and he blinked to do it mentally.

Behind him, the door opened, and Hunter and Elise returned with bags and bags of food. Far more than any of them could eat. Hunt paused, his eyes on his wife. "Let's eat out here," he said. "Let her sleep."

Gray started toward them. Elise looked at Jane. "Can you sit with her and the baby while we eat? I'll come get you in a few minutes."

"Sure, Momma," she said, and Elise's eyes flew to Gray's. She asked him if Jane had spoken to him without saying a word, and Gray slid his hand along her waist.

"I said yes," he whispered as he leaned into her. "Thanks for helping her with all the solutions."

"She's trying," Elise said as they both turned to follow Hunter back out of the room.

"She's great," Gray said. Down the hall, he sank onto the couch with his son. "That is the cutest baby in the whole world."

Hunt grinned at him and handed him a brown bag of food. "Thanks, Dad. I think so too."

"Now, it looks like you got enough food to feed an army." Gray opened the bag to no less than six cheeseburgers. "Which one of these is mine?"

———

A COUPLE OF DAYS LATER, Gray slapped his gloves against his thigh as he left the barn. He'd just finished the evening chores on the farm, all of his goats, horses, chickens, cattle, sheep, and the lone pig he owned fed and ready for the night.

Poppy Harris next door had reported a lynx at her place recently, and Gray had been extra diligent with making sure his fences were strong and tight, as well as keeping more eyes than usual on the pastures. The last thing he needed was to lose livestock because he hadn't been paying attention to a warning.

He only had to stop in the shed and put away the equipment and tools he'd used to help Elise in their vegetable garden that day. He honestly didn't know why she planted one every year. She did it here, and then they'd go to Coral Canyon, and she'd plant again. She loved gardening with everything inside her, and Gray had never been able to tell her no, even when she was angry.

Laughter floated on the air as Gray crossed the road between the farm buildings and the cabins, and he looked down the lane. He loved this life here in Ivory Peaks, and he couldn't believe he'd once driven downtown every day and lawyered day and night for HMC.

At the same time, he'd loved that life too. *Different phases*, he told himself, because it really felt like he'd lived two lives. Sometimes three or four.

Hunt was still the CEO of HMC, and Gray didn't see him quitting any time soon. Michael, Wes's son, was the next oldest grandchild who could possibly take over the company, and he was fifteen years old. He'd be sixteen come November, but he still had a whole bunch of years ahead of him before he could move into Hunt's corner office.

Gray worried about his son constantly, though Hunter had never really given him a good reason to do so. Maybe with Molly, when they were teenagers. But now? Gray really didn't need to worry so much.

He did, though, and he couldn't stop himself. He worried about Jane too, and Deacon and Tucker. He wanted the very best for them, but he also wanted to teach them how to handle disappointment. How to deal with hard situations and people. How to be hard workers and good people.

He reached for the door handle on the shed and pulled open the door, the sound of voices meeting his ears now. A lower voice, clearly male. And then...his daughter.

Gray's heart thumped hard in his chest, and he reached to flip on the light inside the shed. It was a huge space which held lawn mowers, rakes, shovels, a wheelbarrow, bags of fertilizer and potting soil, and anything else Elise needed for their yard and garden, or her business. It wasn't quite dark yet, but the light really brightened everything.

The chatter had stopped, but Gray had the distinct impression he wasn't alone. "Hello?"

Jane came around the corner up ahead. It had been made by stacking bags of bark there, and Gray had no idea why she'd need to be back there. "Hey, Daddy."

"What are you doin' out here, bug?" he asked. Maybe she could help him put away the tools, but he didn't move. He'd heard a male voice out here with her. Not a boy's voice. A man's.

He looked behind her, expecting to see someone. *Michael*, he prayed. *Please let it be Michael.* If the cousins were just out here chatting and wasting time, fine. No big deal. Gray loved having his nephew here every summer, though he went north when Mikey came south.

Wes really wanted his children to have experience on the farm, and Gray had mentioned to him more than once to buy something up there. That's what Cy and Ames had done. Colton didn't have any more children at home, and thus no need for a farm.

"Nothing," Jane said, her eyes dropping to her tennis shoes. Oh, that was bad, and Gray felt his irritation start to bubble.

"Who's here with you?" He started toward a plastic tray that had once held containers of tomatoes. He and Elise had planted them all this afternoon, and he picked it up.

"No one," Jane said just as a man said, "It's just me, sir."

Gray looked at Cord Behr, his pulse flying through his body as if it had been tied to a bullet. Every fatherly protective gene in his body fired. "You're aware my daughter is fourteen years old, right?"

"Daddy," Jane said.

"No," Gray said, taking a step toward the pair of them. They had no reason to be behind the bags of bark.

None. Not in Gray's book anyway. "Jane, you will not argue with me on this."

She folded her arms, her blue eyes blazing fire at him. But she didn't argue.

"Thank you," he said. "You should get up to the house. Momma was asking about you."

She glanced at Cord, who nodded. He wore kindness in his expression, as well as pure guilt. Gray had no idea what to do. He knew the man's story, and he knew he had nowhere else to go.

*This is your daughter*, he told himself as Jane walked toward him.

"It was nothing, Daddy," she said. "We're just talking about the mountains. Cord has a buddy who is a tour guide is all."

"Sure," Gray said, narrowing his eyes at her as she neared. "We're leaving in the morning, so be sure to tell Paisley not to be late."

"She won't be late." Her tone suggested he was the stupidest person on the planet for even suggesting a teenager might not be ready to leave by six o'clock in the morning.

"Maybe we won't take her," Gray barked at her. "Maybe I'll call her mother tonight and tell her you've been grounded for the summer."

"You said she could come."

"You're standing in the dark shed with a man a decade older than you." His chest heaved. "This is not smart,

Jane. This is the opposite of what your mother and I have taught you to do." He didn't look at Cord, because his emotions were all over the place.

He'd never felt so out of his element before. Hunter had never done something like this. Gray hated comparing his son to his daughter, as they weren't the same at all. They were only half-siblings to begin with, and Jane hated the comparisons more than anyone.

Thankfully, she said nothing as she turned and left.

Gray bent and picked up another item of trash, his heart racing and his mind bent the wrong way. "Do I need to let you go, son?" he asked, his head bent.

"No, sir."

"How old are you?"

"You were right, sir. Twenty-five."

Gray lifted his eyes and looked at the man square in the face. "I'm fifteen years older than my wife, but we were both adults when we met."

Cord swept his cowboy hat from his head. "I understand, sir."

"Do you?"

He looked like he was about to burst into tears. "I need this job, sir. Please don't let me go."

"I don't want to find you alone with my daughter again."

"No, sir. It was innocent, sir."

"Was it?" Gray took a step toward him. "Tell me about it."

Cord swallowed, his fingers gripping the brim tightly. "I just came in here to put away the rakes, like Miss Elise asked me to. Jane brought in the hose, and we started talking about your family going to Coral Canyon."

Gray considered him, nothing inside him buzzing that this man wasn't being honest with him. He had to rely on his intuition and feelings to know things like this, and right now, he felt like Cord was being straight with him.

"How'd you get behind the bark?"

Cord dropped his eyes to the ground. "I'd rather not say."

"Son." Gray took another step toward him. "I urge you to say."

"I don't want to blame your daughter," he said, his gaze flicking up and back down. "I'm the adult here, and I take the blame." He looked up again, this time holding Gray's gaze. "It won't happen again, sir, I swear to you."

Gray let a couple of beats go by, his mind buzzing at him not to let this man go. If he did, it might be the worst thing he'd done in a while. He hated this power he held in his hand, and in the end, he had to listen to his gut.

In that moment, he knew it was the Lord talking to him. Telling him to keep Cord close to him and the farm. *Keep him here and teach him. Love him. Help him.*

"All right," Gray said, his heart softening. "Why don't you come by the house after you shower and eat? I think we need to talk some more."

Cord didn't ask about what. He didn't seem surprised

at all. He simply said, "Yes, sir. Thank you." Then he mashed his cowboy hat back onto his head and strode toward the exit. Gray sighed as he left, all the tension in the world leaving the shed and his body.

He pulled out his phone and texted his daughter. *How did you two get behind the stack of bark?*

If Cord wouldn't say, Gray would get the story from Jane.

# Thirteen

CORD BEHR SWORE AS HE FLEW UP THE FRONT steps of the cabin he shared with Travis Thatcher. "Stupid, stupid," he said as he barged through the door. Travis yelped and spun from where he stood in the kitchen.

Cord threw his cowboy hat, planted his feet, and bellowed toward the ceiling. His fist clenched at his sides, and he couldn't believe he'd gotten himself into a situation with the boss's daughter.

The boss's underage—severely underage—daughter.

"Whoa, whoa, whoa," Travis said, coming toward Cord quickly. "What's goin' on? Are you okay?"

Cord was not okay. He seriously felt like crying, then packing everything he owned, and then running. And running fast. If he had any gas in his truck, he might. If he had anywhere else to go, he might. If he didn't love this job with his whole heart and soul, he would.

He looked at Travis, the anger in his storm blowing out. That only left the grief, and Cord broke down into a sob.

Travis blinked once, and then gathered Cord right against his strong chest. "Okay, cowboy," he said. "It's not that bad. It's okay."

Cord clung to him, because Travis was almost old enough to be his father, and Cord had viewed him as one since he'd moved into the cabin with the man last December. "I messed up," he said between sobs. "I just went to put away some rakes, and I got in so much trouble."

"Okay," Travis said again, his voice deep and low and soothing. "Just get it out, and then you can tell me what happened. We'll take care of it."

Cord cried for only another few seconds, and then he straightened and pulled away from his cowboy mentor and friend. He kept his chin down as embarrassment streamed through him. He could talk a tough talk and ride a rough ride. But inside, he was wounded. Bleeding. Dying a little more with every single breath he took.

"I'm so humiliated," he whispered.

Travis went past him and closed the front door. "It's just me and you now, Cord. What happened?"

Cord sank onto the couch, his limbs going numb. "I was helping Elise clean up after the garden planting. She said I needed to put the rakes away, and then I could be done for the night. So I did. Jane came in after me."

Travis sat on the couch too, his knee pressing into

Cord. For some reason, that made Cord feel safe, and another wave of gratitude for the older man filled him. "Go on."

"She'd brought in a hose, and it was too heavy for her to lift onto the hook. So I stepped over to help her." Cord could see it all inside his mind. It *had* been innocent. Sure, maybe he'd flirted with Jane in the past. Cord couldn't seem to help it; he flirted with everyone. Men, women, and apparently children. He hadn't even known he did that until Mission pointed it out to him.

Cord normally loved to laugh and have a good time, but that was because he didn't want to dwell on the darkness in his life. *The past darkness*, he told himself.

"Anyway, with the hose up, I turned to start putting the tools away properly." He shook his head. "Jane asked if I'd seen the new gnomes her mom had bought. I said no. She said I just had to see them, and she took me further into the shed, around this stack of bark."

He dropped his head into his hands and scrubbed his fingers through his hair. "She showed me the gnomes, and we talked about her goin' to Coral Canyon, and the mountains, and the next thing I knew, she'd switched places with me, and I couldn't get past her."

Travis said nothing, and Cord didn't dare look at him. "I knew I was in trouble, but I didn't know how to get out of it."

"Did you touch her?"

"No."

"That's good." Travis exhaled. "Did she touch you?"

"No."

"Also good."

Cord looked up. "Her dad came in. Turned on the light. Called us out. He was not happy, and he wants me to come by the house after dinner 'to talk.'" He made air quotes around the last two words. "He didn't fire me on the spot, but I'm not confident I'll be here past dark." He started to tremble again. "I need this job, Trav."

"I know you do," Trav said, though Cord had never told Trav why he so desperately needed this job. Only Gray Hammond knew that. Well, and his son, Hunter.

Trav sighed, his eyebrows drawn down as he looked past Cord and thought. A timer went off, and Trav got up to go get the food out of the oven. Cord followed him, the thought of being alone unbearable.

"Tell me what to do."

"You're going to eat," Trav said, lifting a pan with bubbling, cheesy pizza from the oven. "Poppy sent over some veggies, and I doctored up this pizza." He smiled at it, and Cord knew he didn't need Cord's problems. He hadn't seen Poppy all week, since things on the farm had exploded lately. Gray had wanted every fence checked, and they'd all been out with the wire stretchers for a week now. Cord had more scrapes and gashes than he'd like to admit, and if he never saw another piece of barbed wire again, he'd be happy.

But not really, as he loved working the land more than anything else he'd done in his twenty-five years of life.

Trav sliced the pizza into triangles with a giant chef's knife and put two pieces on a plate for Cord. He turned and handed it to him, his eyes serious as can be. "Then, you're going to go talk to Gray and make sure he understands how innocent everything was, and how grateful you are to be here, and that you'll not be putting a toe out of line again. Ever."

"I already told him all of that," Cord said, worry still sailing through him.

"He wants to talk to you about somethin'," Trav said.

Cord turned away from the older man. "Yeah. I know what he wants to talk about."

"What?" Trav asked.

Cord didn't know how to tell him. He really didn't want the stupid mistakes of his youth to follow him forever. At the same time, he knew they would. Sometimes things were permanent, even if they'd been a mistake. Even if he'd been young and stupid. Even if he'd been in the wrong place at the wrong time.

"Just like in that blasted shed," he muttered to himself. That was all that had happened. Wrong place, wrong time. He sat at the tiny table shoved in the corner and picked up his food. He ate quickly and said, "Thanks, Trav. Sorry to...break down like that."

"You break down like that any time you want," Trav said. "I don't mind." He'd shown Cord nothing but acceptance and kindness, and Cord appreciated that so much.

"I'm going to go shower and head over to the farmhouse."

"I'll be here," Trav said. "Maybe asleep on the couch, but here." He smiled wearily at Cord and went back to his pizza.

Cord did exactly what he said he would: He showered. He put on his best pair of jeans and the nicest shirt he owned, a light blue collared shirt. No tie. He polished his boots and pulled them on. With nothing left to do, he grabbed his wallet, his phone, and his cowboy hat, and headed out the door.

Trav wasn't out in the living area or kitchen when Cord passed through, and he figured the man could take care of himself for a bit. It was Cord who couldn't.

He made the walk to the farmhouse in quick strides, admiring the cheery lights. When he'd been homeless, he used to look at houses like this and imagine the quaint families inside. They always got along, and everything was warm and bright. The Hammonds fit that to a T, even if Jane had said she didn't want to go to Coral Canyon and would rather stay here.

Cord knew better than most that families had problems, even the best ones. And the Hammonds were one of the best families Cord had ever met.

He hesitated at the back door, and then he simply knocked on the glass and went right in. The family wasn't sitting at the table, but the scent of dinner hung in the air. Elise turned from the sink and smiled at him. "Evening, Cord."

"Hello, ma'am." He took off his cowboy hat and tried to put a smile on his face. It sounded forced and wobbly, and Cord let it fade away.

"Cord," Gray said as he appeared at the end of the hallway. "Come on back."

Cord looked from him to Elise, and she kept her smile on her face. He didn't see Jane or any of the other kids, and Elise twisted back to the sink without saying anything else. Cord saw no other choice but to go with Gray, so he did that.

He'd changed out of his farm clothes, and Cord almost didn't know how to handle the man in gym shorts and a T-shirt, shoeless, without a cowboy hat on his head. He waited for Cord to enter the office, and then he did, closing the door behind him.

"Please, sit." Gray went behind the desk and Cord perched on the front of a chair in front of it.

"I just want to lead with another apology, sir. Honestly. It was just a bad situation that I should've gotten myself out of."

"I talked to Jane." Gray looked up. "I know where the blame lies, Cord, and yes, I'd love for you to continue to be the adult in any future situations."

"There won't be any future situations, sir. I can promise you that."

Gray sighed and shook his head. "We don't know that, so maybe there shouldn't be any promises made."

"I will be better about getting out of any future situations."

"Jane knows better now too," Gray said.

"I didn't mean to get her into any trouble."

"Oh, the girl knows how to get herself into trouble." Gray wore a dark look. "She thinks you're—and I quote, 'adorable,' and 'so cute,' and she assures me she didn't mean to get you into any trouble either."

Cord didn't react, because Jane was fourteen years old. It didn't matter if she liked him or not. "I'm a bit of a flirt," he said. "I maybe led her on."

Gray frowned and leaned back. "Cord, I know who you are."

Cord wanted to challenge him on that, but he held his tongue. He had no idea how Gray Hammond could know who he was, because Cord was still trying to figure it out.

"You're a good worker," Gray said. "And a good man. You'll have to work harder than others to be where you want to be, and until you figure out where that is, I'd love to have you here."

"Really?" Cord asked.

Gray smiled at him, and Cord felt whiplashed around. "Yes, Cord. I feel like you need to be here, and that I can help you. So if you're willing to stay here, I want you to stay here."

Cord simply stared at him. *Gray* was the good man in

this situation, and Cord's eyes teared up again. "Thank you, sir," he whispered.

"You come see me anytime," Gray said. "For anything you need, all right?"

"Yes, sir." Cord stood and put his hat back on his head. "I will." He leaned forward and shook Gray's hand, the grip firm and warm. Then he left the office with his head held high and his spirit soaring. Perhaps his future would be better than he even knew, and he determined he'd keep his head down and his hands busy until he found the path he was supposed to be on, whether here at the Hammond Family Farm or somewhere else.

# *Fourteen*

A WEEK PASSED, AND THEN TWO, AND BEFORE Travis knew it, his phone rang, and Poppy led with, "Well, he's gone." Her voice pinched, and Travis stepped away from the horse he'd just put in the stall.

Cinnamon Roll wasn't real happy about that, and he whinnied and snuffled at Travis's back as he walked away. "He's gonna have a great time," he said, immediately regretting it. "I mean, he'll probably call you from the airport, ready to come home, but yeah." He smiled as he stepped outside. He still had plenty to do that morning before he could take a break. Fixing all those fences had put them severely behind on the upkeep around the barns and stables, and he nodded to Michael Hammond as the boy went by with Mission and Cord.

The three of them weren't joking and talking like they sometimes did. Everyone had plenty to keep them busy, and Travis was glad Hunter had started coming out in the afternoons with Molly, because the man worked hard.

Poppy sniffled and said nothing. Travis looked up into the glorious, blue, summer sky. He had no idea how to soothe this ache. He didn't have children. "How about I bring you lunch?" he asked, his voice real quiet, almost stuck in his chest. "You're off today, right? I'll come over in a few hours, and we'll eat. Then you can come follow me around the farm while I work." The idea made him smile, but he didn't know why.

His relationship with Poppy had been going well—in his book. Slow, but well. He didn't need a racecar relationship, and the work they both had to do in a day kept them apart. He texted and talked to her every day, and they'd been out a few more times. He hadn't kissed her yet, and Travis swallowed hard just thinking about it.

He knew himself well enough, and he suspected once he kissed Poppy, he'd be crossing a bridge he'd then burn to the ground. There would be no going back for him at that point, and he was terrified to take the first step.

"You're working," she said. "But I'd love to see you. How about I run to the grocery store and get a few things? Then I'll cook, and you can come eat and rest during your lunch break instead of rushing all over just to bring me food?"

"I don't mind," he said. "I can hear you're upset."

"Cooking will help that too," she whispered. "I know what you like, Trav."

His grin returned. "Do you?"

"Yes," she said, but she didn't elaborate. "I'll surprise you, okay? Noon? Twelve-thirty? When can you come?"

His stomach growled, and he wanted to go right now. But the sun had stuck only partway up in the sky, which meant he still had a few hours of work to do. "Noon," he said. "I won't be a minute late."

"I'm sure you won't." Her tone lightened, and that made Travis's heart do the same. "See you then."

"Yep," he said. "See you then." He hung up and exhaled in a long, low hiss. He felt perched on the edge of a knife, and he didn't know why.

"Travis," someone said, and he turned.

"Yep." He started toward Matt, who was coming toward him. "What's up? Sorry, I was just talkin' to Poppy for a second."

Matt waved him away. "It's fine. I'm putting together a little party for Boone's birthday, and I wondered if you and I could sit down and chat about it sometime this week."

A smile filled Travis's soul. "Sure," he said. "What are you thinking?"

"Well, his birthday is three days before Chris's." They started back into the stable together, where Travis got the hay Cinnamon Roll had wanted five minutes ago. "So I'm thinking a joint party. I mean, we have enough celebrations around here as it is." He smiled, but a hint of exhaustion hovered right at the edge of his eyes. "It's not for

LIZ ISAACSON

another month or so, but Gray will want to come back from Coral Canyon for it." He fed the horse next to Cinnamon, and that was a chore Travis wouldn't have to do.

"I'm actually thinking of doing it in mid-August, which is a few weeks late, but then Gray won't have to come home early, and he won't have to come home and then go back for a couple of weeks."

"I think that's a good idea," he said. "Maybe all the brothers would come for Chris's birthday. He's going to be eighty-seven. That's a big year."

Matt chuckled and shook his head. "At that age, every year is a big year."

Travis grinned while they finished feeding the horses, and he bounced ideas off Matt. "Hey, isn't Keith's birthday then too?"

"Yes," Matt said. "I'll talk to him about combining too."

"I know he might not want to," Travis said. "I mean, maybe. I don't know." He knew Keith, because the boy used to live here on the farm. He worked with the horses full-time in the summer, and every day after school too.

"Maybe I can offer him this family party, and he can do a separate friend party. We combined both last year, and it was a lot."

"That's because you got married the next day," Travis said.

Matt smiled too. "Maybe that was why last August felt like a marathon."

"August always feels like that around here," Travis said. "It's either too hot or not hot enough, and we're racing some agricultural clock we don't know about yet."

They both laughed, and Travis's mind, body, and soul felt lighter after a good chat with Matt. He always did. "Hey," he said. "I won't be at lunch today, but I can do whatever you need for the party."

"Goin' to Poppy's?"

Travis nodded, his throat suddenly very narrow. "Yeah," he managed to push out. "Her son went on a trip with his grandparents today, and she's...lonely."

Matt pulled off his gloves and flipped on the water in the sink to wash his hands. "Huh. I didn't think anything upset Poppy Harris."

Travis had been about to say goodbye, as he had to get on the ATV and go move the cattle from field six to seven before lunch. Now, however, he paused. "What do you mean?"

Matt looked at him, their eyes meeting in a long look. "I don't know," Matt said. "Nothin' bad or anything." He finished rinsing and turned off the water. He didn't look away from Travis as he reached for a towel. "She's just always struck me as...strong. She's got a tough exterior."

Travis knew that all too well. "Yes," he agreed. "I can see that."

"For example, why was she so upset with you last

year?" He looped the towel through the holder while Travis once again tried to swallow down a too-narrow throat.

"Uh." He checked over his shoulder, but no one had come upon them. "You have money, right?"

"Some," Matt said, though Travis knew he had a lot. Boone too, as the man had just sold his property in Montana for quite a sum of money.

"I have some too," Travis said. "She was havin' a hard time last year—didn't bring in enough alfalfa—and I, uh, helped out with some of her bills."

Matt frowned. "And she was mad about that? Why would she be?"

"I maybe didn't tell her I was going to pay them before I paid them."

Matt's dark eyes widened, and he looked like a catfish for one moment before he burst out laughing. Travis's mood only darkened, and he ducked his head. "Sorry," Matt said. "Honest, I am." He started for the exit, and Travis fell into step with him. "And I can see Poppy bein' upset about that. It's exactly what I mean. She wants to be self-reliant, and she doesn't let anyone in."

Travis frowned at the horses walking in the ring. He had to bring them in too, and he'd somehow forgotten. Julius Caesar had not, and he tossed his head and said so.

"Obviously, I have no idea what Poppy's like, really." Matt's words rushed now. "I'm sure she's very accommodating and open with you. Of course." He cleared his throat. "I have to get over to the counselor cabins. Molly's called a meeting to find out if we need to hire more trainers, counselors, or no one at all." He tipped his hat and practically ran away from Travis.

But his words wouldn't leave his ears. *She doesn't let anyone in.*

Had she let him in? If not, how would he know? If she had, he still wasn't sure he would know. "Maybe ask her," he muttered to himself as he slowed the ring and reached for Julius's lead.

---

HE ARRIVED at Poppy's the moment the clock in his truck flipped to twelve. He unbuckled and got out, because she lived literally two minutes from the Hammond Family Farm, and that wasn't long enough for his truck's air conditioning to truly cool off the cab. He'd rolled down the windows just to keep from suffocating, and he left them down as he got out and headed for the front door.

The scent of something savory and brown and delicious met his nose as he rang the bell. He expected Cotton to yowl and howl, and the blue heeler did exactly that.

"Come in!" Poppy yelled from somewhere inside the house, and when Travis did and found her in the kitchen, she stood at the stove, frying something. "Sorry, I can't leave these."

"It smells amazing in here," he said. He once again blinked and saw such an amazing future with her. He'd come home every day at mid-day, and they'd spend time together. He wouldn't have to tell her how tired he was; she'd know. She wouldn't have to tell him how excited she was to see her bleeding heart doing so well; he'd know.

"That bleeding heart outside is fantastic," he said, joining her at the stove.

She beamed up at him, almost like she hadn't sent her son off on an anxiety-inducing trip that morning. "Isn't is gorgeous?" She leaned into him slightly, and he watched the oil bubble and boil around the items in the pan.

"Are you makin' chicken fried steak?" he asked, true surprise in his voice.

"Yes, sir," she said.

Wonder filled him, and Travis felt his feet slipping. He was going to fall in love with her if she cooked like this for him, but he kept that to himself. "Wow," he said. "I didn't know regular people made that. I thought you had to get it in a restaurant."

Poppy laughed, and that made Travis happy. "My chicken fried steak is way better than any restaurant." She nudged him away from her. "Go on. These are done, and the gravy's hot, so we're ready."

He backed up to give her room to lay the two golden pieces of fried meat on a plate lined with paper towels. She deftly scooped piping hot mashed potatoes onto two plates, then laid the steaks next to them, and then doused everything with the healthiest ladle of country gravy Travis had ever seen.

His mouth watered—positively watered—and not only because of the food. He couldn't look away from Poppy, and when she raised those blue eyes to his, words came shooting up his throat. "Are you keeping me out?" he asked.

She blinked. "What?"

He realized how out-of-nowhere his question sounded. "It's just...I know we've been goin' slow and all that. Summer's real busy for us both." He toed the ground, regretting his outburst already. "But you're... letting me in, right?"

Poppy's gaze cooled as he watched. "I'm trying," she said. Hey, at least she was being honest with him. "It's hard for me, Trav." She picked up the two plates and nodded to the forks sitting on the counter. "Grab those, would you?"

He did, as well as the roll of paper towels, and followed her to the table. One thing about Poppy: she never ate anywhere but at the dining room table. Not the bar. Not on the couch. Heck, sometimes Travis stood over the stove and ate his pizza so the crumbs would just fall onto the sheet where he'd cooked the thing. Not Poppy.

Today, a vase of fresh flowers sat in the middle of the table, and they'd all come from her yard. Travis admired them, and he sat while she went to get lemonade and ice water out of the fridge. He always drank lemonade, and he realized as she set the pitcher of pale yellow liquid in front of him that she made it especially for him.

That had to mean something, right?

"Why is it hard for you?" he asked, laying a paper towel across his knee. He looked up at Poppy as her chair scraped the floor.

She sat and studied her food for a moment. "Do you want me to be honest, or do you want me to sugarcoat it?"

"Be honest," he said. He might need to see a throat specialist for how hard he had to work to swallow after that. Of course he wanted her to be honest. Didn't he?

Poppy nodded, but she didn't speak right away. She cut into her steak, piled on a dollop of potatoes, and stuck the bite of food in her mouth. Her eyes rolled back in her head as she moaned. "Yes," she said. "This is what I needed today."

Guilt gutted Travis. She needed a good, hot, home-cooked meal and good company. Not a boyfriend showing up to ask her hard questions. He wanted to say, "Forget about what I asked. It's fine. Tell me where Steele is right now." She'd know if he was in the air or had landed. All of it.

"Poppy," he started, but she interrupted him with, "I have a hard time trusting men."

What he'd been about to say stuck in his throat. He could only stare at her, and she couldn't seem to look at him at all. "Because of Eli?" he asked.

She nodded, going in for more chicken fried steak.

Travis only had one thought in his head, and he fought against letting it come out. It persisted and persisted, and he finally thought the Lord might be telling him to just say it. He looked down at his own untouched food and cut into the perfectly crispy, perfectly cooked steak.

"Well," he said, keeping all the emotion out of his voice. "It's a good thing I'm not Eli then, isn't it?"

That brought Poppy's eyes straight to his, and this time, Travis slowly lifted his food to his mouth and ate it, waiting for her to speak.

# Fifteen

POPPY'S HEART BEAT IN A WAY IT HADN'T IN A while. Perhaps since she'd learned someone had paid her mortgage and Gray Hammond had insisted it wasn't him. She'd known in that moment that Travis Thatcher had done it. She'd almost driven to the man's cabin to yell at him too, but she hadn't. For a reason she didn't know, she hadn't.

She'd given him a piece of her mind later, though, something she sincerely regretted.

She couldn't take another bite, not when Travis's deep, dark eyes held hers. Not when his interest and desire swam right there for her to see. He knew how to wall that off, and he hadn't. Poppy wasn't sure how to open the door to her inner thoughts and emotions, not all the way, at least.

*Just don't close it*, she told herself, and she at least

didn't slam the door closed, shut down, and then ruin their lunch date.

"No," she said finally. "You're not Eli." The words sounded foreign in her head, but they became true as they settled in her ears. Travis Thatcher wasn't anything like Eli. He didn't speak loudly or at the speed of light. He didn't sleep late. He didn't choose himself over her.

As she ran through several more things that were complete opposites between Trav and her ex, she smiled. At the same time, her heart wailed. "I'm sorry, Travis," she whispered. "I've maybe been a little closed off."

"It's okay," he said easily. Eli hadn't forgiven like that either. "Maybe a good reminder. A baseline to work from. I'm not him, and if I do or say something you don't like that reminds you of him, you just tell me." His eyebrows went up in a silent, "Okay?"

She nodded and went back to their lunch. Everything was brown and white, and Poppy startled. "Oh, my goodness." She jumped to her feet. "I forgot the veggies." She hurried into the kitchen and pulled open the fridge. "I made the best cucumber salad to go with this."

Travis chuckled as she returned to the table and put the glass bowl with the delicious cucumber slaw between them. "I only eat the veggies you feed me," he said, grinning from ear to ear.

She let herself focus on his mouth, because she'd been thinking about kissing him all morning. They'd sat across from each other in the high school gymnasium only three weeks ago. She told herself it wasn't that long, and she'd be horrified if she'd kissed him already. She would've too, if Cotton hadn't spotted that lynx.

Perhaps she'd opened the door to her life, her heart, more than she thought she had.

"That cucumber salad is my great-grandmother's recipe," Poppy said, a bit of bite in her tone. "If you don't like it, don't eat it."

"You love it," he said. He picked up the bowl and spooned some of the crunchy, tangy vegetables right on top of his chicken fried steak.

"It's fantastic," she said. "I made that right after we got off the phone, so it's had plenty of time to marinate."

"It smells good." He stabbed a couple of cucumber triangles and popped them into his mouth. He moaned and let his eyes roll back in his head, exactly the way Poppy had done to buy herself some time before she answered his question.

It had surprised her, to be honest. She'd thought she'd done a pretty good job in talking to Travis, texting him a proper amount, letting him know she liked him without becoming needy or desperate or annoying.

They'd talked about his previous marriage and Eli in the past, and she hadn't realized there was any wedge between them. Maybe there wasn't, she thought. But then, why had he asked?

"It's great, Poppy," he said. "Really."

She leaned forward and forked up a couple of cucumbers too. "I wouldn't put it on my hot food like that, but hey. You do what you want."

He did too, teasing her about mixing her hot food with her cold food for a couple of minutes. They laughed together, and suddenly it was okay that Steele wasn't there. Poppy didn't want to admit it to anyone, but she felt...freer than she had in a long, long time. She didn't have an ex-husband she shared custody with. It had been her and Steele for eleven long years. The task of caring for him day in and day out, hour after hour, all day, every day, had fallen on her.

She'd sobbed the moment she'd come inside the farmhouse after waving goodbye to him, her step-mom, and father, and once she'd calmed down, she'd called Travis.

Travis.

He was a place of safety for her, and Poppy felt the door between them opening further.

She smiled at him as they finished eating, and she stood first and cleared their plates. She loved cooking for people—*for him*, she amended in her head—and she put his cleaned and empty plate in the sink with hers.

"Poppy, you're the best cook in the world." Travis came up behind her and wrapped her in his arms. She smiled and giggled as she turned to embrace him.

"Trav, you're the best...cowboy I know." She finished the sentence lamely, but he laughed anyway. She didn't know what to put in the blank space there. Boyfriend? Was he the best boyfriend?

The best she'd ever had.

"Do you want to take your lemonade outside?" she asked.

"No, ma'am," he drawled. "Do you know how hot it is today?" He pulled back, his smile set on mega-watt. "I'll take it right here in the air conditioning." He returned to the table, filled his glass, and took it into her living room where he collapsed on the couch with it.

He took a long drink and put the glass on the end table. He sighed and leaned back, and Poppy watched him. She could see herself walking across the room and sliding into that empty space at his side.

So she did.

She didn't have to think about where Steele was and if he'd walk in on them. She didn't have to worry about what he might think, or if he'd see something inappropriate.

He lifted his arm around her, and she cuddled into him while Cotton circled and laid at her feet. The warmth from Trav's body seeped into hers, and his chest rose and fell in long, even strokes.

"Baby?" he asked.

"Yeah?" she whispered back, a bit surprised to be called by a pet name. He hadn't done that yet—barring an errant *sweetheart* here and there, usually when he teased her—and it felt intimate and special.

"There's a concert in the park tomorrow night," he said, his voice still only a decibel above a whisper. "It's

George Wilson Jones, and I love him. Would you like to go with me?"

"It's part of the Lazy Summer Days, isn't it?" Poppy asked.

"That's right," Trav said. "We get dinner if we want to do their picnic, and then the concert. I'm fine doing both, if you'd like." He'd closed his eyes, but he opened them and tilted his head down to look at her. "Or you can make me something mouthwatering like you did today, and then we can go to the concert. You choose."

Poppy did love to cook for him, and she'd love to have more time to do it. If she didn't work for Elise doing land-scaping, she could tend to her small farm and then make breakfast, lunch, and dinner for her loved ones.

Her pulse stalled at the thought that she might be in love with Travis. Then it laughed at her. Of course she wasn't in love with him.

Yet.

"I have a busy day tomorrow," she said, and surely only she could hear the strain in her voice. Trav's eyes drifted closed again, so she'd been right. "I better not commit to cooking something mouthwatering."

He grinned and nodded. "The picnic is at six or seven. I don't know. I'd have to look."

"I'll look," she said. "And let you know."

"Mm." He tightened his arm around her as the silence enveloped them again, and Poppy let her eyes fall closed too. Everything in the farmhouse stilled. She hadn't felt this comfortable and this serene in a long, long time.

Maybe she'd never felt this at-peace with herself and her life, and she snuggled deeper into Travis's side, wishing she'd never have to let him go. Of course she did. His lunch hour ended, and he had to get up and walk out of her house.

He paused in the doorway and turned back. Poppy lived out in the country, and no one drove by her house. Her only neighbors were the Hammonds and the people they employed, and they lived a half-mile down the road. He could certainly take her into his arms and kiss her, but he didn't.

Her blood burned hot as he hugged her tight and said, "See you tomorrow night, baby," then he turned and left. She waved to him the way she had to her son, but this time, she didn't return to the farmhouse and cry for several minutes.

She pulled on her work boots and went out into the afternoon heat to check on her goats and horses, feed the chickens, and spend some time with Dorothy. "He's so amazing," she whispered to the donkey.

Dorothy leaned into the touch the way Poppy did to Travis, and she knew how much the animal loved her. Did Travis know how much Poppy liked him?

"Hello!" someone called, and Poppy pushed away from the fence. Dorothy brayed in protest or excitement,

Poppy wasn't sure. "Poppy!" her sister called. "Are you out here?"

She jogged over the gravel path to the road and waved her arms above her head. "Out here!" she yelled to Elora.

Her sister spotted her and came through the gate toward her. Poppy went to meet her, pulling her younger sister into a tight hug when they met. "I told Briggs you'd be out here. He's putting the lemon sherbet in your freezer."

Poppy didn't know what to say. Her sister and her husband had taken good care of her over the past couple of years since they'd gotten married, but Poppy hadn't called Elora this morning after Steele had left.

Elora pulled away suddenly. "Girl, you smell like my husband." Her eyes searched Poppy's face. "Whose cologne is that?"

The temperature outside suddenly heated Poppy from the inside out. "No one," she said. "Come say hi to Dorothy before she loses her mind." The donkey hadn't stopped crying for Elora since she'd called, and the two sisters walked toward the pasture.

"You have been keeping things from me," Elora said.

Poppy kicked at the gravel. "I went to the Lazy Summer Days speed-dating event a few weeks ago."

Elora gasped, as she'd always been a tad overdramatic. "You did not. You're dating someone!" She turned and yelled over her shoulder, "Briggs! She's dating someone!"

"Why are you telling him?" Poppy asked crossly. "And the whole world?"

Elora burst out laughing, her long hair spilling down her back as she tipped her head toward the heavens. "The whole world, Poppy? You live out here alone. No one can hear us who's not within a ten-mile radius."

She looked west, to the farm next door. Her barn obscured the view of the Hammond land, where Travis hailed. He'd brought her goats back several times, and he'd ducked into that barn to shelter from a storm last fall.

"I'm seeing someone who works for the Hammonds," she said, eliciting another gasp from Elora.

"You're kidding. Who?" Her own blue eyes seized onto Poppy's face and wouldn't let go. "Mission Redbay works there. They hired someone new.... Cord-Some-thing-or-other. He's way too young for you." Her mind ran in circles, Poppy could tell.

She sucked in another breath. "It's Travis Thatcher."

"How do you even know him?" Poppy asked. "He doesn't go to our church."

"Mm, I heard a rumor you brought a man to the church potluck a few weeks ago—and that was right after the speed-dating."

"See? You already knew." Poppy reached the fence and stroked her hand down Dorothy's neck. The donkey really wanted Elora, and she'd come back to Poppy once she got her pat.

Elora petted her too, and Dorothy seemed to drift off

in pure bliss. "I didn't know," she said. "Small towns are notorious for terrible gossip."

"Plus, I haven't dated in fifteen years, so you didn't believe the gossip." Poppy didn't mean to speak with a forked tongue, but she had.

"No," Elora said quickly, but Poppy tilted her head and quirked her eyebrows.

"Fine," Elora amended. "I found it hard to believe." She once again searched Poppy's face. "But it's true, so you better start talking now." She held up one hand, her finger pointed almost at Poppy's right eye. "And don't leave anything out."

"First," Poppy said. "We're going to the summer concert series tomorrow night, and I need help with my outfit."

"Oh, so we haven't kissed him yet." Elora wore glee in her face. "Honey, why didn't you call me earlier? I could've helped you so much with a man you met speed-dating." She turned as her husband's footsteps crunched over the gravel too, and Dorothy brayed and brayed like she'd been reunited with her long-lost soulmate.

Briggs laughed as he approached, and he greeted Dorothy first. Then he gave Poppy a quick squeeze, said, "Heya, Poppy," and looked at his wife. "Uh, what did I walk into?"

"Nothing," Poppy said just as Elora said, "I know exactly what you should wear to get your new cowboy boyfriend to kiss you after tomorrow night's concert."

# Sixteen

TRAVIS STEPPED OUT OF THE SHOWER AS HIS phone rang. Yes, he'd brought it into the bathroom with him. He couldn't seem to divorce himself from it. It trilled out his momma's ringtone as he reached for a towel.

He muttered a string of unpleasant words under his breath as he tried to get his hands dry and reach for the phone at the same time. If she needed his help tonight....

He didn't finish the thought. He managed to answer the call before it went to voicemail with a, "Hey, Momma. What's up?" He thought he sounded pretty casual too. After tapping the speakerphone button, he put the phone back on the vanity and started drying himself.

"Travis," she said. "What are you doing for dinner tonight?"

"Goin' out with Poppy," he said instantly. A moment

of fear hit him. Had he told his mother about Poppy? Of course he had. Weeks ago, after their first date.

"Oh, of course." Momma let the silence drape between them. "Well, if you get hungry, Pastor Herald brought over two of the most amazing pizzas I've ever seen."

Travis looked at himself in the mirror, his dark hair shining like oil in the fluorescent light. He grinned and then started laughing.

"What?" Momma asked.

"The pastor—our *very single* pastor—brought over *pizza*?" He laughed again, the idea of it so very funny to him. "Does he know you don't even like pizza?"

"I like pizza just fine, young man," she said, her voice crisp and curt.

Travis simply couldn't stop laughing. "I can't remember the last time you ate a piece of pizza. That man is sweet on you."

"He is not."

"How long did he stay?" Travis asked, his laughter fading. His mother had plenty of male courters; she just wouldn't admit it. She also didn't want to get married again, though he had no objection to it. Both of her husbands had passed already, and she simply didn't want to bury a third. That was what she claimed, anyway.

"Oh, just a couple of hours," she said, her voice indicating she was waving her arm as if swatting a noisy, bothersome fly.

"Sure," Travis said, smiling again. "Well, I can drive over and pick them up tomorrow sometime. Or freeze 'em for me and I'll get them on Sunday."

"Are you going to bring pretty Poppy to church out here with you?" Momma asked next, and Travis hadn't been expecting that question.

"Uh, I don't know, Momma." She was pretty rooted in her church congregation, and Travis hadn't talked to her about attending church together.

"I'd love to meet her."

"Yeah, I know." Travis reached for his shaving cream. "I have to go, Momma. I'll be in touch about the pizza, okay?"

"Okay. I love you, son."

"Love you too." He let her end the call, and then he cleaned up around his beard, brushed his teeth, got dressed, and headed out to the kitchen. Cord sat at the table with his phone in front of him, frowning.

"What's on that thing you don't like?" Travis asked, shoving his device in his back pocket.

Cord looked up, his eyes glazed for an extra beat. He cleared them and said, "Nothing."

"Yeah, I'm convinced." Travis opened the fridge and took out a bottle of water. He twisted the lid and sat as he continued to look at Cord. "You can tell me." He and Cord shared a lot about their lives. He didn't know every-thing that had brought Cord to the Hammond Family

Farm, but what he did was enough to elicit sympathy and empathy for the younger man.

The truth was, Travis could see a younger version of himself in Cord's eyes. He recognized the lost look, the uncertainty with which the man breathed, and pureness of his soul in his attempts to do what was right. He simply didn't know what that was, and that frustrated him to no end.

Travis knew; he'd been Cord once-upon-a-time. He'd made mistakes too. Maybe not as big as Cord's, but again, Travis didn't know the extent of everything.

"It's my parole officer," Cord muttered, his eyes falling to the phone again. "He wants to come see where I work." He ran one hand through his sandy hair. "I don't want him out here. Then everyone will see him."

Travis said nothing, though he hadn't known Cord had a parole officer. That meant an arrest, a crime, possible jail time. "Is it a requirement of the parole?"

"No."

He shrugged one shoulder. "Maybe tell him you don't want to introduce him around to your co-workers? That you're trying to move on? There are pictures online."

"Only of Pony Power," Cord said. He finally looked up. "I don't really dictate to him what he can and can't do. That's what he does to me." He wore fear mixed with defiance on his face. "But it's not a requirement of my parole. I have to submit evidence of my employment, and I have."

So Gray knew about the parole. Travis trusted Gray, so

any squeamish feelings he had suddenly disappeared. "I'd maybe play up the angle that you're trying to move on, that not many people know about your parole, and you work with kids."

"I'm not violating my parole."

"I didn't think you would." Just the look on his face told Travis that.

"Trav." Cord shook his head and exhaled. He transformed from stressed to happy-go-lucky in less time than it took for him to inhale his next breath. "You look nice. Goin' out with Poppy tonight?"

"Yes." Travis got to his feet. "And we're going to be late."

"What are you doing?" Cord stood too.

"The Lazy Summer Days picnic and concert in the park," he said. "It's George Wilson Jones."

Cord grinned like he'd just discovered a treasure chest full of gold. "That guy you're always blasting on Sunday mornings?"

Travis laughed and confirmed that it was indeed the same country music artist.

"Have fun," Cord said, and Travis headed for the front door. He stood on Poppy's doorstep only five minutes later, and she answered the door in the cutest, billowiest sundress Trav ever did see.

Big, bold flowers in blue and purple splashed across the white fabric, and she wore a fun pair of jelly sandals in bright blue on her feet.

"Wow." He drank her in from head to toe, his eyes coming back to hers after he'd feasted. "You're absolutely stunning."

She laughed lightly and put one hand on his chest. "You don't look half-bad either."

"Half-bad?" He glanced down at her hand as it burned into his chest. She'd painted her nails the same purple as her dress, and he marveled at how she'd done that. His lungs screamed for air, and he took a breath, his thoughts spiraling around one thing and one thing only: kissing Poppy.

Right there. Right now. Her son wasn't here. Cotton had yelped at the sound of the doorbell, but he now stood at Travis's feet, panting and looking at him hopefully.

He didn't move, because he honestly didn't know how to initiate a kiss with this woman. She was gorgeous on the inside and outside, and she made him tingle in a way someone hadn't in a while. Maybe ever.

"Are we going?" Poppy asked, and the spell between them broke. She stepped back to pull the door closed, and she had to herd Cotton back inside to do it. She faced him again, and Travis's face had heated beyond hot.

"Yeah," he said. He took her hand and they went down the wide front steps together. "If this is bad tonight, we can leave any time, all right?"

"You think George Wilson Jones will be bad?" She scoffed. "I don't think so."

"The food might be," he said.

"It's a sandwich and chips," Poppy said. "We'll survive."

Travis hoped so, because he wanted this date to be the most magical night of her life. *Probably shouldn't take her to a lame, town-organized picnic then*, he thought.

"What if I said my momma had two amazing pizzas at her place?" He paused at Poppy's door, though the summer evening wasn't cool by any means.

"Pizzas at your mommas?"

"The pastor is sweet on her," Travis said with a smile. "She doesn't even like pizza, and she said I could come get them." He pulled his phone from his back pocket. "If I call her now, they'll be ready when we get there." He held it up, the unspoken question in the air.

Poppy looked at his phone and then him. "Do you want to take me to meet your mother?"

"Yes." Travis just said it. Right out loud. He might as well, as he wasn't getting any younger and he certainly didn't have time to play games. "If you don't want to or think it's too soon, that's fine."

He started to lower the phone, and he'd just tucked it back into his pocket when Poppy said, "I really like pizza."

"I'm sure it won't be as good as yours." He took a tiny step closer to her. "Do you really want to?"

"We can still make it to your concert, right?"

"Yes," he said. "That'll actually give us a good reason not to stay too long."

Her delicious lips—those pink-glossed things that

followed him into his dreams at all times, day or night—curved up. "Let's go, then."

He opened her door and helped her climb into his truck. He wasted no time getting behind the wheel to get the air conditioning blowing, and then he called his momma. "Travis, dear," she said, her voice piping through the speakers.

"You're on a call with me and Poppy," he said, grinning at his girlfriend. "So behave yourself, Momma."

"Oh—I—" She said nothing else, and Travis chuckled.

"Would you put in one of the pizzas for us?" he asked. "We think that would be a better dinner than the picnic in the park."

"I'm heating the oven right now," Momma said. "You're thirty minutes away?"

"About," Travis said.

"I guess I better change back into regular clothes," Momma quipped, her veiled way of saying she wished Travis had given her more notice to meet Poppy.

He only laughed, because she'd called him thirty minutes ago, and he knew she didn't spend all day in her pajamas. He ended the call and looked at Poppy. "She doesn't need to get re-dressed. My momma is...well, you'll see."

"I don't want to see," Poppy said, and Travis realized she was choking her purse. "I want you to tell me."

"She's a bit on the...refined side," he said. "She's...classic. She wears slacks all day, even to garden. If she's 'dressed down,' she'll wear a pair of cotton pants the color of denim. She's got about five men circling her right now, but she's not interested in any of them, and she doesn't like pizza."

Poppy smiled and her shoulders relaxed. "So the pastor is out."

"The pastor will be lucky if Momma opens the door for him again." Travis laughed and pulled onto the highway that would take them up to his mother's. He couldn't believe he was doing this, but at the same time, it felt right.

Perhaps he was more like Cord than he thought. He was still trying to figure out the right thing to do, the right thing to say, the right place to be, and following his heart and gut while he did.

He glanced over to Poppy. "What did Steele do today?" he asked, and she brightened. Travis really wanted more time with her. He wanted to get to know all about her, and get to know her son, and maybe then that vision he kept having of walking into the farmhouse after a long day of work outside and finding Poppy waiting for him with a smile and a sandwich would become his reality.

Travis enjoyed his time with Poppy in the truck. The conversation was easy, and he mostly listened as she told him about her son's adventures in the Big Apple. He finally made the last right turn into an older neighborhood, his momma's house down the street a bit on the left.

He eased up to the curb and looked at the bright blue front door. She'd hung a new wreath since Sunday, when he'd been here last. "This is it."

Poppy didn't hesitate to get out of the truck, but Travis's cowboy boots were suddenly dragging. Still, he met Poppy at the front of the truck and secured her hand in his.

"Nervous?" she asked.

"No."

"Then maybe you could stop strangling my fingers."

Travis realized how hard he'd been gripping them, and he chuckled nervously. "Fine," he said. "I'm nervous."

Poppy grinned at him. "Mothers love me, Trav. Don't worry."

They approached the house together, and as Travis never knocked or rang the bell here, he went straight in, calling, "Momma?"

She had an old dog who never barked, but Pigeon came around the corner that led back into the hall just to see who'd come to visit them. Travis couldn't help wondering how many other visitors his mother entertained during the week. Apparently the pastor, among others.

"In the kitchen," Momma called, and Travis took Poppy through the living room and into the back of the house. It was sectioned into rooms, the way century-old homes were, and she turned as his boots hit the tile.

She wore a perfectly pressed pair of black slacks, which

she'd paired with a bright green sweater. Polished, as always. "Hey, dear," she said, leaving the stovetop to come hug him.

He released Poppy's hand to do that, something tense between him and his mother for a reason he couldn't name. *Of course you can*, he told himself. *This is the first woman you've brought home in a decade.*

Travis swallowed as he stepped back. He indicated the beautiful blonde he'd brought with him. "Momma," he said. "This is Poppy Harris. Poppy, my mother, Melanie."

"Oh, aren't you the prettiest thing in Colorado?" Momma gushed. She took Poppy into a hug too, and Poppy wore a warm smile as she retreated back to Travis's side.

"It's great to meet you," Poppy said.

"The pizza is almost done," Momma said, spinning back to the stove as the timer went off. "See? There it is." She bustled the few steps to the oven and picked up the gloves. "You two go on out back. I've got the table set up for you there, and I'll bring out dinner."

Travis's first thought was to refuse, and then he snapped his mouth shut. He nodded Poppy toward the door sitting to the left, and she moved that way in her fun, girlish shoes. He followed, and only a few seconds later, the back yard opened up to them.

Momma had an army of mature trees standing guard along the west side of her yard, which bathed the whole thing—grass, deck, pergola—in glorious summer evening shade. The scent of honeysuckle and other flowers filled the air, and Travis took a deep breath and let it all out.

"This is the most amazing thing ever," Poppy said, going all the way to the edge of the deck. "Look at this yard, Trav."

"It's great," he said. "My mother happens to like gardening, same as you." She didn't have a vegetable garden, and Poppy's was quite large. But she did tenderly care for the trees, bushes, plants, and flowers in her yard, and she chose each one carefully.

"Sit, sit," Momma said as she came outside. Travis noticed the table only had two spots, and he silently thanked the Lord above for such a good mother. "The pizza is hot, and the salad is cold."

Travis went to Poppy's side and leaned down. "She'll talk your ear off about the yard if you ask," he murmured. "But I kinda want to eat with you alone."

She looked up at him, that glint of attractiveness in her expression, and she nodded. They turned as a unit back to the table, and Travis just caught sight of his mother hurrying back inside. "She'll have salad and drinks and dessert," he said with a quick laugh. "We best not waste it."

"No, sir," Poppy said. She allowed him to hold her chair for her while she sat, and once he'd taken a seat across from her, she took both of his hands in both of hers. "This is amazing, Trav. Way better than the Lazy Summer Days picnic."

"You think so?"

She looked at the pizza and then up to Momma as she came bustling back onto the deck with a big bowl of green salad in her hands. Poppy pulled her hands back to her lap, and Travis did the same so his mother could put down the food.

Momma smiled at him—the biggest, healthiest smile he'd seen on her face in a while—and said, "Okay, I'll leave you two to it. I'll have brownies and ice cream when you're ready."

"Thank you, Momma," Travis murmured, but Poppy said, "Thank you, ma'am," in a loud voice full of enthusiasm.

Momma smiled her way off the deck, closing the back door behind her and leaving Travis to his hometown date with the prettiest woman in Colorado. He looked at her, and she looked at him, and he took a gander at the pizza.

"Good thing I brought some gum," he said, reaching for the first slice of the pie—which held plenty of onions, peppers, and meat. Not exactly the best for having fresh kissing breath later.

"Oh?" Poppy asked. "Whatever would you need that for?"

Travis's gaze flew back to hers, his heart suddenly pounding too hard in his too-small chest.

# Seventeen

POPPY SURE DID ENJOY TEASING TRAVIS. THE way his eyes widened and that vein in his neck throbbed.... She laughed loudly and held out her plate as he put the first piece of pizza on it. She wanted to say it looked great —not at all like something a pastor would make. Maybe the pastor's wife, but he clearly wasn't married.

She scolded herself for stereotyping men as unable to cook. Of course men could cook. Travis served himself some pizza and stirred the salad before her laughter died out. He served her some of that too, then put a few leafy greens on his plate, before he looked at her again.

"Was that a serious question?" he asked.

Poppy's pulse paraded through her body now. "Maybe," she said. She'd packed a tin of mints in her purse, because she felt certain she and Travis had been going down a path toward kissing. And they'd arrived at the waterfall.

Travis shifted in his seat. "I don't know," he said. "Just that pizza breath isn't the best for slow dancing."

Slow dancing. She cocked her head and studied him. "Do they dance at these concerts in the park?"

"George has some real good dancin' songs," Travis said as he lifted his pizza to his mouth. Mesmerized, Poppy watched him take a bite and begin to chew. He covered up his mouth with a napkin as he wiped his lips, and that broke her concentration on that part of his body.

"You know what I think?" he asked after he'd swallowed.

"What?" she murmured.

"I think you're thinkin' about kissin' me, and you want my breath to be as fresh as can be." He grinned at her.

Poppy had started this teasing, but now, her face flamed hotly. "You're thinkin' about kissin' me," she shot back at him, throwing in some of his cowboy drawl for emphasis. "That's why you brought gum."

He gazed back at her, his smile going nowhere. "Guilty."

Poppy dropped her head and let her hair hide some of the flame in her face. She cooled quickly under the shade, with the evening breeze, and she bit into her pizza. Though the crust was store-bought, whoever had made this knew what they were doing. She nodded as she chewed and swallowed. "This is amazing. Your momma should go out with the pastor."

Travis laughed again, but he shook his head. "She won't. She doesn't want to get married again."

Poppy sensed some stories there. "Why not?"

Travis shrugged one shoulder and finished his slice. "She's been married twice. Both of her husbands have died. She doesn't want to attend a third funeral."

Poppy could only blink. "Oh, right. I remember you said that."

He nodded. "My daddy died a long time ago. Decades now. She met someone else and moved out here, which is why I came here after New York."

She'd known he wasn't from Colorado, but North Carolina. He did have a stronger cowboy accent than most men around here, some of whom just wore the hat and thought that made them a cowboy. Poppy did love the big black hat perched on Travis's head, and he wore it like a pro. Everything he did screamed of confidence and ability, though she'd seen him nervous before. Apprehensive. Vulnerable.

All of those softer things only endeared him to her faster and easier.

"She's a lovely woman," Poppy said, glancing toward the house. "I see why she has men calling on her."

"She's headstrong, though," Travis said. "If she doesn't want to do something, she won't."

"Would you be upset if she got married again?"

Travis shook his head and picked up a piece of ham that had fallen off his pizza. "No," he said. "Like I said, my daddy died a while ago. She's alone, and while she says she likes it, there are times when I know she's lonely." He met her eyes. "She's got a couple of cats and that old dog." He smiled. "And friends here in the neighborhood, at church. I think she's doing okay."

"She has you," Poppy said, adding him to the list, because he'd literally just described her life. But hidden behind his seventy-year-old mother. She had animals to keep her company. Maybe not cats—the barn cats didn't like anyone, least of all her—but a donkey and a dog. A couple of horses, and goats she vented at every single day.

She had friends at church and friends next door. She had Steele to look after, and her parents and sister to keep her entertained should she get too lonely.

And she had Travis.

"Oh, I come once a week," he said. "And more if she needs something heavy done."

"You guys still have a good bond," Poppy insisted. "I can feel it."

Travis didn't deny it, and Poppy leaned forward. "You know, you just described my life too."

His face went blank for a moment, and then it filled with a ruddy color that made her smile wider and wider.

"Like, I'm good with all of my animals and friends—and you if you stop by once a week."

"I didn't mean that for you," he said, obviously horrified.

She giggled and enjoyed teasing him—maybe a little too much. "I know," she said. "But I think you're more important to your mother than you just made it sound." She reached over the big bowl of salad and clenched her fingers around his. "You are to me."

That sobered everything, and Travis's embarrassment drained out of his face. "You're important to me too, Poppy," he said, his voice tight in his throat. Poppy hadn't brought in her purse, where she'd placed the mints. She had finished eating, as had Travis.

She stood and rounded the table—such a quaint little round thing that barely held their two plates with a pizza and a bowl of salad between them. Travis pushed away from the table, and Poppy sat on his lap. He wrapped his arms around her, and despite her curves, Poppy felt safe and secure in his embrace.

She knew his mother could see them from the kitchen window, but she didn't care. The breeze played with her hair, which she'd spent a few minutes putting a wave in, and the silence in the privacy of the backyard spoke to her soul.

Travis's breath swept along her neck, and Poppy shivered at the introduction of it into her life. She could easily turn her head and kiss him. Her heartbeat went wild as indecision raged in her head. Did she want her first kiss with him to be right here? On his momma's back porch?

"Poppy," he murmured, the tip of his nose pressed into her cheek.

She turned in slow motion, facing him. Their eyes met, and his face had to be only six inches from hers. Oh, she was ready to kiss him. One-hundred percent ready, and her eyes drifted closed.

"It's been a while, but—"

"Brownies," his mother announced, and Poppy nearly toppled off Trav's lap.

"Momma," he said, his voice loud in her ear. She stood quickly, her legs feeling like the jelly in her shoes. "You scared me."

Poppy turned away from Melanie, because pure humiliation drove through her. She shook her head as she hugged herself. *Bad idea*, she silently yelled at herself. *You should've known better, Poppy.*

And she did, but she'd gotten so caught up in Travis Thatcher. Everything about him called to her, and even last year when she'd been so short and unpleasant to him, she'd been attracted to him.

It suddenly felt like she'd been waiting for an eternity to kiss him.

"We'll take them to go, Momma," Travis said behind her. His bass voice said something else, but he'd lowered it enough that Poppy couldn't make out the words. When she turned around, she found him frowning at his mother, who looked at him with wide eyes.

"We'll be late if we don't get goin'," he said. "And I

don't want to miss any of the concert." He slid Poppy a look out of the corner of his eye that said he didn't want to be interrupted again, and she couldn't blame him.

She did her best to put on her gracious face as she approached the pair of them. She could see his momma's beauty in his face, and she smiled at Melanie. "Thank you so much for dinner," she said. "It was fantastic. Whoever brought that to you should be applauded."

"Travis says you're quite the chef yourself," Melanie said, her smile genuine too. She linked her arm through Poppy's. "Come get the rest of the food."

"Momma," Trav said behind them. "We're leaving like, right now."

"Two minutes," his mother said, and he huffed out his breath.

Twenty minutes later, they finally had everything Melanie wanted to send home with him, and Travis had the look of a man about to explode. He marched to his truck with Poppy at his side, and she let him open her door for her. She met his eye, but he still looked one step away from a rabid grizzly bear, so she scampered into the cab and waited for him to get in the driver's seat.

The moment he started the truck, she said, "Your mother is amazing," while watching the house. "I really liked her." She swung her attention to him. "Do you think she liked me?"

He softened noticeably, his fingers releasing the

steering wheel and his shoulders drooping. "Yeah," he said. "I think she really liked you."

"Don't sound so happy about it," Poppy teased. She thought of her own parents—and Elora—and she simply knew they'd adore Travis. What wasn't to like? His proper manners? His good looks? His tender care for her, the animals he worked with, and his mother?

She laughed, some of it a bit forced. But it did its job, and he relaxed further. "I'm happy about it," he said as she quieted.

"You just want to kiss me," she sang.

He looked over to her, his eyes practically blazing with energy. "You're the one who climbed into my lap at my mother's house."

Poppy pressed one palm to her chest. "You make it sound scandalous." She shook her hair over her shoulders and played with the end of one curl. "I thought it was romantic. Peaceful." She sighed. "It felt nice."

Several beats of silence went by before Trav said, "It was nice, Poppy," in a near-whisper. When he spoke like that, she did want to touch her lips to his and pull—just to see if she could get him to talk a little louder.

She reached into her purse and plucked out the mints. She put one very deliberately in her mouth and offered him the tin. He took it and took a few mints before passing it back. With that back in her purse, she folded her hands in her lap, right over one of the biggest, splashiest flowers on her dress.

Her thoughts wandered to Steele, and she'd texted her father to say she'd be out with Trav that night. Her son had called only a minute later, and she wouldn't hear from him until tomorrow. They were going to the Statue of Liberty and Ellis Island, and Poppy couldn't wait to hear all about it.

Before she knew it, Trav came to a stop in a parking spot in the overflow lot at the downtown park in Ivory Peaks. Main Street ran for three blocks, north and south, and Poppy could find everything she needed to live in this quiet, out-of-the-way small town in Colorado. Everything she didn't grow on her own farm, that was.

"Wait, and I'll come around," he said, and then he dropped out of the driver's seat. Poppy checked her hair as he circled the truck, and she pressed her lips together. They didn't hold quite as much gloss as she'd have liked, but it would have to do. She probably wouldn't know many people in the park anyway. People from all the surrounding towns and suburbs came out to Ivory Peaks for their Lazy Summer Days, and Poppy told herself she already had the attention of the one person she wanted to have it.

Trav opened her door and crowded into the space instead of creating room for her to slide to the ground too. One of his hands landed on her hip as she twisted toward him, and the other moved swiftly and surely up her arm, lighting on her shoulder, and then carving a path of fire up her throat and around to the back of her neck.

He held her there, his gaze as strong and as electric as the current between them had always been. "I sure like spending my time with you," he whispered just before he pushed his cowboy hat back a bit and lowered his head toward her.

She pulled in a breath and took his face in her hands just before her eyes closed, and then, she waited. It felt like another age before his breath brushed her skin, and then a century before he matched his mouth to hers.

Fireworks and national anthems went off then, and any nerves he'd had over kissing a woman again after a long hiatus surely disappeared. He knew exactly what to do, his mouth dictating how fast they moved and how long they kissed.

They breathed in together, and Poppy couldn't get enough of him. Enough of his cologne in her nose. Enough of the feel of his hands against her skin, in her hair. Enough of the taste of him—minty, sure, but with another note of something fresh and desirable. What that was, she didn't know.

She simply wanted to keep kissing him to find out.

She sank into the kiss, further and further, until Trav had roped her heart completely. Only then did he pull away, both of them taking a breath and then sighing it out.

"Okay?" he asked.

"Yes," she said, her eyes still closed. She didn't want anything or anyone to break this moment, because she knew it could never be recreated. After all, how many life-changing, earth-shattering first kisses could she have?

In her lifetime, to date, she'd had one. This one.

She wanted another one, so she inched forward, searching for him behind closed eyelids. He found her and kissed her again, and Poppy prayed she never had a first kiss again. Because it wouldn't hold a candle to this one.

# Eighteen

TRAVIS HADN'T GONE DOWN IN FLAMES BY kissing Poppy. In fact, she seemed to like it, and he sure wasn't going to argue. Those shiny, pink lips had been taunting him for days, and he couldn't believe he was kissing them.

It felt like he'd swallowed fire, from the tip of his tongue all the way down to his toes. It ran through his veins as if his blood had been replaced, and once that had smoldered out, all that remained was the passion and mutual respect between him and Poppy.

She'd started another kiss with him, and though he heard people talking and laughing around him, they sounded far away. Everything existed outside of him and Poppy, Poppy and him, and Travis didn't want to ever let anyone else in.

He broke their kiss again, tenderly and slowly, so she'd

know he was reticent to do so. He leaned his forehead against hers, and they simply breathed together. They'd done that before, and she'd said that it was "nice" between them. There were better words for it, Travis was sure, but right now, he didn't care.

To him, being able to be with someone else without having to stuff the silence with sound was nice.

Being able to talk to Poppy and tell her real things—that was nice. Taking her to meet his momma without it being a national event: Nice.

So much between him and Poppy felt so nice, and Travis wanted to hold onto it for a long time. He was comfortable with her. Not only that, but he felt like he could be himself and that was okay. Okay, and enough.

"I hear them starting," she whispered, and Travis straightened. He opened his eyes, realizing that there was a world beyond Poppy Harris and that magical mouth. "The band," she clarified. "I can hear them, and I don't want you to miss it."

He backed up and gave her room to get out of the truck, which she did. He collected a blanket from the back, as well as two camp chairs, and they started for the stage that had been set up in the middle of the park. It wasn't hard to find, as people streamed toward it.

Travis noted that everyone seemed to be part of a couple. There were no children that he could see, and while he didn't check for wedding bands, he was willing to bet he wouldn't find any.

He found a spot near the center-right side of the stage, about a hundred yards back, and he set up their chairs there. Poppy sat, and he spread the blanket over her legs. It wasn't too chilly yet, but even summer nights in the Rocky Mountains could require a blanket or a jacket.

He took his seat just as someone said, "I give you... George Wilson Jones!" The man—the legend—walked onto the stage, and Travis whistled between his teeth. The shrill noise lifted into the air, barely as loud as the whooping, hollering, and applause from everyone else.

He put his hands together too, and he grinned over to Poppy. He really did love George Wilson Jones.

She shook her head like he was a naughty little boy in a candy store, and she'd let him get whatever he wanted—just this once.

He stopped clapping and took her hand in his, lifting it all the way to his lips. She wore appreciation on her face when he looked at her again, and he sure hoped she'd once again find her way onto his lap before the night ended.

George Wilson Jones started with the headlining song on his platinum album, and the crowd once again went wild. Travis had Poppy's hand in his, however, so he simply patted out the rhythm on his opposite thigh, his spirits soaring somewhere up in heaven.

———

A COUPLE OF HOURS LATER, he couldn't stop yawning. The concert wasn't quite over yet, but one glance at Poppy told him she wouldn't mind if they left early. She didn't look bored, but rather, she'd just finished yawning too.

"Let's go," he said, straightening his spine to get his mouth closer to her ear.

She bent down to hear him, as she had been sitting with him for about twenty minutes. Once she'd noticed how chilly it had gotten, and that he'd only brought the one blanket, she'd claimed her spot on his lap and spread the comforter over both of them.

"You're ready?" she asked. "He's going to do a big finale."

"You have to work tomorrow morning," he said. "So do I. We can beat the traffic."

She still didn't move. "You sure?"

For him, it was either sit here for another twenty minutes to end the concert, and then take her home. Or take her now and kiss her on her front porch for those twenty minutes. He knew which he wanted to do.

"Sure," he said. "I've seen you yawn about ten times in the past ten minutes."

"I just need a cup of coffee," she said, smiling at him. "Do we have time to have coffee at my place?"

Travis wasn't sure if that was such a good idea. "If I have coffee now, I won't sleep," he said.

She stood, and they packed up swiftly. He led her

away from the spotlights and the crowd, the darkness pressing in closer and quicker around them. He kept a good hold on her hand, and though they didn't speak, Travis felt as if they belonged together. Everything that night may not have gone perfectly according to a script, but it had gone perfectly well.

The drive out to her farm took fifteen minutes, and he walked her up to the porch under the glorious Milky Way. He paused just before he thought her motion-sensing lights would come on. "Look at the sky," he murmured, his head already tipped back. He admired the stars, the great splash of them across the sky. "It looks like God Himself painted it in gold, white, and silver."

They must be the Lord's favorite colors, because he never used much else with the stars.

"They're beautiful," Poppy agreed.

"I always wanted to go to space," Travis said, chuckling. "I think every little boy does."

"As a matter of fact, Steele's talked about being an astronaut," Poppy said.

Travis smiled and looked at her. She too had her head back, her eyes drinking in the glory of the night sky. She was easily the most beautiful person he'd ever met, and Travis's heart filled with...love for her.

*It's too soon*, he told himself, and he kept his voice caged. He didn't love her; he knew that. He sure did like her though, and he did want to see her more and more. He wanted to get through all four seasons with her, maybe take a road trip together, celebrate birthdays and holidays, and talk about everything and anything.

Then, if they could somehow see meshing their lives, traditions, and families together, that was what Travis wanted to do. But he knew he couldn't go too fast. He knew he needed more time to see if combining their two lives into one would really work.

So he swallowed the words and held onto the feelings as they continued up to her front door. "That was the best date I've been on, ever." Poppy pressed her purse to his chest and tipped up onto her toes. She kissed him, and Travis sure did like that.

He brought her flush against him and kissed her back, deepening it when she felt ready to go with him. Travis could honestly kiss her forever, but he forced himself to stop after several long seconds. "When can I see you again?" he whispered.

"Tomorrow," she whispered back, her fingers fiddling with the buttons on his shirt, near his throat. "I'm only working until lunchtime." She looked up at him with those stunning blue eyes. "Can I come find you on the farm?"

"I'd like that." He kissed her again, and then reluctantly, he let her drift inside her house and close the door, a soft, sexy smile on her face.

He somehow made it back to his cabin, which was dark save for a single light burning above the sink. He flipped the switch there and went down the hall to his bedroom, happier than he remembered a man could be.

As he knelt to pray, he could only think of one thing to ask for help with. His blessings abounded, and he went through those with God, and then he paused. "Lord," he whispered. "I don't know what might come between me and Poppy, but when it comes up, please bless us to be able to overcome it."

He'd like to think that nothing could come between him and this woman he was steadily falling for, but he knew better. Travis had been down this road before—a couple of times—and there would be something hard they'd need to overcome. Probably more than one thing. Now, in the future, even after they got married.

"*If* we get married," he said aloud. His thoughts then went in that direction, and Travis only remembered to end his prayer and get in bed when his knees started to ache.

———

THE FOLLOWING DAY, Travis sat with Chris at his desk as lunchtime neared. He loved looking over the man's portfolios, and he'd learned a thing or two in the years he'd been at the Hammond Family Farm. If nothing else, he'd learned to love the older gentleman like a grandfather, and as Travis didn't have a father figure in his life, his relationship with Chris meant a great deal to him.

"Grandpa," Hunter called as he entered, and Chris immediately started to lumber to his feet. Travis shot to his and helped the older man until he was steady. They didn't exchange a look and Chris didn't thank him. The motion was so normal and natural, Travis wasn't even sure either of them even realized he assisted Chris from time to time.

He stayed at the desk as Chris went to get his great-grandson from Hunter. Molly came into the house behind him, her oversized hat hiding her face. "Phew," she said, and since the house where Chris lived was small and the main area served four or five different functions—including that of an office—Travis heard her. "It's so hot out there today."

"It won't be as hot in Coral Canyon," Hunter said.

"We're not going to Coral Canyon," Molly retorted. "Next year, Hunt, okay?"

"It's nice there."

"They need you at HMC," she said. "I need you out here still." She took off her hat and then swept baby Ryder's off his head too. Chris arrived, cooing at the child, and he took the three-week-old from his father.

Travis tidied up the desk, closing folders and stacking papers. Chris got up every morning and went through his stocks. He had pages and pages of handwritten numbers and notes, the likes of which only he could decipher. Travis had learned his system over time, but it wouldn't be the way he did things at all.

That didn't matter. Chris did things his own way, and

he knew what they meant. He'd made incredibly smart investments over the years, and while he'd started out rich, he was definitely in the upper echelon of wealthy thanks to his keen mind, diligence in paying attention to the numbers, and his ability to make unemotional decisions.

Once Travis felt like he wouldn't be intruding on the family get-together, he stepped out from behind the desk. He approached Hunter and shook his hand. "How's downtown life?"

"Busy," Hunter said with a smile. "Even though I'm technically not going into work, I still go into work every day." He laughed, and Travis knew the feeling. He'd spent a decade in the finance sector in busy, bustling, cutthroat New York City. There were no off-days, even when the markets weren't open.

"That's a choice," Molly said, obviously continuing a conversation they'd had before.

"She and the baby sleep until mid-morning," Hunter said, no amount of regret in his voice. "I figure, I'm up at six anyway. I head into the office and work for a few hours, and then I'm free the rest of the day."

Travis knew that wasn't quite true. Everyone knew it when Hunter's phone shrilled out, and he looked at it. He frowned, silenced it, and said, "All right, Gramps. What's for lunch?"

Chris hadn't had his mind anywhere near lunch, but Travis had also been in the house long enough to know Chris had checked something in the slow cooker an hour ago. Molly currently walked with the older gentleman over to the couch, where he sank into the cushions, the sleeping infant in his arms not even giving a grunt.

Travis smiled at the pair of them. Chris was almost eighty-seven years old. Ryder was probably close to twenty-five days old. And yet, they belonged together. They were clearly related, and Chris loved his great-grandson with his whole soul.

"He made pulled pork," Travis said. "I think he was going to do carnitas." He took a few steps toward Chris. "Right, Chris?"

"Everything is in the fridge," he said. "Corn tortillas, cheese, lime wedges. I did it all this morning." He barely looked away from the baby while he spoke, and Travis did take an extra second to watch the two of them.

He didn't have any children of his own, and in that moment, he wanted one. A tiny baby who needed him. Who depended on him for everything. He closed his eyes, and that baby had his dark eyes and hair...with a hint of red in it.

Startled, he turned toward the kitchen and walked over to the fridge. Everything they needed for the tacos sat on a sheet tray. He slid it out and put it on the counter just as someone knocked on the door.

"That'll be Poppy," he said, his pulse firing through his body like a cannon.

"Poppy?" Molly asked. "Poppy Harris? Who lives next door?"

"Yeah." Travis abandoned the tray and lunch prep in favor of answering the door. Hunter and Molly didn't live here, and Chris obviously wasn't going to get up. He didn't want him to, and he arrived at the door a few seconds later.

He opened it, and sure enough, Poppy stood there. "You found it," he said.

"Right where you said it'd be." Her eyes met his, dazzling and sparkling, and then she looked past him and into the house.

"Hunter and Molly are here," he said, keeping his voice low. "They brought their baby. And Chris, of course."

"No Matt or Boone?"

"Chris said they were busy today," Travis said. "C'mon in." He'd invited her here for lunch, because she'd said she was only working half the day and would come find him. It wasn't uncommon for him to eat lunch with Chris, Boone and Cosette, Matt and Gloria, and anyone else who happened to stop in.

Today, that was Hunter and Molly.

Poppy entered, and Travis closed the door behind her. He stepped to her side and said, "I'm sure you know everyone, but everyone, this is Poppy Harris. We're seein' each other. Poppy, you know Hunter and Molly." He nodded to them, noting that Molly's face had been lit with delight. "And Chris—and he's got little Ryder."

"Oh, he's adorable." She hurried over to the couch

where Chris sat with the baby. "Molly, he's just amazing." She looked at Molly, who went to join them in the living room. "You haven't brought him to church yet."

"No," Molly said. "Too many germs there, though we bring him out here every day, and there are a ton of kids in and out of Pony Power."

The women continued to talk about church, babies, the equine riding facility, and Poppy's farm while Travis and Hunter got lunch ready. Hunter wasn't the type to ask a bunch of questions, which Travis appreciated.

He had one on his mind, and he needed to ask Poppy if she wanted more children. She was younger than him by several years, and judging by how she glowed when Chris passed her Ryder so he could come put the finishing touches on their lunch, Travis suspected Poppy indeed wanted more kids.

He'd ask later. Today, he just wanted to enjoy lunch with her and his friends.

# Nineteen

GERTRUDE WHETTSTEIN WATCHED COSETTE sweep the mascara onto her eyelashes. They fluttered and moved, and yet Cosette's head stayed deathly still. There was no way she could do that. She wasn't even sure why she wanted to.

She switched her gaze to her reflection in the mirror, and all she saw was the color pale. She smiled, and even her teeth were white. They were supposed to be, but Gerty was pale from head to toe. No matter how many hours she worked in the sun, moving horses, feeding horses, riding horses, her forearms only held the barest hint of a tan.

Michael, her summer boyfriend—and she only called him that inside her head and never out loud. Her dad would go *ballistic*—seemed to turn another shade of brown every time she saw him. Which was every day.

"And then you're done." Cosette stuck the wand back

into the tube and twisted it tight. She blinked at Gerty, her smile wide and warm. Gerty did love Cosette for a lot of reasons. One was that she loved Daddy, and sometimes he was really hard to love. Gerty knew, because her father seemed to be the big, hulking obstacle in her life at every turn.

At the same time, she loved him with a fierceness she couldn't ever imagine feeling for another person. Her daddy had been there for her through every single thing in her life. Good, bad, terrible, awful, heart-wrenching, and then back to good, joyful, fun, arguments, forgiveness, sadness, depression, and back to pure happiness.

She couldn't imagine ever loving someone as much as him, though her crush on Michael only seemed to grow with every summer they spent together. This was their third here at the Hammond Family Farm, and he only had one more before he'd become a senior and graduate from high school.

Gerty was younger than him and just going into ninth grade this fall. She wasn't sure why any of it mattered. She already knew she wanted to work with horses for her whole life. It was almost like she had some equine blood in her veins, and she simply understood horses almost better than people.

Uncle Matt's wife was like that, and Gerty loved spending time with Gloria too. She worked with all of the horses at Pony Power, training them to be the best therapy animals they could be for the kids who came to get the help they needed at the farm.

Gerty herself was one of those kids, and she'd been seeing a counselor for the past month—since Daddy had asked Cosette to marry him. She'd said yes, of course. She worked here at the farm too, and once they got married in January, Gerty's life would change again.

She and Daddy lived on the farm now, in a cabin alongside the other cowboys who worked here. But Cosette had a house in town. Just like Uncle Matt had taken Britt and Keith to live in town with Gloria as one big happy family, Gerty and Boone would do that once the I-do's were exchanged.

Gerty didn't let herself think past January. She knew Daddy wanted more kids, and somehow, that made her feel like she wasn't enough. Her dad never held anything back from her, and he'd told her several times that she'd always be number one to him—and she believed that too.

Thus, the counseling sessions had started. Gerty actually liked them—unlike the way Cosette held the mascara toward her. "Do you want to try it?"

"Uh, I don't think so." Gerty gave her a smile. "Maybe one day. I don't know. It looks so good on you. I think it'll make me look like a clown." Or like she was trying too hard. She and Mikey didn't "go out."

First of all, her father would have a conniption fit. Secondly, neither of them was old enough to drive without an adult. And taking her daddy on a date with her? That was about the worst thing Gerty could imagine. Mikey wouldn't be sixteen until November, and that meant he was only allowed to drive a ranch truck along the super slow dirt roads here on the farm. Gerty couldn't even do that yet, and she'd had it on her list to talk to her father about for a week now.

First, though, she needed to make sure he knew she was going out with Keith and Kassidy...and Mikey that night. Sans mascara.

"You sure?" Cosette asked. "I could do it if you're worried about poking yourself in the eye."

Gerty was, so she only nodded. "Go light," she said. "I'm like a ghost, Cosette, and I don't want to look like a goth ghost." She set her jaw, then told herself to release it. She didn't like how manly it made her look with such a square jawline.

"Just look straight at me," Cosette said. "Focus on my nose."

Gerty did, but her eyes blinked when a foreign object got too close no matter how hard she tried not to let them. Cosette said nothing, and five minutes later, she stepped back. "I think it's beautiful," she said in a soft voice. Everything about Cosette was soft, and while Gerty's memories of her own mother were muted and blurry around the edges, Cosette reminded her of Mama.

No wonder Daddy had fallen in love with her.

She giggled nervously, still focused on Cosette. "I don't dare look."

Cosette smiled and gestured toward the mirror. "Look." She moved behind Gerty, who had no choice but to face herself then. She did, and...she didn't hate the girl looking back at her. Cosette had gone light, but the black makeup still shone like a sore thumb on Gerty's face.

"I don't hate it," she said.

Cosette wrapped one arm around her waist and hugged her. "You look beautiful," she repeated. "With or without the makeup. But this is the best place for a girl your age to start."

Their eyes met in the mirror. "Do you think my dad will let me pierce my ears?"

Cosette smiled but she shrugged. "I have no idea, Gerty. Sometimes I can't predict what's in that man's head."

"I can never predict that," Gerty said dryly, then she smiled with Cosette. She'd promised both of them she wouldn't try to work one of them against the other, so she said nothing else. "Well, he's going to see me sooner or later, and I still haven't asked if I can go to the movies with Keith and Mikey." She took a deep breath and turned to leave her bathroom in the cabin.

Her dad sang along to a song in the kitchen, which was only a step or two down the hall. Gerty made those and said, "Daddy."

He looked up from the frying pan on the stove and froze. "Oh, this is not good for my heart." He clutched at his chest with his free hand, the other still holding the spatula he'd been using to scramble eggs.

Gerty rolled her eyes, her default when it came to Daddy's theatrics. "It's a little tiny bit of mascara," she said.

He grinned as he came closer to her. She'd grown a few inches this past year, but he still towered a good foot over her. "It makes you look so old," he said. He pressed a kiss to her forehead. "But I like it. Looks normal." He smiled to Cosette as she entered the kitchen too, and Gerty tucked her hands into her back pockets.

"Uh oh," Daddy said.

"What?" She looked between him and Cosette.

"You only tuck your hands like that when you're about to ask me something I'll want to say no to." He turned his back on her and returned to the stove. "And now the eggs are burnt."

"Let me," Cosette said, hipping him out of the way. "Go talk to your daughter."

Gerty swallowed as Daddy let Cosette take over with the cooking. He faced her and gestured at her with one wide sweep of his hand. *Go on, Gerty*, he was saying.

"Keith is taking Kassidy to *Storm Wars* tonight," Gerty said, her hands automatically seeking out one another. Her fingers intertwined, and then she pulled them apart. "I want to go with Mikey. It starts at seven-fifteen, and Keith said we could go a little early and get

McDonald's. It's cheap, and I have enough to pay for dinner and the movie. I'd need a ride into Uncle Matt's, as Keith left early for his baseball practice today." Her eyes flicked over to Cosette, but the woman wasn't looking at her.

"Cosette said she might be able to take me, if you didn't have something ultra-romantic planned for tonight. She said she wanted to call her daddy, and she has to finish making something for her friend she walks with in the morning." Gerty swallowed again, her throat sticking together for a moment too long. "So yeah."

Daddy appraised her. He folded his big arms, which only made his biceps twice as big. There he was, standing between her and a fun evening with the boy she liked way too much. Probably. That was what she told herself sometimes.

*You like him too much.*

And she did.

He was a nice boy, though. He was smarter than anyone Gerty had ever met, and he worked dang hard around this farm he didn't even own. He lived away from his family—and all of his friends—for months every year, and he could kiss her like he had to have his mouth against hers to keep living.

Yeah, she definitely liked Michael Hammond too much.

She couldn't predict the future, but the Hammonds

practically had theirs written for them. Mikey had told her that lots of times. His cousin, Hunter, was the CEO of the family company right now, but Mikey would be grown up and ready to take over in another decade. She'd be almost twenty-five then, and she knew the love story of Molly and Hunter Hammond better than almost anyone.

In her head, it was Gerty's love story with Mikey too, though she had no idea what the twists and turns the road ahead of her held. For herself, or for him. Or for either of them. She was also aware that plenty of people dated in high school, graduated, moved out and on, and never saw one another again.

That could be her too.

"What time does the movie end?" Daddy asked.

"It's an hour and fifty-seven minutes," Gerty recited. "With previews and maybe ice cream after, I should be home by ten-thirty."

"Who's going to bring you home?" he asked.

Gerty swallowed. "I should've said I'll be ready to be picked up at ten-thirty. *Mikey and I* will be ready to be picked up at Uncle Matt's at ten-thirty. He needs a ride into Uncle Matt's too." She held very still, because she'd already anticipated all of her father's questions, and she had answers ready.

An offense was the best thing to have when it came to him. She watched him crack right in front of her, and she wondered if he knew he did that. Gerty certainly wasn't going to tell him.

"All right," he said. "Since apparently laying on the couch and watching TV with me isn't very 'romantic,' I suppose you can go."

Gerty grinned at him and threw herself into his arms. "Thank you, Daddy."

He caught her and lifted her right up off her feet. It honestly wasn't hard. Gerty didn't weigh ninety pounds soaking wet, and she sometimes hated how straight up and down and rail thin she was. At least no one here made fun of her chicken legs. Of course, Gerty hadn't worn shorts in over a year, so no one could actually see her bird-like appendages.

"Gerty," he said as he set her back on her feet. "Is this a date?"

"Yes, sir," she said. It was always better to tell her father the truth. Not only would the guilt eat her alive before the movie started, but he had a sixth and seventh sense when it came to her telling him a lie.

He cocked an eyebrow. "Then you better not be payin' for dinner or your movie ticket."

"No, sir," she said. She wouldn't either. Mikey had plenty of money too, and he'd already said he'd pay for her. She liked being at his side. She liked spending time with him. She liked that he took care of her, and Gerty realized that she liked him for a lot of the same reasons she felt so safe with her daddy.

So maybe, one day, she could love someone as much as

she loved her father. Maybe she could find someone who was the gentle giant he was. Maybe.

———

LATER THAT NIGHT, she sighed as she curled into Mikey's side, the movie about halfway done. She wasn't keeping track now. She'd given her father a pick-up time over an hour after the movie ended, just to have more alone time with Mikey.

He kneaded her closer and squeezed her shoulder. "Are you okay?" he whispered.

"Mm. It's cold in here," she whispered back. They always blew the air conditioner so dang hard in places like this. She'd known that, but she'd forgotten before she'd left the cabin that night. Mikey had a way of scrambling her thoughts—just like her first kiss with him where she'd run off afterward without saying a single thing. Not one word.

She banished the memory from her thoughts, because she couldn't go back and change it, embarrassing as it was.

Mikey hadn't worn a jacket either, but he had brought a backpack. She sat up as he leaned forward and retrieved it. He unzipped it and tugged a blanket out of it. Handing it to her, he smiled. "Here you go."

She took the blanket, wonder flowing through her. Had he been thinking about her while they weren't together? Obviously. He'd anticipated her needs, and everything inside Gerty melted. She'd never considered herself very girly or feminine, but Mikey brought out all of those things inside her.

He'd said nothing about the makeup when she and Cosette had stopped to pick him up, but she'd seen the way his gaze had lingered on her eyes. She wasn't sure what to make of that, and she'd told herself there was nothing to make of it. If he didn't say anything, she didn't have to try to guess at his thoughts.

"You brought this for me?" she asked.

He sat back and lifted his arm, a clear invitation for her to rejoin him and steal from his body heat. Gerty did, settling right into his side and then covering herself with the blanket. It wasn't very big and barely went over her hip, but Mikey tugged it down until it lay flat. "There," he said. "Better?"

"Yes." She laid her arm across his stomach and really leaned into him, her focus on the film completely gone now. She had no idea what it felt like to fall in love, but she knew she felt something—and something strong—for Michael Hammond.

————

AN HOUR LATER, they followed Keith and Kassidy out of the theater, all of them talking excitedly about the

LIZ ISAACSON

ending of the movie they'd just finished watching. Gerty talked as much as anyone, but as they approached the ice cream parlor, she quieted. Keith did too, and she supposed it was the Whettstein in them not to call attention to themselves in big groups. Daddy sure didn't seem to mind it, but he was definitely the more outgoing out of him and Uncle Matt.

Once they got their ice cream, they couldn't find a table for all four of them, and Mikey said, "There's space for us over here, Gerty." She caught Keith's eye at the corner table he and Kassidy had found, and her cousin nodded.

She went to join Mikey outside, and she smiled as she sat across from him at the tiny, tin table. "Okay?" he asked.

She nodded, as she already had a mouthful of ice cream. He grinned at her, and she once again hated that he didn't live here full-time. Did he flash that grin at other girls in Coral Canyon?

Of course he did, and she couldn't control that. He'd told her he went out with girls there. Dances and such. But that he didn't have a girlfriend. She'd been too big of a chicken to ask if *she* was his girlfriend. He'd only been back in town for a few weeks now, and she was honestly still trying to figure out where they stood.

"Hey, I wanted to ask you something." He cast a look toward the door before his eyes came back to hers.

Her pulse leapfrogged, but she said, "Okay."

"I'm going home for the Fourth of July." He licked around his ice cream cone, catching a drip the heat had caused. "My family does a big thing for the holiday every year. I was thinkin'...maybe you could come with me."

Gerty's eyebrows practically flew off her forehead. "To Coral Canyon?"

Mikey gave her that sexy grin he had. "Yeah. To Coral Canyon."

"With you." She didn't ask this time. "And I'd...what? Stay with your family?"

"My dad is coming on Monday," he said. "To pick me up. I'll be gone all of next week. Then he'll bring me back. We have a big house and a big truck. It wouldn't even be hard for you to come."

She could think of one major thing standing in her way. And Daddy was big, strong, and hard to get anything by. A week out of town wasn't something she could hide from him.

"I don't know," she said. "I'll have to talk to my dad about it." And she'd had to psych herself up for a couple of days to ask him about coming to this movie.

"Yeah, I have to ask my dad too," Mikey said.

"You haven't asked him yet?"

"Nope." He didn't seem concerned about it either, but Mikey never got terribly excited about much of anything. Perhaps that was why he could leave behind his siblings, mama, and friends and come work down here.

"Well, let me know what he says," she said. Gerty

wasn't going to bring it up with her daddy until she knew for sure she could go. And once she got that word, she'd have to figure out what to do and say....

Fear blipped through her, and Gerty wasn't ready for this turn in the road, but she also didn't know what to do about it.

# Twenty

MICHAEL HAMMOND LOOKED UP FROM THE BOOK he'd been reading on the front porch of his uncle's house. He knew that growling engine.

He set the sci-fi book aside and got to his feet as his father's enormous black truck rounded the bend and came through the pines which stood sentinel at the end of the road. A smile burst onto his face. Tears pressed behind his eyes, and he thanked the Lord that the road leading to the farmhouse was so long. It always gave him time to compose himself and re-box up his emotions before his dad arrived.

He flew down the steps and slowed his jog to a walk as his dad came to a stop. Daddy flung aside his seatbelt and flew from the truck, and Mikey ran toward him now. They laughed as he reached him and Daddy picked him right up and hugged him tightly.

"Oh, I've missed you," Daddy said, and Mikey once again felt loved beyond measure. He lived with his grandfather during the summers, and Grandpa was amazing. He made Mikey whatever he wanted for lunch, and he didn't have to make explanations when he wanted to spend time with Gerty, on or off the farm. As long as he got his chores done and came home when he said he would, Grandpa didn't give him a hard time.

His father did, and Mikey honestly missed him so much. He sniffled, and his father stepped back. "Hey, are you okay?" He peered at him, and Mikey simply shook his head.

"Yeah, I'm fine." He swiped at his eyes. "I don't know why I'm crying." He honestly didn't. He didn't like showing his father his emotions, but his dad had never belittled him for having them. He smiled up at his dad. "How was the drive?"

"It's eight hours across nothing," Daddy said, his own grin kicking in. "So great."

"I haven't eaten yet," Mikey said. "Can we go to The Burger Babe?" Daddy never missed an opportunity to go see Hilde—or order the Double Hammond burger.

Daddy chuckled and indicated the truck. "Let me go say hello to my daddy and see if he wants to come. You can wait in the truck if you want."

Mikey nodded and did just that. He watched his father climb the steps to the farmhouse and go inside. Grandpa lived out the back door and to the north, and they'd be at least ten minutes, especially if Grandpa was coming. He probably would, as he knew his eldest son was coming into town today.

Mikey sighed and leaned his head back against the rest, the familiar scent of his father like a balm to his weary soul. He didn't know how to tell his father that living here in Ivory Peaks was hard on him. He'd told his mother, and the three of them had talked about it. In the end, Mikey still thought they believed he simply didn't want to leave his friends.

That was part of it, sure. He thought he'd acted decently mature about that, and he didn't have nearly as hard of a time as Jane did. She lost all of her friends every summer when she went north to Coral Canyon, and she had to start over every September. Mikey had been able to merge back into his friend group fairly easily.

The truth was, nothing about his life was all that easy. Everyone thought he was a spoiled rich kid, and he worked hard not to act like one. His friends didn't tease him at all —it was everyone else who looked at him like he was some kind of pariah because his family had money. Or they nominated him for things because they knew his father would pay for whatever needed to be paid for in order for the activity to happen.

He'd felt used several times over the years, and he'd learned to choose his friends more carefully. He hadn't told Gerty or anyone in Ivory Peaks about his family's wealth, but they all knew. The difference was, no one here gave him a hard time about it.

He worried constantly about what his life would be like after high school. He didn't want to let his father down. He didn't want to worry his mother. He didn't want to make Hunter keep doing a job he didn't want to do.

Mikey closed his eyes and let all of his stress—his very name—roll off of him. Several minutes later, he jolted awake when his father opened the door and said, "Get in the back, Mikey. Gramps is comin'."

Mikey hurried to do that, and he helped his grandfather up into the truck before getting in the back seat. Once everyone was buckled, his father backed up. "How's the summer goin'?" He met Mikey's eyes in the mirror.

The emotional slip should've told him that, so Mikey just said, "Fine."

"Dad?" Daddy looked at his father, and Mikey looked at the back of his head too.

"He's wonderful," Grandpa said. "Helps me every morning and evening. Is always home on time. Texts me with what he's doing. He's doing fine, Wesley."

Daddy didn't seem satisfied, and Mikey didn't blame him. He couldn't believe he'd teared up and then let his dad see. At the same time, he started to think that perhaps he could spin that into an advantage for himself.

He let the idea simmer in his head through the drive to The Burger Babe. Through all the cheers and hellos that filled the air upon his father's arrival. Through the delicious meal of burgers and fries. He wanted to bring Gerty here, but seeing as how neither of them could drive, he hadn't yet.

"Let's get going," Daddy said a while later. "I've been on the road all day, and I'm old and tired." He flashed a smile at Mikey, who returned it.

"I've got to use the bathroom," Grandpa said, and he slid out of the booth to do that.

Mikey watched him go, his moment right in front of him. All he had to do was seize it. "Dad," he said, his voice careful and measured. "I was wondering if I could bring a friend home for the Fourth."

His father's eyebrows went up. Mikey said nothing more. His father had run HMC for decades. He had two degrees. He wasn't a stupid man. "If by 'friend' you mean Gertrude Whettstein, the answer is no."

Mikey opened his mouth to argue, but his dad shook his head. "No, Mikey. It's too early. You're too young."

"I really like her, Dad." He kept his voice quiet, and he dropped his gaze to the table. "It's working for Hunter and Molly."

"Maybe in a decade, the conversation will be different." Daddy spoke in his no-nonsense, *I'm-not-changing-my-mind* voice, and Mikey knew he wouldn't. He'd been in this situation before, and his dad didn't budge.

"Are you kissing her this summer?" Daddy asked.

"Yes," Mikey whispered.

"How many other girls have you kissed?"

Mikey raised his eyes to his father's. He didn't have to say the answer for it to be out there in the open. None. He hadn't kissed anyone but Gerty.

His father shook his head again, and he did have the decency to look tired and worn out. He certainly wasn't enjoying this conversation any more than Mikey. "Son," he said. "I really think you should go out with other girls."

"I like *her*." And she liked him. They talked throughout the school year too; he helped her with her math, and she sent him funny memes.

"Hunter dated a lot of other girls," Daddy said quietly. "So when the Lord brought him and Molly back together, he knew the difference between her and them. Right now, Michael, you don't know the difference. You've tasted chocolate and you like it. But you might like butter pecan more."

"That's Hunt's favorite flavor," Mikey said, rolling his eyes. "And Gerty doesn't even tan, Dad. If we're going to compare her to ice cream, she should be vanilla."

His father's eyes glinted with laughter but also pure determination. "There might be some rainbow sherbet out there that you'll fall madly in love with."

"There might be," Mikey said evenly. He simply didn't want to try it. Not right now.

"Have you thought about life beyond high school?" Daddy asked, and Mikey suddenly wanted to roll his neck and stretch everything out.

"Ready," Grandpa said, saving him from answering. But Mikey knew the question wouldn't go far. It would sit silently for now, but he had an eight-hour drive ahead of him—with just his dad and himself—in only a couple of days.

He had some idea of what he'd like to do once he graduated, and it wasn't anything either of his parents would like.

He slid out of the booth and started helping Gramps back to the truck while Daddy gave everyone who worked at The Burger Barn one more hug. That took forever, and Mikey could admit he admired his father for his philanthropic efforts. He had a lot of qualities worth emulating, and Mikey would be lucky if he ever became half the man Wesley Hammond already was.

Starting with a safe, secure, comfortable place for Mikey to exist. He slept with his dad that night, both of them in Uncle Gray's bed, and Mikey wouldn't want to be anywhere else. The way he felt about his family told him he'd be right back here in the Denver area eventually, ready to don the suit and tie and take his place in the top-floor corner office.

But first, he had to figure out what to do about Gerty, if anything, and if he could really tell his parents that he was seriously considering learning how to fly helicopters for the Army.

# Twenty-One

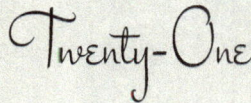

Wesley Hammond looked over to his sleeping son, all of his sixty-plus years streaming through him. He'd seen plenty of early mornings, and even more late nights. He'd operated on a global clock while running HMC, and he knew how to take a power nap better than anyone.

Since he'd retired, Wes had found a new brand of happiness. He'd gotten up early with the babies when they cried, and he'd taken them to his wife in the middle of the night so Bree could feed them.

Mike was almost sixteen now, but Wes still felt like he needed all the tender loving care of a newborn. The uncertainty streamed from him, and Wes sighed as he got up. The sound morphed into a groan, which Wes tried to stifle. He padded into the master bathroom and flipped on the shower.

His parents had lived in this house for decades before Gray had taken over the farm and they'd moved into the generational house just behind this one. Wes had never lived in this house as an adult, and he didn't mind that fact. He loved the country life of a small town, a house further from town, and the quaint little streets and shops that lined them. But he didn't want to farm. He didn't want to run a farm and manage all the people and pieces it took to do that.

Gray had a foreman, and Molly ran Pony Power, but it all seemed like a heap of work to Wes. He loved his slow-paced life in Coral Canyon, as he was technically retired and had labeled himself a househusband the day Mike had been born.

Bree still did a few things up at Whiskey Mountain Lodge, but not many. She loved behind a mom as much as he enjoyed being a dad, and they'd been raising their children together for a decade and a half.

He showered and went back into the bedroom to get dressed. Mike hadn't moved, and he didn't as Wes rifled through his bag to find his clothes. He tiptoed out of the room and closed the door behind him. In the kitchen, he set the coffee to brew, and then he went out the back door and took a deep breath.

The air smelled different here, though the Grand Tetons were part of the Rocky Mountain Range that existed here too. The farm air wasn't the same as the mountain lake air he breathed in every morning, his cup of hot coffee in his hand and the sun barely filtering through the trees.

The sun hadn't risen here yet, as Wes had gotten up early. He couldn't seem to sleep past six most days, and once again, his napping skills came in clutch when he needed them. He crossed the deck and went down the side steps. Then crossed the lawn to his father's house. Mike normally slept and lived there, but he'd wanted to be with Wes that night.

He knocked on his dad's front door as he twisted the knob. "Daddy," he said, fully expecting his father to be up. He was getting up there in years, but he'd likely be sitting at the computer, checking his stocks.

He wasn't, and Wes frowned. "Daddy?"

"Coming," his father called, and Wes looked toward the bathroom door. A moment later, his father came out, tucking in his shirt.

"Morning, son." He smiled widely, and Wes was struck by how old his father was. Gray had said as much, but as Wes didn't see him as often, it always came as such a shock. He wasn't the same, stern, dark, determined father he'd been when Wes was growing up.

The thought gave Wes hope, actually. "Morning." He embraced his father, both of them laughing. "You look great, Daddy."

"Lies," his father said. "I know I'm losing hair by the day, and it's all white now."

"It looks great." Wes stroked his beard. "I've got plenty

of gray in my hair too." He grinned at him. "I've got coffee on at the farmhouse, and I'm going to make bacon and eggs."

"Let's go." Dad smiled them out of the house, and Wes asked him how Mike was doing on the way across the grass. His father moved slowly, and Wes adjusted his stride to match.

"He's doin' great, son," Dad said. "Really. You and Bree have done such a great job with him."

Wes nodded. He hadn't been looking for praise. "What about him and Gerty?"

"They come to dinner sometimes," Dad said, his voice casual. "They're cute together."

"They're young," Wes said, frowning.

"Don't worry so much," Dad said. "Boone's here, and he's a great dad too. He's not going to let anything happen that shouldn't."

"Do you think it's innocent?" Wes watched his father so he could judge his real reaction. "I just...he's so young, and he has so much in front of him." Wes knew the road Mike was on, and his father did too.

"Remember when you were fifteen or sixteen?" Dad asked.

"Barely," Wes mumbled.

"You came to me and said you wanted to run for student body president when you were a senior."

He had to be older than fifteen or sixteen then, but he

didn't say so. He simply held his father's elbow as they took the first step up to the deck.

"I wasn't so sure, because we'd just gotten a new crop of cattle that needed work, as well as six new horses. I was deep in the throes of negotiating some deal that was probably the most important one at HMC, and I wasn't home, ever." He panted as he reached the top of the steps. "I relied on you boys so much. Too much, I know that now."

Dad wore regret on his face as he looked at Wes, who shook his head. "You were a good father, Dad."

"I did my best, but I was a much better businessman than a father." His mouth turned down. "Anyway, I didn't want you to run. I thought it would pull you from the farm too much, and your mother needed you. You were the oldest."

Wes nodded, and they got moving again toward the door. The first rays of sunshine kissed the wood at his feet, and he looked up into the sky. He loved the sunrise in Ivory Peaks, and he took a moment to feel the warmth on his skin. "I ran anyway," he said.

"That you did," Dad said. "And you won. It was then that I started thinking you should run for Mayor one day."

Wes chuckled, though that had been a sore spot between him and his father. "I didn't do that."

"That's because you had an opportunity in your

youth that formed your opinions and gave you experience."

"That's exactly what I'm worried about Mike missing out on," Wes said. "Dating other girls."

"He says he dates in Coral Canyon."

"He does...a little." He went to the junior high dances and now the after-football game sock hops at the high school, as well as proms and anything else he wanted to.

"He's young," Dad said as he went into the house. "He'll figure out what he needs to figure out, and he'll be better than you one day."

Wes suddenly found the comfort he needed, right there inside those words. He wanted his children to be better than him, and he changed his prayers from *Help me with Michael*, to *Help me live long enough to see all the amazing things my son is going to do with his life*.

He laid bacon in the pan, his thoughts only half on the conversation with his father. He thought about Mike and the difficult conversations they still had ahead of them. But Wes could have them. He wanted his son to come to him, the way he went to his dad even now.

"Hey, hey," Hunt called, and Wes looked up from the eggs he was scrambling. "Breakfast smells good." He entered the kitchen, his infant boy in his arms, and everything in Wes's life became clear.

In ten years, this could be his son walking through the door, his grandchild in his arms. Wes abandoned the eggs, as he hadn't put them in the pan yet, and practically jogged to Hunter. "Look at this baby."

He'd seen the boy on video chat, of course. But there was nothing as good or as wholesome as a month-old baby in person. He took the boy from Hunter, both of them laughing. He gazed at the baby, his love overflowing and overflowing. He looked up at Hunter, his eyes filled with tears. "I love him. I love you, Hunt."

Hunt threw his arm around Wes and hugged him, the moment tender and silent between them. It lengthened, and Wes didn't step away until Molly said, "I'll put the eggs in, okay?"

"No," he said, turning with the baby. "I'm making breakfast this morning for everyone." He strode back toward the stove, but he didn't want to give up Ryder.

Molly quirked her eyebrow at him. "Are you going to scramble the eggs with that baby in your arms?"

The infant gurgled in his arms, and Wes looked down at him. His smile touched his mouth again, and Hunt clapped him on the shoulder. "Let her make the eggs. You've done the bacon and the coffee."

"I can set the toast with a baby in my arms," Wes said. He did that while Molly scrambled the eggs, and soon enough, they all gathered around the table.

"I'll go get Mikey," Hunter said, a wide, gleeful smile on his face. "Don't tell them until I get back."

"I wouldn't dream of it," Molly said, setting the huge bowl of eggs in the center of the table. Hunter left the room, and she mock-whispered to Wes. "We're coming up to Coral Canyon for several weeks this year. He hasn't told his father or family."

Wes grinned at her and let her take her son. "That's great, Molly."

"We'll see how long he can stay away from work," she said. "He's already been gone almost a month."

"I heard he still goes in," Wes said, holding his father's chair steady while Dad sat down.

"Every morning," Molly said with a sigh. "Except today." She placed Ryder back in his car seat and set him near her. Then she sat too.

Wes had just glanced toward the hallway when Mike and Hunt appeared, both of them talking and laughing over one another. They looked very similar, what with all that dark hair and that long, sloped, Hammond nose. Despite their age difference, they'd always been great friends. Wes knew that came from Hunter and his deep, deep goodness, and he appreciated the man his nephew had become so much in that moment.

"Let's pray," he said as they reached the table, and Wes took his seat and then his son's hand. "Mike?"

He nodded and bowed his head. "Dear Lord," he said. Nothing else followed, but Wes kept his eyes shut. His son was so much like him, and sometimes he had some trouble getting the right words out in the right order.

"Thank you for family," Mike finally said. "Thank you for this food. Bless us to travel safely when we go back to

Coral Canyon, and bless my momma and siblings that they'll be happy to see me." He cleared his throat and added, "Amen."

"Amen," Wes added to the prayer, and he deliberately didn't look at his son as he reached for the plate of bacon.

"Mike," Hunt said. "Tell me what's goin' on with Captain. Molly says you've been workin' on something with his gait?" He glanced at his wife, then spooned some eggs onto her plate.

"Oh, right," Mike said, and his voice grew more animated as he spoke about the horse. Wes recognized a spark of love for farming and ranching—or at least horses—inside his son, and he wondered if Mike knew it.

He'd find out. He'd ask him on the drive home what he was thinking for the future, and then he and Bree could talk about the best way to support their son.

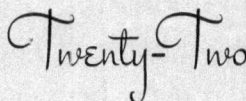

Twenty-Two

"THERE THEY ARE." POPPY LAUNCHED HERSELF out of the camp chair Trav had set up for her in the shade of her big cottonwoods in the front yard. She felt like she hadn't seen her son for a decade, not just eight days.

Her father's truck came around the corner, but Poppy's keen ears had already heard it. She strode down her dirt driveway, the evening sun so hot that heat waves lifted into the air. Once that went behind the big Rockies, things would cool off considerably, but they still had about an hour before that happened.

"Momma!" Steele called as they approached. He'd rolled down his window, and he wore the widest smile Poppy had ever seen on his face. "Look at this otter I got!" He held up the stuffed animal, and Poppy waved and waved as they went by.

She followed them back up the driveway, and the moment her son slipped from the back seat, she drew him into a hug. "Oh, I missed you so much." She wanted to squish him tight and hold him close to her forever. "I can't wait to hear all of your stories."

Boots landed behind her, and Poppy stepped out of the way so Trav could come to her side. Her step-mom got out of the passenger seat, and the door on the other side of the truck slammed too. Her daddy walked around it, and Poppy slipped her hand into Trav's.

"How was the flight?" she asked. She did let go of his hand to step into her step-mom's embrace. "Things went okay?"

"Fine," she said. "We gained some time coming home, but I'm going to use it sleeping." She laughed lightly as she stepped back. "I'm an old lady, and that was a packed trip."

"It sounded like it," Poppy said. "Thank you so much for taking him." Her heart and soul swelled with gratitude, and in that moment, she realized how much Iris loved her—and her son. "Daddy, thank you."

Poppy hugged him too, and then she had no choice but to return to Trav's side. She told herself that she wanted to be there, and she had nothing to be embarrassed about. Iris and Daddy looked at him—and only at him—and Poppy took a quick peek too. He smiled at them, his hand in hers tight.

"Travis," she said, and then she cleared her throat.

"This is Travis Thatcher." She looked up to him again. "Trav, this is my daddy, Whit, and my step-mom, Iris. You know Steele, of course."

"Can I go take Cotton out to the goats?" Steele asked. "I missed them so much!" He ran for the corner of the house without waiting for Poppy to tell him yes or no. She would've said yes anyway.

"We're eating in ten minutes!" she called after him, and her son waved to indicated he'd heard her.

"Nice to meet you, sir," Trav said, taking a step forward to shake her father's hand. He did the same to Iris, repeating himself with "ma'am" tacked onto the end. "Poppy's been tellin' me all about your adventures in the Big Apple."

"You're the one who told us where to eat in Chinatown," Daddy said. He slid his eyes to Poppy for confirmation. She nodded, and her dad finally relaxed and smiled. "How long have you two been an item?"

"That's not what it's called anymore, Daddy." Poppy rolled her eyes and turned toward the house. "Come on inside. Dinner's almost done, and Elora will be here any minute." She couldn't believe she'd invited her sister and her husband for dinner too, but at the same time, if she wasn't dating Trav, she would've. He was just one more mouth to feed.

That so wasn't true, because he was so much more to Poppy. So much more, she didn't want to admit it to herself. Or anyone else. "We've been dating for about a month."

"Oh, over a month," Trav said from behind her. "The very first of June, sir. Five or six weeks now."

"That's wonderful," Iris said, her voice bordering on gushing.

It was wonderful, and Poppy relaxed as she climbed the steps to her front porch. The scent of pot roast met her nose upon entering the house, and Poppy could allow the meal prep to distract her in the kitchen.

Trav talked about his life in the city, and Poppy's parents told stories about their trip where they fit in the spaces.

"Call Steele, Daddy, would you?" Poppy asked as she switched off the mixer. The potatoes were whipped. The roast ready. The salad unbagged and mixed together. "I wonder where Elora is."

"Right here," her sister sing-songed, and then she stopped short. Her gasp should've sucked up all the oxygen in the farmhouse. "My goodness, you didn't tell me your *boyfriend* would be here."

Poppy rolled her eyes as Trav turned toward Elora. "Yes, I did." She wiped her hands on a kitchen towel and went around the island to make the introductions. "Trav, this is my younger and far more dramatic sister, Elora, and her husband, Briggs. Guys, this is Travis Thatcher."

"Great to meet you, man." Briggs shook Trav's hand while Elora studied him. Poppy didn't like that appraising look on her face, but her son had just come inside, and she had to wrangle him into washing.

That took a few minutes, plus Elora and Briggs saying hello to Daddy and Iris, and it took too long to get everyone at the table. Poppy's nerves frayed when she finally sat. She looked at Trav, who gave her a small smile in return. She should've started smaller, but she couldn't take back the invitations now.

"Let's pray," she said.

"I have an announcement first," Elora said. Her face glowed, and Poppy knew what she was going to say before she said it. "I'm pregnant."

Poppy didn't have time to cover her ears before Elora shrieked. Cotton barked like the devil himself had come inside, and Trav startled. Daddy complained about Elora's screaming, as did Iris. Steele looked around at everyone like they'd lost their minds—and Poppy nearly had.

She shook her head at the commotion, wondering how four extra people could cause so much of it. Then she reached over and hugged her sister to her side. "That's so great, Elora. Congratulations." She smiled at Briggs. "So exciting."

"When are you due?" Iris asked.

"December thirty-first," Elora said. "A New Year's baby." She giggled. "Isn't that so cool?"

Poppy might not have used the word "cool" to describe a due date, but she only nodded. "That's great," she said.

"When's your birthday?" Trav asked, and she swung her attention to him.

"March," she said.

He nodded, didn't volunteer his birthday, and awkwardness descended on all of them. "Let's pray," she said again, and she met her father's eye. "Would you say grace, Daddy?"

He nodded, and cowboy hats came off and heads got bowed. Her father never said more than what needed to be said, and once Poppy had learned that, she'd learned to listen to what came out of her dad's mouth.

Tonight, he said, "Lord, we're grateful for Thy bounty in our lives. We're grateful for safe travel, and to be home tonight. We're grateful for a healthy baby for Elora and Briggs, and bless them that all will develop properly during El's pregnancy." He paused for a moment, and he breathed in deeply. "We're grateful Poppy has someone new in her life too, and bless her and Travis to find their way toward each other in a world that likes to pull people apart."

She went over that line again in her head. *Bless her and Travis to find their way toward each other.*

She wasn't sure what it meant. They'd found each other. They *were* together.

"Amen," Steele said at her side, and Poppy opened her eyes. She'd missed the last part of the prayer, but it didn't matter. She'd heard what she needed to hear—now she just needed to riddle out what it meant.

An hour later, she handed her father a cup of coffee and sank into the chair beside him. "Thanks for dinner, honey bear," he said, smiling as he lifted his cup to his lips. He smacked them after he drank. "You make the best coffee."

"Don't let Elora hear you say that." Poppy hid her sarcasm behind her own coffee mug and watched Steele open the back gate. He went through it, Trav right on his heels. Her boyfriend had been helping her around the farm for the past couple of weeks, and she could admit that it was nice to have pens that latched properly, and fences that didn't need mending, and a barn that didn't leak. In fact, everything around Poppy's farm this summer was going swimmingly well, and she'd likely bring in her full harvest of alfalfa, which would sustain her well for another year.

The fact that she still owned this farm meant a great deal to her—and it was all because of Travis's selfless sacrifice in paying her mortgage last year. Her stomach wobbled—that still didn't sit right with her. She'd thought about offering to repay him, but she didn't think he'd let her. For one. For another, she didn't have the money to repay him.

Yes, she worked, but she needed that money to pay her bills until the alfalfa actually came in. Until she actually sold it and had that money in hand.

"He seems nice," her dad said. "Travis."

"He is nice," Poppy said, her voice pitching up

strangely at the end there. She liked him, but she didn't say so out loud.

Dad didn't say anything else, and that honestly set Poppy's teeth on edge. She wasn't sure why, only that she knew her father must have some thoughts bubbling in his head. She wasn't going to ask him what he was thinking, because he'd never truly held back with her before.

After her mother had died, he'd stepped right into her life, learning how to put her hair in ponytails and do French braids. He'd become mother and father to her, and it was because of his example that Poppy had known she could raise Steele alone. It hadn't been easy, and watching him with Travis showed her that she might have been wrong.

A single person couldn't truly be both mother and father. She'd tried, and she'd tried hard. She'd done the very best that she could—and she knew the Lord had given her Steele for a specific purpose.

"He's good with Steele," Dad finally said.

Poppy nodded and took a slow sip of her coffee. "I'm not gonna go too fast with him, Daddy."

"I'm sure you won't."

"He helps around here," Poppy said. "He's kind. He works hard. He's a good man. But we need...time." Maybe she'd rushed into things in her previous relationships. She wasn't sure. What she knew was she wanted to go through several events with him. Months with holidays and months without. She wanted to have him around when

Steele started school, and when the harvest came, and then the first snow.

She wanted to see him on good days and on bad, on happy days and on sad. She wanted to talk to him all the time and really get to know him. Truly know him. She wasn't sure she'd ever truly known Eli, and she didn't want to repeat those mistakes.

"It's okay to take some time," Dad said. The back door screeched as it opened, and he looked over his shoulder. "Hey, hon." He got to his feet. "Steele said they got a few new chickens with funny feathers on their heads. You wanna go see 'em?"

"I sure do." Iris threaded her fingers through Dad's, and they walked away from Poppy. Elora wasn't terribly outdoorsy, and Poppy wasn't surprised when her sister didn't come out onto the deck. She nursed her coffee for several minutes, and then she set down her mug and got to her feet.

She wandered out onto the farm, easily finding everyone by the laughter. She paused as they came into view, wanting to take a picture of the scene in front of her. Her parents, standing near the chicken pen, with Steele throwing them feed. Trav leaned against the fence too, his smile wide and his face full of light.

He was so handsome, and so good, and Poppy wondered what about her had caught his eye. What about her interested him? Did he truly like her, or was she a charity case with shiny pink lips?

Trav caught her eye and straightened. His smile didn't dim, and she walked toward him, tucking her hands into her shorts as she did. "What's going on out here?" she asked. "It's almost dark, and those chickens have been fed already."

"I like the black and white ones," Steele said. "You didn't say you got new chickens."

"Travis brought them a couple of days ago," she said.

"Rescued 'em from a farm south of here," he said. "Matt said we have too many next door, and your momma said she could always use more eggs." He smiled at her and reached for her. She slid her fingers between his, feeling like she now held the world in the palm of her hand.

"He eats a lot of eggs for breakfast," Poppy said.

"We have to get goin', bean," Dad said, and Steele turned away from the hens. He hugged his grandfather and then who he knew to be his grandmother. Poppy did too, her emotions swirling through her whole body.

"Thank you," she whispered to both of them. They nodded and started back toward the house. "We need to get in too," she said to Steele. "Church in the morning."

He groaned, but he only threw one more handful of feed to the chickens before doing as she said. She kept her hand in Trav's as they all walked back to the farmhouse. "Are you going out to your momma's tomorrow?" she asked.

"Yes, ma'am," he said. "Did you want to come out there for dinner? I'm sure she wouldn't mind."

"I'm not going to make your mother cook for me and Steele," Poppy said, actually mildly horrified at the thought. "I'd cook for you if you wanted to come to dinner here."

"No potluck? It's the first Sunday of the month."

"It's a holiday weekend," she said.

"Should we go to the fireworks tomorrow night?"

"Can we, Mom?" Steele peered out past Trav, his eyes wide and hopeful, something she could see even in the dimming light.

She hesitated, because Poppy didn't love fireworks. She wasn't sure why, only that they scared her a little. "I suppose," she said. "We could eat here and head over to the park afterward."

"If you don't want to, that's okay," Trav said quietly.

"Please," Steele said. "Please, Mom. I'll help with the dishes so we can go faster."

"Like you said you'd help tonight?" she asked, her eyebrows going up.

Her son dropped his head, and Trav chuckled. "I'll help too," he said, and that brought Steele's face back up. He looked at Trav, obviously searching for something. Trav nodded, and then Steele did too.

"We'll clean up," Steele said. "Completely. And I won't whine for the long licorice ropes."

Poppy burst out laughing, because she'd forgotten about those—and that Steele did whine for one every time he saw them. "I don't believe that," she said among her laughter. "You love those things."

"You can ask me," Trav said. "I might say yes."

"Oh, don't you dare ask him," Poppy said. She nudged Trav with her hip. "You can't buy him everything he wants."

"Not everything," Trav said. "Just one of those long licorice ropes. Did you get the corndogs from that cart near Central Park?"

"Yes," Steele said, skipping ahead of them. "It was *so* good, Travis. I love the hot mustard."

Trav grinned at him. "I love that too."

Poppy simply walked along, listening to the two of them talk. Back at the house, she told Steele to go change into his pajamas, and she noted that Elora and her husband had left. El had left a note on the counter that said, *Thank you for dinner. I'm tired, so we're heading home. Love you, sis.*

She always liked hand-written messages more than texting, but Poppy pulled out her phone and sent her a good-night message. She couldn't help turning her back on Trav and typing out, *Did you like Travis?*

"I should head home too," he said, and she turned back into him. Her phone forgotten, she set it on the counter and moved into his waiting arms. He bent down and kissed her, and while she'd kissed him several times now, this one felt new and different. It wasn't rushed, and there wasn't fireworks and explosions.

Plenty of heat though, in the slow, sensual way he let her know how he felt about her. She held onto every stroke, hoping she let him know she was falling for him too.

"I'll be here around six?" he asked, his voice soft and deep and wonderful.

"Sounds good," she said.

"'Night, Miss Harris." He straightened his cowboy hat, smiled at her, and headed for the front door. Cotton walked him out while Poppy watched, and then her blue heeler came trotting back to her, his eyes inquisitive.

Her phone buzzed, and Poppy picked it up. *Yes, Briggs and I both liked him. He's great, Poppy.*

She'd barely finished reading the text when another one came in. *You sure seem to like him, which I think is so cute.*

"Cute?" Poppy asked herself. What did that mean? She yawned, and she was honestly too tired to ask El what she meant. She was obviously obvious in her feelings for Trav, and she wondered if that was a good thing or a bad thing as she switched off lights and locked doors. Then she went upstairs to check on Steele.

He'd changed and was leafing through a comic book. "Lights out, bud," she said, reaching to do that for the main overhead light. He snapped on the lamp, set his book on the nightstand, and climbed under the covers.

She tucked him in and sat on the edge of the bed. "I'm

so glad you're home." She leaned down and hugged him hard. "I'm glad you had fun, but I'm glad you're home."

"Me too, Momma." He clung to her, his arms skinny but strong. She released him, and he sank back onto his pillow. "It's okay with me if you marry Travis."

Poppy sucked in a breath. "What?"

Her son blinked at her. "Iris and Dad said you might marry him, and I've been thinking. I like him. The chickens like him. Dorothy ran to him like they were old pals." He smiled at Poppy. "Even Cotton likes him, so I decided it's okay."

Poppy gave her son a smile. "That's great, buddy," she said. "But we're just dating right now. It's like...we're getting to know each other. It takes time. We're not going to get married right away."

"Okay," Steele said as if he understood all the intricacies of intimate relationships. "But when you do, just know it's okay with me."

Of course she'd consider his feelings, but Poppy hadn't considered getting her eleven-year-old's permission. So she smiled, tucked him as he rolled away from her, and padded downstairs to her bedroom.

Poppy had never been married before, and she could admit the little girl fantasies of lace and long dresses, veils and vats of flowers, a big cake and the biggest, best outdoor ceremony appealed to her. She could see Travis—her knight in shining cowboy boots—standing at the altar, and she couldn't wait to get to him and say I-do.

She didn't know what any of that meant, and a twitch of fear accompanied her through her nighttime routine of brushing her teeth and changing into pajamas. She wanted her knight, her prince, but she felt some part of her resisting it.

If she married Trav, she wouldn't live here alone. The farm wouldn't just be hers. She'd have...help, and Poppy honestly didn't know what to do with that thought.

# Twenty-Three

TRAVIS TURNED AS SOMEONE CALLED HIS NAME. That didn't sound like Matt, Boone, or Cord, the three people who usually came to find him in the stables. The month of July wore on, almost a blister on his heel with the heat and the long hours of daylight.

He didn't normally mind having the sun come up by five-thirty and stay in the sky until ten p.m. But this year, something nagged at his soul. He honestly couldn't wait until winter, when there would be more darkness and more hours to sleep.

He took a couple of steps away from the stall he'd been scooping. The horses spent so much time in the pastures in the summer that he didn't have to clean stalls as often. He didn't mind the work, because he loved the good, earthy smell of shavings and horses. He liked the quiet time with just him and the sound of the tools, his

LIZ ISAACSON

thoughts, and the promise of a light breeze outside once he finished.

He stepped outside and found Steele Harris shading his eyes as he looked out over the fields between here and the houses across the way. "Steele," he called to the boy, and the child turned toward him.

They weren't doing therapy riding lessons today, so the farm seemed quiet. Travis knew plenty of people were doing their jobs, both inside the barns and stables, and outside, and he had a long list of tasks to finish that day too.

Right now, however, his heart beat slid through his chest and right up his throat. Steele had never come next door unexpectedly, and he rarely reported to Travis anyway. Had he missed a call? He thought quickly through Poppy's schedule and what she was doing that day.

Landscaping somewhere, he knew that.

"Heya, Trav," Steele said, jogging toward him. "I finished with Maisy and Daisy, and Gloria said I could come find you." He arrived in front of him, his disposition sunny and bright. "She said you'd have some work for me."

Travis smiled at him. "Sure thing," he said. "C'mon. I'm just in here doing this last stall, and then we'll take the wheelbarrows to the Dumpsters."

"I can do that," Steele said. "Right now."

Travis wasn't so sure the boy's spindly arms could

wield the wheelbarrow, but he didn't argue. He went back into the stall, pulled on his gloves, and got back to work.

"Should I take it now?" Steele asked.

"Sure," Travis said. "You know the way?"

"I helped Boone with his stalls last week." Steele grunted as he lifted the wheelbarrow, and his first couple of steps wobbled. Then he righted the load, and Travis smiled as he walked away. He'd spent more and more time with Steele, and he liked the boy a whole lot. He wasn't sure if Steele liked him, but he'd never given any indication that he didn't.

Travis thought about how he could possibly step into shoes he'd never tried on before, his mood darkening as he moved the spoiled material out of the way and started laying down fresh shavings. Steele still hadn't returned when he finished, and Travis wiped his brow.

"Shouldn't have let him go alone." He took his shovel and pitchfork with him, because if he came upon a spilled mess and Steele, he'd need a way to clean it all up. It was just stall shavings, and while he didn't want to do the work twice, it wouldn't be the end of the world.

He went all the way to the Dumpster and didn't see or find Steele. Confusion bubbled inside him, and Travis turned in a full circle, looking for him. The boy had a cell-phone, but Travis didn't have the number, and he leaned his tools against the metal Dumpster—which radiated heat, by the way—and headed inside the administration barn.

"Cosette?" He stuck his head inside her office. Empty.

He went through the whole building and didn't find another person. Frowning now, Travis pulled out his phone and dialed Matt. "Boss," he said when Matt answered. "Where is everyone? I was here with Steele, cleaning out the stalls in the back, and he took a load to the garbage, but he never came back. Now I can't find him anywhere." He stepped outside, the circles where they walked and exercised horses to his left and right.

They sat dormant and unmoving, but he hadn't expected them to be active. They wouldn't exercise the horses in the heat of the day. His stomach growled, and Matt said nothing.

"Matt?" Travis pulled his phone away from his face to see if the call was still connected. It was.

Matt's voice came through the line garbled, and Travis almost growled. He honestly felt like a starship had come to the farm, loaded up everyone, and he'd been left behind. The breeze blew. The grasses swayed. In the distance, he found Captain and Cinnamon munching grass. So at least the horses hadn't been abducted.

He reminded himself that he'd seen cars and trucks parked in front of the admin building, though there definitely wasn't as much activity this week as there had been. Molly and Hunter had gone to Coral Canyon for the summer, and they'd reduced their therapy to riding on Mondays and counseling on Tuesdays. It was Thursday, and Travis honestly didn't know where else to look.

"...tell you," Matt said.

"What? I lost you."

"Mikey's coming," Matt said, obviously yelling and trying to enunciate clearly. The line beeped and the call ended before Travis could say anything. He lowered his arm and walked past the rings so he could see more of the farm. He didn't see a discarded wheelbarrow anywhere, and he still had a pile back in the stables to clean up.

He kept moving toward Chris's house, because he figured he could take refuge from the sun there, get something to eat, and text Michael to meet him there. He'd no sooner done that, the shade from his cowboy hat making it possible to see his screen in the bright sunlight, when someone called his name again.

He spun at the sound of Poppy's pretty voice, his pulse high up in his head now. She waved to him from the fence line near the farmhouse, and he instantly changed his stride to move toward her.

She wore a smile and a pretty pink sundress—so not landscaping clothes—and Travis told himself not to run to her. He'd already been ultra-obvious in his feelings for her—which he didn't regret—but he'd noticed that they'd slowed and cooled in the past week or so.

He still saw her often—almost every single day. They talked all the time. He took her out. He hung out at her house with her and Steele and Cotton. And Dorothy. She loved that donkey with everything inside her, and Travis didn't mind cleaning up buckets, moving hay, feeding chickens, or wandering the paths of her farm with her and her son.

In fact, he loved it, and he wanted it to be his full-time reality.

"What are you doin' here?" he called as he got closer.

She boosted herself up onto the bottom rung of the fence. "Are you surprised?"

"Beyond," he said, and he did take a hop, skip, and jog to close the distance between them. He took her face in his hands and kissed her, the heat between them doubling under the July sun. "You're a sight for sore eyes."

"You saw me last night." She grinned at him, those lips pink and shiny and oh-so-delicious.

"I can't find anyone around here," he said. He swallowed hard. "I lost Steele."

Poppy's smile slipped, and she looked past him. "He's around somewhere, I'm sure."

"Yeah." Travis turned and surveyed the pasture too. "But he was workin' with me, and he didn't come back with the wheelbarrow. I can't find anyone in the admin building. I called Matt, but he must be out on the farm doing something, because the service was terrible."

He faced Poppy again, finding a glimmer of laughter in her eyes. "What?" he asked.

"Nothing."

He tilted his head as her smile exploded onto her face again. "This isn't nothing," he said.

"Have you had lunch?" she asked innocently. "I finished really early this morning, and I'm starving."

"I can throw in the leftovers you gave me last night. I only ate a few for breakfast."

"How you can eat the same food over and over, I'll never know."

He grinned back at her. "You deliberately make ten times too much food, just you can have leftovers." He chuckled as she pretended to look like he'd insulted her.

"Ten times too much?" She scoffed. "It's not that much."

"How many pizzas did you make when I came that one time?"

"We each like a different kind." She dropped down to the ground from the rung. "Come on, let's go to your place."

He ducked through the rungs in the fence and took her hand. They started around the farmhouse to the back yard, but there were a lot of trees here, casting plenty of shade. He slowed and when Poppy looked at him, he pressed her right into the side of the house and kissed her.

She seemed a bit surprised at his actions, but then she melted into him. Then she kissed him back like this secret make-out session in the shade was the best idea he'd had. Maybe it was.

"Trav," she whispered as he slid his mouth along the column of her neck.

"Hmm?"

"You really don't know where Steele is?"

That got him to raise his head. "Matt said he'd send Michael to find me."

"So maybe you shouldn't be kissing me back here," she mock whispered.

Travis ducked his head, a hint of embarrassment squirreling through him. "Did you need help on your farm today? I thought you needed to move those sprinklers." She sure wasn't dressed to work on the farm, which she normally did after she did her landscaping job.

"Steele will help me tonight."

"I can come help."

"Sure," she said, her voice far too high for his liking. Travis wanted to call her on it, but yet again, someone called his name.

He stepped away from Poppy and went into the back yard. Michael Hammond caught sight of him and swung down from the horse he was riding. Grace stood where she was as he came toward Travis. "Hey," he said. "Boone grabbed Steele for lunch, and he wanted you to come too, so we can talk about Matt's party."

"Where's Matt?" Travis asked as Poppy joined him.

"He's out at the retreat site," Mikey said. "Getting ready for this weekend's group." He looked like he'd ridden all the way in from out there. Perhaps he had. "I'm supposed to grab lunch from my granddad and head back out, so he won't know about the party."

Travis nodded and said, "Thanks, Mikey."

The teen turned and swung back into the saddle. He went around the shed to his grandfather's, and Travis looked at Poppy. "Maybe Boone will have food."

"Sounds like it," she said, slipping her hand into his. Feeling less frantic now, Travis walked down the dusty road with outbuildings and barns on one side, with cabins on the other. He passed his and Cord's and continued to Boone's which was the second-to-last one on the end.

Laughter came from the house, further lifting Travis's spirits. He and Poppy went up to the porch, and he knocked on the door. The laughter had started to die, but now it muted completely. Whispers filtered out through the open windows, and Travis looked at Poppy.

She cocked an eyebrow back at him, and they both stood there.

"Boone?" Travis finally called.

"Come in!" Boone yelled.

Travis almost felt like he was walking into a trap, like perhaps Boone had rigged a bucket of ice water to tip onto his head the moment he stepped inside. He twisted the doorknob and pushed open the door without moving.

Nothing splatted on the ground in front of him. He couldn't see anyone in the cabin either. His heartbeat skipped a few times, and then he committed to entering. He'd only taken one step when a whole crowd of people jumped up from behind the couch and the island in the kitchen, all of them shouting, "Surprise!"

Travis yelped and fell back, stepping right on Poppy's

sandaled foot. She cried out, and everyone started shouting and laughing. Through the chaos, Travis got the jist of the party.

It was for him, which strangely made his face heat furiously, and it had to do with his hiring anniversary here at the Hammond Family Farm. Gray and Elise weren't there, but Matt sure was.

The faker. He hadn't been out at the retreat site. He had perfect service here. Steele stood with Keith and Britt, and Mikey walked in the back door only a moment later. He wore a beaming smile, and he moved to stand beside his grandfather, who applauded with pure joy on his face.

Travis finally relaxed and let himself smile. "Thank you, everyone," he said. His stomach gave a loud roar at the sight of the six-foot sub sandwich on the counter, and the piles and piles of potato chips.

"Your favorite," Boone said, lifting up a bag of the salt and vinegar kettle chips that Travis loved. He could seriously eat an entire bag by himself, every single evening.

"Root beer in the fridge," Cosette said, opening it. Her smile told Travis that she loved and appreciated him, and suddenly all the pieces of the past twenty minutes came together. They'd all flocked here, sent Steele to give him a reason to abandon his chores, and then Poppy to make sure they got over to the cabins.

"Everything is still good and cold and ready," Matt said. "Though it did take you a bit longer to get here than we anticipated." He looked at Travis, but Travis didn't want to explain why he'd taken a "bit longer" to get over to the cabins.

He took Matt into a hug and said, "Thank you," then did the same for Boone and Chris. If there were two other people on the earth who liked to plan and throw parties more than the two of them, Travis had never met them.

People started piling salads, sandwiches, and chips onto plates, and Travis didn't hesitate to join them. Matt sidled up to him and said, "We need to finalize things for Boone and Chris. I'm talkin' to Gray in the morning, and he wants to know a date."

"I can come over tonight," Travis said out of the corner of his mouth.

"Maybe I can stop by before Gloria and I leave." Matt put a chunk of sandwich on his plate. "Keith's fine to share the date, and he's going to be doing a friend party on his actual birthday."

"Perfect," Travis said.

"Maybe around six?" Matt said. "The farmhouse?"

"Sure." Travis separated from him then, turning toward the table where Boone eyed him suspiciously.

He took the seat at the head of the table and looked up at the other Whettstein brother. "Your birthday is next week."

"Is that what you two are conspiring about?" Boone asked. He never did pull punches.

"They're not conspiring," Cosette said with a hefty roll of her eyes. "They're probably talking about work."

"Zelda," Travis said, because he knew Boone's favorite horse would distract him from anything he and Matt had really been talking about.

"What about Zelda?" Boone practically bellowed. His dark eyes blazed too, and Travis could only laugh.

"She's fine, Boone," he said. "But I do want her picking up that switch faster."

"Yeah, well, she's fightin' me on it," he muttered. He turned to go get his own food, and Boone shook his head as he said, "Mikey, give Gerty some blasted room to breathe, would you? You don't need to stand so dang close to my daughter."

He met Poppy's eyes, and she giggled into her hand. Then she picked up her sandwich, looked at her son, tousled his hair with her free hand, and smiled back at Travis before taking a big bite of her lunch.

"You're sneaky," he told her before tucking into his own sandwich. Poppy didn't confirm or deny it, but she'd definitely lured him here. He'd honestly go anywhere she wanted him to, but that was a secret he was going to keep for a while longer.

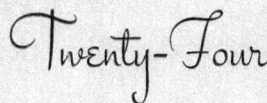

Twenty-Four

"I CAN MAKE THE CAKES," POPPY SAID. "REALLY." She watched Trav as he sank onto her couch. He'd been putting in long summer hours on the farm next door. Then he'd come over here and do the same thing for her animals. For her fences and outbuildings. Heck, he'd even mowed her lawn last week when she'd been so over-whelmed with a huge retaining wall she and the crew she worked with had had to do three times before it was right.

Elise had videoed in from Coral Canyon, and she'd almost come back just to make sure it got done right.

"It's fine if you can't," he said. "I talked to Matt and said I'd ask you, but we really can order them."

"For a party that's next week?" She shook her head and twisted to open the fridge. He just needed some lemonade and a friend. She could provide both. "I don't think you can get custom cakes made that fast. I'll do it."

"It's Boone and Chris," Trav said tiredly. "Nothing special."

Boone had thrown a fun luncheon for Trav's anniversary at the Hammond Family Farm—six full years he'd worked there—and Poppy loved baking. "I can do it," she said again. She'd stop by the offices next door and talk to Cosette. Find out what Boone liked. "Are all the Hammond brothers coming down for the party?"

"Yes."

She nodded though she moved behind him and he couldn't see her. She collapsed onto the couch too and handed him the ice-cold can of lemonade. He gave her a smile and a kiss on the forehead as he said, "Thanks, hon."

He popped the top on the can and took a long drink while Poppy watched. "Dinner is almost ready," she said.

"You don't have to feed me every night, you know," he said.

"I know." She didn't feed him every night anyway. "I didn't see you hardly at all last week." He made space for her against his side, lifting his arm and putting it around her. "It's just that shredded cream cheese chicken. Don't get excited."

"Did it come from a box?" he asked.

"No."

"Then I'm excited."

"Mama!" Steele exploded into the house, Cotton right at his heels. Poppy barely had time to swing her attention from Trav to the back door before her dog was upon her.

Her very muddy dog. "Cotton!" she yelled, trying to push him down and stand up at the same time. Thankfully, she still wore her gardening clothes from that day. She wasn't sure when she'd stopped changing and dolling herself up before Trav came over, but nothing had changed between them. Not the heat, not the sizzling arc of electricity every time she looked at him, nothing.

"What's going on?" she demanded as Cotton jumped up onto the recliner next to her. "Get off, Cotton. You're a mess. Steele."

Her son dripped muddy water onto the floor, but at least he had enough sense not to come further into the house. "There's a leaking pipe in Dorothy's pasture. You should see her. I think she's a new color." He grinned like this was fantastic news.

To Poppy, not so much. Her stomach plummeted toward the floor. The timer on the pasta went off, and she looked into the kitchen, not really sure which disaster to take care of first.

"I got it," Trav said. "C'mon, Cotton." He spoke with authority, and the blue heeler did exactly what he said. "Outside with me. Come on, Steele." The three of them left the house, leaving Poppy to herself.

She frowned, not sure why having Trav take control of the disaster on her farm bothered her. But it did.

She stood still and watched them cross the deck and go down the steps before she thawed. Then she hurried into the kitchen, silenced the timer, and drained the pasta through a colander she'd put in the sink.

In the slow cooker, the chicken waited, and Poppy shredded it and mixed together the Italian seasoning, the melted butter, and the cream cheese. She added the pasta and stirred it all together. She pulled the heavy crock out of the hot pot and put it on the counter. It might overcook slightly, but she had no other choice. Leaking pipes couldn't just be left to turn the ranch into a mudhole.

Poppy pulled open the back door and hurried out onto the deck. She couldn't hear anything besides the usual farm noises of rustling tree branches and the squabble of chickens. The closer to Dorothy's pasture she got, the more noise met her ears.

The donkey was positively singing, and Poppy froze when the animal came into view. She was drenched in mud, as if she'd laid down and rolled around in it—which of course, she had.

Steele had tied her to the near fence post, and Dorothy wasn't too happy about that. Poppy got herself moving again, and she said, "Dorothy, stop your bawling." The donkey tossed her head and looked at Poppy with baleful eyes. "Look at you." She lifted her hand as if she'd pat the donkey, but she didn't. She pulled back, because she didn't need to end up covered in mud too.

"To the wash stall," she said. She went down several yards and through the gate. She unlooped Dorothy's lead and took her toward the smaller of her two barns. She didn't really have a wash stall, not like the big fancier farms did. The horse stables and boarding areas had them too. She just had a open-ended stall with a spigot nearby. She'd hose down Dorothy to get the worst of the mud out of her coat, and then she'd set her back into a dry pasture to get all the water out of her hair.

Dorothy sang and brayed as Poppy got the job done, and she could barely hear herself think. "All right," she finally yelled over the animal. "Enough." The other equines Poppy owned had come to see what all the racket was about, and they all stood as close as they could get, their heads draped over the top of the fence.

"Isn't she naughty?" she said to them. "None of you would ever roll in mud, would you?" She gave them all a smile, because of course they would. They didn't care how much trouble it caused Poppy; they loved to flop down and get dirty. They were like great big dogs, and Poppy looked around for Cotton. He'd have to be washed outside too. Steele probably would as well.

Laughter carried on the air, the distinct sound of an older man's with a child's. Poppy smiled at the sound of it, but at the same time, it rubbed at her wrong. She should be the one out there getting the pipes fixed with her son. The two of them had never really needed too much help.

Sure, she allowed Gray and his cowboys to come help in hugely busy times. She went next door and helped them bring in their hay too. She'd gone on a cattle drive or two for the Knickers down the lane in the other direction.

They helped each other here in Ivory Peaks, but Poppy didn't like relying on others.

"You aren't reliant on him," she told herself as she put Dorothy in the pasture with the other horses. "He's your boyfriend, and he's just helping." She went to see what she could do to get the pipe mess fixed faster so they could eat, but Trav, Steele, and Cotton had just exited the pasture.

"All good?" she asked, secretly hoping it wasn't. She didn't know why. She didn't want to get covered in mud. Even Trav had the stuff all the way up to his shoulder and all smeared down the front of his body, as if he'd laid down on the ground and stuck his arm into the earth as far as it would go.

"All good," he said with a smile. He turned the beam in Steele's direction. "Steele here did a fine job gettin' the water off, and the new fitting on."

Steele likewise looked up at Trav with stars in his eyes, and when he looked at Poppy, he bounded toward her. "It was awesome, Mama."

"Awesome." She cocked one hip and folded her arms. Her fingers were freezing from the hosing down, and she couldn't believe buckets of mud was "awesome."

"Let's hose off, son," Trav said, moving past her. Poppy couldn't even turn around and watch them head for the hose.

*Son.*

Steele wasn't *his* son. He was *hers.*

A new kind of possessiveness filled her, and she spun

around to tell Trav she'd do it. She could take care of her own child. He should just go on home and get in the shower.

Her chest heaved while she worked to calm herself. She gave herself credit for that, because the Poppy of almost a year ago would've marched after Trav, lectured him, and then driven him off her farm.

Steele yelped and then started to laugh, and she watched from a distance as he got rinsed until the water didn't drip brown. Trav did the same to Cotton, who wasn't very happy about it either, and then he turned the hose on himself.

She wouldn't have any clothes to fit him, and she wasn't sure how long she stood there watching him hop around as he tried to get the mud off without getting too much cold water on himself. Long enough for everyone to get de-mudified and for Trav to come back to her. "I'm gonna run home and change." He leaned forward and swept his lips along her cheek, branding her with fire. "I'll be back in ten. You guys don't have to wait for me to eat."

He turned and left, seemingly unaware of her inner turmoil. Poppy prided herself on that too, because what she felt usually showed right there on her face.

"Come on, Mama," Steele said, and those words got her to move. They left Cotton in the back yard to finish drying, and she made Steele wait on the deck for her to get a few towels. She mopped him up the best she could, and then she told him to go get in the shower. "Dinner will wait," she said.

Trav returned before Steele was fully ready, but he said he didn't mind waiting for him. So they waited. The silence between them wasn't right, but Poppy couldn't put her finger on what exactly was wrong. Her chest stormed, she knew that. Tears pricked her eyes for no reason she could name. Her hands shook as she lifted the lid on the slow cooker and stirred everything together again.

"Why are you upset with me?" Trav asked.

Not two seconds later, Steele came bounding down the steps. "Ready," he announced.

Poppy let him distract her from Trav's question. She couldn't really avoid his gaze, and their eyes met for a long moment. *Later*, she pleaded silently, and he turned toward Steele.

"All right." He clapped his hands together and then gave a fist-bump to Steele. "Let's eat, shall we?"

Poppy was still reeling from the fist-bump. She'd never seen her son do that with anyone. Not a friend who'd come to the farm to play. Not a cowboy next door.

*Yes, a cowboy next door*, she told herself as she joined Trav and Steele at the table. *Trav is a cowboy next door.*

Oh, how she didn't like that thought. He'd told her at the beginning of the summer that he didn't like the label of "friends" or "neighbors." He wanted to be more than that. Poppy wanted him to be more than that.

She really did.

Why then, was she suddenly regretting letting him so far into her life? Into Steele's life? Why did she feel like she had to do everything herself and be everything for her son?

She wasn't sure, and she had no idea how to answer Trav's question. Why was she mad at him?

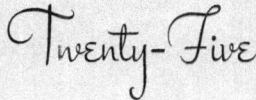

# Twenty-Five

TRAVIS WASN'T ENTIRELY SURE WHAT HE'D DONE wrong that evening. Poppy had gone still and silent out on the farm, and she hadn't reacted to his kiss before he'd left to shower. He'd hurried, and he'd beaten Steele, even with the drive.

Still, something was wrong with Poppy. Travis didn't want to speculate, because that rarely turned out well. At the same time, he needed a detective certification or a whole lot of brains to come up with a pretty good idea for her ire.

He'd helped her too much.

He'd been trying not to go out on the farm after dinner. Steele wanted to show him this, then that, and when Travis saw something that needed to be fixed, repaired, moved, or taken care of, he did it. It was almost second-nature to him.

Poppy hadn't ever come right out and said he shouldn't. He'd seen her throw him a look or two from time to time, but then she'd recover. They'd be fine.

Things between them didn't feel fine right now.

"Trav," Steele said, and Travis blinked out of his thoughts. He'd barely eaten, but Steele's pasta was almost gone.

"Yeah, bud?"

"Will you come to the Dads and Doughnuts this year?"

Travis sucked in a breath at the same time Poppy did. "Steele," she said sharply. "Trav, I'm sorry." She shook her head at her son. "He's not your father."

Steele looked between her and Travis. He had no idea what to say. The truth was, he really liked spending time with Steele. They'd worked on this farm and the Hammond's next door together for several weeks now. He saw Steele as often as he saw Poppy, because even if they went out alone, he came to pick her up. The boy was always here, and he'd chatted several more times with Elora, Poppy's go-to babysitter, as well.

"I just thought you guys might get married," Steele said.

"Dads and Doughnuts is at the beginning of the year," Poppy said, stabbing at a piece of chicken. "How fast do you think people get married?"

Steele wore a blank look on his face.

"Boone and Cosette aren't even married yet," Poppy

carried on. "They've been engaged for two months. There's dating, Steele, and then there's engagement, and that can be long. *Then* you get married." She seemed out of breath, her chest heaving. She wouldn't look at him, and she got up from the table in the next moment. "Are you finished?"

"Yes," Steele said, pushing his plate closer to her.

She didn't touch it. "Bring your dishes over then."

Travis wasn't finished, but he also didn't want to put more food in his mouth. He stood and took his plate into the kitchen, only a couple of steps behind Steele. They cleaned up in silence, the awkward tension Poppy had brought from her snarky tone and harsh words hanging over everything.

"Go get in the tub," she said to Steele.

"I showered before dinner," he said.

Travis thought Poppy might blow, and he stayed out of the way. This was clearly an issue with him, not Steele, and he didn't need to make things worse by trying to parent for her. He rinsed out the washcloth and laid it beside the sink to dry while Poppy said he could go get his game machine and play for a few minutes.

Travis wanted to leave before he could be alone with Poppy, which was the exact opposite of almost every other night with her.

The boy left, and Travis had no choice but to face her. She watched Steele disappear up the steps, and then her shoulders drooped as she exhaled.

He didn't need to ask her what was wrong. "I'm sorry I helped with the pipes." He'd wanted to get down on the ground and get the broken fitting out. Then Steele had zipped over to the shed and found another one. Travis had coached him on how to put it on, and then the pipe stopped leaking. It had been an easy job, one Travis had done countless times before. At least it hadn't happened in March, when everything still froze and a man could lose a couple of fingers to frostbite while hosing off outside.

"It's fine," Poppy said, tossing a kitchen towel onto the counter.

"It's not," he said. "You're upset with me."

She started to move to leave the kitchen, but Travis darted in front of her. "Talk to me," he said.

Her eyes held that fire they'd had last Thanksgiving. He sensed she was going to burst into tears about five seconds before it happened, and he got transported back almost a year to that fateful rainstorm that had paired them up in her leaking barn. He hadn't known what to do then.

He did now.

He took her into his arms and held her against his chest while she raged against herself. He couldn't pretend to know what was in her head, and she didn't speak. She did calm after only a few minutes, and she sniffled as she stepped back.

She led him to the couch, and they sat down together. It wasn't the close kind of cuddling he liked from her when they normally made it to the couch, but rather, they kept distance between them, and he didn't relax back into the cushions.

Poppy perched on the edge of the sofa, studying her hands as they twined around one another. "I just...I don't like that I need help."

"It wasn't me helping," he said. "It was just...a thing. I was here already."

She nodded, but he knew she didn't see the situation the same way he did.

"It's not charity," he said.

She nodded again, but frustration filled Travis. "Poppy."

She didn't look at him right away, but Travis had learned so much about her in the past couple of months. If he waited, she would. So he waited. Sure enough, after several seconds, she lifted her chin and met his eyes.

"I'm too old for games," he said evenly. "So I'll just say it." He swallowed, not sure if the right words would come out in the right order. He prayed quickly that they would, and then he dropped his own chin to his chest. "I'm falling in love with you. When I think of this time next year, we are married. Me and you. I live here. This is *our* farm."

He ran one thumbnail over the other, his bravery failing him. He shook his head. "I guess...I guess I just need to know if you'll ever see it that way." He looked up, hoping and praying that she'd affirm that of course she would.

She said nothing. He searched her face, growing more and more agitated with every second of silence.

"I'm adjusting," she said. "It's been me and him for so long, Trav. You don't get it."

"No," he said quietly. "I don't." He got to his feet. "I don't get this pride inside you. I don't get why me putting away feed buckets bothers you. I don't get why the three of us working together to solve the problem tonight upsets you. You took care of Dorothy. We took care of the pipe. It was no big deal. That's what families do."

"You're not his father."

Travis shook his head, as she wasn't even hearing him. "I know that, Poppy. Everyone knows that." He rounded the couch and kept going. "But I could be. But not if you won't let me."

"You're leaving?"

"Yep."

"Trav," she said, and he spun back to her. She'd stood too, and his abrupt change in motion stalled her at the corner of the couch.

"You're not being fair," he said. Everything inside him pounded and thundered like a herd of wild horses stampeding. "You want me here at night. You like cooking for me. You text me all day long. You kiss me like you mean it. But I'm not allowed to help on the farm? It's ridiculous.

I'm not allowed to form a relationship with your son and try to be a good father figure for him? Why not?"

His fingers clenched into fists, and Poppy stood there blinking at him.

"You don't need me," he said. "I get it. No one needs me." Travis hated that he had this deep-down desire to be necessary. But he did. He suspected all humans did. They wanted to belong, didn't they? They wanted to feel like they mattered to someone, didn't they?

Honestly, he felt like he could leave this farmhouse right now, and the wind could whip him up into the sky, and not a single person in Colorado would miss him.

*Maybe Momma*, he thought.

He loved his momma, he did.

But he didn't want his momma to want him. He wanted Poppy to be falling in love with him too. He wanted Poppy to need him to come home to her every evening, and to want his help with the house, the farm, her son, dinner, the cars, the goats, all of it.

And she didn't.

"I'll see you tomorrow," he said, turning to leave again.

"I've managed for a long time without anyone," she said behind him. "It's just an adjustment for me."

"You punish me and him in the meantime," Travis said as he went down the hall. "It's not fair," he muttered under his breath, hoping she wouldn't hear him.

"Travis," she said, and at least it wasn't the sultry, sexy way she used his nickname.

He sat on the bench beside the front door—which he'd bought a few weeks ago—and started to pull on his boots. "I know you don't *need* me, Poppy," he said, all of his frustration and irritation leaking into the words. He should stop speaking, but he didn't know how. This had to come out, because it had been boiling inside him for a while now. "I want you to *want* me."

His chest heaved, and Travis stood and turned away from the woman with her chin held high and those blue eyes blazing. "I have to get home. Early day tomorrow." He yanked open her front door and walked out, everything too bright in this blasted August heat.

She didn't call him back, and Travis didn't look back up to the porch as he got behind the wheel. He simply jammed the truck into reverse and got out of her driveway as quickly as he could.

He also didn't make the first right-hand turn he came to. He didn't go back to the Hammond Family Farm. He didn't go home, despite the fact that he did have an early morning tomorrow.

He simply kept driving, wondering how long it would be before someone missed him.

For his momma, days.

For Poppy, at least until tomorrow.

For Cord—well, it would probably be Cord who called Travis in about an hour if he wasn't home by then.

And that wasn't the person Travis wanted to have worrying about him.

"I want her to want me," he said again, this time to the radio, to his silent phone in the console, to himself. He took off his hat and tossed it onto the passenger seat, the wounds inside him which Poppy had started to stitch closed with her loving hands, tender kindness, and beautiful heart all bursting open and starting to bleed again.

"Why doesn't she want me?" He looked out the windshield and up into the heavens, begging the Lord to help him.

*Go home.* The words came to him, and Travis didn't fight them. He flipped the truck around and went back to the Hammond's farm. He arrived behind Cord's truck just as the last of the twilight faded into darkness, and he caught sight of the man standing at the window, the curtain fluttering.

Travis wasted no time getting out of the truck and into the house, where Cord now paced. "Hey," he said, setting aside his own problems for a moment. "What's going on?"

Cord threw him a look full of nerves and...disgust. Yeah, something was definitely bothering him. "My brother wants to come here," he said. He turned away from Travis. "He wants a job."

Travis had never heard Cord talk about his brother. "Okay," he said. "That must be bad to have you actin' like this."

"It's not good," Cord said. "I don't' know how he found me, either. That bothers me."

"You have a parole officer, right?"

"Yeah." Another turn, and Cord came toward him again.

"Maybe through them."

"Probably." He turned and went back into the kitchen. He pulled out a chair and dropped into it. "Trav, I don't get along with Whit."

"Okay," Travis said, joining his cabinmate and friend in the kitchen. "Then you tell him there aren't any spots here."

"He saw the seasonal job board." Cord rubbed the back of his neck. "He called Matt, and he said I could put in a good word for him."

Travis took a moment to go over some options. "Maybe you can tell Matt you don't want him to be hired."

Cord met Travis's eye, pure fear in his. "Trav, he's still into all that stuff that got me into trouble the first time." He whispered, his eyes bright and glossy with unshed tears. "The drugs, and the money, and the...I can't go back to that. I can't."

Travis reached over and covered Cord's hands with both of his. His brain fired at him, and he knew the Lord had just inspired him. "Can you even be around him? Is it against the conditions of your parole, maybe?"

Cord brightened then, and he said, "I don't really know."

"Do you have a copy of your parole terms?" Travis asked. "I'll help you go over them. I used to read a ton of tedious documents for my job in New York City."

"Gray's a lawyer," Cord said, a touch of hope in his voice now.

"He won't be home for a couple more weeks," Travis said. "But I bet we could email him. We can ask Chris too. He's a lawyer."

"He is?"

"Was," Travis said with a nod. "Get the documents, Cord. Let's see what we can do."

The younger man shot to his feet and went down the hall to his bedroom. Travis stayed at the dining room table, the space not quite big enough to hold his broad shoulders and all the misery pouring off of him.

He could help Cord, and that would ease the ache inside him for a while. His friend needed him. His work around this ranch was needed and appreciated. Why then, did Poppy hold so much power over him, and why did he have to crave only her approval?

"It's not fair, Lord," he whispered to the darkness beyond the window. "I'm a good person, and it's not fair that she can't allow herself to see it."

Cord returned, and the sound of his boots on the floor forced Travis to stuff away his own inner turmoil. He'd done it before, and he could do it again.

At least for a little while.

# Twenty-Six

MATTHEW WHETTSTEIN PULLED UP TO THE
Harris farm and put the truck in park. This place was
beautiful, with the big maple and cottonwood trees in the
front yard. Rose bushes and bleeding hearts lined the
front of the farmhouse, the blooms bright and colorful
against the gray siding on the house.

He picked up his phone and got out of the truck. The
party for his brother and Chris Hammond sat on the
calendar for tomorrow, and Matt had never been more
grateful to have Gray and his family back at the farm. He
always missed them during the summer, but the wind had
kicked up in the past couple of weeks, bringing in an early
cold spell that had left them all scrambling.

Squashes had to be covered. Fences had blown down.
Trees too. Horses who usually didn't mind storms had
shrieked through the night.

Matt had very nearly canceled this party—more than once. But Travis and Gray had stepped in to help on all fronts, and Matt just needed to pick up the cakes and get them in his freezer. Poppy had given him explicit instructions for when to get them out and how to display them, so he felt confident they'd be perfect for tomorrow night's party.

He glanced back at his wife and children in the truck, and Keith got out of the back seat to come help him. He'd turned almost the color of tanned leather that summer, what with all his work on the farm. Matt smiled at him as he waited for his son to approach.

"Okay?" he asked, and Keith nodded.

"I think I saved three thousand dollars this summer." He handed Matt his phone, where a number sat. His bank account, which had swelled a lot with his full-time work this summer.

"That's amazing," he said.

"You'll still match it, right?"

"Yep," Matt said. Keith had turned seventeen last week, and he'd had all of his guy friends over for a game night. Matt had rented a pool table and a swimming pool, and they'd had the time of their lives. At least it had looked that way to him. Keith had been talking about the party for a solid week—and that meant something, as his son didn't vocalize anything he didn't absolutely have to. "One more year," he said.

"I can work the farm next summer too, can't I, Dad?" Keith preceded Matt up the steps.

"Of course," he said. "Gray always needs people."

Keith nodded and fell behind Matt as he knocked on the door. A dog barked inside, and Matt shifted his feet. He wished Travis would've come to pick up the cakes, but the cowboy said he and Cord didn't have room in their fridge or freezer, and then he'd been swarmed by Wes and Colton Hammond, who'd arrived this afternoon.

Matt loved the Hammond men, all of them. But he was glad he and Gloria had their own place off the farm. It was nice to not always be at work, and he hadn't realized how free he'd feel until he'd moved out of the on-site cabin a year ago.

The door opened as Poppy said, "Back up, Cotton. They're just here to get the cakes." She looked up from the blue heeler at her feet, and Matt's first thought was that she looked absolutely thrashed.

A smear of white frosting went across her left cheek, and the bags under her eyes told him she hadn't slept in a while. "Poppy," he said as pleasantly as he could. She had to be suffering with a lot of the same problems on her farm as they were next door. Matt suspected Travis had been pulling double-duty for a while, and perhaps that was why Poppy looked so ragged.

"Come in," she said, her voice also pleasant. She backed up, and the blue heeler came to sniff them.

Deeming them bomb-free, he too turned and trotted into the house.

The air conditioning blew out, because while it had been windy stormy, by evening, the sun still heated everything. The weather really was unpredictable and Matt couldn't keep up with the temperature shifts.

"The harvest might be early this year," he said as he crossed the threshold into her house.

"Unfortunately," she said.

"Gloria says it'll leave time for the gardening." Matt chuckled, but something tense hung in the rafters here. Keith said nothing, and Matt paused in the back of the house. "Poppy, these are stunning."

He moved toward the two cakes on the countertop. One had been molded and shaped to look like a horse, complete with all four hooves on the ground, legs extending upward toward the body. He marveled at it and went all the way around the island so he could see every inch of the chocolate brown creature.

He gazed at Poppy next. "It's life-like."

"That's Boone's," she said. "Cosette says he only loves two things more than horses." She put a tired smile on her face. "Gerty and her, and well, I thought sticking candles in your fiancée's face was a little weird."

Matt laughed with her, though hers died out quickly. He switched his attention to the other cake, this one a two-tiered affair that Matt quickly recognized as the farmhouse next door. "Wow," he said. "Look at that."

"Did you see the porch?" Keith asked, and Matt circled the cake to get a better look.

"Unbelievable," he said. The roof seemed to pitch up exactly like the house's did, and if she'd made some pine trees and the fence that ran up to the house, it would be a miniature replica of it.

He turned toward Poppy and grabbed onto her. He pulled her into a hug and said, "Thank you so much. These are going to make the party."

"You'll have to do a cake for Britt's birthday," Keith said. "She would kill for one of Gingerbread, wouldn't she, Dad?"

Matt released Poppy, who'd gone quite stiff in his arms. "Defniitely," he said. He tugged his phone out of his pocket. "How much do I owe you?"

"Oh, nothing." Poppy waved her hand like anyone could make cakes as fabulous as these. "It was my pleasure."

"But it's a lot of ingredients," Matt said. "They're not free. I didn't expect you to make them for free." He frowned as he navigated to his payment app. When Poppy still said nothing, he glanced up. "I want to pay you."

She wore lasers in her eyes. "Why does everything have to come with a price tag?" She gestured toward the cakes again, nearly hitting the horse. Matt almost yelped and dove for it ninja-style, like if she'd happened to hit it, he could save it.

Thankfully, she didn't, and she didn't seem to notice

his panic over her touching the masterpiece as she continued with, "Why can't *I* do something nice for someone for once? Why won't anyone let *me* do that?"

Matt had no idea what was going on, but he sensed it was bigger than him. Bigger than these cakes. "You can," he said gently. "I'd absolutely pay for them. I thought Travis told you that."

Poppy spun away from him. "He did."

Matt looked at his son, whose eyes had gone wide. He wasn't going to help, and Matt wouldn't expect him to. "Okay," he said. "If you tell me your username on Cash-Out, I'll send you what I think is fair. Or if you'd rather I didn't pay at all, that's fine too."

"You don't need to pay me," Poppy said, and Matt tucked his phone away and nodded to his son.

"All right, Poppy. Thank you so much." He and Keith picked up the farmhouse first and started for the door, the cake balanced perfectly on the board between them. If they could get these back to the house without them smashing or melting, it would be a miracle in the month of August.

Gloria had moved Britt up to the front seat with her, the waif of a nine-year-old able to sit in the middle of the bench seat without an issue. They put the farmhouse directly behind Gloria, and Britt got up on her knees to look at it.

"Daddy," she said. "That's the m-m-most beautiful

cake I've ever seen." Her eyes shone with sparkles, and Matt grinned at her.

"Just wait," he said in tandem with Keith, and they grinned at one another. Back in the house, Poppy stood at the stove, scrubbing something. Matt wanted to fold her inside his arms and tell her everything would be okay. He didn't dare, because the anger emanating from the woman told him not to.

He didn't know Poppy very well as it was, but he really wanted to encircle her in comfort and peace. He looked at Keith and chin-nodded toward Poppy. He took a deep breath and said a prayer.

"Poppy," he said.

The woman looked up, surprise in her eyes as if she hadn't realized that Matt and Keith were still there. "Hmm?"

"What can I do for you?"

She simply blinked at him. Matt cleared his throat and stepped right into the sink. "I can finish the dishes. Where's Steele? Do you guys need anything out on the farm? The wind's been murder this week."

Poppy stared at him blankly, and Keith went toward the back door. He walked outside, and Matt swallowed. "You don't seem...right, Poppy."

As if someone had slid a mask over her face, her eyes blinked, and something snapped into place. "I'm fine, Matt," she said. "Steele's feeding the chickens and horses, and then he'll be in. We're fine."

Matt had been married for a little over a year, and he knew that the version of "fine" Poppy had used meant the opposite of okay. He didn't know what to say to her, and he finally dropped his head in acquiescence to her. "Okay," he said. "I'm happy to come over and help with anything the wind blows down. Or I can send someone. We have people next door."

"I'm aware." She went back to the pot in the sink, and Matt looked to the back door. Keith didn't come through it, and he wasn't sure what he should do. He couldn't get the horse cake out to the truck by himself.

"I'll go check on Keith." Matt kept his head down as he escaped out the back door, pulling it closed behind him. Thankfully, Keith and Steele walked across the back lawn, both of them smiling. Steele did come over to the Hammond Family Farm quite often to work, though he'd stop soon. School started in just ten or eleven days, and Matt was looking forward to getting back to a normal schedule. Breakfast, school, work, dinner, baths, homework.

*You'll have a new baby*, he reminded himself, and Matt couldn't help smiling. He loved being a dad, and he met both boys at the top of the steps. "How's the farm, Steele?"

"Good," Steele said, knocking his knuckles against Matt's. "We got the fences back up, and the animals are in the barn for tonight."

"Good, good," Matt said, looking past him and out at

Poppy Harris's farm. Nothing seemed to be in too much disarray, and he determined he could text Travis and find out if Poppy needed something she hadn't wanted to admit to.

He went inside with the boys, and he and Keith hauled the horse cake out to the truck. Gloria wore a hint of worry on her face, which quickly morphed into relief when she met Matt's eyes.

He heard Britt's shriek from inside the truck, and he chuckled with his son. They took the cake around to the driver's side, and Keith got in first, and then Matt slid the horse cake onto the seat beside him.

"I'll do my best," Keith said. "Don't drive crazy, Dad."

Matt promised he wouldn't, and he got behind the wheel. Britt grinned at him like she'd just met the real Santa Claus, and Matt patted her skinny little leg as he laughed.

"I want a horse cake like that for my birthday," she said.

"You want a unicorn cake," Gloria said.

"It's kind of like a horse." Britt turned and looked at Gloria. "Just with a horn."

Gloria smiled at Britt, and Matt loved how she loved his kids. With his ex-wife completely out of their lives, Gloria truly acted like Keith's and Britt's mother. She helped them with the troubles in their lives, and even as the baby inside her grew, she'd taken Britt and several other kids rollerblading in the stroller.

She took the horses and dogs with her, and everyone loved a good run down the highway in the Ivory Peaks countryside.

"Maybe a cake shaped like Pearl," Matt suggested, and Britt whipped her attention back to him.

"Could she make one like Pearl, Daddy?" Her eyes held bright hope, and Matt couldn't deny her anything.

"I'll ask Poppy, okay, baby?" He met Gloria's eyes and started to back out of the driveway. He got them home without any cake accidents, and then he and Keith put each cake in the deep freezer in their garage.

That task done, Matt blew out his breath. "Okay," he said. "Now we just have to decorate, but we can do that in the morning."

"Dad, can I go over to Ella's?" He looked up from his phone. "She's having some people over for movies and games." He waited for Matt to give his permission, but Matt couldn't tell if he wanted to go or if he'd accept a no.

"Ella?" Matt asked.

Keith reached up and took off his cowboy hat. "Yeah, I should shower first." He went up the few steps from the garage floor to the entrance and into the house.

Matt hurried after him. "You need to shower first?"

"I've been working the farm all day," Keith said over his shoulder.

"Keith." Matt planted his feet in the kitchen, his voice loud enough and firm enough to get his son to turn around.

"Dad," he said.

"Gloria said we're ordering pizza," Britt said as she skipped in between them. She wobbled on her feet, but neither Keith nor Matt lunged toward her. He might have in the past, but he'd learned to let his daughter fall.

She didn't anyway, as she grabbed onto the back of the dining room chair. "Do you want the meaty one, Daddy? Or the dessert one?"

"Both," he said, and Britt turned to go back to Gloria, who'd settled on the couch in the living room. He closed the distance between him and his son. "Ella? Is Kassidy going to be there?"

"I don't know," Keith said. "Maybe."

"Be straight with me. Did you break up with her?"

Keith sighed out the entirety of the air in his lungs. "Yes, okay? Rob has already asked her to homecoming, and when she told me, I could tell she wanted to go with him."

Matt heard a hint of frustration in his son's voice, and he put one hand on his son's shoulder. "Are you upset?"

"Kind of?" Keith said, guessing at it. "I mean, I really liked her. We've been dating for a while." He kicked his toe along the floor. "But we're seniors, and she wants to date other people. So." He met Matt's eyes. "What am I supposed to do about it?"

"Nothing," Matt said, the word ghosting out of his mouth. "There's nothing you can do about it." He took a deep breath and braced himself to say something his son might not like. "But I don't think rushing into something with Ella is a good idea."

Keith shook his head, his smile spreading slowly across his face. "Dad, Ella is like my sister. I'm not interested in her." He turned and started down the hall to his bedroom.

"Who's going to be at the party that you need to shower for, then?" he called after his son.

"No one," Keith said back, but Matt wasn't convinced. He made a half-turn and faced Gloria and Britt. His little girl had curled into Gloria's very pregnant belly, and she had both hands flat against the baby.

"Daddy, she's kickin'," she said, and Matt walked over to them. He loved his girls, and he couldn't wait to have another one. He put his hand over Britt's, her skin so pale despite how much time she spent at the farm, out in the sunshine. The baby did thump against his palm, and he grinned at both of them.

"I ordered pizza," Gloria said. She leaned her head back and sighed. "I'm exhausted, Matt."

"I know, sweetheart." He sank onto the couch beside her. "The baby will be here any day now."

"I hope not until after the party." His beautiful wife gave him a gorgeous smile, and he leaned forward to kiss her.

"I love you," he whispered. "The party, school starting, and then the baby."

She smiled against his lips and said, "Chloe? Do you like the name Chloe?"

"Chloe Whettstein." He tried the name out with their last name. "I don't mind that."

"You still like Olivia."

Matt laid back against the couch. "I do," he said. "But I like Chloe too." His own exhaustion pulled through him, and the windows to his right rattled with more wind. "Do you think this wind will ever stop?"

"I hope so," Gloria said. "Can you imagine having all of those Hammonds inside, unable to go out on the farm?" She laughed lightly, and Matt joined her. He closed his eyes and relaxed, the feelings of peace and contentment moving him toward sleep.

"I'm headed out, Dad," Keith said, and Matt jolted awake.

"It's windy," he said, getting to his feet. They ached, and he needed to get out of his boots, his jeans, his hat. Gloria hadn't changed either, and he should help her get down the hall before the pizza came. "Be safe. I want a text when you get there, and I want a text when you're leaving."

"Yes, sir," Keith said.

"Help me up, baby," Gloria said.

Matt extended his hand to her and helped her stand. "Let's change before the food comes, and then we'll put something on the TV and relax."

She nodded, and as Keith left through the front door, Matt and Gloria went down the hall to their room to get out of their farm clothes. "Britt," he called over his shoulder. "Don't answer the door, okay? Come get me."

She said nothing, and Matt turned back. "Britt."

"Okay, Daddy."

"Okay, what?" he asked. "What did I say?"

She turned toward him, her eyes wide. He loved her dearly, but she struggled to listen and comprehend sometimes. "Come with us, baby," he said. "Once the pizza comes, we'll put on a movie."

"Can it be the singing one?" she asked, scrambling to come after him.

"Not the singing one," Gloria whispered, and Matt said, "We'll see," which was about as close to "no" as he could get when it came to Britt.

"Daddy, can I go look at the horse cake?" she asked.

"Not tonight," he said. "In the morning, okay? You can help me get it over to the farm for the party." He gave her a smile, and she grinned on back. Britt couldn't really walk anywhere she went, and she hop-skipped along while they went to change their clothes.

Matt prayed that Gloria would make it through the next ten days until their baby was born. He prayed the party he'd been working on putting together for the past several weeks would go off without a hitch. He prayed for the safety of his son.

Then he remembered he was going to talk to Travis about Poppy, and he prayed for the two of them as he sank onto the bed. He called Travis, who answered with, "If you want me to go back out onto the farm, I can't. I've broken both of my legs."

Matt burst out laughing, because they'd all been working around the clock lately. "I don't want you to go back out onto the farm."

Travis exhaled. "All right, then. What's up? You got the cakes okay?"

"Yes," Matt said. "It's actually Poppy I wanted to ask you about. She seemed...upset."

"Yeah." Travis sighed. "She wasn't too happy with me for helpin' her get the animals in the barn."

Confusion ran through Matt. "She was?"

"She...doesn't like needing help."

Pieces clicked together inside Matt's head, and his head hung down. "So me offering to help her with something on her farm probably wasn't wise."

"Did you offer help?"

"Yes," Matt said. "She seemed like she could use it."

"I'll find out if she does," Travis said. "I've been over there every night, and I think she's probably okay."

"Okay," Matt said. "If she needs something, I know we're willing to help, and all the Hammonds are here for a few days."

"Right," Travis said. "I'll let you know."

"Great, well, then I'll see you in the morning." The call ended, and Matt laid back on the bed. No sooner had he don't that then the doorbell rang, and he sprang right back up.

"Pizza," he said. "I'll get it." He left Britt on the bed with Pearl, and Gloria had just changed into her sweatsuit. He took a couple of steps to her, kissed her again, and said, "I think Chloe is the winning name so far."

She beamed at him and said, "It's at the top of my list too, but we'll see."

Matt went to get the pizza, his thoughts still lingering on Poppy and her son, Steele. *Let Travis deal with it*, he thought, and Matt determined to do just that. After all, he knew her better than Matt did, and Travis would let him know if Poppy needed anything.

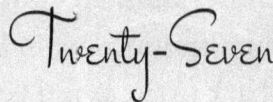

# Twenty-Seven

GRAY SAT UP IN BED, THE CRY OF AN INFANT loud in his ears. Beside him, Elise didn't move, and he looked at her and then the ajar door before flinging off the covers and heading for the hallway. He'd definitely heard Ryder, and it was definitely still the middle of the night.

Hunter came out of the bedroom right as Gray turned into the office where they'd put the baby. "I've got him," he whispered to his son. "Go back to sleep."

"You sure?" Hunt followed him to the playpen.

"Yeah," Gray said. He bent over and picked up the little boy. "He'll go right back to sleep." He put the baby over his shoulder, the soft, squishy human melting right into him. Pure love filled him, and he gave Hunt a smile. "You're tired. Go back to bed."

Hunt nodded, patted his son's back, and left the office first. Gray had spent a lot of time in this office, as had his older brother Wes, and their father. He didn't stay here right now; instead, he took the baby into the main living area of the house, where a light shone above the stovetop.

Gray settled into the couch, shifting Ryder into the crook of his arm as they both lay down. He breathed in and out, evenly, a hum starting low in his chest. The little boy had gone right back to sleep, and Gray could hold him like this forever.

He'd loved his babies exactly the way he loved Ryder, and he dozed, the goodness of life moving through him.

Sometime later, he woke. The sunlight had started to stream into the house from the back windows, and the scent of coffee filled the air. He kept his eyes closed, though he was aware of movement in the kitchen. Elise's delicate steps moved about almost silently, and she said, "Hush now. Daddy's asleep on the couch with Ryder."

Littler feet came toward him, and Gray got the very real sense that one of his sons was peering at him over the back of the couch. He smiled and opened his eyes to find Tucker watching him. "He's awake," he called to Elise.

"Shh," she said, coming into view too. "Don't wake up Ryder." She guided Tucker away, her smile meant only for Gray. She whispered something to their son, and Gray stayed right where he was. He wouldn't be able to do that for much longer, but hopefully another hour or so.

All of his brothers had followed him and his family from Coral Canyon back to Ivory Peaks. They'd only be here for today and tomorrow, and then they'd all make the eight-hour drive north again. School was starting soon, and Gray focused on drawing in a deep breath, holding it, and then releasing it.

Hunt would be going back to work full-time next week. He and Elise had already talked about making sure Molly had the support she needed with their son. She'd be out here at the farm all the time in the afternoons, running the children's therapeutic riding program she and Hunt had founded a few years ago.

Elise had a metric ton of paperwork and projects to catch up on. There would be parent nights, and new teachers to meet for their three children still in the house. Gray really wasn't looking forward to Tucker going back to school. The boy struggled mightily, and he worked even harder to cover up the fact that he struggled.

Gray and Elise hadn't even known until springtime last year, and the boy was going into sixth grade this year. He said a quick prayer for his son, more footsteps coming into the kitchen.

"He's on the couch," Elise said, and Gray knew his oldest son was approaching. Hunt had turned into a tall, talented, full-grown man while Gray watched, and he grinned up at this boy too.

"Look at you," Hunt said with a smile. "Stay right there." He pulled out his phone and took a picture, Ryder still snoozing like he needed Gray's chest to keep him warm and comfortable. "Thanks for lettin' me sleep. He's been a beast lately."

"He's teething," Elise said. She stepped to Hunt's side and looped her arm through his. "Why are you dressed like you'll be going into the office? It's Saturday."

"This is how he dresses now," Gray said.

"I—" Hunt snapped his mouth shut and looked from Elise to Gray. "I can go change."

"Into what?" Gray teased him. "A different pair of slacks and a red polo? The blue one is fine." He'd brought Molly and Ryder to Coral Canyon for the summer, and it was a rare day that Hunter wore jeans. Even when they'd gone fishing on the lake their house overlooked, he'd worn black slacks and an even blacker polo.

Hunt's eyes narrowed. "I have jeans and T-shirts. I just didn't bring any of them."

"He wants to look nice for the party," Elise said, her blue eyes boring into Gray's darker ones. "Don't tease him."

"I'm just saying, we probably need to do some work on the farm today, so everyone can take time off for the party."

Matt, Gloria, Cosette, and Travis had planned a huge birthday bash for Gray's father, as well as Boone and Keith. They all had birthdays in a three-week window, and they'd waited to celebrate until Gray could return with his family.

"I do have a conference call this morning," Hunt said, the truth finally out. "Just with my advisory board, so I thought a polo was fitting."

"You look nice," Elise said as she turned to leave. "I'm making buttermilk pancakes and bacon."

"I'm going to lay here with the baby," Gray said, letting his eyes drift closed again. "Someone wake me up when my brothers get here."

"You won't need to be awakened," Hunt said dryly. "They're like a circus you can hear from fifteen miles away." He chuckled as he left, and the house went mostly silent again. Elise made some noise as she cooked, and the bacon sizzled in the pan. It actually lured Gray back to sleep, and the next time he woke, it was because someone had just slammed a door.

The back door was glass and slid open and closed, so it had to be the front door. He yawned, and Ryder squirmed in his arms. He opened his eyes and looked right into the boy's dark, dark features. "Hello, baby," he whispered.

Ryder lit up like the sun, his smile wide and instant. He babbled and his arms and legs flailed. He'd been born without a single hair on his head, but he had some dark, soft fuzz now. Gray chuckled as he got baby-fist punched in the chin, and he lifted his head so he wouldn't be the recipient of any more blows.

"I'll take him," Wes said as he appeared over the back of the couch. "You better get up, brother. Dad's expecting us in the stables in thirty minutes." He lifted Ryder off Gray's chest, his smile morphing for the baby. Everyone in the Hammond family adored Ryder, and Gray couldn't help thinking it was because they all loved Hunter so very much too.

He sat up and rubbed his eyes. "Yep, I'll shower fast." He did, got dressed, ate some hot pancakes and leftover bacon, and kissed his wife. "We're just goin' out to the west fence and back. Daddy can't do much more than that."

"You guys be good to him," she said, eyeing Cy and Ames, two more of Gray's brothers who'd shown up while he'd been showering. Elise had fed them all, and their wives sat at the dining room table, a couple of high chairs holding their children surrounding them.

Gray loved everyone in his family, and he'd have them here at the farm every day, all day, if he could. Out of the five of them, he and his family were the only ones who didn't live in Coral Canyon full time, and sometimes he longed to sell the farm to Hunter, pack up everything he needed, and make the move permanent.

Elise had a thriving landscaping company here, which she loved, and Gray didn't want to leave his father here alone. He didn't want to abandon Hunter in that downtown high-rise building, especially not with the stress of being the CEO of the family company and a new father.

The back door slid open, and Colton walked in with their father. "Dad has a question," he said in a loud voice, which drew everyone's attention.

Gray looked up from his phone. He'd been texting Hunt to see if he could come horseback riding with all of them. He knew the moment he saw his father's face that he'd found out about the surprise party.

"Boys," he said slowly, just the way he did when they'd been younger and one of them had done something or gotten into something they shouldn't. "Why do I have to be back here at six, but I can't come early?"

Wes looked at Gray, who took a step forward. "Because, Dad," he said. "Matt and Gloria need to decorate for your birthday party."

Dad shook his head. "I don't want a party."

"It's not for you," Wes said. "It's for Boone and Keith."

"And you," Colton said, grinning at his brothers. "Matt's spent a lot of time on this, Daddy." He made a beeline for the bacon, of which only a few pieces remained. "Don't ruin it for him."

"That man," Daddy said. He shook his head. "He treats me like...." He paused, and every person in the room could've filled in the silence.

*His father.*

Matt didn't have a father—Boone either—and they did spend a lot of time with Daddy. Gray wasn't quite old enough to be their father—maybe if he'd become a dad at age seventeen—but he felt wildly overprotective of both Matt and Boone.

His thoughts drifted to Mission, Travis, and Cord too. All of the men who came to work and live here became part of the Hammond family—they became Gray's—and he absolutely would be their father figure if they needed him to.

Dad sniffled, and Gray continued toward him. "Did you eat this morning, Dad? It's real hot out there this morning." He wasn't sure if it was or not, but he assumed by all the sunshine pouring in through the windows.

"It's windy too," Wes said. "You'll need a jacket."

"I've ridden horses before." Dad wiped at his eyes.

"Not as an eighty-seven-year-old," Ames said. He moved right into his father and hugged him. "Now, come on. I got a text from Matt that said he'd love any help he can get today to get a few things put back together while we're all here."

They'd all pitch in and help too. Gray and all of his brothers had grown up right here on the farm, and they knew the chores well.

Dad scoffed. "I can still ride."

"Let's go see," Gray said right as Hunt entered the kitchen area. "You comin', Hunt?"

He wasn't carrying his baby, and he looked down at his clothes. "If I can borrow something from you, Dad." He surveyed the other men who'd gathered in the farmhouse that morning. They all wore jeans and T-shirts, leather jackets and cowboy hats. Boots and belts and buckles. No slacks. No polos. No shiny shoes that looked professional polished.

"Sure," Gray said, exchanging a glance with Wes. "We'll be right behind you, okay?"

"I'm sure Matt has Dad's horse saddled," Wes said. "So I can help with yours and Hunt's."

"Smells like bacon in here," Boone boomed, and Gray grinned as he went down the hall with Hunt. Boone might not be super happy about the surprise party, but for how much attention he called to himself, he likely would be. Gray supposed he'd find out later that day.

———

BY FIVE-FIFTY-FIVE, Gray was ready for the party to start. The whole farmhouse dripped with streamers in blue, gray, black, white, and yellow, and stacks of paper plates and cups waited for the party-goers to arrive and get eating.

"Last one," Gloria said as she and Cosette slid a foil-covered pan onto the counter.

"I could've come and brought that in," Gray said, guilt tripping through him. Gloria was due with her baby any day now, and she didn't need to be carrying big aluminum trays of food.

"It's lettuce," Cosette said. She smiled at him. "No big deal."

"We do need a spot for the cakes," Gloria said. She slid a few things closer together. "Matt and Keith are bringing them in right now."

Sure enough, Matt came into the kitchen backward.

He and Keith moved slowly, and they slid an exact replica of the farmhouse onto the counter.

"Oh my word," Gray said, breathing out. His little boys played a video game in the living room, only fifteen feet away, but the world silenced to just that house. "This is incredible."

"Poppy Harris," Matt said.

"Wait until you see the horse, Mister Gray."

He looked down at Britt, who slipped her hand into his. She smiled up at him, and he loved the innocence of the little girl. The back door slid open and Michael came inside with his siblings. The noise level was about to go off the charts, and Gray took Britt and got out of the way as the house started to fill.

All of his brothers arrived within seconds of each other, each with their wife and children. Dad came with Colton and Annie, as he already knew about the party. Hunter and Molly and Ryder went right into the living room with the other grandkids, because they all adored the couple. And they adored the little kids in the family.

Cosette came inside with Matt this time, and the horse cake was something beautiful to behold. Gray couldn't look away from it, even when Elise asked him a question about Travis and Poppy.

"Gray," she said again, and he finally looked at her.

"Do you see that cake?"

"Do you see how Poppy is glaring at Travis?" She nodded toward the couple who stood over at the corner of the dining room table. Matt and Keith had set up tables so everyone would be able to feast from the taco bar, but it wasn't hard to see the way Poppy's eyes cut right into Travis.

Gray was reminded of Thanksgiving Day last year, when the woman had lectured Travis out on the deck. "I thought they were dating," he said under his breath.

"They are," Elise said. "Something's wrong." She wrung her hands together, and Gray wanted to tell her she couldn't fix everything for other people. She wanted to, and he loved that about her, but it wasn't possible.

She hated it when other people hurt, but she didn't know what to do. Gray didn't either. "Elise," he said, and she switched her gaze to his. "They have to work it out."

"They're just so perfect for each other," Elise said. She moved into Gray's arms, and he wrapped her up tight. She was absolutely perfect for him, he knew that. "I don't want her to be upset. She's such a good person."

If he could, Gray would shield the people he loved from all disappointment and hardship. He couldn't do that, so he simply held Elise tight while Matt came back into the kitchen. He startled when he saw Gray's father there already, and his eyes narrowed as a smile touched his mouth.

"Someone told you," he said.

"I figured it out," Dad said, opening his arms wide. "Thank you, son." Matt easily stepped into Dad's arms, and Gray found himself tearing up as the two of them hugged. He knew Travis shared a special bond with his father too, and Gray wouldn't have it any other way.

"Just come on," Gerty said, and every eye went to the back door.

"I just don't see why—" Boone cut off as he entered the house.

They'd arrived a little early, but it wasn't hard to tell a party had been put together.

"Surprise!" Keith stepped forward, and Gray quickly added his voice to the fray with the same word.

It rippled through the house, and Boone started to laugh. The sound of that joy filled the house, and he grabbed onto his fiancée and twirled Cosette around.

"It was all your brother," she said.

Boone gripped Matt next, and Gray understood that strong, brotherly bond better than anyone.

"All right," Matt said, sniffling. "This is a party for Boone, Chris, and Keith. There's a ton of food, and Boone, the horse cake is for you."

"Ho-ly cow," he yelled. "Who did this?"

Every eye moved to the corner of the room, and Poppy lifted her hand halfway up. Boone scooped her into a hug too, and that got her to thaw and laugh, at least a little. She did return to Travis's side and slid her hand into his, so maybe they'd just had a teensy argument. Gray and Elise had had plenty of those.

"Cake first," Boone said. "Gerty, will you put in the candles?"

Gray couldn't stop smiling at all the love in his farmhouse. There were so many people from different walks of life, and he met Cord's eyes. The man wore joy on his face, and that slipped when he caught Gray watching him. Gray lowered his head, because he didn't want to cause any alarm in the man.

When he looked up again, the first refrains of *Happy Birthday* filling the farmhouse, Cord's smile had returned. Gray tucked Elise tighter against his side, pressed a kiss to her head, and joined his voice to the song celebrating his father and his friends.

# Twenty-Eight

GLORIA WHETTSTEIN BENT TO PICK UP THE brush she'd dropped. She'd just finished combing out Lady, and the lessons for the day had ended a half-hour ago. School had started on Tuesday, and Gloria had made it through the first week of Britt's fifth grade year and Keith's senior year. She loved being their mother, and she worried constantly about how she could add a baby to the mix.

She wasn't sure what her days would look like once her little girl arrived in the world. She had work here at the farm, in the stables, and they'd just gotten a new horse to train at the beginning of August. Everyone knew she was pregnant, and she'd made plans with the other trainers and cowboys who worked at Pony Power for her upcoming absence.

Her official due date was tomorrow, and Gloria's eyes

filled with tears at the prospect of going past the twenty-fourth. Everything in her body hurt, and Lady nosed her in a gentle way, her way of saying, *I'm right here, Gloria. You can cry if you want to.*

She wanted too, and the first tears splashed down her face as she brought her hand up to cradle Lady's cheek. "I'm okay," she whispered to the horse. She was, but she also wasn't. Her back hurt. She couldn't sleep more than a few hours at a time. She hadn't seen her feet in weeks. They were swollen and tight right now, the heat that had returned to Colorado only exacerbating that.

She was thirsty, and exhausted, and she just wanted Matt to appear, sweep her into his arms, and take her home. He'd take care of her, feeding her and bringing her something to eat, and he'd lovingly rub the tension and tightness from her feet. Britt would bring her a cookie from the freezer, and Gloria would sleep as they watched TV and then Matt worked with his kids on their homework, chores, and anything else they needed.

The man was seriously a superhero, and Gloria loved him so much. More than her horses, which said a lot. She stroked Lady's face, and the horse kept her head tucked against Gloria's neck.

A pain ripped through her belly, and Gloria cried out. She gasped in her breath, holding it, and then trying for more oxygen. She grabbed onto Lady's hair to hold herself upright, because everything from the chest down had ignited in pure fire.

Lady guffawed and whinnied, stomping as she backed away from Gloria. She fell forward to her knees, her hands immediately moving to her belly to cradle it and try to hold her skin together. She seriously felt like the baby was going to claw her way out of Gloria's belly button, and she couldn't move to get her phone out to call Matt.

The horses she'd already brushed down and put away made a sudden racket, all of them whinnying and crying, and Gloria lifted her head to look at them. "I'm okay," she gasped out, the pain starting to subside. The doors down on the end of the row stood open, and she needed someone to walk by so she could get their attention.

No one did, and she groaned as she inched forward to put her hand on the front of the stall where she'd put Lady. The mare leaned over and lipped Gloria's hair, giving another quiet whinny.

"I know," Gloria said as she stood. A breeze kicked through the stable, and Gloria felt wet in the wrong places. She looked down, but she couldn't see past her baby belly. Instinctively, she knew her water had broken.

Shocked, she looked into Lady's eye. She was one of the calmest, most gentle horses. She worked with some of the harder children here at Pony Power, because she could tolerate them. Now, though, she wore a wild look in her eyes.

She reared up, and as Gloria cowered away from her, Lady bellowed out a neigh that set the other horses into a frenzy too. She snuffled and snorted while Captain beside her nickered over and over.

"Gloria?" someone asked.

She kept one hand on the stall as she turned. Cord stood there. "My water broke," she said, her voice barely her own. "Can you get Matt?"

Cord's eyes widened exponentially as he looked from her face to her feet. "He's on his way in. I'll get him now." He spun and dashed outside. He whistled through his fingers, and Gloria sagged against the stall door.

Lady returned to her, pressing her into the door with her huge head. Mission ran inside, his expression wild too, and he came right to her side. "You're okay," he said, as if he'd delivered a dozen babies right there in the stable. "Matt's seriously two minutes out."

"Maybe we should head for the parking lot," she said. She and Matt parked in front of the admin building, and right now, it felt like a ten-mile hike to the truck they drove to the farm every day. "Britt's here somewhere too."

She'd only taken one step when another slicing pain pulled through her. Then cut. Then jabbed, jabbed, jabbed, and settled into a tension she couldn't breathe through.

"Gloria," Mission said. "Cord!"

The other cowboy ran toward them, and he shored Gloria up on the left side.

"She's contracting," Misson said. "Just stay here, Gloria. We've got you."

"Britt's with Elise," Cord said. "Keith said he'd stay with her, and Chris said they could stay with him tonight."

"They have school tomorrow," Gloria said through clenched teeth.

Cosette appeared, her gaze also full of fear. "Gloria." She ran toward her. "Boone said you're going into labor." She glanced down, resolve entering her expression. "You certainly are. I'll take the kids home with me and get them to school tomorrow, okay?"

Gloria nodded in quick bursts, the contraction so tight. "I'm going to pop."

"Gloria." Matt entered the stable, his brother following right behind him. "Let's go. Can you walk?"

"I think so," she said, though she didn't dare try to take a step. Several seconds later, she did, and she made it to the truck without another contraction. When she and Matt were alone in the truck, tears streaked down her face again. "Hurry, Matt, okay? I don't like this."

He reached over and squeezed her hand. "We'll be there so fast."

She closed her eyes, as they burned so badly, and she focused on breathing in and out. Doing that allowed her to make it through one contraction in the truck, and then she was surrounded by doctors and nurses. Matt never strayed more than six inches from her, and Gloria experienced a powerful wave of gratitude for that.

He wanted to be a dad again as much as she wanted to

be a mom. Both of his children were in therapy, and Gloria hoped they knew that they were so, so important to her. This baby wasn't going to be more than them.

She got the epidural, and then everything lifted. The doctor finally told her to push, and Gloria did. She'd been around plenty of horses and cows as they'd been born, and when her baby girl's cries filled the air, another round of tears flowed down her face.

The nurses took her a few steps away, but they quickly brought her back, all bundled and wrapped up in a pale pink blanket.

"Oh, wow," she said, marveling at how much a human heart could love, and how instantly it happened. She felt like she'd been waiting decades to meet the tiny girl in her arms, and she studied her perfect button nose, her long, dark eyelashes, and the soft wisp of pitch black hair on her head. Both she and Matt were dark, so she wasn't surprised to have a brunette daughter. She looked a lot like Keith, but none of Britt at all.

Gloria looked up at Matt. "She's not a Chloe."

He shook his head, his chin quivering with his emotion. "Nope."

"What are we going to name her?" She gazed back at the precious bundle in her arms, all of the names she and Matt had discussed gone. None of them fit. Not Elly, not Chloe, not Olivia.

*Who are you?* she wondered, and her baby squirmed and gave a quick yelp.

For some reason, Gloria laughed, her eyes filling with tears again. She had the very distinct feeling this girl was going to be like a wild mare, and Gloria would have to break her and then they'd be the very best of friends.

"What about Roxanne?" Matt suggested. He slid his big, weathered hands beneath his daughter, and Gloria relinquished the girl to him. She wished she had a camera to capture the pure, unadulterated love in his face as he bent closer and closer to the infant.

His eyes drifted closed, and he kissed the baby's cheek. "Yeah," he whispered as he settled her into his arms. "I think she's Roxanne."

Neither of them had ever mentioned that name, but it felt...good. Right. Gloria reached up and wiped her face. "Yeah," she said. "And we can call her Roxy."

Matt grinned at her, leaned down and matched his mouth to hers, and murmured, "You are amazing. I love you so much."

"I love you too," Gloria whispered, and then she laid back, ready to finally, finally get some rest. And maybe when she woke up, she'd be able to see her feet as she took their daughter for a walk around the maternity ward.

# Twenty-Nine

POPPY POURED THE LEMON CUSTARD OVER THE crust and gave the pan a good slam against the counter to get all the air to come to the surface. She then covered it with plastic wrap, tucking it into all the crevices so that a skin wouldn't form while it chilled in the fridge.

She should be outside, working on the farm. She had two downed trees that still needed to be cut into chunks. She'd have to rent a splitter from the hardware store to turn it into manageable firewood she and Steele could bring in to burn this winter. She had a chainsaw outside, but she didn't want to do the job.

Because she only had a few animals, she'd been able to put them all in the same pasture while she and Steele worked to get the fences fixed in the other two. The wind had swept through the valley for a couple of weeks, and

Poppy was still trying to catch up on all the extra work Mother Nature had caused for her.

Trav had done all the fences bordering the Hammond Farm, and she'd caught him going along hers inch by inch with a wire stretcher. That had been the day of Boone's surprise birthday party, and she hadn't been happy. She could fix her own fences, and Trav had plenty of his own work to do.

He'd argued back with her, which Poppy didn't hate. She sometimes needed someone to check her and not let her get too out of control, and Trav was really good at that. At the same time, she hadn't been able to find a bridge from where they were now to where they'd been before he'd gone out onto the farm with Steele to fix the broken pipe.

Poppy also needed to get on the mower that day. She had four fields of hay to cut, and the sooner she did it, the sooner she could bale and sell. The cold snap that had come through town a couple of weeks ago hadn't done too much terrible damage. She'd probably have a couple of fields of hay that wouldn't grow as well, but it wouldn't be as bad as last year, when she'd only brought in half as much alfalfa as she needed.

She frowned as she opened the fridge to find a place to put the lemon bars she'd just made. She hadn't had to work for Elise today, so she'd spent the morning baking— her happy place. She loved the work on the farm too, and as soon as she got this chilling, she'd head outside.

After making space in the fridge, she slid in the lemon bars, and then she sighed. Matt Whettstein had offered to help too, and Poppy wondered why she couldn't take it. Why couldn't she just say, "Yes, that would be great, Matt. Please send over as many men as you can, and let's get my fences fixed. Let's get the shingles back on the barn. Let's get the hay mown. Thank you."

The words literally choked her, and Poppy couldn't say them. She and Trav hadn't truly spoken of her attempt to get past her extreme need to be self-reliant, because things between them had been so strained. He still called and texted. When she planted a beautiful row of bulbs that no one would see until next spring, he was the first one she wanted to text and tell.

She needed to swallow her pride and tell him she needed him. That was what he wanted to hear, but she didn't know how to make her voice say those words. They balled up in her throat as she left the farmhouse and went toward the equipment building. At least all of her machinery worked this year, and she figured she could mow during the hottest part of the day since the tractor had moderately functional air conditioning.

Poppy couldn't think about anything else while she went back and forth in the fields, getting all the alfalfa down in perfectly neat rows. She did love this farm, and of course she'd thought of living here with Trav. In the winter, he'd go out and de-ice the troughs for the horses. They'd have enough money to get more goats, a few beef cows, pigs, and all the chickens in the world. She'd have rainbow-colored eggs for days and days, and she'd be able to pass them out to all the ladies at church for free.

Before she knew it, Poppy was sniffling, and her vision had blurred through the tears in her eyes. "You better not lose him," she told herself in a stern voice. She gained control of her emotions and gripped them tightly as close to her heart as she could. Tonight. She'd tell him tonight that she needed him, and could he please come help her get the other pastures fixed so the horses didn't have to live with the goats and Dorothy?

By the time she got back to the farmhouse, Steele had returned from school. Gray had picked him up that day, and he stood outside the chicken coops, tossing in the feed. "Hey, Mama," he said.

"Baby." She took him into a hug and squeezed him tight. "How was school?"

"Okay," he said, which was about as excited about school as Steele got.

"Your teacher said she was sending home a project today," Poppy said, watching him.

"It's a reading thing," he said. "It's in my backpack."

He'd probably dumped that the moment he'd come inside the farmhouse, and Poppy would have to get it out herself after dinner that night. Steele had made it through the first couple of weeks of school, and it hadn't gone very well already. He had a couple of boys in his class he didn't get along with. Rather, they'd singled him out in the first couple days of school and started picking on him. His teacher had stepped in instantly, and Poppy was grateful for her.

She stepped away from Steele, and she didn't know what to say next. "I'm going to go start dinner."

"Okay," Steele said.

She walked away from him, Cotton on her heels. The dog sometimes trotted through the fields as she mowed them, but today, he'd stayed with the horses.

Poppy washed up and got moving on the ground beef for the meatballs. She'd just put them in the oven when Steele's laughter floated on the air. She straightened, first glancing to the back door as he should be coming in soon. He didn't come through it, and she side-stepped to the kitchen window. She'd looked through it so many times to check on her son, and she felt the same way she always did. Like she was a good mom.

Outside, Steele ran in a wide arc and then he caught a football. Poppy felt the *thunk!* of it as it hit his chest way down deep in her soul. She had never played outside with her son. They worked on the farm, and she might play a card game with him on an errant Sunday evening. He loved video games, and he'd go next door and play with Tucker and Deacon from time to time. They all lived busy lives out on their farms, but as Trav came into view, his grin wide and his hand lifted for a high-five, Poppy saw a completely different scenario.

Perhaps Steele didn't need a bunch of brothers or

cousins or friends to play with. He simply needed some-where safe where he could be himself. Trav clearly adored her son, and Poppy had no idea what to do about it.

They turned toward the house, and she ducked out of the way. Her pulse hammered in her chest, and she didn't know why. She pleaded with the Lord to make her normal, for her reactions to having a great man in her life —and her son's—to be what Trav needed.

She buried herself in the fridge when the two of them came inside, and she said, "The meatballs just went in. It's about thirty minutes until dinner."

"Mom, Trav brought a football." Steele hurried toward her, and he tossed the ball into the air as he did. Poppy's breath caught in her throat again, but this time because her eleven-year-old was going to break something with that ball. Probably her nose—or his.

"You don't throw it in the house," Trav said, booping it and bobbling it away from Steele. He tucked it into his chest and lifted his eyebrows. "I told you that."

"Yes, sir," Steele said.

Trav nodded and palmed the ball down on the island. He leaned into Poppy, still frozen in the open door of the refrigerator, and kissed her quickly. "Hey, sweetheart. I thought we were going to Game Time for dinner tonight."

Poppy's eyes widened. "Oh no." She moaned and moved away from the fridge. "I forgot."

Trav stepped out of the way too, and the door on the

fridge swung closed. "They're showing the college football opening game."

She knew. She'd just forgotten. "I'll get changed. Steele, go clean up." She reached to turn off the oven.

"It's fine, Poppy," Trav said, his voice very quiet. "We can eat here and then go. Hunt says he's not going to be on until halftime."

Steele headed for the half-bath around the corner, and Poppy turned to face Trav. "No, we can go. I'll just turn off the meatballs and make them when we get back."

Trav looked at her, and Poppy wanted to say and do the right thing. Her thoughts scattered, and her throat closed right onto itself. He nodded and said, "The fences are still down out there, Poppy." He dropped his chin to his chest. "Can I come fix them for you this weekend?"

Poppy fought against the urge to tell him she could do it. Of course she could do it. He knew she could do it, but so could he. "Yes," she said, the word carving a trough in her throat as she spoke it.

Trav jerked his head up. "I can?"

"Yes." She put one hand on his chest. "I would really like it if you came and fixed them for me this weekend."

He took her into his arms, and Poppy finally felt the last of the tension she'd put on them weeks ago drain away. "I'll feed you meatballs and Spanish rice. Maybe see if I can get a few ears of corn ripe enough for corn on the cob."

"With that spicy garlic butter?" he murmured, his eyes solidly locked on her lips.

"If that's what you want."

"It's what I want."

She tipped up and kissed him, and Poppy maybe allowed herself to fall for the first time since she'd started dating Trav three months ago. The world blurred around her, and the floor went right out from under her feet. Kissing Trav had always been magical, but this felt like she'd reached a new level.

"All right." He pulled away as the sound of the bathroom door creaking met his ears. "Let's get goin'. Steele?"

"Ready," her son said, and Poppy watched Trav walk over to him. He made a big show of making sure Steele had washed all the way to his elbow, saying, "My momma used to smell my hands, my elbows, and my neck." He chuckled as Steele led the way toward the front door.

Poppy hurried to turn off the oven, trying not to think about the half-cooked meatballs sitting inside. She could deal with them later. Just like she'd deal with the animals, the downed fences, the newly pregnant barn cat, and her feelings for Trav.

Later. She could deal with it all later.

———

A COUPLE OF DAYS LATER, Poppy took a folding table out to her deck. Trav had brought Mission and Cord with

350

him to get the fences fixed, and when Poppy had seen the three cowboy-hatted men working on her farm, she'd quickly whipped up a huge batch of her grandmother's famous potato salad to go with the sweet and sour meatballs she'd made earlier in the week.

She spread a dark gray cloth over the table to hide the faded orange stains from when Steele had once spilled spaghetti on the table. She went back and forth from the deck to the house as she brought out plates, cups, silverware, and then finally the food. She'd gone to the grocer that morning and found the broccoli slaw bagged salad she liked, and a big bowl of that went in the middle of the table.

The meatballs went next to it, and then the potato salad on the other end. She brought out the bottle of pink lemonade Trav liked, as well as a pitcher of peach iced tea she loved. She'd told Trav to come in for lunch at noon, and the clock ticked past that.

No cowboys came in, and Poppy went down the steps, whistling for Cotton to come with her. If left unattended, he might jump up and gobble down the meatballs. He was a very good dog, but the scent of red meat almost undid all of his human training.

He ran ahead of her and jumped the gate without waiting for her. She giggled at his theatrics, and she followed him at a slower pace as Cotton ran toward Trav, Mission, and Cord. They weren't in the fields anymore, but hammering together part of the fence in the goat pen.

"Lunch is ready," she said, drawing all three pairs of eyes. The men had to be a decade apart as she looked at them. Cord was clearly in his twenties—early twenties if the baby face told Poppy anything. Mission was more her age, with a hint of experience in the lines around his eyes. Travis was seven years older than her—and therefore Mission—and she adored the sexy silver in his sideburns. He had it growing in his beard too, and Poppy smiled at him.

"Let's go, boys," he said, reaching up to take off his hat and slide his hand through his hair. "We don't want Poppy waitin' on us." He gave her a smile as he abandoned whatever part of the job he'd been doing.

Cord and Mission followed him out of the pen, and Trav latched it so her naughty goats wouldn't follow him back to the deck. He'd told her that they just followed him like rats did the Pied Piper, and she'd laughed and laughed. Sure enough, all eleven of her goats crowded near the gate, and Trav looked down at them.

"Stay here," he told them. "I'm lookin' at you, Joe. No funny business." He gave the tallest goat a look that meant business, but it softened when he turned it on her. "I think they'll stay."

"What else did you guys get done out here?" Poppy didn't look too closely, because there was always something to do on a farm.

"All your fences in the pastures are up," Mission said.

"So Trav put the horses in the west one, where he said they went."

Poppy pressed her lips together and nodded. "Thank you, Mission."

"We got the pine tree off the equipment building," Cord said. "But we still need to get all of that chopped up."

"We don't have time today," Trav said. "Molly needs all of us for the lessons this afternoon."

"You can go any time," Poppy said. "I can do the chopping." She wouldn't use an axe or anything, but a chainsaw. She had gloves and protective goggles, and she actually liked wielding the power tool and taking something huge and tall like a tree trunk and making it into manageable pieces.

"Wow," Mission said as he went through the gate from farm to yard. "This yard is gorgeous, Poppy."

"She's a horticulturist," Trav said, a hint of pride in his tone.

"I do love gardening," Poppy said. "And cooking and baking. So eat as much as you want."

Cotton's nails clicked up the steps first, and Poppy stuck her head into the house and called to Steele, who she'd put on the computer that morning to do a math video and get his homework finished. He didn't come, and Poppy turned back to the cowboys. "Go ahead and eat. I'll go grab Steele."

He tended to get too involved in things, and he'd

probably finished his math and moved onto one of his games. He hadn't asked, however, and irritation flashed through Poppy. She went into the office and found Steele slumped forward over the desk.

Her heart dropped to her feet. "Steele." She rushed toward him and put her hand on his back. He was breathing, and he stirred at her touch. Relief spread through her, and she dropped into a crouch. "Hey, baby. You fell asleep and lunch is ready."

She looked at the screen, where the saver danced around. Steele had been off the computer for a while, and she doubted that he'd finished his math video or homework.

Steele wiped his eyes as he sat up. "My head hurts."

"Come get some medicine," she said, straightening to help him. She kept her hand on his back as they went into the kitchen. She got down some tablets for him and watched him swallow them. She had plenty of work to do in the yard and on the farm that afternoon, and she really didn't have time to take Steele to the doctor. Plus, on the weekend, she'd have to pay more to take him to the after-hours clinic.

She kept all of that to herself as she poured the children's syrup into the little cup and handed it to him. Steele took it, shivering as he swallowed the last drops. "Ugh." He gave her the cup back, and Poppy put it in the sink.

"I have to get the hay turned today," she said. "If you don't feel better after lunch, I'll have you take a nap."

"Trav said I could come help him next door," Steele said, his eyebrows bunching down.

"Not if you aren't well." Poppy turned him toward the back door. "And you know, Trav doesn't always get to decide what you do."

"He's going to be working with the horses," he said. "I can lead them back and forth for the kids, and I love doing that. They have a new pony and everything."

"Ponies will bite your hand off just as easily as they breathe." Poppy reached past her son and opened the door.

"Leo's nice," he said. "He doesn't bite."

They went outside, and Poppy paused the conversation. She sat beside Trav and gave him a smile. "Steele has a headache, so he might not be able to come work with you this afternoon."

Trav's gaze flew to Steele, who growled at Poppy. "I'm fine, Mom."

"You were asleep—and you didn't finish your math." She picked up the serving spoon and put some meatballs on her plate. In that moment, she realized that no one had any food on their plate. She looked at Cord across from her. "You guys didn't eat."

"No, ma'am," he said. He looked like he might bolt at any moment. "It looks amazing though."

"Do you want to say grace?" Trav asked.

Her face flamed, despite the shade covering the deck. She hadn't wanted to keep them waiting, and she'd said they could start eating. "All right," she said, but she couldn't bring herself to look at either cowboy across from her. "Steele, will you?"

"Fine." Her son huffed at her, and that only ignited Poppy's irritation again. If he kept that up, he wouldn't be going next door to help Trav with the pony even if his headache went away. "Dear Lord, we're grateful for this food. Bless us to be strong and healthy. Help me to not have a headache so my mama won't freak out. Thank you for Trav and Cord and Mission coming over to help us with the farm. Amen."

He said all the words in one big string, and Poppy had barely made sense of them—horror driving through her—when Trav started to chuckle.

Poppy frowned at him and then Steele. "We usually breathe during a prayer."

"Does this potato salad have peas in it?" Mission asked, and Poppy's attention switched to him.

"Yes," she said. "And carrots. My grandma used to make it like that."

Mission looked up, clearly dumbstruck. "It looks amazing."

Poppy loved getting complimented on her food, and she pushed Steele's rushed prayer out of her mind. When the meal ended, he claimed to "feel way better," but

Poppy suspected he'd be saying that even if he had a splitting headache.

She had work to do too, so she let him go with Trav and the other boys to lead ponies to children for their therapy lessons. She herself had plenty to do, and since she'd mowed three days ago, if she could get this raking done today, she could bale tomorrow. If she had proper working headlamps or another person on her farm, they could follow behind her in an hour or two and bale the windrows.

Since she didn't, Poppy would rake it all today, giving the hay another chance to get nice and dry, and she'd bale after church.

She didn't mind the hours behind the wheel of the tractor, the raking mechanism behind her. Cotton rode with her today, and Poppy enjoyed the blue sky with the wispy white clouds running through it.

By the time she got back to the equipment shed, the sun had started to go behind the mountains. Since the Rockies were so huge, that didn't necessarily mean it was terribly late yet. "Late enough for Steele to be home."

She cut the engine on the tractor and got down. Something still buzzed somewhere, and Poppy frowned as she turned toward the huge door she'd just driven through. "That sounds like a chainsaw...." She strode away from the tractor, saying, "Come on, Cotton."

The dog jumped down and trotted up to her, and Poppy went outside and toward the barn. Dorothy hee-hawed at her, but Poppy didn't detour over to her. Someone was here cutting her trees into logs.

Not just someone.

Trav.

Sure enough, she found the man just as he sliced off another section of the trunk. He wore safety goggles and gloves, and Poppy came to a stop across from him and put her hands on her hips. "I told you I could do that," she yelled.

He looked at her and let the chainsaw whine into silence.

"Where's Steele?" she asked. "Was he really okay?"

"I fed him hot dogs at my house," Trav said, and that only made Poppy realize how hungry she'd become. Lunch had been hours ago. "He was playing video games with Cord when I headed over here."

She indicated the logs he'd sawed. "I don't need you to do this."

"You were busy out in the fields."

"Then you rest while you wait for me to come back," she said. "Or you text me, and I'll come in faster."

"You don't get to rest."

"It's my farm." She pointed at him. "And you don't get to rest either. You were up early to do your chores next door, I know that. Then you worked over here all morning. Then back over there all afternoon and evening. Then back here. It's enough."

Trav's eyes darkened with every word she said, but she

meant it. "I worry about you," she said. "No one can work as much as you do and not feel it."

"I'm okay," he said.

"I'll believe you when you believe me."

He simply stared at her for another moment, and then he pulled on the chain and fired up the machine again. Shocked, Poppy stepped back. "Go shower," he yelled at her. "I'll be in after this is done."

"I don't want you to do this," she called, trying to make her voice as loud as his had been. At least loud enough to be heard over the chainsaw.

He pretended he hadn't heard her and he bit the chain into the wood. She couldn't stand too close, or she'd get hit with the shavings, and helplessness filled her. A terrible well of guilt filled her, and she couldn't stand here and watch him do her farm chores.

They were hers.

She still hadn't fed the animals that night, so she got that job done, barely making it to the farmhouse before darkness fell. Still, the whine of the chainsaw filled the air. How Trav could cut without light, she had no idea.

She did shower, and she took a long time in the hot spray. She wasn't sure why. She didn't even know what she thought about. She only knew she needed some time to herself and her thoughts. Out in the kitchen, Trav's soft snores filled the air. Poppy found him prostate on the couch, and she didn't want to disturb him.

But he couldn't sleep here. Steele couldn't stay at his

place. So she leaned over and touched his shoulder. "Trav," she said quietly. "You need to go."

He jolted away, and Poppy pulled back quickly. "Just me," she said. "It's just me."

Trav sat up. "Sorry." He reached for his cowboy hat and smashed it on his head. "The wood is done. I can get a splitter and help with the firewood next weekend."

"I can do it," Poppy said.

Trav ignored her and headed for the front door. "I'll have Steele back in ten minutes."

"I'll text him."

"I just did," Trav said. He left while Poppy stewed in her frustration. He was feeding her son dinner. Texting him. Working around the farm. All the things Poppy didn't want him to do. She'd been letting him, but she swallowed, trying to find the reason why it was okay for him to work himself so hard...for her.

Several minutes later, Steele came inside looking refreshed and happy. "Heya, Mama."

"Bedtime." She expected Trav to come inside too. He didn't. "Is Trav outside?"

"I guess." Steele went upstairs, and Poppy headed for the front door.

Trav was outside, sitting in his truck. She approached, her heartbeat pouncing through her whole body. She opened the door and got in. Neither of them said anything.

Time ticked by, but Poppy wasn't sure how much. "Trav," she said at the same time he said, "Poppy."

The ice broke, but the tension remained. He shook his head. "Do you need anything?"

"No," she said. "Trav, please stop trying to do everything. It's not necessary. The logs would've been fine. I don't have time to do the splitting right now anyway. They're *fine*."

He nodded, his gaze stuck out his side window. Poppy really wanted him to look at her, but he didn't. She didn't dare reach over to take his hand in hers. He exhaled and said, "Can you get out, please?"

She wasn't sure what she'd expected him to say, but it wasn't that.

"It's late, and I want to go home." He turned his weary eyes on her. "I won't be back to help."

"Thank you," she said. She reached for the door handle.

"Ever," he said in a deathly quiet voice. "This is it for us, Poppy. I don't think it's going to work out."

She twisted back toward him, warring emotions marching through her. Part of her would never be okay without him. Another part couldn't handle any more tension, any more silent fighting about what he could do around the farm and what he couldn't.

"I'm real sorry," he said, his head hanging down. "I know you're a good woman, but well." He exhaled heavily. "I don't think you're ever going to 'adjust' to havin' me around, and frankly I'm tired of tryin' to fit into a space where I don't fit."

Poppy didn't know what to say. "Steele is going to be devastated," she blurted out.

He brought his head up, and his eyes locked onto Poppy's. "If this is just about me and Steele, that doesn't have to change." He spoke with power, and his expression blazed with dark fire.

"I—"

"I can't believe this," he said, understanding dawning in his eyes. "You like what I do for Steele more than what I do for you."

"No."

"You don't want me to do anything around the farm, but sure, take Steele next door and let him work."

Poppy swallowed, the vitriol and sarcasm in his voice almost punching her in the throat. The silence stretched between them, until he said, "Please, just go."

Poppy turned and slipped from the truck, the door already hanging open from when she'd unlatched it before. She somehow pushed it closed, the resulting slam like a gunshot in the quiet night.

Travis backed out of her driveway and left, leaving Poppy to stare after his red brake lights until she couldn't see them anymore.

# Thirty

TRAVIS FLIPPED THE SECOND EGG IN HIS FRYING pan, the yolk breaking. He growled under his breath, because Cord had been asking him if he needed help with every single miniscule noise he'd been making for the past few days.

Since he'd ended his relationship with Poppy.

Cord knew Travis had broken up with her, and honestly, Travis would be surprised if everyone on the farm didn't know. Thankfully, Matt, Boone, Gray, and everyone else hadn't asked him any questions about it. He wouldn't know what to say anyway.

"The truth," he muttered to his frying eggs. He'd already cooked the sausage links, and he did love a big breakfast for dinner. Cord sat in front of his laptop at the dining room table, as the man had started taking college courses online when the fall semester had started.

He spent almost all of his time in the evenings doing homework now, and Travis helped him as much as possible. Cord didn't have a problem with getting the assistance, and of course, Travis's thoughts went back to the one person who did.

Poppy.

He regretted breaking up with her. Nothing too terribly bad had happened. The truth was, Travis simply didn't want to have to look into her eyes every time she caught him doing something for her and find that defiance.

She'd asked for his help, and for a few days, he'd thought she might actually be able to change. She might actually allow him to be her hero. She might actually welcome him onto her farm, and he might actually be able to carve a place for himself there.

He'd definitely have to carve it, as Poppy had a rock-hard exterior that required him to constantly chip away at it.

Which was why he'd broken up with her. He was tired of fighting with her, even when they weren't verbally fighting, and even when he wasn't doing anything she didn't want him to do.

*The real truth is she doesn't want your help*, he told himself.

He pulled the eggs from the pan and slid them onto a plate. "I broke one," he said.

"I'll eat it," Cord said. "I don't care."

Travis wanted the runny yolk, and for as foul of a mood as he was in, he happily served Cord the hot eggs and cracked three new ones into the pan. He salted and peppered them as they hissed and fried in the hot pan, and he managed to turn the trio of them without breaking a single yolk.

Finally, something going right in his life. He joined Cord at the table, but his cabinmate had finished his eggs by that time. "How's the reading?" Travis asked after he'd caught a glimpse of Cord's screen.

"Good enough." Cord sighed and closed the laptop. "I hate it, actually." He didn't smile at Travis, but their eyes met.

Travis nodded, appreciating how real Cord was with him. "One class at a time. I could read you some of it, if you wanted." He'd done that once last week, and Cord had said it had helped a lot.

He had trouble making sense of things when they were written, but he could listen and comprehend better. He'd done push-ups while Travis had read the boring mechanical text, and he'd aced that week's quizzes and assignments.

"I have to go get some tools at the hardware store," Cord said. "Maybe you could come with me and read in the truck on the way there and back?" His eyebrows went up, his gray eyes full of hope.

"Sure," Travis said. The couch had been calling his

name for a nap, but he could help Cord. It would be better than staying home alone.

Cord brightened and speared another sausage link. "Thanks, Trav."

He finished dinner, collected the text Cord needed, and they headed to town. Travis donned his reading glasses and started reading about the inner workings of a diesel engine. Cord stopped and asked him a couple of questions, and Travis underlined a few things for the man to look at later.

Cord bought the tools he needed, and he dropped Travis back at the cabin before he went to the equipment shed. He was studying to be a ranch and farm equipment mechanic, and Gray had said he could work on their machinery.

Travis knew Poppy had had some issues with hers too, and he'd thought for about point-four seconds about mentioning it to her that Cord could fix anything she needed as he studied.

Then he'd remembered that he'd broken up with her. He frowned as he went up the steps and toward the front door. A dog barked down the lane, and Travis turned that way.

Pearl ran to the edge of Boone's yard, her eyes focused on something on the other side of the dirt road. Travis looked that way too, and the next sound that met his ears made his heart leap and then deflate like a punctured balloon.

Goats.

"Maa!"

Travis froze, because Gray and Elise didn't own any goats. Those were Poppy's.

Maybe someone else would find them. He watched Pearl and Boone's cabin, fully expecting the man to come out and notice the goats. Two of them—Graybeard, the devil, and another ungulate named Cloudy Skies—came out from behind the shed.

They were on the wrong side of the farm to have come from Poppy's. Or else they'd been snacking on the grasses over here for a lot longer than just a few minutes. Travis guessed that was the case, and when no one else made any appearance, he decided he couldn't just go inside and do nothing about the goats.

"Graybeard," he called as he reached the bottom of his steps. The goat looked his way, his crazy eyes locking onto Travis. "You shouldn't be over here, bud."

The goat didn't mind at all that he was out, and he was completely unrepentant as he "maa"'ed and came toward Travis.

The goats had always loved Travis, and both of them came right up to him. He patted the tall, gray one and asked, "Is it just the two of you? Or am I gonna have to walk around and round up all your friends?"

"Mmm-aaa!" Graybeard said. Travis took that to mean all the goats were out, and the herd leader would help Travis round them up if he wanted him to.

Travis didn't want to do any of this tonight. Still no one else had appeared, and Travis felt like everyone on the farm had deliberately stayed indoors.

He had no idea what Poppy was doing tonight, but he suspected she was simply at home. Steele didn't do any sports or activities, and she had a farm to run after her full-time job pruning, landscaping, and planting other people's yards.

"Lord, I can't run into her," he said. "If I take these goats back, can You please make sure Poppy isn't outside?"

The Lord didn't answer, and Travis looked down at Graybeard. "Call your pals," he said. "I'm not makin' this trip more than once, and I'm not wandering the farm to find y'all."

Graybeard bleated again, and Cloudy did too. Travis started walking toward the Harris farm, which was to the east and a bit north. It wouldn't take him long, and with every step, the leader of the herd called for his goaty friends to join him.

Poppy owned eleven goats, and Travis had nine or ten with him when he reached the fence separating the two properties.

He went through the rungs and down to the gate to let the goats in, but several of them had hopped the fence without waiting for him.

Only Cloudy and one of the smaller kids had come with him, and Travis sighed at the same time his heartbeat started to bounce around erratically.

He used to love coming to this farm. He loved Steele. He loved Poppy.

"No," he told himself, but he couldn't deny it out loud. He did love her, and just because he hadn't told her —or even himself—didn't mean it wasn't true.

He glanced in the direction of the farmhouse, but the barn, chicken coops, and equipment building mostly blocked it. He could just make out the roof, and the only way Poppy would see him was if she was out on the farm.

Steele fed the chickens, but Poppy took care of the horses. She also loved Dorothy the donkey with her whole heart, and Travis had never been jealous of a donkey before.

Dorothy brayed as Travis led the goats past the stables, and the coward inside him paused and checked the farm spreading in front of him for any sign of Poppy.

Steele stood near the chicken coop, working to refill their water. The hens squabbled under the shade of the trees, and he stepped into the pen with the chickens to get his evening chores finished.

"Ho, there," Travis called, because he didn't want to scare the boy.

Steele looked up, his face splitting into a smile. "Trav." He abandoned his task and came toward Travis. "What are you doin' here?"

He vaulted the fence keeping the chickens inside, and he flew right into Travis's arms. Travis's whole heart broke, and he knew in that moment he needed to call Poppy and try to work something out. Anything.

"Your goats are out again," he said gruffly, trying to hide his emotion. He couldn't really, but Steele kept hugging him, so Travis didn't have any eyes on him.

"I saw," he said after another couple of moments. Steele stepped back, his chin toward the ground. "I was almost done with the chickens, and then I woulda come and gotten them."

"It's not a problem," Travis said. He glanced toward the farmhouse, but he could only see the path leading to it. "Where's your mama?"

"Someone from the library came to talk to her." Steele turned and went toward the goat pen. "Come on, guys."

A single goat remained in the paddock, over in the shade of a tree, and as Travis went into the pen with the goats, his concern increased. "Steele, how long has Lucky been lying down?"

"I don't know," Steele said.

Travis went over to the goat, but she didn't get up. She bleated at him pathetically, and Travis suspected something was wrong with her. Perhaps she was pregnant, or perhaps she was sick. No matter what, she needed to be looked at.

He crouched in front of the goat and put his hand on her belly. "What's with you?" he asked. He couldn't diagnose goat health with a single touch, and he twisted to look at Steele. "Tell your mama, okay? She needs to have the vet come look at Lucky."

"Okay." Steele came up behind him while Travis studied the goat's eyes and ears. Everything he could see looked okay as far as he could tell, so a veterinarian was definitely needed.

He straightened and put his arm around Steele. "Don't tell her I brought the goats back, okay?" He looked down at the boy, who lifted his head up, his cowboy hat letting the evening sunlight hit his face. "Just tell her you got the chickens fed and the goats done, but that Lucky's down."

Steele nodded, his jaw tight. "You two broke up."

"Yes," Travis said. "I'm sorry, son."

"She's just really stubborn," Steele said. His voice pitched up. "That's what Grandpa said, and he's right. She's too proud, and she's too stubborn."

"She's a good woman," Travis said quietly. "You listen to your mama and do what she says, and you'll be all right."

Steele leaned into him. "Will you come throw the ball with me?"

"No," Travis said, his grip on the boy's shoulders tightening. "But you can come next door if your mama says it's okay."

Steele sniffled and nodded. "Okay."

Travis drew in a deep breath, not sure what else to say to Steele. He didn't want the child to hurt, not because of him. "I better get back," he said. "You should too. It's gettin' close to dusk, and I know your mama doesn't like you out too late."

"Yeah."

They left the paddock together, and Steele made sure the gate was latched properly. Travis went west and Steele went southeast. "See you later," Travis called.

"Yep," Steele said, and Travis couldn't help feeling like the boy had sounded just like...him.

He kept his head down as he walked back to the cabin, and as he passed Boone's, the flicker of firelight caught his attention. He detoured toward it, because that light meant Boone would have hot dogs, marshmallows, graham crackers, chocolate, and Starburst, all ready for roasting.

Chatter met his ears, and Travis was welcomed to the crowd which included Mission and Chris.

"There you are," Chris said. "Cord was looking for you." He put his arm around Travis, and because Travis needed the love and support, he leaned into the older gentleman.

"I'll text him." He did, and then he looked at Chris. The firelight jumped and danced across the man's face, but his joy still exuded from him.

Chris met his eye. "What's wrong?"

"Nothing."

The older man frowned. "You seem unsettled."

"He broke up with Poppy," Mission said, immediately

taking a bite of his hot dog. He just said it so casually, and Travis growled again.

"Oh, I see." Chris's shoulders rose and fell. "I'm sorry, son."

Travis had said those exact words to Steele only a half-hour ago, and he nodded in acceptance.

"None of us know why," Mission continued. "And Cord won't say."

"It's not our business," Boone said. "That's why." He threw Mission a look that told him to be quiet, but Mission was already taking another enormous bite of his hot dog.

Travis looked at Boone, then Mission, then Chris. Gerty sat there too, her phone mostly illuminating her face. Michael had left the farm a couple of weeks ago, and she'd been moodier than normal since then.

She looked up, her eyebrows raised, and Travis dropped his gaze. "I broke up with her, but I'm starting to think it was a mistake."

"Call her," Chris said.

Travis shook his head before the man stopped speaking. "I can't."

"Sure you can," Boone said.

They didn't understand. Poppy hadn't changed, at least not as much as she probably needed to for Travis to be happy with her. At least long term.

"When I was dating Bev," Chris said. "She broke up with me, because I was always falling asleep on our dates."

He chuckled like this was funny. "I was working so much, and every time we got together, we'd get food or she'd make dinner, and then I'd fall asleep on her couch. Or rather, her aunt's couch, as she lived with her Aunt Angie at the time." He shook his head. "I was so comfortable with her, but she wanted to talk. She wanted to go dancing. She wanted to play games. Go for walks. I wanted to put on the radio or a movie and fall asleep. I guess she didn't find me romantic."

Travis said nothing, riveted as he was to the story. He'd known Bev, but in his mind, she and Chris had always been together. They'd been blissfully happy since the day they met, and while he knew that of course couldn't be true, it also felt true.

Cosette came outside with a tray at the pause in Chris's story, and she started handing out rice crispy treats. They smelled like chocolate and peanut butter, and Travis didn't mind the additions.

"How'd you get her back?" Boone finally asked.

Chris startled and said, "I showed up at her house with my hat in my hands, and I begged her to forgive me. I told her I wouldn't work so much, and that I'd take her dancing, and if she'd give me a second chance, she wouldn't regret it." He drew in a long breath and eased it all out of his lungs again.

"I disappointed her again, of course. I had five boys and ran HMC. I worked a lot. Like, a lot. But when I came home, I talked to her. I worked and played with the boys for any scrap of time I could find. I took her dancing."

Travis thought of Poppy and what they had between them that was the equivalent of dancing. She loved to cook for him, and he loved to go out on her farm and work it for her. If only that wasn't the one thing she didn't want him to do.

She loved it when he brought her flowers, and Travis hadn't done that in a while. She liked it when he sat with her on the porch. She liked it when he chuckled at her while she talked to Dorothy.

"And she took you back?" Gerty asked. "Just like that?" She kept her focus on Chris even when Cosette sat next to her and offered her a treat.

"Yes," Chris said. "I wouldn't say 'just like that.' We dated for a long time afterward. Beverly used to say she wanted to get through every major holiday, and every major event at the company, so she'd know if she could handle them as they reoccurred. At the time, dating for as long as we did wasn't really what young people did."

"How long did you date?" Travis asked.

Chris smiled at him. "Fifteen months. I suppose she figured she could live with me after that, and when I asked her to marry me—for the third time, I might add—she said yes." He chuckled, the sound quickly becoming sad. Tears glistened in his eyes, the firelight illuminating all of them. "I miss her so very much."

Travis reached over and patted the older man's hand. "I miss Poppy too."

"Maybe you just need to go see if she'll take you back," Gerty said. "That's what my daddy did." She did grin at Cosette then, and she took another treat from the tray.

Travis said nothing, because he wasn't sure showing up at Poppy's right now was the right decision. She was a unique woman, and a good woman, and he closed his eyes against the bright orange flames and told the Lord, *I'll go when You tell me it's the right time.*

Satisfied that God would do that for him, Travis finally took a bite of his rice crispy treat. He made room for Cord when the man came to join them, and he enjoyed his evening with the found family at the Hammond Family Farm who loved him and accepted him just the way he was.

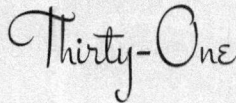

# Thirty-One

POPPY WATCHED HER SON AS HE CAME IN FROM the farm. Steele had been going out without complaining with surprising regularity. He usually had to be asked at least twice to attend to the chickens and goats in the evening, but for the past week, he went without her asking him even once.

Every night, right after dinner, close to seven-thirty. The days were getting shorter now that September had arrived and almost a month of school was behind them.

He came in before full dark, and he reported that all was well with the animals. Something had changed with him, though, and she determined that the moment he left tomorrow night, she'd follow him.

*Or you could just talk to him,* she told herself.

"How's Lucky?" she asked. The goat had recently become pregnant, and Steele had been the one to alert her to the goat's condition. She'd called the vet, grateful she had enough money to pay that bill, and now she tended to her every morning right before she left for work, and every afternoon when she got home. Steele checked on her in the evening, and so far, Lucky had been doing well.

"Great," Steele said. "Can I ride my bike next door? They're doing a bonfire."

Poppy's first thought was to deny him. Her second had to do with the text she'd gotten earlier in the week. Travis's mother had actually texted her and said she'd found the recipe for the hamburger hash she'd made while Trav was a boy. His favorite weeknight meal, and Poppy had asked her about it weeks before they'd broken up.

She still hadn't answered Melanie, Travis's momma, and if she said Steele could go to the bonfire, he'd be gone for a couple of hours. That was more than enough time to get out to Melanie's house, visit, and get the recipe.

Why Poppy wanted it, she wasn't sure. An idea niggled at her in the back of her mind, and as she sat on the couch in her own living room, it became a full-fledged fantasy.

She'd make Trav's favorite meal, call him and ask him to help her with something, and then surprise him with the food and an apology.

Getting him to the house wouldn't be too hard. She could say her dishwasher had malfunctioned, and she didn't have anyone else to call.

*No*, she told herself. That wasn't what Trav wanted to

hear. He didn't want to be her last resort. He wanted to be her first.

He didn't want to only be allowed to come to her house when she needed help. He wanted her to want him.

And want him, she did.

She'd learned that in the past three weeks since his sudden departure from her life. She'd been diligent in talking to her online counselor through an app her sister had recommended, and a day didn't go by that she didn't talk about Trav with Elora. In fact, she'd been about to call Elora when Steele had walked in.

"You're back fast," she said. "Everything is done?"

"Yes," Steele said. He flopped onto the couch with her. "I saw Deacon, and he said they're doing a bonfire, so I hurried." He looked at her. "There's no school tomorrow."

Poppy admired her son. He was growing up so fast, and she smiled as she reached over and bumped back his cowboy hat. "All right," she said. "Take your phone and text me when you get there. I'll text Elise too."

Steele whooped and jumped to his feet. How he had so much energy after such a long week, Poppy didn't understand. Of course, he was a child, and he didn't carry quite the mental load she did.

He tore out of the house, and Poppy sighed as she texted Elise to let her know Steele was on the way.

*We'll take good care of him*, Elise sent back. *If it's too late for him to come back alone, I'll make sure Gray or Hunt brings him.*

*Thank you,* Poppy told her. That done, she then dialed Elora. She'd run her insane idea by her sister, and then she'd know if it was worth pursuing or not.

"Sissy," Elora said. "I just passed Steele on his bike. Does this mean you're home alone?"

"Yep." Poppy popped the P in the word, and then she heaved herself off the couch. "Is Briggs with you?"

"Nope," Elora answered. "Just me. I had to come down here for my hair appointment, and I thought I'd swing by for ice cream and coffee. Where'd Steele go?"

"The Hammonds are having a bonfire." They had them often in the summer and fall, in fact, and Poppy had gone to one or two.

"Oh, that sounds fun," Elora said. "Too bad you can't go over there and make up with Trav."

Poppy sighed and went into the kitchen. "I wanted to talk to you about him, actually."

"Brew the coffee. I'm here." Elora hung up, and Poppy got the coffee pot rinsed out and reset before her sister came inside. She had a barely-there baby bump that everyone could see, because she didn't normally carry much extra weight and every article of clothing she owned was skin-tight.

Poppy brightened and hugged her. "It's good to see you."

"You've been calling me every day for weeks."

"I appreciate it." Poppy stepped back. "I have a little dilemma."

"Have you finally admitted that you're in love with Trav?"

"No," Poppy said, though a smile touched her face and her soul at the thought of being in love again. She'd realized that one of the things she was absolutely terrified of was falling in love. She'd been there before, and it had not ended well. She had never been able to imagine a different ending for her, Steele, and Eli, and therefore, she had no future with a man who loved her.

Even Trav.

"His mother texted this week." Poppy tapped and swiped to get to the message from Melanie. "Read it. I haven't responded."

She moved back into the kitchen to get down mugs, and to pull out the sugar and cream. Her sister liked warm cream with a hint of coffee flavoring, and she poured a healthy amount into a measuring cup and put it in the microwave.

"This is easy," Elora said. "You tell her you want the recipe." She glowed as Poppy faced her. "Then, you make this for Trav and tell him what we all know." She handed the phone back. "Cooking is your love language, Poppy. This is how you make things right with him."

"He loves lemon bars too," Poppy said.

"You can make those in your sleep." Elora slid onto a barstool. "Do you like my hair?"

"It's adorable," Poppy said, immediately realizing that she'd used the wrong adjective. "I mean, it makes you look a little older. No bangs."

Elora swept her fingers through her sandy blonde hair with only a hint of the red Poppy had flaming in hers. "I feel like my forehead is a fivehead without the bangs."

Poppy grinned, because while Elora wasn't all that much younger than her, she constantly used phrases and sayings Poppy didn't understand. "Fivehead?"

"You know, a forehead that goes on forever; it's actually a fivehead." Elora covered hers with her palm. "My forehead is huge."

Poppy burst out laughing, because her sister did not have a "huge" forehead. "I've literally never thought that about you," she said.

"Well, it's true." Elora sighed, and Poppy served her a cup of coffee. She pulled a bag of cowboy cookies from the freezer and put them on the counter too. "These thaw really quickly."

"Ooh, do they have walnuts or pecans?"

"Pecans," Poppy said, as she liked pecans in her cookies far more than walnuts. "Walnuts make my mouth a little itchy."

"Briggs too." Elora reached for the zipper bag. "He went and got some allergy testing done, and he's going to start the shots."

"Is he?" Poppy looked at her phone, her thoughts scattering as Elora started talking about her husband's allergies to grass, pollen, basically every tree in Colorado, wheat, and some mild aversions to nuts.

She tapped out a quick message to Melanie. *I'd love to come get the recipe and surprise Trav with it. When's a good time?*

She'd have to have a miracle to make it work out between her busy schedule with the landscaping, the farm, and her son. Poppy found herself praying for that miracle.

Melanie said, *Any time, dear. I know how busy you are. I don't have anything planned in the near future.*

Poppy didn't either, and she looked up from her phone and met her sister's eyes. "She says I can come get the recipe any time."

"Let's go." Elora hopped down from the barstool as she had always been up for any adventure. Her smile said she couldn't wait to meet Trav's mom, and Poppy decided it sure would be nice to not have to go alone and pretend everything between her and Trav was hunky dory.

She was going to make it that way, and maybe his mother would never have to know of her fatal flaws that had driven Trav away.

"Elora," she said very seriously. "Promise me you won't say anything about me and Trav breaking up."

"I won't." Elora crossed her heart and took one more swig of her coffee. "I'm taking two of these cookies to go."

Poppy laughed and shook her head. Then she took two cookies too, and she said a half-dozen silent prayers as she followed her sister outside to the driveway.

———

A WEEK LATER, Poppy hadn't been this nervous since she'd attended the speed dating event four months ago. She looked around her kitchen, her stomach rolling every other second. First to the right, then to the left. Left, right, right, left.

She and Steele had been home from church for forty-five minutes. The hamburger hash sat in the oven getting toasty and brown. The timer said she had twenty-two minutes until it would be ready.

Her son had gone upstairs to change his clothes, and he hadn't come back down yet. She'd call him for lunch, and he'd come running.

But first, she needed to call Trav.

Her throat rebelled, and she couldn't swallow nor speak. She tried clearing it, and she reached for the iced tea she'd poured herself. She gulped it until her throat ached from the cold.

"Come on, Poppy," she said. "You want him back. Make the call."

She wasn't even sure he'd answer. Oh, how she hoped he'd answer. Feeling brave and adventurous, she finally tapped the phone icon to make the device dial.

His line rang once, then twice. She paced away from the island, one finger in her mouth as she chewed the nail. Three rings. She would go to voicemail soon.

On the next ring.

"Howdy," a man said, and it wasn't Travis.

"Oh."

"It's Cord," he said. "Trav just ran out to the truck to bring in the ice cream we forgot about."

Poppy didn't know what to say. She barely had anything prepared to say to Trav, let alone his cabinmate. "Could you—?"

"It's melted." Trav's voice came through the line. "We'll have to get more."

"Here he is," Cord said. "Phone for you, Trav."

"Who is it?" Scuffling came through the line, and then silence. Poppy's pulse sped with every second where neither of them said anything.

Finally, she heard something, and it was someone breathing out. "Hello, Poppy."

The deep, beautiful sound of Trav's voice saying her name made her breath catch. Her emotions spiraled, and she pressed her eyes closed against the hot tears.

"I need you," she whispered.

"I'm sorry?"

Poppy opened her eyes and paced toward the back door. She couldn't breathe inside. She couldn't breathe without Trav. She'd been slowly suffocating since he'd broken up with her weeks ago.

"I was—I need some help with my fridge, and I wondered if you could spare a couple of minutes to look at it." She burst out of the house, her heartbeat doing the same thing. Bursting, over and over again.

"Cord's taking a machinery class," Trav said. "I can send him over."

Desperation caught in Poppy's throat. "I have lemon bars and ice cream as payment, but I want you to come."

*I want you.*

She pulled in a breath and held it, praying Trav would come. *Please, please,* she prayed.

"Right now?" Trav asked.

"Lunch is almost ready," she said as casually as she could. "If you came right now, you could stay and eat."

"Cord hasn't eaten either," he said.

Poppy swallowed hard, but she had to get him over here. "He can come," she said.

"We'll be there in a few minutes." The call ended, and Poppy practically threw her phone onto the island as if it had grown fangs and might bite her.

"A few minutes," she repeated. She hurried to the front door and nearly tripped over Cotton when she turned right back around. "Oof." She grabbed onto the back of the wingback chair there to steady herself and looked down at her dog. "Sorry, buddy."

Poppy took a moment to breathe, and then she returned to the main part of the house. "Steele," she called. "Come help me set the table."

She'd already pulled out four plates, cups, and utensil settings by the time her son came downstairs. "Who's coming over?" he asked.

"Cord and Trav," she said without looking at her

child. She hadn't told him much about what had happened between her and Trav, and he'd only asked once why the cowboy had stopped coming around. She'd said he was very busy next door at his real job, and she'd ignored the raised eyebrows of her father and step-mother.

"Are you getting back together with him?"

Poppy paused in laying out the forks. Instant excuses popped into her mind, but she bit them all back. "Yes," she said simply. "I'm going to try to get him to go out with me again."

Steele grinned from ear to ear, which also surprised Poppy. "Good. He likes you so much, Mama, and I like him, and he likes me."

"Steele," she said with plenty of warning in her voice. She didn't have to ask anything else.

Her son dropped his head, and that was all the answer she needed. Steele had seen and been talking to Trav for who knew how long. "I have his number," Steele said. "He brought the goats back once or twice."

"Was it once or twice?" Poppy asked, shocked Trav had been on her property, and she hadn't known it. She felt so tethered to him, despite the distance between them. Distance she'd caused. Distance she was going to erase.

"Twice," Steele said. "And once this week too. So three times."

"Three times."

The doorbell rang, and Cotton went into a frenzy. She jerked her attention toward the hall leading to the doorway, and she reached out and put one hand on Steele's shoulder as he started to move toward it.

"I want to get it," she said slowly. "*I* have to make things right with him."

Steele nodded; she dropped her hand but didn't move. "Go on then, Mama," he said. "Hurry up."

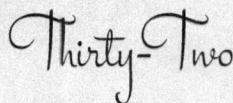

## Thirty-Two

TRAVIS GLANCED OVER TO CORD, WHO MET HIS eye. "I know she's here," he said. When she'd called, Travis had wanted to leave immediately. He'd given himself some moments of pause so he could listen to the Lord.

He'd been waiting for the feeling and signal that he should show up right here, on Poppy's porch, and he'd gotten it the moment he'd heard her voice. God had told him to come, and now he needed the woman to answer the door.

Cord nodded and looked back at the door. Cotton had quieted, but no one had come to let them in. Travis had only brought himself and his phone, but Cord carried his toolbox in case he could tweak something and fix Poppy's unknown problem with the fridge.

"You look like you're going to throw up," Cord hissed. "Calm down. She called you."

"To help her," Travis said.

Cord nodded. "Right. So you're good. You're back in the game."

Before Travis could answer, the door swung open, and both him and Cord looked to it. Poppy stood there, and she still wore her dress from church, with one of her white aprons tied around her neck and waist.

She wore pure apprehension on her face as her gaze flitted from him to Cord and back. "Hey," she said.

Cotton came right out onto the porch, and Cord grinned, put down his tools, and bent to pat the blue heeler. With him busy, Travis could only stare at Poppy.

"You look great," he said. For some reason, he'd hoped she'd be as miserable as he'd been. He reminded himself it was the Sabbath, and Poppy always wore more makeup to church.

Poppy pressed her palms together. "Trav," she said. "I lied. There's nothing wrong with my fridge." She cut a glance over to Cord as he straightened. "I just wanted you to come over, and I didn't know how else to do it."

Travis could only stare, so it was Cord who asked, "Why did you want him to come over?"

"Because." She swallowed. "I want him here." She shook her head, her eyes falling closed for a moment. "I want you. I want you *here*. I love you, and *I want you*. I want this to be your farm. Not mine. I guess not yours either, but ours. *Our* farm." Poppy looked down at her son as Steele moved into her side.

"Hey, Trav." Steele held out his fist for Travis to bump, and numbly, he did it.

He looked back to Poppy, still trying to catch up to everything she'd said.

"I made hamburger hash," she said, stepping back. "Your momma gave me the recipe, and I'm hoping it, along with the lemon bars and the ice cream, will be enough to convince you to give me another chance." She switched her gaze back to Steele. "The timer's going off, baby. Go check it for me, would you?"

"Okay, Mama." Steele left, and Cotton trotted back into the house too.

"I'm gonna take these tools back to the cabin," Cord said in a loud voice. He bumped Travis hard with the black, metal box. Travis grunted, but Cord only said, "Oops."

Their eyes met, and Cord glared at him. "Unfreeze, Trav," he muttered, and then he left him standing there on Poppy's porch all by himself.

*Unfreeze.*

He did, so much in his head that he needed to clear up with Poppy. "You called my mother and got the hamburger hash recipe?"

"Sort of," she said with a smile. "I'd asked her for it a while ago, and she couldn't find it. When she did, she texted me, and I went up to get it last weekend."

"Last weekend," he repeated. "She didn't say anything about it."

"She may think we're still together." Poppy toed the floor with her black heel. "Unless you told her we'd broken up."

"No," he said. "I didn't."

"I didn't either." Poppy faced him now, all shyness gone. "I miss you so much." She moved into him. "I've been talking to someone on an app, and I know I love cooking for you. I'd do it even if I was drop-dead tired— and that's how you are with me and this farm. I know you mean well, and let me tell you, I have peaches from here until the Atlantic Ocean I'm going to need your help with."

Travis started to smile, letting it slowly sink into his soul. He put one hand on her hip. "Did I hear you right, Miss Poppy Harris? Did you say you love me?"

"You're not deaf," she said. "Unless that happened in the past couple of weeks."

"Twenty-four days," he murmured. "It's been twenty-four days since I've spoken to you. Every one has been agony for me."

Poppy wilted in his arms. "I'm sorry, Trav. I really am."

"I am too," he said. He slid one hand up the side of her face. "I'm in love with you too. That's why I've been so miserable, because I don't want to live without you."

She smiled up at him. "I haven't even had you try the hash yet."

"I don't care about the hash," he said. "I mean, I do. I

can't wait to try it." His gaze dropped to her lips. "But Poppy, it's you I want."

"I want you too," she whispered.

"Really?" he asked. "Like, really-really?"

"Really-really, with my whole heart." Tears filled her eyes. "I won't lie; I'm a little scared. But I'm working through it, and if you can be patient with me, I will be the woman you want."

"You already are," he said, lowering his head. He touched his lips to hers, and Travis's blood ignited with that sweet, chaste kiss. He accelerated it quickly after that first touch, and he only slowed and stopped kissing her when he remembered Steele was somewhere nearby.

"I'm sorry," she whispered.

"Let's try again," he said back. "If you need four seasons and a road trip to know, I'm fine with that. Really."

Poppy nodded, stroked her hand down the side of his face, and said, "I love you. I want you here. I want you, because you're you."

Travis captured her hand in his and pressed it to his pulse. "Thank you, Poppy." He kissed her again, the beating of his heart between them. "I love you too."

———

"THAT'LL BE POPPY AND STEELE," Travis said several weeks later. He quickly turned off the water in the kitchen sink and reached for a towel to dry his hands. Before he could yell for them to come in, Steele had opened the door.

He walked in wearing full cowboy gear from head to toe. The hat, the old western vest, a plaid shirt in black and white, chaps, boots, spurs, everything. Travis started laughing at the way he sauntered as if he'd just stepped into a saloon where he expected big trouble.

"Wow," he said as he chuckled. "Look at you."

"Did you win?" Cord asked. He closed the laptop and got to his feet, his face full of hope. Steele had borrowed Cord's chaps—as well as the biggest belt buckle Travis had ever seen. Steele too.

Cord had apparently ridden in the rodeo for a year, and he'd won enough to get a belt buckle the size of a dinner plate.

Steele remained steely and grim-faced while Poppy entered. She carried a huge chocolate cake, and Travis hurried to help her.

"Let me have it," he said.

She handed him the cake and did a double-take at her son. "Is he in full persona *again*?"

Cord chuckled, and Travis couldn't help grinning at the boy. "Seems like it."

"He won't even talk," Cord said.

"He says that's because John Wayne doesn't talk unless he has to." Poppy rolled her eyes. "Steele. Talk to the boys."

Travis put the cake on the counter and looked up just as Steele broke from character. "I won!" He jumped into the air and pumped his fist while Cord whooped and whistled. Travis applauded too, and he went to hug the boy.

"That's great," he told Steele. "Are you going to stay in costume all night?"

"Yeah," Steele said. "It's a Halloween party, right?" He looked up at Travis, who nodded.

"But just for people here at the farm," Poppy said. "There's no one to impress."

"Jane will be here," Steele said, and Travis watched as Poppy froze right where she was. Her face paled, and Travis ducked his head to hide his smile. Steele would be twelve by Thanksgiving, and while Jane was a couple of years older than him, that age difference wouldn't matter once they became adults.

"Jane?" Poppy screeched.

"Jane's nice," Cord said, grinning at Steele.

"I, well, of course she's nice." Poppy looked like she'd never even considered that Steele would like a girl.

Travis chuckled as he went into the kitchen. He swept one arm around Poppy's waist and leaned in to kiss her. With other eyes on them, he kept it tame and then pulled away. "So, what are you?"

Poppy stepped back and did a twirl, but she wore clothes he'd seen many times. A pair of jeans. A plaid shirt that looked suspiciously like one he owned. It was blue and yellow and black, and it definitely didn't fit her very well.

She wore a pair of dark brown cowgirl boots, and she reached up and took his cowboy hat from his head. Travis didn't appreciate that too much, but when she settled it on her head and cocked it at him, those glossed-pink lips spreading and grinning.... He could barely remember his own name.

"She's you," Cord came to stand beside Travis. "And you're staring," he hissed out of the corner of his mouth.

Travis jolted and blinked, because Poppy had dressed up as him. "Well." He took her hand in his. "I think you pull me off pretty well."

She giggled too, and the front door opened again. They all turned that way as Jane Hammond said, "Knock, knock." She pretty much sucked the air right out of the cabin, and Travis's smile slid away.

Jane surveyed the group there. "Uh, sorry. I knocked, but no one came, and I could hear you, so...." She straightened in the doorway and cleared her throat. "Daddy says y'all can bring the desserts over any time."

She looked the most at Cord, and she didn't even seem to notice that Steele stood there, looking all fly and handsome in his cowboy costume. She herself wore a historical dress like the kind Travis had seen in the Regency movies Poppy had shown him. Jane even had a bonnet over her fair features, and Travis couldn't see a hint of Gray in her at all.

Jane clasped her hands all proper-like as well. "Okay." She cleared her throat. "I need to go tell Mission and Boone too, before I get Granddad."

"Can I come?" Steele asked. "I can help spread the word that you're ready."

She nodded and smiled at him, and Steele followed her out of the house, closing the door behind him.

Travis felt like he could get a full lung full of air then, and he switched his gaze to Poppy. "He's eleven," he said. "It's fine."

Poppy narrowed her eyes at the door as if she'd march after Steele and chew him out. In reality, she'd probably do that to Jane, not her son, and Travis put both hands on her shoulders and forced her to look at him. "Hey," he said. "It's nothing."

She blinked, the scary part of her retreating. "Yeah, he's eleven."

"Molly and Hunter started dating when they were eleven," Cord said.

Travis spun toward him. "Hey. Not helping."

Cord grinned and said, "Sorry. But I'm just sayin'." He squeezed past Poppy and Travis to open the fridge. "Now, look at this cheesecake."

He pulled the concoction out of the fridge, and Poppy's eyes went wide. "Cord." She pressed one hand to her chest. "Did you make that?"

"Yes, ma'am," he said at the same time Travis said,

397

"No, he did not." His voice hung in the air, and Cord gave him a speared look.

"I did," he said.

"You *decorated* it," Travis said, grinning at his best friend. "You didn't make the cheesecake."

"It's a cake *decorating* contest," Cord said. "No one ever said you had to make the cake too." He held his head high as he moved past them. "Come on. They're doing the cake walk first." He took his vampire-inspired cake to the front door and walked out.

Poppy looked at her chocolate cake—of which she'd made every single part. The three tiers. The haunted house on the top. The knobby trees with bare branches and creepy owls in them.

"That graveyard is terrifying," Travis said, drawing her attention from the cake to him. "You're going to win."

"That looked like real blood," she said. "And I've never seen someone get frosting so black. It's like, impossible." She wore worry in her eyes now, and Travis laughed as he wrapped her in his arms. Everyone was gone now, and he could kiss her the way he wanted to.

"Honey," he whispered. "Who's the only one who needs to know you're the best cook and baker in town?"

She softened and studied the buttons at his throat for a moment. "You," she said.

"Mm." He touched his lips to her forehead. "Who's the only one you want the share the farm with?"

She looked up at him. "You."

He let his love for her stream through him, and he sure hoped it showed in his eyes. "Who's the one who loves you, loves you, loves you, whether you win a small-town cake decorating contest out on a remote farm or not?"

Poppy tipped up onto her toes and pressed her lips to his. Travis kissed her back, taking the stroke deeper and deeper until he felt her passion for him way down deep in his soul. She finally pulled away, both of them a little bit breathless. "You," she whispered, pressing her forehead to his. He kept her flush against his body as they swayed to a silent song in his head.

She looked up at him and added, "And I love you too, you know."

He nodded, smiling all the while. "Yeah," he said. "I know."

# Thirty-Three

POPPY COULDN'T KEEP UP WITH THE BUBBLING, boiling, steaming, stewing pots and pans on the stove. "Trav," she called over her shoulder while she drained cooked potatoes into the sink. "I need help."

He silenced the timer on the oven before she'd said the last word. "I got it."

On this Thanksgiving Day, he'd also been out to the animals to feed them. He'd thrown the football with Steele, Briggs, and her father—their own small version of a Turkey Trot—and he now entertained everyone with stories from his life in the city, as well as helped her in the kitchen.

Poppy loved having him here, in her house and in her life. She hadn't had to put the leaf in the dining room table by herself. That chore had always reminded her of how there were simply some things in life that required two people, and she had always been a party of one.

Until now.

With Trav, putting the leaf in the table and spreading her grandmother's hand-sewn tablecloth over it had taken a few seconds. He'd hauled in the fifty pounds of potatoes and peeled half of them. He'd stuffed the turkey—under her watchful eye, of course. Trav was a decent cook, but he excelled at putting things in the oven, setting a timer, and then taking them out. Much more, and Poppy had to instruct him.

She'd done several lessons with him and Steele, and her absolute favorite one was the pork potstickers. Both of the boys in her life could now fold them faster than she could cook them, and they'd started having Potsticker Sundays after church.

Poppy invited her parents and her sister and Briggs, and Trav brought his momma and most weeks, Cord. Sometimes Chris or Mission or both would come too, and Poppy welcomed anyone who wanted to walk through her door.

Before, she didn't want anyone to see the state of her home and farm. She'd felt like a seriously stiff Rocky Mountain storm could've knocked everything she held dear to the ground, but as she and Trav and Steele worked the farm together, it only got better and better.

She'd sold over half of her hay now, and Black Friday was supposed to happen under the threat of a major snowstorm. Since Poppy didn't shop much, it wouldn't impact her either way. She had no plans to set her alarm to get up and hit the mall. Instead, she had an alarm set so she could make her delicious buttermilk bars for breakfast.

Trav slid the perfectly baked and golden rolls onto the countertop and asked, "Butter?"

"Yep." Poppy grinned at him and pointed with her chin. "Right there."

He picked up the pastry brush in the melted butter and stirred it around. He painted the baked bread with it as Poppy put the potatoes into her stand mixer. She added heated cream, butter, and sour cream, then pulled the plug on the pressure cooker so she could get the potatoes out of it too.

"What else?" Trav asked. They both turned toward the back door as the wind rattled the glass, trying to get in. "Storm's startin'." He went that way while Poppy twisted the lid on the pressure cooker. The creamy, yellow potatoes inside made her mouth water, and Poppy remembered that she hadn't eaten that day at all.

The clock ticked closer to one—witching hour—and Iris came over to help. "I've got the condiments on the table, Poppy," she said.

"Thank you." Poppy wrestled the heavy pot out of the cooker and dumped the potatoes into the stand mixer bowl as well. Several stuck to the bottom, and Poppy left them. They'd have brown bottoms, and she didn't want the color in her creamy Yukon Gold mashed potatoes. Not on Thanksgiving Day.

The doorbell rang, which set off Cotton. "Hush," she barked at the dog, her stress coming out suddenly.

"It's my momma," Trav said as he went past her. "I'll put Cotton in the bedroom?"

"He's a little anxious," Poppy said. She was too. She reminded herself this holiday meal—with everyone in her or Trav's life that they loved and wanted to be with—was part of her journey with Trav. She wanted to experience a full year of holidays, events, and family gatherings with him. They needed to know how they blended together. She needed to see how she fit with her own family when she was part of her-and-Trav. She wanted to see where he fit with her and his momma, his job, and his friends.

She wanted to know if he'd keep working for the Hammonds once they got married, and Poppy's vision blurred as she finally lowered the whisk into the potatoes and started them whipping. She'd just thought of marrying Trav without an "if" anywhere in sight. It wasn't even in her mind.

Melanie entered the room on Trav's arm, and he glowed. He always did as he escorted her anywhere they went. She hadn't wanted to leave her congregation, which Poppy understood. She didn't want to leave hers either. Trav had started attending church with her a couple of months ago, and if it wasn't Potsticker Sunday, they went to his momma's after church.

"Steele, get Miss Mel's cookies."

Her son jumped down from the barstool without continuing with his video game for even another moment. He loved Trav's mom, because she always brought him a gift. It could be something simple like a bag of Reese's Pieces—his favorite candy—or the promise that she'd get him a pair of rabbits come springtime.

When Poppy had looked horrified at the thought of multiplying rabbits on her farm, Melanie had told her every boy needed rabbits to tend to as they grew up. Trav had told a couple of stories about his own rabbits, and Poppy had decided she could handle having bunnies—if Trav was there to help.

"Are these the monster cookies?" Steele asked, his voice full of hope.

"They sure are, young man." Melanie smiled at him. "Tell me about Lucky. How's she doing?"

"Good," Steele said. "Trav thinks she's going to have twins."

"You should see her, Mama," Trav said. "She's huge, and she still has a month to go, probably."

Poppy stopped the mixer and pulled the bowl from it. "We're ready." She met Trav's eyes, and he nodded. He guided his mother to the table, and they'd put her next to Daddy, with Iris on his other side. They took up one side of the table, and then Poppy, Steele, and Trav sat opposite of them.

Cord sat at the head of the table, and Elora and Briggs

shared the other end of the table. Mission had gone home to California, and everyone else next door had family or other celebrations to attend.

Poppy didn't need a huge gathering at her farmhouse. Last year, she'd had her parents and her and Steele. Elora and Briggs had gone to his parents' for the meal, and Poppy hadn't seen her sister until the following day.

Tears filled her eyes, and she arrived at the table last. Everyone looked up at her, as she hadn't taken her seat yet, and she blinked in quick surprise. "Thank you for coming today," she said. Her voice broke slightly, and she put one hand on Trav's shoulder. "I appreciate all the things everyone brought, as well as all the help around the farm I had this morning so I could stay inside and cook."

She meant every word too, and her voice and emotions didn't waver as she said them. To get out the next part, though, she had to take a long pause as her heartbeat accelerated and her throat closed.

Trav slid his arm around her and said, "I'm grateful to be included here on this farm for Thanksgiving this year." He looked up at her, his dark eyes like falling into a warm cup of coffee, sans cream and sugar. He was dark from head to toe, but absolutely delicious. "I'm grateful I have Poppy and Steele in my life this year, because last year I was just wishing I did."

"That isn't true," Poppy said, getting jolted out of her trance.

"Oh, it's absolutely true," Trav said, chuckling.

"I lectured you from here to the Mississippi last Thanksgiving." She blinked at him, sure he hadn't *liked* that.

"You've been in his head for a long time," Cord said quietly. Poppy looked at him, and he gave her a small smile. "I'm also grateful to be here at this farm this year. I've spent Thanksgiving in some...interesting places, and this is definitely one of the better ones." He nodded. "Thank you, Poppy, for having me." He looked to Melanie, and she reached over and patted his hand.

"I'm grateful I get to spend this holiday in such a warm home, with all my favorite people."

"Don't let her fool you," Trav said, grinning. Poppy slid into her chair while he teased his momma about the many male suitors who'd tried to get her to come to their Thanksgiving meals.

"I'm grateful for my girls," Daddy said, and Poppy's heart melted again.

"I'm grateful to be part of this family," Iris said, and Elora already had tears streaming down her face as every eye turned to her. Poppy was a sympathetic crier, and no one affected her like Elora.

She sniffled and wiped her eyes. Elora said, "I'm grateful I get to be a mother, and I hope I can be half as good as Poppy."

"You will," Poppy promised her. Number one, she had a good husband at her side already. Poppy hadn't had that, and she'd done the best she could. She hoped the

Lord wouldn't expect any more than that from her, and she knew He didn't.

Briggs pressed his lips to his wife's cheek and said, "I'm grateful for my wife."

Poppy looked at her son and nudged him with her elbow. "Your turn, baby. We're sayin' what we're grateful for." She realized how very much she sounded like Trav as she dropped the G on one of her words.

Steele blinked up at her. "I'm grateful for this farm and that I get to go outside and do chores."

Poppy's eyebrows shot up. She giggled as Iris said, "Nice one, Steele."

She looked at Trav. "You coached him on that."

Trav laughed and held up both hands. "I did not."

The attention came back to Poppy, and she had to say something. She'd had a few thoughts rolling around inside her head for days, and she still didn't know what to say. She looked around at everyone, so many doors opening in those few seconds.

"I'm grateful my goats kept getting out," she said, nodding. Her voice quit on her then, but the one person who knew how significant loose goats could be put his arm around her and kissed her temple.

"So am I," he whispered.

"And leaky roofs," she whispered. "And that I couldn't pay my mortgage last year."

He smiled softly at her, touched his lips to hers for

only a breath of time, and then said, "Poppy asked me to say grace. We ready?"

She nodded, glad for the excuse to close her eyes so she could keep all the burning tears contained and not ruin her carefully drawn-on makeup. Trav's deep rumble filled the farmhouse, as did his special spirit and good soul, and Poppy fell a little bit more in love with him simply by having him at her side on this holiday.

# Thirty-Four

BOONE WHETTSTEIN WOKE SLOWLY, NO LIGHT beyond his closed eyes. It was the first week of January, which meant it could be far past time for him to get up and he wouldn't know. The sun didn't rise the way it did in the summertime, and he craved the warmer temperatures and burning sunshine.

At the same time, he wouldn't be waking up alone again.

Because today was his wedding day.

That thought caused a smile to cross his face, and he did open his eyes. Light came in through the crack in his door, but that didn't mean Gerty was up. They left the hall light on all night long, because she didn't like getting up in the middle of the night in the dark.

Boone moved slowly, and by the time he picked up his phone, it was just after six. *Plenty of time*, he told himself.

He never was one to lay in bed once he was awake, and he got up and stepped into the shower.

Gerty found him in the kitchen only a few minutes after he'd started brewing the coffee, her pink camouflage pajamas loose even though Cosette had gotten the smallest size available. The fact was, his daughter was made of bone, muscle, and sinew, and not much else. Sass, maybe.

He grinned at her. "Morning, bumblebee."

"Morning." She wiped her face. "Why do we get up so early when we don't have to?"

"Habit," he said. They'd done the same thing over the Christmas holiday, but they'd still had their chores on the farm to do. Today, they didn't.

"I got a text from Jericho," she said. "He said the heaters are on in the barn already."

Boone grinned and nodded. "Great." He and Cosette had eaten tacos in Jericho Johnson's barn on their first date, and when they'd talked about where to get married, Boone had suggested the barn.

Cosette had seized onto it, and Boone had called Jericho instantly. The man was nicer than any other human on the earth, and the ceremony would be small. Cosette only had one sister, and Boone only had one brother. All the cowboys from the farm would come, and Gray and Hunter and their families.

But other than that, there wouldn't be many guests. Forty or so, which felt huge to Cosette. She'd been talking to her therapist about being in the enclosed space with so many people for a couple weeks now. She said she could do it, and Boone wasn't worried she wouldn't show up because of him.

He was a tad nervous she'd have a hard time with everyone looking at her. She'd grown and changed a lot, and she absolutely was ready to marry him, but she had some trauma that could rear its head at unexpected times.

Her daddy had been dealing with some health problems for several months now, but he wasn't doing his chemotherapy treatments right now, and they'd gone to the barn last night to practice the walk.

It was only eleven steps from the door to the altar, which Boone and Matt had carved together out of a huge log from one of Poppy Harris's downed trees. Cosette had put the carved piece up on black iron legs to represent the melding of Boone—a country boy who might be a little rough around the edges—and her—a more refined person than Boone.

"What about the orange marmalade?" he asked. "What's the status on that?" For their wedding luncheon, the first course was French toast bites with orange marmalade. His grandmother's recipe.

"We got it all done," Gerty said. "Elise and Poppy are so fast in the kitchen." She wore something on her face Boone had seen plenty of times before. She had something she wanted to ask him, something she thought he might not like or might say no to. He stirred sugar into his coffee and gave her time and space to ask him.

"Poppy said she could teach me how to cook." Gerty cleared her throat. "I was thinkin' I should do that."

"Are you saying I don't teach you things?" Boone looked up and smiled at her.

Gerty rolled her eyes. "I'm saying Poppy's really good at things inside the house, Daddy. Me and you, we're outdoor people."

"Cosette knows how to cook. Maybe she'll feel bad if you take lessons from Poppy."

"That's why I'm asking." Gerty blinked, her bright blue eyes full of fear and hope. "It doesn't have to be either-or. Aren't you always telling me that?"

"I may have said it a time or two," Boone said. Or twenty or thirty. Or more. He'd spent a lot of time in the past year or so talking about hard things with Gerty. Boys, grades, horses, the future. Getting married again. Her mom.

Boone and Cosette were getting married only eight days before the anniversary of Nikki's death. Boone went to Montana every year to see his first wife, and this year, Cosette was going with him. They were stopping by on the way home from their honeymoon. They'd all go back once school got out, as January in Montana was like visiting the arctic in the worst month possible.

Gerty needed to see her mama and talk to her about the year's events, and Boone hoped she'd do that for her entire life.

"I'm gonna go shower," Gerty said. "If you think it'll upset Cosette, I can ask her too."

"I'll talk to her," Boone said. "I'm sure it'll be fine, bumblebee."

"If Mikey gets here before I come out, don't torture him, okay?" She cocked one eyebrow at Boone, who pretended to be offended.

"I do not torture the boy."

"Just being in your presence is torture for him," Gerty said dryly. She headed down the hall.

"That says something about him," Boone called after her. He wasn't all that upset about Gerty's relationship with Michael Hammond. He didn't really see where it was going, but he knew that teenagers thought everything that happened today meant that was how things would be forever. Boone knew far better than that.

He finished breakfast and retrieved his tuxedo from his bedroom before someone knocked on the door. He answered it to find the tall Hammond boy standing on the porch.

"Morning, Mister Whettstein," Mikey said. He stuck out his hand for Boone to shake.

He did. "Howdy, Mikey." He stepped back and let the teen inside. "How was the drive?"

"My dad made me do it," he said, a ghost of a smile coming to his face. "So it was long and tense."

"Wow," Boone said. "But you did it."

"I begged him to take over about ten times. The man's made of steel."

Boone burst out laughing, because he could just see Wes Hammond refusing to take over the task of driving.

"He complains incessantly about how slow I'm going," Mikey said next, his tone turning a tad dark. As dark as Boone had ever heard. "He made me pay for the extra gas." He shook his head and rolled his eyes. "Would you mind if I had a cup of coffee?" He indicated the pot in the kitchen, and Boone gestured for him to go ahead.

"I'm staying with my granddad, and he wasn't up yet," Mikey explained as he opened the cupboard to look for a mug. "I didn't want to wake him."

"Your dad's not up?"

"Not yet," he said, turning his back on Boone. "He's getting older too."

Wes Hammond was about two decades older than Boone, and they had children the same age. Wes had simply gotten started on his family much later than Boone.

"You're okay if I take Gerty to breakfast this morning?" Mikey looked up from his coffee.

"She's goin', isn't she?" Boone wasn't going to complain about the relationship. As far as he knew, Michael was nothing but respectful. He could talk to Boone like a regular person, and he worked like a dog all summer long, apart from his momma and family. He took care of his grandfather, and he'd been absolutely adorable with Ryder, Hunter and Molly's new baby.

Seeing Michael, Gerty, and Ryder this summer.... Boone could admit it had been like looking into a crystal ball that was showing him the future. He wasn't sure if that would happen, and again, he knew that just because one thing happened didn't mean it would stay that way. Life had a way of throwing in hairpin curves, fastballs, and all kinds of other twists that a person couldn't anticipate.

"I won't keep her late. I just wanted to talk to her about something."

"What?" Boone asked, and the word did come out a little aggressively. He told himself this was the "torture" that Gerty had reference.

Mikey sighed and settled his weight onto the leg furthest from Boone. "Next summer," he said without looking up from his coffee. It must've been the most fascinating thing he'd ever looked at for how hard he stared at it.

"What about next summer?" Boone asked.

"Dad," Gerty said as she entered the room. She wore a soft blue dress with a square neck that Boone thought showed a lot of skin. No curves. Nothing inappropriate. Still. Little white and yellow flowers dotted the fabric, which fell all the way to the floor. She wore cowgirl boots with it, and some of that mascara that Cosette had taught her to apply.

Boone thought she was the loveliest girl in the whole

world, and one glance at Mikey told him the boy did too. "What?"

"You ask too many questions."

"He's fine," Mikey said. He moved toward Gerty and wrapped her in a hug. "You look great." He spoke the last sentence in a near-whisper, but Boone heard it anyway. The words held tenderness and happiness, and Boone could admit that if he had to give up his little girl to a man one day, he wanted it to be someone like Michael Hammond. Someone who clearly cherished her. Someone for whom the world stopped when Gerty walked into the room.

"Thanks," Gerty said, her eyes falling closed. She wore eyeshadow today too, and Boone told himself it was because it was his wedding day, not because she was going to spend the next hour at breakfast with Mikey.

In reality, it was probably both.

They both looked at Boone. "I'm okay to go, Daddy?"

"Yep." He too went to hug her. "I love you, bumblebee." He wasn't sure why he felt so emotional about this moment, but he did. It felt like he and Gerty had always been on the same path, just the two of them. But today, when he said, "I do," to Cosette and pledged himself to her, he'd be stepping to a different path.

It would still be adjacent to Gerty's, but she had her own roads to drive very soon. Very, very soon, as she was fifteen years old now. She only had three years of high school left, and then her whole life would open up for her.

She'd be doing things without him, and Boone suddenly wanted to freeze time and hold her right there in his arms forever.

His chest hurt, and he couldn't rope time the way he wanted to. So he stepped back, and their eyes met. "It's okay, Daddy," she said, and Boone wasn't sure why she'd felt the need to reaffirm that to him.

He nodded and cleared the emotion from his throat. "Go. Have fun. I'll see you at the barn."

"Everything will be ready," she said. "I promise."

Boone didn't doubt his daughter. She did what she said she would, and she worked really, really hard. She'd been involved in the wedding planning more than Boone, and she'd helped Cosette plan every tiny detail.

He just wanted to show up and get the ceremony done. He didn't care about what sat on the table, or what color anything was. If Matt, Chris, Gray, and Travis were there, Boone would be good.

Oh, and if Cosette showed up.

———

A FEW HOURS LATER, Boone let Matt straighten his tie. "It's good," he finally said, because Matt kept touching it. "Why are you more nervous than me?"

"I don't know," Matt said, finally stepping back. He looked from the tie to Boone's eyes. "I love you, brother. I guess I just want this to be perfect for you." He drew

Boone into a hug, and the sleeves on his jacket pulled tight as he lifted them around his brother.

They stood there together, the silence and tight grip between them saying so much. Boone loved Matt with everything he had. He adored his brother, and he'd followed him here after a very difficult time in Montana. They'd been through so much together, and Boone cleared his throat and stepped back.

"Thanks, Matt."

"This is your new beginning."

"I've been waiting for it for a long time." Boone could admit the past eight years had been terribly difficult for him. Not since he'd come to Ivory Peaks and this farm, and Boone was convinced there was something magical about the land—or the people—here.

"Today's the day." Matt grinned at him and turned as the door behind them opened. They had no one else in the room with them. No father. No grandfather. No other brothers or brothers-in-law.

"Dad," Keith said. "Roxy's throwing a fit, and Gloria wants you to take her." He came into the room with the fussy baby, and Boone's world brightened.

His brother lit the world with joy whenever one of his children came around, and especially this precious little girl God had given him and Gloria last fall. Boone wanted another baby as quickly as Matt had gotten one, and he reminded himself that he didn't need to compete with Matt. His life wasn't a race.

Behind Keith came Gray Hammond and his father, then Wes, Mikey, Travis, Mission, Cord, and then Gerty, who hung onto Cosette's father's arm, her face glowing like she was the one walking down the aisle today.

Just like that, the energy in the room went from somber and solo to full of vibrant energy. Boone grinned at Gray and Wes, hugged them both, and then took a longer moment with Chris. He ate lunch with the man almost every day, and he'd been like the father Boone had never really had. He knew Matt felt the same way, and for some reason, it meant a great deal to have Chris here to tell him, "I'm just so happy for you and Cosette. You're perfect for each other."

Boone agreed, and then Gerty tapped her wrist. Matt had managed to quiet his fussy baby, and Boone nodded at his daughter.

"All right, everyone," she said in her loud, horse-commanding voice. "It's time to get out to the barn. Daddy needs to be at the altar in about seven minutes, and since he's such a politician, he'll need every one of them."

"I'm not a politician," Boone said, grinning at Gerty.

"It's time to go anyway." She looped her arm through Jeff's and bent her head toward his. She'd deliver him to Cosette and then come into the barn, and Boone's rest-lessness suddenly tripled.

He left everyone leave the room ahead of him, and Travis stepped to his side. "You good?" he asked.

"Cosette's here, right?"

"Yep." Travis smiled at him, and they hurried through the cold from the guest house to the barn, where Boone lost Travis to Poppy Harris and her son. Boone went to the altar and shook the pastor's hand.

People took their seats. Molly played the piano in the corner, the music perfect for a country barn wedding in the winter.

Boone looked toward the doors as they opened. No one stood there for a few moments while the guests got to their feet. Molly increased the volume of her playing, and Boone coached himself to breathe, to clasp his hands pleasantly in front of him, and to keep his smile hitched in place.

Cosette didn't appear after what felt like a reasonable amount of time, and his feet shifted. He wasn't going to go find her. She'd said she'd be there. That she could do this, because it was *him* waiting for her.

He swallowed, his anxiety nearly getting the best of him, and then she stepped into the doorway. It framed her perfectly, and Boone's smile sprang to his face.

She was absolute perfection. The angel he'd been waiting and waiting to find. The exact woman God had led him to—and she'd overcome some of her own fears to be there with him.

Their eyes locked, and her smile beamed at him from eleven paces away. He held out his hand, and she took the first step toward him.

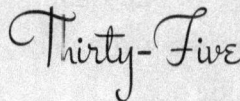

# Thirty-Five

COSETTE BRIAN GRIPPED HER DADDY'S ARM LIKE he alone could save her if she went down. He couldn't, and they both knew it. Gratitude and joy streamed through her that Daddy was at her side at all. After the news of his cancer last year, she hadn't been sure she'd ever get to have him do this for her.

This, being walk her toward the best-looking man in the state. The country. The world. The exact right person for her. The man who simultaneously made her heart rejoice and her stomach swoop and her lips tingle with want of kissing him.

Boone Whettstein.

She took step three and moved past the cowboys she worked with at Pony Power. Another step had her smiling at Molly Hammond, though she didn't take her eyes from

Boone. She couldn't. It was like he held her captive—the way he always had.

Nothing about their relationship had been rushed, and that was partly due to the healing she'd needed to do, and partly because of Boone's daughter. Cosette did tear her eyes from Boone for a moment, only to look at the teenager walking beside her.

Gerty glowed too, and she looked up at Cosette. She wasn't much taller than the girl, and they shared a special bond that the past year had cemented tightly. She didn't know how to be a mother, but she did know how to be kind. She knew how to listen. She knew how to do some girly things that Boone didn't. She knew how to love now, and she thanked the Lord above for that.

She walked past Gray and Elise, as well as Wes, his wife, and Michael. The Hammonds from Coral Canyon weren't staying long, and Gerty had already gone out with Mikey that morning. She'd stay with Matt while Cosette and Boone went on their honeymoon, as he'd watched Matt's kids when he and Gloria had gotten married.

Another step brought her to Matt and Gloria, who had front-row seats, on one side, and Louisa—Cosette's best friend—and her sister, Raven, who had an empty spot next to her on the other. Daddy would sit there, and Cosette felt flushed with the love here in the barn today.

They arrived at Boone, and he first leaned down and kissed Gerty's cheek. He whispered something to her, a true whisper, and Cosette hadn't thought the cowboy could do that. Apparently, he could, and when he straightened, his eyes shone with unshed tears.

He looked at her, spread his arms wide, and engulfed her and Daddy into the same hug. They all laughed, and Cosette should've known and planned for her wedding to be less than formal.

She had, because she knew Boone, and the man was fun, flirty, loud, loved to laugh, and somewhat irreverent. He also knew when to have a serious conversation, and when to back off, and when to simmer down. Cosette loved everything about him, and after he'd helped Daddy to his seat in the front row, he returned to her side.

The rest of the crowd had sat too, and Boone tucked her hand into the crook of his arm, patted it, and they faced the pastor together. The clunking of the barn doors told Cosette the cold had just been locked out, and she smiled warmly up at Boone.

"I love you," he whispered.

Her eyes drifted closed as the words washed over her. She felt loved, and that meant a great deal to her. Boone had been nothing but careful and respectful with her, and her heartbeat hammered at the thought of being intimate with him. She hadn't done that for a long, long time, and it hadn't been loving and kind in her previous experience.

She shuttered out the fear, literally seeing a pair of dark green shutters closing over the thoughts. Not allowing them in. It was a visualization tactic her therapist had taught her, and Cosette took a deep breath, feeling the air rush past her nostrils and fill her with life.

"I can feel the love between the two of you," Pastor Stone said. "It fills this barn to the rafters, and God Himself rejoices at the union of Boone Carter Whettstein and Cosette Leslie Brian. What a unique experience for me." He paused here, his face shining and good. He pressed one hand to his heart. "I can *feel* it. Can you all *feel* it?"

A couple of people gave low murmurs of assent, but Cosette just basked in it. She'd spent so much time feeling unloved, and that had been a dark, terrible place to be. This barn, with the tea lights, the white roses woven through them, and the lampposts to make it look cheery and outdoor when no one wanted to be outside, was the exact opposite of that.

Everyone here loved her. She loved everyone here.

"It's so amazing to feel this kind of energy and love," Pastor Stone said. "I just want you all to bask in it for a moment. Really see how it settles in your soul." He looked at Boone and then Cosette. "If I may?"

"Go ahead, Pastor." Boone filled the barn with his voice, and Cosette certainly didn't need to add hers to his.

"I just have this feeling...." He stepped to the side so he could see the congregation better. "Someone here needs to hear this. Maybe I need to say it. Maybe it's Cosette or Boone, though this wasn't in my original speech." He smiled and took a deep, long breath.

"The Lord loves each of us. I know it. I can feel it so deeply right now. Someone here might feel lost, or overlooked. Adrift. Wondering what the purpose of their life is. Where they should be going. Or doing. Or if they should be making a change at all. I don't know the answers for each of you personally, but I know Cosette and Boone, and I've seen such marvelous changes in each of them as they've fallen in love and been engaged this year."

He surveyed the crowd, and Cosette's eyes caught on Gerty's. Tears ran out of her right eye, and she made no move to wipe them. Cosette's chest trembled, and she wanted to go to the girl. Gerty did feel a little lost, especially now that Cosette would be a full-time fixture in her life. They'd gone for ice cream, and shopping for makeup, and to get their hair cut, and they'd talked about anything Gerty worried about.

Cosette had assured her over and over that she wouldn't become second. She wouldn't lose her dad. She was only gaining a mother.

Maybe she hadn't felt the truthfulness of that until now. Maybe she was still worried, and the Pastor's words could calm her. Or maybe she was simply missing her mom, and Cosette could respect that and give her the space she needed.

She sat beside Britt, who looked up at her with ten-year-old innocence. She hugged Gerty, who embraced her cousin as well.

Cosette looked to Keith, who had his head down. Matt wiped his eyes. Gloria did as well, despite trying to keep her five-month-old baby from crying.

In that moment, Cosette realized that the pastor had just spoken to *every* person in the room. Including her.

They *all* felt a little lost here on Earth, removed from God, from their heavenly home.

"I guess I just want to say—don't give up. The Lord knows you. He is aware of you. He will guide you, direct you, and preserve you, if you follow His voice." He nodded like something that powerful was easy, but Cosette knew it wasn't.

It had taken her fifteen years, and a loud, mouthy cowboy with a huge heart of gold for her to feel loved again.

Pastor Stone returned to his place and looked at Cosette and Boone. "All right. Are you two ready to get married?"

"Yes, sir," Boone yelled, and the whole barn laughed, Cosette included.

"I believe you wrote your own vows."

Boone cleared his throat and reached into his jacket pocket. He wore a deep, dark tuxedo, somehow specially tailored for his wide shoulders and slim waist. He'd shaved for today's wedding, and Cosette wanted to run her hand along the smooth skin on his face. She would. Tonight, after they were alone.

She shivered at the thought, but this time, it was a

good kind of shiver. The kind she didn't shutter out and close off.

"Cosette," he read from his paper. He looked at it and then her. It and her. He crumpled it in his fist. "I'm in love with you. I've been in love with you for a solid year, and I'm so glad this day is finally here. I will do my best to love you the way *you* need to be loved, support you the way *you* need me to support you, and cherish you the way *you* need to be cherished."

He leaned forward and brushed his lips along her cheek, to which Pastor Stone said, "We're not kissing yet, Boone."

More laughter came from Cosette's mouth, and while she'd written out her vows, she hadn't had anywhere in her dress to conceal them. Her dress hugged her bodice and shoulders, her waist and hips, only flaring when it reached just above her knees. She felt like a fairy mermaid in it, and she'd adored it from the moment she'd seen the lace and straps.

"Boone," she said, her voice strong and sure. She felt more like herself than she ever had, and she felt herself rising in height a couple of inches. Or maybe it just seemed that way internally. "You have made me want to be a better woman. I know I have not been easy on you with my demands for more time, more conversations, more distance between us. I am thankful the Lord blessed you with patience, kindness, and the biggest heart out of any man on the planet."

Boone's smile didn't diminish a single ounce, but he did shake his head, ducking it so the cowboy hat he wore obscured his face. She reached up and lifted his chin, the electricity between them as hot and instant as it had always been.

"I love you," she said, pouring everything she had into the words. "I will do my very best to be a good wife for you. Loving and supporting and firmly kind."

He chuckled, and she lowered her hand. He didn't look away from her again.

"I am dedicated to being the best mother for Gerty that I can be. I'm going to need a lot of help on that one, but I have the best partner in the world to do it—you."

He nodded now, his gaze strong and powerful.

"I appreciate your past and where you both come from, and I count myself lucky to get to be in your future."

Boone started to lean toward her again, and Pastor Stone said, "Okay, since we're heading for another kiss, I now pronounce you man and wife." He rushed the last several words, and they were almost unintelligible.

Boone laughed, the sound silencing as he pressed his mouth to Cosette's. It wasn't a good kiss. It wasn't sensual and hot the way some of theirs had been.

It was the best kiss of her life, because it sealed her to him, and him to her, and from this moment on, they'd get to be a family.

# Thirty-Six

TRAV PULLED UP TO POPPY'S FARMHOUSE, glared at the sky, and jumped out to go help her with the luggage. "It's supposed to be spring," he said as thunder growled in the sky.

"Mother Nature missed the memo." Poppy bumped a suitcase down the last steps on the porch before Travis arrived.

"Let me," he said, and she did. He loved that about her now. She asked for his help, and she truly wanted it. She wasn't just giving him tasks to do to make him feel important. She had, at first. He'd called her on it, and she'd gone to see her counselor, and she'd gotten better.

Steele came outside too, and Travis hurried to get all of their luggage and backpacks, purses and bags of snacks into the truck before the storm started. Thankfully, they were headed south, where there was no snow in the forecast in Phoenix.

It was a long drive—over thirteen hours—but they weren't doing it in one day. He and Poppy wanted to travel together, and he knew this was his final test before she might be ready to tell him yes when he got down on both knees. Truth be told, Travis wanted to get Poppy off her farm too.

He knew her here. He knew how she operated, and he could've predicted the way she ran back up the steps to double-check that the front door had gotten locked. As she came back down to the sidewalk, he said, "Dorothy is going to be fine."

"I just worry about her," she said, looking over her shoulder, though the donkey couldn't be seen.

"I put her in the stable myself," he said. "You should've seen her; flirting with all the other horses. Mares and geldings." He laughed, and to his relief, Poppy did too.

"She's noisy."

"The stables aren't by the house, honey." He guided her to his truck. "Now, come on. You haven't had a vacation in seven years, and we're going to have an amazing Spring Break in the sunshine."

He'd survived another winter in Colorado by the skin of his teeth. In all honesty, probably because of Poppy and Steele. He loved seeing them in the evenings, even if it was to sweep her deck or haul in a load of firewood. Or to help get an errant chicken out of the mud, or to talk to Dorothy while his fingers, toes, and nose froze in the winter air.

He'd gladly suffer through winter after winter with Poppy at his side.

A fat snowflake landed on the windshield as he closed her door. He darted around the truck, determined to outdrive this storm. He jumped in and buckled, saying, "Let's hit the road." He looked in the rearview mirror and smiled at Steele. "Buckled in, bud?"

"Yep." He snapped his belt across his chest and went back to his video game. Travis didn't try to make the boy talk. He did plenty at other times, and Travis looked over to Poppy, who rolled her eyes.

He took her hand, smiling, and kissed the back of it. "Ready, sweetheart?"

"So ready."

Travis let his gaze linger on her for a moment. He'd looked up jewelry stores in Phoenix, after the one time they'd talked about getting married. One time, a few weeks ago. He wanted to see what he could learn from her now, and if her position had changed on the status of their relationship.

"This is a road trip," he said casually.

"Sure is." Poppy kept her voice just as casual and nondescript.

"You said we just needed to see how the road trip went, and then we might be able to put a date on the calendar." He glanced at her as he looked behind him, though there wouldn't be anyone there. No one lived down this way, and no one would've followed him here.

"Did I?"

Travis chuckled and said, "You most certainly did."

Poppy grinned at him as he got the truck moving along the highway. He flipped on the windshield wipers to clear the precipitation. It hovered between rain and snow, a horrible, wet slushy sleet, and he really wanted to be out of it.

"Well, 'went' implies that the road trip is over, and we're evaluating it."

"Maybe we could just talk about a wedding then," he said. "Like, what does that look like for you?" She'd told him precious little, and Travis really wanted to give her everything she wanted. "And, uh, I don't really think I need to say it, but I'm going to say it. Money's no obstacle. So if you had all the money in the world, and you were planning your wedding, what would that be like?"

He looked at her with hope, and the flirty smile on her face had faded into a different kind. One with joy and wonder and happiness. "I know this might be kind of silly," she said. "But I love my farm so much." She met his eye, but he couldn't hold her gaze for long. This highway may be mostly abandoned, but the weather wasn't cooperating. "I'd love to be married there."

"Okay," he said. "With Dorothy as your Maid of Honor?"

Popppy laughed, which made Travis smile. "Definitely," she said between the giggles. "And Elora, of course."

"Of course."

Her sister had had her baby a couple of weeks ago, and Poppy had spent countless hours there, helping her with the nursery, with breastfeeding, with making dinner. Travis didn't mind so much, because he got fed too, and it was only another twenty minutes of driving. He was glad to have her right next door again.

"There's a really big cake," she said, her eyes drifting closed. "And it's made of all white frosting and red roses and bark."

"Did you make it?" he asked.

"No," she said. "My dress isn't white, but it's blue. Pale, dusty blue, like that first hint of sky in the morning when the summer sun comes up. You know that moment?" She opened her eyes and looked at him.

He fell in love with her all over again, the wonder and excitement on her face more than he could take. "I know it," he whispered.

"Like that." Her voice lowered too. "And you're there, and it's summertime, and we have an evening wedding, where we serve dinner afterward to all of our family and friends."

"With lemonade?"

"So much lemonade," she said. "I don't make the dinner, Trav. Someone caters it, but it's really nice. Meat and potatoes nice. Steak. Lobster if you want. Really high-end food."

"You're making me hungry," he teased, but the majority of him really loved this picture she painted for him.

"We won't eat at the farm. We'll only get married there. But we'll eat somewhere really fancy, with chandeliers in the ceiling and a dancefloor for after dinner. You'll set the playlist to all your favorite country music, and we'll dance for a while before we sneak away on our honeymoon." She glowed now, and Travis really wished he wasn't driving. He'd like to kiss her, and he told himself he'd have the opportunity later.

"And where's that?" he asked.

"In the summertime?" She cocked her head and watched the road in front of them. "You know, I don't know." She threaded her fingers through his. "You've traveled more than me. Where would you go in the summertime for a honeymoon?"

"Europe," he said. "A river cruise. Italy and Germany and France. It would be amazing."

"It sounds amazing." Poppy sighed, and the silence enveloped them. Travis liked it, and he drove while Poppy looked at her phone, Steele played his video games, and the country music played on the radio.

This was a good life, and Travis sure was glad to be living it.

———

"Go on," he said to Steele a couple of days later. "Go find a friend." He dropped the bag Poppy had handed him from the back of the truck. The house they were renting had three bedrooms, so they each got their own. She'd packed lunches for all of them, and Travis turned to go help her with the cooler.

He and Steele had found a shady spot in the park, and the twelve-year-old now ran toward the splash pad. Travis prayed, "Help him find someone to have some fun with today."

He wasn't sure, because he hadn't asked, but Steele didn't seem to have a lot of friends. He didn't have boys his age over to the farmhouse much, but he spent his afternoons and evenings with his mother, Travis, and the animals on the farm. He sometimes played with Deacon and Tucker, Gray's boys, but not often enough for Travis to think they were good friends.

Nothing had come between him and Jane, of course. Travis wasn't even sure the boy still had his innocent crush on her. Probably not. At that age, those things came and went like lightning.

He took the cooler from Poppy just as her phone chimed. It sounded like a cha-ching with a high-pitched flourish, and he asked, "What was that?"

"I have no idea." She tugged her phone out of her shorts pocket and looked at it as she walked beside him to the shade. He'd just set the cooler on the ground at the base of the tree when she sucked in a gasp. "Oh, my goodness." She looked up, her eyes brighter than he'd ever seen them. "I sold The Traveler."

Travis's eyes widened too. "You did?" He rushed to her side and peered down at her phone. He wasn't sure what he was looking at, other than an amount of money for the custom piece Poppy had done with a couple of chainsaws and one of the bigger logs she'd salvaged from the trees that had blown over last fall.

She'd wanted to carve it, and she'd had his feet flow down into the stump so the art could stand on its own. She'd posed it in her own garden—both vegetable and flower—and listed it on a local artist's board in Ivory Peaks.

The Traveler had been sitting there for at least three months, unsold.

"And they want more," she said excitedly. She'd sawed out three more pieces, but she hadn't put any of them up for sale yet. "Trav, this is incredible." Her fingers flew across the screen as she started messaging with the buyer.

"Sure is," he said. He wouldn't be lying if he said he'd like something Poppy could do from home. She liked working for Elise, and she was very good at landscaping and mowing grass, but she came home exhausted and still had more work to do.

If they had kids....

Travis shelved the thought. He hadn't asked her to

marry him, though in his opinion the road trip was going very well. They'd had a great three days so far, this one being their first full day in Phoenix.

The sun shone hotly overhead, and Travis set up the chairs they'd found in the rental. He sat and reached into the bag for sunscreen. His skin tanned like leather, but he still tried to protect it whenever he could.

"Come sit down, sweetheart," he said. " You're going to burn."

She did, barely looking at him. She finally looked up a couple of seconds later. "Did you spray Steele?"

"No." He stood and whistled through his teeth. Steele turned toward him, and Travis waved him in. The boy came running, water droplets flying from his wet hair.

"What?"

"You need sunscreen," he said, and then Travis proceeded to get the boy covered.

"There's a boy named Chuck out there." Steele panted from the run. "He's eleven, and he has a twin sister. Her name is Nellie."

"That's great," Travis said. He rubbed the lotion into Steele's back. "Arms up." The boy did what he said, still so much like a child. Once he was covered, Travis sent him back out onto the splash pad.

He sank back into his seat, and Poppy pocketed her phone. She said nothing, but the excitement built within her. "How many did you sell?" he asked.

"All of them." She burst out laughing. "Trav, I sold all

of them!" She threw herself into his arms, and he laughed with her as she settled into his lap. She wrapped her arms around his shoulders and sighed. "And guess what?"

"I'm dying here," he said.

She smiled at him, so much happiness pouring from her. "They want me to come do a carving of a tree that was struck by lightning. It's still standing—well, partially—" She rolled her head back and forth. "And they want me to carve it into a piece of art, right there in their front yard."

Travis beamed up at her. "That sounds like your dream job."

"Right?" She looked toward the splash pad. "And Trav...what if it can be?"

"What do you mean?"

"I mean, what if this is what I do? I work the farm with you and Steele, and I get to do chainsaw tree art around the Denver area." She wouldn't look at him, which was how Travis knew the idea still existed in its infancy in her mind.

"That's an interesting thought," he said, hoping she'd go on.

"I have a degree in horticulture," she mused. "I can evaluate the life and health of the tree. Then I can shape it into something beautiful, even though it's been broken." Her voice faded. "Even though it's been damaged. Even though it's been hurt, and malformed, and other people might just cut it down and cut their losses."

Travis nodded along with her. After the first sentence, he didn't think she was talking about trees, but herself. "Maybe what Pastor Stone said at Boone's and Cosette's wedding was meant for you."

"Maybe." Poppy would stew on it in her head for a while. She'd talk to him eventually, once she thought she had all the pieces fitted where they belonged.

"You have the chainsaws."

"Yes."

"You have a client now."

"I've sold the four pieces."

"So you've started," he said. "Maybe you see where it will go, like us. Like the way we did."

She looked at him again, and Travis stretched his neck to kiss her. "I love you, Poppy. If you want to carve sculptures out of injured trees, I will support you." He thought of what Boone had said in his vows.

*I will do my best to support you the way* you *need me to support you.*

That was what he wanted to do with Poppy. If that meant with money, he was okay with it. Time, fine. Love, guidance, acceptance, advice—all fine with him.

Poppy didn't like to be pushed to talk about something, or to tell him things she wasn't ready to vocalize, so he didn't press the issue.

Only one question kept coming to his mind while they watched Steele splash, run, and yell with the other kids several yards away. He swallowed, but it wouldn't go away.

"Poppy," he said.

"Mm?" She turned toward him and then stood up.

He took her hand into his. "Will you go look at diamonds with me tomorrow?"

Her eyes widened. "Here?"

"Yes," he said. "Here. I think people get engaged in Phoenix, just like they do in Ivory Peaks." He smiled at her. "I want you. I want to be with you and Steele on the farm. I want to be your husband, and I want you to be my wife." He stemmed the flow of words and swallowed. "If it's too early, that's fine. I just want you to know how I'm feeling, and I want to be engaged." He dropped his head and kicked off his flip flops to let his toes be free in the grass. "If you're envisioning a summer wedding, sweetheart, are we talking this year or next summer?"

If she said next summer, Travis might die. He could do it, but it would be hard on him.

Poppy's fingers in his tightened. "We better go look at diamonds tomorrow."

His gaze flew up to hers. "Yeah?"

She smiled down at him, and he pulled her back onto his lap. He kissed her, and she didn't have to confirm for a second time. Her kiss said, "Yeah," in a way her voice couldn't.

# Thirty-Seven

POPPY SWITCHED THE LAUNDRY FROM THE washer to the dryer, wondering when it would end. She and Steele had been home from their Spring Break road trip to Phoenix for a couple of days, but every time one of them went out onto the farm—so each of them at least twice per day—they came back with mud on their pants. Usually their hands as well, but those washed up in the sink.

Trav said he'd been running his machines constantly too, as was everyone in the state who owned farms or ranches, as snow had fallen for a few days while they'd been out of state, but now the spring sunshine had melted it all into muck.

That chore done, Poppy stirred the simmering soup on the stove, thinking this would probably be the last time she made soup until autumn, and then she faced the back door again. She'd been out to check on her cattle who'd given birth earlier this year, and she had one horse who'd gone into his spring colic early.

She really just needed to check the goats and then visit with Dorothy. She pulled on her jacket, drew a breath, and went outside. She'd sprayed the deck down yesterday afternoon, but more muddy tracks had been left. Steele had gone to his scouting meeting that night, and one of the other parents would bring him home in about a half-hour. Which meant Poppy had thirty minutes to figure out how to get Trav to ask her to marry him.

She knew he wanted to. They'd spent a lot of their trip to Phoenix talking about weddings, proposals, and diamonds. While Steele played video games in the rental, Trav had snuck her to a jeweler, and they'd looked at rings. He hadn't bought anything, and now that they'd completed their first road trip together, Poppy had checked off all of her requirements.

They'd gotten along well on the trip, even when Steele whined for double hot dogs at the baseball game and then hadn't eaten both of them. When she got upset with her son, Trav balanced her. When he looked blankly at the boy, Poppy knew just what to do.

Now that they'd been dating for almost a year, Poppy felt like she had a good grip on how to be half of a couple, half of a parenting unit, and still be herself.

"Dorothy," she called, and the donkey brayed in response. She came tromping through the mud, and she didn't care at all that it splashed up on her forelegs, where Poppy's cuffs and pantlegs would've been.

"Hee-haw, eee-haw," she said, plowing right into Poppy's outstretched palm.

"Yes, I'm here." She smiled at her and stroked her ears back. "I just saw you this morning." She peered down at the donkey. "Have the horses been tormenting you?" She looked to the paddock next door, but none of the other equines could be seen. They weren't dumb, and they'd make themselves scarce if they thought Poppy might lecture them.

She looked west and hoped Trav would make an appearance. "Should I just tell him I'm ready to get engaged?" Surely Trav had to know. She stood with Dorothy for several minutes, the two of them listening to the sounds of the farm in the spring evening.

"Well, I have to go check the soup," she told Dorothy. "You've got dinner, and I'll see you in the morning."

She turned and she saw Trav walking toward her. He carried the biggest, brightest assortment of flowers Poppy had ever seen, and the bright orange from the daisies filled her soul with delight. "Hey," she called.

He grinned at her from beneath that sexy cowboy hat. "Are you talkin' to Dorothy?"

"Yep."

The donkey started calling and nickering to Trav, because she loved him too. It really helped that he always seemed to have a candy or plum in his pocket. He chuckled as he reached the pair of them. "Yes, hello, Dorothy." He gave her a healthy scratch, the flowers tipping as he held them with one hand.

Poppy eyed them, so glad to see him. "Are those for me?"

He took the blooms into both hands. "Yes, ma'am." He held them for her while she leaned forward to smell them.

"I love the brightly colored flowers."

"She put in some of the green tulips. You love those." He touched one of them, and Poppy ran her fingertip along the petals too.

"I do." She whispered the words, the meaning of them not lost on her. "It's not my birthday." That had been a couple of months ago, and Trav had done everything exactly right that day. Mornings were some of her busiest times, and he'd been at the farmhouse when she'd gotten out of bed.

He got Steele off to school, and he'd made her Belgian waffles with fruit and cream and powdered sugar. He'd purchased her a really expensive blender, which she was fixing to use to make tonight's soup as smooth as possible.

She'd baked him a cake made of all the finest chocolates on his birthday, and she'd snuck over to his cabin long after Steele had gone to sleep to eat it with him. She'd only stayed for a few minutes, because her son was home alone, but she'd enjoyed tasting her cake on his lips.

"I saw them at the market," he said. "And they reminded me of you, so I got them for you."

She took them from him and buried herself in the fragrance of the flowers. "I love them. Thank you."

"I got two rounds of sourdough too," he said. "They'll go with the soup, and you guys can have your sandwich party this weekend." He grinned at her, his hand sliding along her waist easily. He drew her against him as much as he could with the bulging blooms between them.

She smiled up at him. "You're staying for dinner, right?"

"Do I ever not stay for dinner?" He leaned down and kissed her, the movement slow and steady and perfect. "Cord's here," he whispered. "He stayed at the house, though, because I have something very important to talk to you about."

He straightened, his throat moving as he swallowed. Poppy found him adorable when he got nervous, but she wondered what he could possibly have to be anxious about. He held up a ring—a diamond ring with a bright gold band.

"I'd get down on both knees," he said. "But this is my last pair of clean jeans, and I don't want them to get all muddy."

"Get down on both knees!"

They turned to see Cord standing on the edge of the gravel, not committing to getting dirty by stepping into the muddy area.

Trav chuckled, and Cord waved his hand and held up his phone. Poppy couldn't help laughing, but her own pulse danced and pounded. Trav was asking her to marry him. She wanted to blurt out "Yes!" right now, but he wouldn't like that.

"Fine." Travis dropped to both knees. "Wow, that's colder than I thought it would be."

Poppy giggled and held her flowers in front of her. "You really don't have to do this."

"Dorothy." He looked over to the donkey. Her name sent her into another fit of braying, and when she stopped, Trav said, "She said I did. So." He held up the ring again, and it had the big, bright white square-cut diamond she liked, and she really had no idea how much something like that cost.

"I love you, Miss Poppy Harris," he said. "I'd kneel in mud for you every day of the week if you needed me to. I love your son, and I want to be his dad and your husband. I've wanted to live and work on this farm for months now, and you'd do me the biggest favor if you said yes to bein' my wife."

"Hee-haw!" Dorothy punctuated the proposal perfectly.

Poppy leaned forward and touched her mouth to his. "Yes," she whispered. "I can't wait to be your wife."

Trav slid the ring onto her finger with steady hands, and he used the rungs on the fence to help himself get back to his feet. Then he took the flowers and held them over his head, effectively blocking them from the camera on Cord's phone. He kissed her, every stroke of his mouth against hers testifying of everything he'd just said.

He pulled away after several seconds and said, "I can't hold my arm like this." He chuckled, and Poppy did too, burying her face in his chest as he lowered his arm.

"I love you," she said quietly. She lifted her eyes to his. "I love you so much, Trav. I want you here on this farm, with me and Steele, as soon as possible."

"So what are we lookin' at?" he asked. "June?"

It was a third of the way through April now, and Poppy thought she could probably pull off a wedding in a couple of months. "Let me see who I can get to cater the dinner and make the cake," she said. "Then we'll see."

"I'd marry you tomorrow," he said. "Tonight, in these muddy jeans, if you wanted to."

She grinned at him and stroked her hands down both sides of his face. "I'd marry you tomorrow too," she said. "I love you, I want you, and I can't wait to be yours."

He smiled, as she'd just said all the things he liked to hear. He kissed her again, and Cord whooped, but Poppy didn't care. He said, "I'll go pull the soup off the stove," and the faint sound of his footsteps retreating met her ears.

She met Trav's eyes, and both of them smiled like fools. She wanted to kiss him for a good long while still, and with Cord here, someone would be there for Steele when he got home. Dinner could wait.

What couldn't was kissing Trav, and Poppy did that.

# Epilogue

CORD BEHR DROPPED HIS HANDS AND LOOKED AT himself in the mirror. Trav had helped him put it up on the back of his door in the cabin, and Cord looked absolutely miserable.

He was absolutely miserable to be losing his cabinmate and best friend to marriage. He told himself for the tenth time that day—"He's going to be next door. You have his number. You can call or text him anytime."

Then he hitched a smile to his face and left his bedroom. Gray Hammond hadn't hired anyone else to take Trav's place yet, so Cord would live alone until he did. To be honest, Cord wasn't looking forward to it. He didn't like being alone, because then his thoughts could come in and take over, and he never liked where they went very much.

He much preferred staying busy. Engaged in conversation or work with others around over being by himself or alone with his thoughts. Enrolling in school for the past year had helped a lot with that, and Cord had really enjoyed his first year of technical training to become a ranch equipment repairman.

He loved working outside. He drew calm energy from the animals around him. He liked the cowboy way and the good feelings he got by hanging around with good people. That was why having Trav all moved out already made his smile turn upside down before he'd taken the three steps down the hall to the kitchen.

Trav turned from the sink, and he grinned instantly at Cord. That brightened Cord's spirits slightly, and he smiled too. "Wow," Trav said. "Look at you."

"It's nothing more than I wear to church." Cord tugged on the end of his sleeve, because it wasn't quite right.

"It's completely different with a jacket," Trav said as he approached. "You look so old. So refined."

"You're the one pushing fifty," Cord joked.

Trav burst out laughing, but he didn't deny it. He also wasn't pushing fifty, though technically, if someone wanted to round up from forty-three, they wouldn't land on fifty...something Trav had told Cord in the past when he'd joked about his age.

Cord was twenty-six now, and still as lost as ever. *Not*

*true*, he told himself as Trav brushed his hand down the front of his jacket.

"You look fantastic," Trav said. "A real best man." He drew Cord into a hug, and Cord gripped him tightly. Trav knew Cord didn't want him to leave the Hammond Family Farm. He was literally five minutes away, but Cord couldn't shake the feeling that everything was about to change.

Of course it was. Trav was marrying Poppy today, and they'd start their new life together.

"You'll still read to me in the evenings, right?" Cord asked, his voice so broken. "I'll come to you."

"Every night if you need me to," Trav said. He pulled back, and Cord dropped his chin to his chest. He wasn't wearing his cowboy hat yet, and he didn't want Trav to see him crying. The man felt like a father to him—what a real father should be like—and Cord had told him that in the past.

"You're going to be okay here, Cord," Trav said, his bass voice slow and serious. "You're a good man."

Cord nodded, because he desperately wanted to believe Trav. "I'm trying."

"That's all that matters," Trav said. "Gray knows you, and he knows what you need. Don't worry so much about who he puts in the cabin with you."

"I might move in with Mission." At least Cord knew Mission, and he wouldn't have to start all over getting to know someone. His past experiences had taught him that even when he'd grown up with a person, he didn't really know them.

He saw life through so many colors now, and he was slow to connect with people because he didn't trust them. He and Trav had gotten off to a great start, and they had a stellar friendship. Cord didn't want to lose that.

He wouldn't. It would just change, and Cord could handle change. God had certainly thrown plenty of that at him in his short lifetime.

"You could," Trav said. "But maybe see how it goes here first." He smiled at Cord as he raised his eyes from the ground. "I don't even recognize you from when you first started here." He raised his eyebrows. "You've changed that much. All right?"

"Yes, sir," Cord whispered.

Trav shook his head good-naturedly. "Don't call me sir." He picked up his keys from the counter. "Come on. We best be gettin' over to the farm."

"Poppy didn't want you to come help?"

"She said she didn't need me," Trav said, his voice steady and even. "She wants it all to be a surprise."

Cord nodded and followed his friend out of the cabin. They loaded up and drove the dirt roads to the highway, then went down about a mile, and hit Poppy's dirt lane. Bright blue, yellow, and white balloons drifted in the summer evening breeze, and Cord smiled at them.

He wasn't sure when he'd lost the innocence of his youth, when balloons floating on the air personified the simple things in life. The celebration of a baby or a wedding. The joy of a birthday party. The wonder of helium.

Trav pulled into Poppy's driveway, which had the far post holding down another bundle of balloons, and a big sign with a big red arrow on it pointing people further down the lane. Everything in Poppy's yard always looked absolutely amazing, and this summer was no different. Her roses, tulips, and other flowers bloomed like they'd come up just for this mid-June wedding. The grass glowed an emerald green and had been clipped to a precise height. The front door on the farmhouse had been painted bright blue, and the whole house had been recently repainted a bright white.

Cord knew, because he'd helped Trav do it for a solid fortnight. Just the fact that a high school dropout now knew what a fortnight was told Cord how very far he'd come. He suddenly believed Trav, and he pulled down the hem of his jacket after getting out of the truck.

They went into the farmhouse, which boasted blessed air conditioning, and Cotton barked a couple of times to greet them. "Howdy, fella." Cord adored this dog, and he wondered if Gray would let him get a dog. His parole officer had liked that Cord was accountable to someone besides himself, and he'd encouraged Cord to continue to surround himself with people or things that required his constant care.

Then his focus wasn't so much on himself, but the horses who needed him. The cowboys relying on him. The plants which would die without his tender loving care.

Determined to ask Gray if he could get a dog, he straightened and followed Trav into the rear area of the farmhouse. Poppy wasn't anywhere to be seen, because she believed it was bad luck for the bride and groom to see each other before the ceremony. Trav stood at the island, where he and Cord had eaten lunch or dinner plenty of times, and read something.

Cord joined him, and Trav handed him the card after he'd finished.

*Trav - Don't come outside until the specified time. That's five fifty-seven, by the way. I'm synchronized with the clock on the stove.*

"Wow," Cord said, glancing up and looking at the clock. Trav had almost thirty minutes before he needed to be outside, and one look from Cord told him that it was going to be a long half-hour.

*Cord – I'd love your help ushering. You can come out any time you get here, but that'll leave Trav inside alone.*

"So she wants me to go out now." Cord looked back at the card.

*Trav – I made you a chocolate cream pie to pass the time. It's in the fridge. Just don't spill on your tuxedo, please.*

That was the whole note, and Cord looked up as Trav opened the fridge. He pulled out a full-sized pie, and Cord's mouth watered. "I've got to find a girlfriend who can cook," he said.

"Or a girlfriend at all," Trav teased.

Cord nodded, his smile cemented in place. He had very specific reasons he didn't date, but Trav and Poppy's happiness had shown him that perhaps he could have a future with someone too. Who, he didn't know. He worked a lot of hours at the farm, and he didn't mind them. Maybe he just wasn't ready yet.

Trav didn't bother to cut the pie. He simply opened a drawer opposite of Cord and pulled out a fork. He went straight into the pie, leaning over it in case something dropped off the utensil.

Cord chuckled, shook his head, and went to the back door. Poppy had gone so far as to tape a big piece of poster paper over the window, and Cord slipped outside while Trav took another bite of pie. The cowboy wouldn't ruin anything for Poppy on her wedding day, and she hadn't needed to make him a pie.

She'd done it because she loved him and wanted him to be happy.

Cord stalled only one step outside the farmhouse, an absolute wonderland opening up before him. He'd helped Trav re-stain the deck last week, and he'd done plenty of chores around this farm too. He'd never seen it look like this.

The grass in the back held chairs now, with an aisle down the middle of them. Trellises had been set up on the deck, with flowers braided through them. Streamers and lights hung from the tops, and Cord felt like royalty as he walked across the deck with all the décor around him.

Vines and garlands of bright orange daisies had been looped around the railing on the steps that went to the grass, and every chair had a white cloth over the back of it, with a bright blue bow on it.

The altar at the end of the aisle was a huge saddle atop an old metal barrel, and it looked like it had been aged to appear ancient. Cord loved the energy flowing from the ground itself, from the few guests who'd started to gather, and from the scent of flowers in the air.

"Cord," someone said, and he turned toward the weathered voice to face Poppy's father.

"Hello, sir." He shook the man's hand. "Poppy sent me out to usher."

"Guests should be arriving soon," Whit said. "Iris will tell you what to do." He indicated his wife. "Poppy's inside, and I'm supposed to go help Trav with a pie?" He looked a little confused, but Cord only smiled and nodded as he went to talk to Iris.

He didn't want to do anything to mess up Trav's wedding day either, and his smile became more and more natural with every person he interacted with.

Gray and his family arrived with about ten minutes to

spare, and Cord had been instructed to put them in the second row, behind Trav's sisters and their husbands, and his mother.

He did, smiling all the while. Jane caught his eye, and he ducked his head. His first instinct was to flirt with her, the same way he did everyone, but he would not allow himself to do it. He valued his job, he valued the trust Gray placed in him, and he valued his life more than flirting with her.

Jane, however, didn't seem to care about her father at all. She put her hand on Cord's arm and said, "You look great, Cord," before she went down the aisle and past her parents. She didn't look back at him, and Cord turned and walked away before he found himself in a horrible situation like what had happened in the shed last year.

Away from Jane, he could breathe better, and he continued to do what Poppy had asked him to until the flow of people arriving slowed. Almost every chair had been taken, but Cord didn't need one. He'd stand at the altar with Trav.

His phone buzzed, and he pulled it out. *It's five-fifty-seven*, Trav had said. *I need you in here.*

Cord dashed back toward the house, taking the steps to the deck quickly and hurrying inside.

"Let's go," Trav said. "It's supposed to be me and you and Steele." He faced the door. "And now we're one minute late."

———

Travis looked at Steele, who'd come downstairs about ten minutes ago. That was right when Poppy's father had gone down the hall to her bedroom, and Travis had figured out she had been back there the whole time he'd been eating pie.

"Ready, son?" he asked Steele, who nodded.

"Ready."

Travis took the boy's hand and smiled at Steele. "They're all gonna be staring at me," he said, swallowing.

"And you look great today," Cord said, swiping his hand along Travis's collar. "Well, now that I've gotten that collar to lay flat." He met Travis's eyes, and Travis nodded. He knew this wedding was not Cord's first choice of events for today. Travis worried about him the same way he worried over Steele, and he marveled that a person could feel so connected to someone who wasn't a blood relative.

His sisters had made the trip back to Ivory Peaks for his wedding, and his momma would fillet him alive if he put even part of his pinky toe out of line and upset Poppy's schedule. The wedding was supposed to take twenty minutes or so, and they had reservations for twenty-five at a fancy Italian restaurant at seven p.m. They absolutely could not be late to that, and Travis estimated they'd linger around the farm for a few minutes accepting congratulations and taking a few pictures.

He took a breath and stepped to the door. He opened it, letting in the evening breeze—which was hot, as it was summertime—and he led the way outside. The deck looked absolutely phenomenal in the new redwood stain he and Cord had done. "Wow," he said, looking up. "You guys have been busy."

"Mission came over and did them," Steele said, gazing up at the trellises too. "Mama and Grams did all the flowers. Elise did the lights."

Travis smiled at him. "What did you do?"

"I had to mow the lawn, and you should've seen my mother." He rolled his eyes. "She was out there with a ruler to make sure it wasn't longer than three inches."

Cord laughed, the sound drawing attention from the guests down in the backyard. Travis walked under the lights and the streamers, the flowers and the scented air, to the top of the steps. He smiled at everyone as Cord came up to his right side. With Steele on his left, and everyone smiling back at him, Travis felt like he'd landed in the absolute right place.

That made walking down the aisle easy, and Steele peeled off to sit with his grandfather while he and Cord waited at the altar with the pastor. Pastor Benson shook Travis's hand, and Travis touched his palm above his heart as his eyes met his mother's.

He noted the wide aisle, as well as how every end-seat held a woman holding a significant number of flowers. Something was up with that, and seeing as how Poppy adored flowers with her whole heart, Travis suspected she would gather those as she walked toward him.

His heart filled with love for the cowboys from the ranch where he worked. He'd kept the job, so he'd definitely be seeing Chris and Cord every single day. But he'd live here, and he'd do a lot more here, and he honestly didn't know how long he'd stay at the Hammond's. For now—that was what he knew.

Poppy hadn't kept her job with Elise's landscaping company this year, which meant she'd had more time to dedicate to her farm, her animals, and the wedding planning.

A gasp rose into the air, and Travis jerked his attention away from the guests and toward the deck. He expected to see Poppy there in her sky-blue dress. She hadn't told anyone but him she wasn't wearing white to the wedding, and he honestly expected quite the gossip to fly.

She wasn't there, however. Her father approached the steps, with Dorothy on a simple lead. The donkey had clearly been bathed, for her hair shone almost a gray-blue in the evening light. She brayed, which caused several people to laugh.

Travis did too, because he should've known Poppy couldn't marry him without involving Dorothy. Even if she hadn't detailed that part of her fantasy; he knew that donkey meant a great deal to her.

He'd been joking when he'd said the donkey would be her Maid of Honor, but apparently Poppy hadn't been.

Elora entered from the left side, and the three of them—Whit, Elora, and Dorothy waited, all eyes trained up on the deck.

The back door opened, and Poppy stepped out. She took great care to close the door and then arrange her dress before she took a single step, and Travis straightened so he could see past all the standing guests to his bride-to-be.

The photographer Poppy had hired moved around, going *click, click, click*, and Travis couldn't stop smiling. At least that would be in the pictures.

Poppy came into view, and a wave of murmurs flew through the crowd. Travis met her eyes when she paused at the top of the steps, and he bowed his head to her. She was stunning in that blue dress, which complimented her fair skin and blue eyes, and all the gems she'd pinned in her up-do.

She didn't wear shoes—but he only knew as she hitched up her dress and swung one leg over Dorothy. The donkey didn't wear a saddle, but she also didn't move a single inch as Poppy settled herself on her back. She seemed almost bored, her eyes halfway closed.

She nickered and called, and Poppy stroked the side of her neck, leaned down, and said something to her. Her dad turned Dorothy toward him, and Dorothy whinnied now.

He chuckled and said, "Go slow, Dorothy. I'm not goin' anywhere."

Whit led the donkey slowly down the aisle while Elora paused at the end of every row to collect the flowers. The bouquet got bigger and bigger, all of the flowers brightly colored in shades of orange, pink, blue, purple, and white.

Dorothy paused when she reached the first row, and Poppy slid off her back. She gave the donkey a hug, then embraced her father. He said something to her, and then Poppy stepped back. Her eyes shone like sapphires as she took the enormous bouquet from her sister and finally—finally—faced Travis.

"I am speechless," he said right out loud.

She shook her head, everything about her soft and wonderful. Travis's love for her doubled and overflowed, and as he tucked her hand into his arm, he thanked the Lord above for his good fortune in getting this woman to marry him.

———

POPPY COULDN'T HOLD the bouquet by herself. She'd known she wouldn't be able to, and she took Trav's right hand and guided it to the slipping stems. He buoyed up the side that she couldn't, and together, they managed to hold the bouquet in front of her.

The saddle and barrel were stunning, and she'd never imagined she'd get such a dreamy wedding. It wasn't the biggest one in Colorado. She'd heard tales of Hunter and

Molly's event, with hundreds of people and all of his uncles dancing down the aisle.

She had her son here, and she reached over and squeezed Steele's hand. Her parents. Her sister and brother-in-law and their baby. A couple of her closest friends from church. Everyone else in the audience came from Trav, and most of them Poppy adored too. All of them, actually.

They were taking the Hammonds and all the cowboys who worked the farm to dinner after this. Her family and Trav's, of course. Not the friends from church, and that was about all who'd come.

"Poppy and Travis," Pastor Benson said. "Marrying two amazing people is the highlight of my job." He clasped his hands together and beamed at them both. "I am honored to be here doing this for you."

"Thank you," Poppy murmured. She'd attended Cosette and Boone's wedding, and their pastor had said such wonderful things. They'd given beautiful vows. Neither Poppy nor Trav liked being in the spotlight very much, so when they'd met with Pastor Benson, they'd told him to say what he wanted.

Poppy had never thought of herself as a traditionalist, but she'd been learning more and more about herself. Turned out, she did like things to be a tad more traditional—her wedding dress notwithstanding.

She was actually surprised Iris hadn't fainted at the

sight of it, and she giggled internally at the thought of her step-mom doing so at her wedding.

"I want to join my voice to that of Poppy's and Travis's when I say welcome to this farm for the marriage of the two of them, before you and me and God Himself." Pastor Benson had a powerful voice, and he could project well. "It's such a beautiful evening out here, and it reminds me to get out into God's great outdoors more often."

Poppy did love her farm, and the silence that descended on them after his words meant so much to her. Behind her, Dorothy bumped her with her head, and she looked over her shoulder.

"Even Dorothy the donkey loves Poppy with her whole heart," Pastor Benson said with a chuckle. "Just like everyone gathered here to witness this union." He looked between the two of them again. "I've known Poppy Harris and her son Steele for a great many years. Twelve or thirteen, I believe."

Poppy nodded and let her smile soften. She couldn't keep it so wide, and her cheeks started to ache. She'd been very deliberate in her placement of the chairs today, and she'd personally tied every single bow after Elora had put a white drape over the chair. Her mom and daddy had been there since noon, helping to decorate, feed the animals, and take care of Steele.

"Travis is a newer figure in my life, but you know how you feel when you meet a giant of a man? That's how I feel around Travis. He's good to the core, and he exudes the air of one who knows who he is and what he wants and why he's here on the earth."

Poppy glanced at her almost-husband. He was good to the core, and describing him as a giant of a man felt so appropriate. She'd been cowed in his presence that day he'd brought the goats back, because his spirit was so tall and upright.

"Steele is a lucky boy to have Travis as a father, and I know Travis wants to be the best dad he can be for the boy."

"I do," Trav said, and Pastor Benson grinned at him.

"Come right here in the middle, Steele," Pastor Benson said.

Steele moved behind Poppy and came between her and Trav. He too grabbed onto some of the stems, and the three of them held them. "I always give a bit of counsel at every wedding I perform," the pastor said. "I think long and hard about it, and sometimes I don't know what I'm going to say until I'm standing right here. Today, I want to encourage the three of you to always hold tight to one another. Life will bring storms. There will be good times and bad times. Times of health and times of sickness. When we cleave to our families and loved ones, we don't have to weather those things alone. We are never alone when we're part of a family."

He nodded to Steele. "When you don't know what to do, Steele, I'd advise you to go to your parents.

Counsel with them. Talk to them. Allow them to help you."

Steele nodded back. "I will," he said somberly. Poppy sincerely hoped he would, once life wiped some of the innocence from his eyes.

"Travis, don't go to your cowboy friends about something in your marriage. Go to your wife." Pastor Benson looked at her. "Poppy, I've never known you to be a gossip. Not ever. But I have a suspicion you tell secrets to Dorothy that no one else gets to hear."

Poppy's heartbeat slowed and nearly stopped. She couldn't deny it, but she desperately wanted to deny it.

"That's okay," Pastor Benson said, grinning at her. "You look like I just told you every member of the congregation here is a ghost."

Several people laughed, Poppy included.

"But," Pastor Benson said. "I would encourage you to also tell Travis the things that trouble you. Dorothy will always love you, no matter what. Travis needs you to talk to him, include him, and confide in him. You do that, and I see many long years of happiness for the two of you."

Poppy gave a single nod, properly chastised. "Yes, sir," she said.

Pastor Benson clapped his hands together. "Okay, onto the nuptials." He focused on Poppy once more. "Poppy, will you have this man to be your husband; to live together in the holy covenant of marriage? Will you love him, comfort him, honor and keep him, in sickness and in health, and forsaking all others, be faithful to him so long as you both shall live?"

"I will," she said.

"Travis," he said. "Will you have this woman to be your wife; to live together in the holy covenant of marriage? Will you love her, comfort her, honor and keep her, in sickness and in health, and forsaking all others, be faithful to her so long as you both shall live?"

Travis looked right at her, his eyes a deep, dark mystery. "I will," he said, kicking a bit of light into them as he smiled.

"I now pronounce you, Poppy Marie Harris, and you, Travis McArthur Thatcher, husband and wife, by the power vested in me by the state of Colorado." He grinned at them and the whole crowd gathered in the backyard. "Join me in praying for this couple, for their health and safety, and for the longevity of their family."

"Amen," the people seated behind Poppy chorused, and then Pastor Benson's face took on a hint of giddiness.

"You may now kiss your bride," he said.

Travis turned toward her in one fluid motion, gathered all of the flowers into his hands and passed them off to his sisters. Before she knew it, he held her in his arms, his handsome face full of light and joy. "I love you, Miss Poppy," he whispered.

"I love you too," she managed to say before he kissed her, all of their friends and family cheering behind them.

———

Read on for a sneak peek at the next book in this family saga & Christian Romance series, **HIS FIFTH KISS**, to find out how things have been going on the Hammond Family Farm over the past 13.5 years - and find out who the hero and heroine are in the next book!

*Read it today by scanning the QR code below with your phone!*

# Sneak Peek: HIS FIFTH KISS, Chapter One

A PIECE THAT HAD BEEN KNOCKED LOOSE INSIDE Michael Hammond found the right place to be as the familiar pine trees lining the road went by. "I've missed Ivory Peaks," he said.

"Mm." His father drove, and Mike's memories ran at him fast and hard. He'd come to work this farm every summer since the age of twelve. He'd met a pretty girl here —Gerty—and he'd kissed her. His first kiss. Hers too.

They'd been real friendly for years, but the past two times he'd come back to the family farm, she hadn't been here. The first time, he'd tried to find out where she'd gone. Her father, who still worked for Uncle Gray, had said she was down in Texas, doing farrier school.

Gerty would always work with horses, Mike knew that. For some reason, he'd expected her to stay right here in Colorado, on his uncle's farm, and wait for him to get out of the military.

She hadn't, unless she was waiting at the familiar farmhouse around the bend in the road Mike knew by heart. His pulse jumped, but he told himself she wouldn't be there. Why would she be there? He hadn't spoken to her in thirteen and a half years, after that last summer after his senior year, when he'd gone to college and then enrolled in the Marines.

He'd become a helicopter pilot, just like he'd told his father he wanted to become. Now, at age thirty-one, he had to have his daddy drive him home after his honorable discharge from the military.

"Looks like they've got everyone in off the farm," Dad said as the big red barn where Molly, Mike's cousin-in-law, ran her children's equine therapy program. Stables and more barns, horse rings, paddocks, and pastures ran to the west, and across the wide pasture sat the farmhouse, as well as the generational house where Mike's grandfather had once lived.

He'd come back to the farm for his grandfather's last few days on earth, and then the funeral. Forty hours later, he'd been back in the Middle East, with completely different people and a completely different climate.

Oh, how he missed Colorado.

Dad rolled down his window, and the cheers and whistles of the cowboys and cowgirls gathered along the fence came in through the window. Mike's face heated, and he wanted to turn away.

"I don't need this," he murmured.

"They miss you," Dad said. "Be nice."

"I am nice, Dad." Mike used to swallow his tongue when his dad told him to be nice. Now, he didn't have to. He wasn't fifteen, or even twenty-five. He was a grown man, and just because he had a hurt shoulder right now didn't mean he needed to be lectured by his daddy about how to be nice. "I just don't know any of them that well."

"You know Matt," Dad said, his voice aged and gravelly. Mike hadn't gotten married yet, but his younger brother Easton had. Mike had come home for that too, and he'd been back in Coral Canyon for about four months, recovering. But now that summer had arrived, Dad had brought him to the farm.

Always the farm.

"Oh, there's Elise," his mom said from the back seat.

Mike saw his Aunt Elise, and she'd aged gracefully. She was far younger than Dad or Uncle Gray, and she still wore pretty sundresses that made her seem more youthful than she was. None of Uncle Gray's younger kids had gotten married, though Jane had been engaged for about eight months last year.

He caught sight of Hunter, and a dose of extreme guilt punched Mike in the gut. "Dad," he said, but he couldn't get his voice to say anything else. He knew he'd disappointed his father by joining the military instead of coming back to the greater Denver area to take over the family company.

Hunter had been running it for close to seventeen years now, and he and Molly had four children. Mike had looked up to Hunter for his entire life. He couldn't see himself anywhere near Hunter's stature in only ten more years, which was how many years older Hunt was than Mike.

He wouldn't be married with four kids in ten years. He wouldn't be running the huge family company, with a beautiful wife running her own business. He wouldn't own this farm, live in this beautiful farmhouse, or have any of the serenity or happiness Hunt had.

In truth, Mike was absolutely miserable.

*That's not the right word*, he thought as Dad brought the truck to a stop. He rolled up the window, and Mike waited patiently for his mother to come help him unbuckle his seatbelt. He hated this part, and he locked his jaw while Momma opened the door.

Their eyes met, and Mike did his best to put a smile on his face. "Thanks, Momma."

"I know you hate this," she said, reaching across his lap to undo the belt. "But I have a really good feeling about this summer." She gave him a smile. "Easton and Allison will be here in a couple of weeks, and Opal has a week or two off from her residency, and she just told me she'd come to the farm."

She smiled at Mike like this was just fabulous news,

and Mike supposed it was. He really just wanted to be shown to his cabin; he wanted to close the door behind him; he wanted to be alone.

As the cowboys who'd cheered for him crowded around the truck, Mike didn't think he'd be alone for at least a few hours. Aunt Elise had likely been cooking for hours—days, even—and Mike stayed in his seat as his mother stepped back.

*Lord*, he thought, but he couldn't finish the prayer. He didn't know what to say anyway, and he realized that he wasn't miserable.

He was lost.

"Come on, son," Daddy said, and Mike slid out of the truck and landed on his feet. He could walk just fine. His right shoulder just didn't work anymore, and no amount of therapy, painkillers, surgery, or prayer had healed him.

He hadn't given up, but he didn't know where else to turn. Thus, when his parents had suggested they come to the farm for the summer, Mike hadn't had any reason they shouldn't.

"Mikey," Uncle Gray said, and Mike didn't have the heart to tell him he didn't go by that nickname anymore. He was an officer in the Marines, and he hadn't been Mikey for over ten years.

Uncle Gray grinned at him, every strand of hair on his face and head the color of his name. He pulled Mike into a hug, and Mike put his good arm around his uncle. For some reason, his eyes burned with tears, and he clung to

Uncle Gray so no one would see until he could compose himself.

"Welcome home, son," Uncle Gray said, and when he stepped back, Mike actually felt like he'd come home. His cousins came to greet him, and then the cowboys. Mike did his best to smile and laugh with all of them.

Cord Behr was still here. Travis Thatcher. Cosette and Boone. Matt and Gloria. Keith and Britt hugged him simultaneously, and Mike felt a new kind of kinship move through him with the Whettstein kids. Keith was only a year older than him, and Mike looked him in the eye.

"You're here," he said.

"Yeah." Keith nodded. "Been back about two years?" He looked at his father. "Almost three, I guess."

To Mike's knowledge, Keith wasn't married either, and he suddenly didn't feel so alone.

"I'm a counselor here now," Britt said, her absolutely bright personality exactly the same as it had been as a child. She was tall and billowy, with long, thin limbs, and bright blonde hair, a pair of blue eyes to go with it.

She reminded him slightly of Gerty, and Mike found himself looking around for her. It seemed like the news of his return to the Hammond Family Farm had reached far and wide, and perhaps Gertrude Whettstein would be here.

He didn't want to ask Keith or Britt, so he walked with them toward the steps that led to the porch. Aunt Elise hugged him and put an arm around him. "Come eat," she said, smiling all the while. Aunt Elise was the epitome of kindness, and his mother had been best friends with her for decades.

He didn't want anyone to feel sorry for him, but he couldn't hide the sling his arm sat in. He didn't want eyes on him, but everyone stared at him. He did his best to talk to everyone, eat everything his aunt and mother put in front of him, and laugh with as much authenticity as he could muster.

After an hour, he met his father's eyes, and Dad stood up from the table where he'd been sitting with Hunt and Uncle Gray. "Let's go see the horses," he said, and he opened his arm for Mike to step into.

He nodded and did just that. Dad went outside with him, but he didn't come down the steps with Mike. "You go on," he said, and Mike didn't hesitate. He walked the length of the fence alone, his steps somewhat halting because he couldn't swing his right arm.

"Mike!"

He turned and found Jane jogging toward him. She made him smile, and he laughed as she reached him and threw her arms around him. She wasn't careful with him, and Mike appreciated that. Sometimes his parents looked at him like their eyes alone would shatter him. Jane didn't treat him like that, and he hugged her hard with his left arm.

"There's so many people inside." She exhaled and ran

her hands down the front of her body. "So many questions."

"Tell me about it," Mike said. They started walking again, and he didn't want to start in on the questions for Jane either. "Are you staying here for the summer?"

"Uh, yeah," Jane said, her voice pitching up. She exhaled again. "I just quit my job actually. I'm starting at HMC next week. Accounting."

"You're kidding." Mike felt like someone had hollowed out his chest. "That's great, Jane."

"Do you really think so?" She looked at him, and Mike cut her a glance out of the corner of his eye.

"I mean, it makes me feel like a loser, but yeah. It's great."

"You're not a loser," she said quietly but with plenty of emphasis. "You're an amazing pilot, and you served your country for almost eight years." Every word she spoke filled him with more confidence. "Just because you don't get a check from HMC doesn't mean you're not amazing."

Mike wanted to show her his dysfunctional arm; he wanted to argue; he wanted to tell her all his fears. He didn't say anything as they continued toward the barn.

"You datin' anyone?" he asked.

"Oh, now you sound like my mother," Jane said dryly.

Mike laughed. "At least she's askin'. My momma knows everything I do, all day long. Every day." He needed space, and the wide open sky, and to get lost in these mountains. His soul settled as a pretty bay horse looked his way.

Jane's phone rang, and she said, "Speak of the devil." She answered the call and said, "Yes, Momma, I just got here." She rolled her eyes at Mike and went back the way she'd come. "I'll be right in."

Mike smiled at her back, because Jane could be a touch overdramatic sometimes. She was a genius with figures and numbers, and she knew exactly who she was. That was why she'd called off her wedding only five weeks before the I-do's, and why she could quit a good job and go to work at HMC.

He went down the footpath between the administration barn and the pasture, his goal the very last stable. He surely wouldn't know any of the horses here at Pony Power now, but his pulse settled into a slower rhythm as he approached the bay at the fence.

"Hey," he said, reaching to let the horse smell him. The animal ducked his head and nosed Mike's shoulder. "Yeah," he said. "It's not really working right now. I can't ride you or anything." He gave the bay a sad smile. Mike couldn't drive. He couldn't ride a horse. He couldn't do a lot of things, and he had the distinct thought that he needed to start learning how to do things one-handed, because his shoulder wasn't ever going to be all the way better.

He didn't want to accept that, and he left the bay at the fence and headed for the far stables. Maybe he could lead a horse out to the remote cabin where he'd first kissed Gerty.

The pasture beyond the last stable held several horses, all of them spread out and dotting the area. He put one foot up on the bottom rung and watched them graze. A couple of them looked at him, and a deep, dark black horse came plodding toward him.

Mike smiled at it, but the horse didn't seem to be looking at him. It nickered and called, and Mike twisted to look over his shoulder.

"Mikey."

When Gertrude Whettstein said his teenage nickname, Mike didn't mind at all. He could only stare at the woman standing twenty feet from him. She wore jeans, and she was just as straight up and down as she'd always been. Thin and lithe, strong and sexy, and he wasn't embarrassed he'd thought that.

She wore her dirty blonde hair in a ponytail high on top of her head, and she tucked her hands in her back pockets, her bony elbows poking out to the sides as she studied him.

He turned fully and stumbled toward her. "What are you doing here?"

Something hard crossed her face. "Am I not allowed to be here?"

"No, it's just—just—" He couldn't find the words. "I —the last couple of times I've been here, you haven't been."

"I've been in Texas," she said. "Montana. Up in Calgary. Around." She shrugged one shoulder, and Mike sure did like her blue and white tank top. It was simple and beautiful, which was Gerty through and through.

"How long are you going to be here?" he asked.

Gerty looked across the pasture, her shoulders and chest lifting with a big breath. "I don't rightly know."

Mike grinned, the world suddenly brighter and more open than it had been five minutes ago. "You don't *rightly know*?" he teased. He'd never heard her talk like that before.

She faced him again, a smile flickering against her lips. Gerty fought against giving him that grin, something she'd done in the past. She'd present him with it eventually, and Mike moved toward her until he stood only a pace away.

"Go out with me," he said, feeling braver and stronger than he had since his helicopter had gone down.

"You don't even know if I'm single," she said, raising that chin he'd once held in one hand just before he kissed her.

"Are you?" he asked.

Gerty pressed her teeth together, and Mike had his answer. He wasn't going to let her off the hook, though, and he waited. And waited. A smile came to his face as he…waited for her to tell him she was, in fact, single.

# Sneak Peek! HIS FIFTH KISS, Chapter Two

GERTRUDE WHETTSTEIN COULDN'T RESIST THE gravitational pull to Michael Hammond. She hadn't seen him in thirteen years, but the tether that had always drawn her toward him had not diminished. Not even a little bit.

Did he know he stood over six feet tall? He must.

Did he know he exuded passion, charm, and confidence all at the same time? Probably not, as he'd never been arrogant about his handsomeness or his brains—and he had plenty of both. So much, in fact, that Gerty had only passed her math classes in the early years of high school because she could send Mikey the problems, and he'd call her and work through them with her.

After he'd left and gone to college, she'd felt too insignificant to call him. He hadn't reached out to her either, but because of the farm that connected the two of them, she'd known he'd gone to officer flight training and then become a pilot in the Marines. A helicopter pilot.

Did he know that was the sexiest job a man could have? She doubted it. To him, he'd just wanted to first, fly, and second, serve. He'd done both, and she could hardly believe he was standing right there in front of her.

"Gerty," he finally said, chuckling. He dropped his gaze to the ground, and she knew he didn't have any idea how adorable that was. She'd asked him about it before, and he'd said he had no idea being more submissive made him more attractive. He looked up at her without truly moving his head, his eyelashes fluttering. "You know how to make a man wait."

And a man now, he was. She supposed she wasn't the same thirteen-year-old who'd met Michael Hammond out near these stables for the first time either. He'd filled out in the shoulders and chest; he'd grown a couple of inches since she'd seen him last. He had to shave every day now, and it was obvious that this morning, he hadn't.

She'd added a few inches to her height since they'd met for the first time, but her spirit felt just as wild as it always did. She hadn't gained any curves as she'd matured, and she folded her arms and cocked her hip just to give herself some shape that wasn't straight up and down. "Fine," she said. "I'm not seeing anyone right now."

"Then we can go out."

"No," Gerty said instantly. She wasn't sure why she couldn't just give into the fire raging between them.

"I'm...." She swallowed hard. "I just got out of a relationship with someone I really...liked, and I'm not ready to start dating someone again."

Mikey nodded, though he didn't look convinced. "Well, I'll be here all summer," he said, and with that, he stepped past her. Actually went by her like the conversation was over. Done. Like he had nothing else to say to her.

"I'm sorry about your grandfather," she blurted out.

He turned back to her, his face showing shock. He cleared it quickly, swallowed, and said, "Thank you. It's been a few years, but yeah. Thanks."

Gerty missed Chris Hammond greatly as well. "He was my favorite person here," she whispered.

"Oh, don't be sayin' that, Miss Gerty," he said, and he sounded like the men in Texas Gerty had known. He'd never drawled like that before, and she had the distinct impression that he was teasing her. He took a step back to her and reached out with his left hand, the one that wasn't in a sling. He brushed his fingers along hers and finally caught the very tip of her pinky before bringing his hand back to his side. "All this time, I thought I was your favorite person here."

Gerty swallowed, her throat suddenly as narrow as a drinking straw. "You weren't here that much, Mikey."

"I go by Mike now."

"Okay."

"You're still Gerty?"

"Yes, sir," she drawled out.

He chuckled and shook his head. "You know I don't like it when you call me sir."

She couldn't help smiling with him, and with that action, he brightened like she'd made his day. "You'll only be here for the summer?"

He shrugged his good shoulder. "There's a specialist here my parents wanted me to see. They're hoping I can get some more mobility in my shoulder." He sobered, and Gerty switched her gaze to the sling.

"I'm sorry about the accident."

"They happen," he said as if he really was okay with his physical condition.

"You can't ride, I suppose," she said.

"Not yet," he said. "The best I can do is walk alongside the horse."

She looked over the pasture again, drinking in this farm. This place she loved with her whole soul. This place where her father and step-mother lived and were raising Gerty's two half-siblings. She'd always felt at-home here, and that hadn't changed despite her absence.

She wasn't sure if she'd regret spending the afternoon with Mikey—oops, Mike—or not. Her daddy wouldn't be happy about it, but Gerty had come to terms with not being able to please everyone. Sort of.

Her heart ached at the blueness of the sky, at the way she and James used to lie in the fields and laugh, kiss, and watch the world roll by. Then they'd get up, dust off, and go take care of the horses.

Gerty loved horses with her whole soul. They loved her back. Behind her, Tennessee—who she'd originally come out here to see—nickered and called to her. She twisted and looked at him, giving him a look that said, Give me a minute, you rascal.

She looked at Mike again. "What's your schedule like today?"

He swept his good hand in front of him. "This."

"I have to take Tenney out," she said. "Maybe you'd like to walk alongside him."

Mike grinned, those straight white teeth dazzling her. Everything about this man dazzled Gerty, and it always had. "Depends on how far you're goin'," he said. "I think my momma gets nervous when I'm more than fifty feet from her."

Gerty's heart ached for him too. She wasn't great at expressing her emotions, but once Daddy had married Cosette, she'd gotten a lot better at talking about them. She loved her step-mom with her whole heart and soul, as her biological mom had been gone so long, Gerty could hardly remember her. She called Cosette "mom," and she loved her younger brother and sister. Her absence had been hard on all of them, and Gerty regretted that it had taken her so long to see James for what he was.

"You decide," she said to Mike. "I think I'm gonna

ride him out to the retreat cabins and back. It's a good couple of miles."

"I can call Hunt if I need a ride back," he said. "I haven't been doing much physical activity since I've been home."

Gerty wanted to ask him everything. Thirteen-plus years was a long time, and they hadn't kept up. She suddenly had a mouthful of words to tell him, but she managed to turn toward the stable first. "I'll get his tack."

"I'll text my momma so she doesn't worry."

Gerty walked away, her heart pounding beneath her breastbone. Once inside the shady stable, she shook herself. "What are you doing? You vowed you would not date for a solid year. To find yourself. To figure out where you should be."

She'd ended things with James only a month ago. One month. A single turn of the moon through its phases. She'd stayed in Montana with her maternal grandparents for a few weeks, and had she known Mike would be here on this farm when she arrived, Gerty...well, Gerty didn't know what she'd have done.

Daddy had questions she didn't want to answer. Cosette watched her with dark eyes, biding her time. Her siblings didn't much care why Gerty had come back, but Walter wanted to show her his stunt tricks all day long, and Amy had definitely inherited their daddy's penchance for talking and laughing. And laughing and talking. And then talking some more.

She sighed and reached up to rub her forehead. She'd just wanted some peace and quiet, and she'd made an excuse about Tennesee and left the cabin as her parents both watched, each with a very different expression on their face.

Mom had smiled her out of the house and would likely text her a couple of questions, and Daddy had frowned mightily, which meant he'd stay up until Gerty came home, and then he'd make her sit next to him on the couch while they talked it all out.

She honestly didn't mind either of those, but she just wanted solace. "Dear Lord," she whispered as she looked up into the rafters of the stable. "I just need to find some peace. Please."

Everything in her life had been shocked, blitzed out of place, turned around, and then shaken up. She'd quit her job in Montana when she'd discovered James's infidelity, and Molly had been more than willing to take her on this summer.

So she'd come back.

Mike had a specialist to see in the city. So he'd returned.

Was it serendipitous? Should she go out with him?

Her heartbeat ricocheted through her body, as if it were three distinct pieces, each trying to beat on its own. She wasn't sure how to be in a relationship with a shattered heart, and she'd told Mike the truth.

She wasn't ready.

Her phone buzzed, and she looked down at it. Mom: *What time do you think you'll be back? Do you want me to hold dinner, or are you riding for a while?*

*A while*, Gerty thumbed out. She wanted to tell her mother that she was twenty-eight years old and certainly knew how to feed herself. She owned a truck, and a horse trailer, and four horses of her own. Gray and Hunter had been more than gracious to allow her to house them here, and she heard Tenney calling for her again.

Mom: *I'm worried about you.*

"Join the club," Gerty grumbled under her breath.

Mom: *Will you at least tell us about your stay with Carrie and Kyle? Your daddy wants to know.*

*Yes*, Gerty sent back. She'd have to tell her parents everything, she knew, but some of it she didn't know how to put into words quite yet.

Thus, her need for a horseback ride. In Gerty's experience, they could fix almost anything. Maybe not a cheating fiancé, but a lot.

Gerty collected Tenney's tack and took it outside, her arms straining with the weight of his saddle. She was strong, and she knew it. People everywhere had underestimated her, and Gerty had almost gotten used to it. She didn't call attention to herself, and she'd worked two ranches in Texas while simultaneously becoming a barrel racer before she'd gone to Calgary to compete in the Stampede there.

She wasn't rodeo queen material, but she could ride a

horse that was for dang sure. She'd won second place, and then she'd gone to Montana to work at a ranch there. She'd met the owner at the Stampede, and he wanted someone to train his horses to carry riders the way hers did. She'd worked at the Johnson Manor Ranch for the past five years, where she'd met her boss's son, fallen in love, and had expected to get married atop two horses and ride off into the sunset.

She should've known her life wouldn't be that easy. Her own mother had died of a rare blood disease when Gerty was only seven years old.

"Gerty," Mike said, and she looked at him. He reached out and touched her cheek. "Where were you?"

Gerty didn't know how to answer. "I just...I need it to just be quiet," she said. "It's so loud inside my head."

He nodded, his eyes harboring a serious edge. She'd seen it before, right before he kissed her that first time. And the last. He was a fun guy—now a man—and a hard worker. Everything he did seemed effortless, even with his arm in that sling.

Tenney took the bit easily, almost reaching for it, and Gerty swung into his saddle. "You're okay to just walk?"

"Yes'm," he said.

"Oh, boy," she retorted. "You're not a cowboy, Mikey."

"I'm wearin' the hat," he said.

She scoffed and shook her head. "That doesn't make you a cowboy."

"I'm working for Pony Power this summer," he said. "I'll figure it out. It's like riding a bike." They started off, and Mike didn't say anything. Gerty appreciated that, as well as the lilting breeze that kept the worst of the summer temperatures from overheating her. She'd been wearing copious amounts of sunscreen since birth, and her skin didn't seem to know how to hold a hue.

One of her farrier trainers had dubbed her The Pasty Gangster, because Gerty could shoe a horse better and faster than anyone, even the most finnicky of equines. She'd loved wearing the leather aprons and working on horse's hooves. She'd told Molly she could do all of that here, and Molly had readily agreed.

The grasses waved around them, making soft swishing noises. Mike's feet on the ground added to they symphony, as did the heavy snuffle of Tenney's breathing. He wanted to go faster than Mike could, and Gerty held him back. He finally gave in to her after about five minutes, and he settled into a slow walk.

Gerty could relax then too, and the world around her turned soft. She loved the blues and greens together, only broken up by brown wooden fences and the occasional puffy white cloud. "Everything in Montana is a bit washed out compared to here," she said.

"Mm?" Mike didn't ask a full question, but then, he'd never had to. Gerty remembered everything with him, and her heart played leapfrog with itself. He'd been good and kind. He'd been helpful and respectful. If anything, the years he carried now had only added to his allure and his charm and his stunning spirit.

"Yeah," she said, deciding it wouldn't be so bad to talk if he was the one listening. "I worked there for the past several years. There's a lot of beige and yellow in Montana."

"It's not fall here yet," he said.

"Then there's only more color," she said, looking west to the Rocky Mountains. They punctured the sky, and the memories of her and Mikey in Coral Canyon when she'd gone with him for a few weeks in the summer flooded her mind. "The trees are pretty in Montana. Lots of color then, but it's just like that here."

"I bet."

"You ever been to Montana?" she asked.

"No," he said. "Just Wyoming and Colorado. I did college here in Denver, and then Officer Training in Georgia. After that, I did the flight training on a base in Florida."

Gerty hadn't been to any of those places, and she knew Mike had been all around the world. Her doubts piled on top of each other, the inner voice in her head whispering, *Why would he want to go out with you?*

He'd served his country. He'd listed his dreams and done them.

She'd hopped around, grabbing at any opportunity that came her way. She'd learned what she needed to learn whenever the situation called for it. She'd enjoyed her life, and she told herself she couldn't get down on herself for not owning her own farm.

"It's cold in the winter," she said. "My daddy used to tease the cowboys here that they didn't know cold, that they'd never really farmed in the winter." She gave a light laugh. "He was right."

"But you liked it there?" Mike looked up at her.

Gerty gazed down at him, that fire licking up the tether between them. She actually wanted to reach for it and see how badly it would burn her. Daddy had always told her she played too close to the fire, but Gerty didn't know how to be someone else.

"I did," she said. "My mom's parents are there, so I got to see them a lot. I'd go talk to my mom whenever I was just...lost."

Silence fell around them again, and Gerty couldn't help wondering if Mike felt lost right now too. "What are you going to do after the summer ends?" she asked. "Work at HMC?"

"I don't know." His voice reminded her of something haunted, and it came out too low. "I have a business degree, but I...don't know."

"I understand that," Gerty said quietly. And she did.

They reached the retreat, and Gerty slid from the saddle. She looped Tenney's reins over the fence and looked at Mike. Something zipped and arced between them, and Gerty got transported back in time about fifteen years.

Her first kiss. Right here behind this cabin, where later, Gray had arranged summer camp retreats for teens. Gerty had helped with those too, and she had loved her life here at the Hammond Family Farm.

"Do you remember my favorite food?" she asked.

"Assuming your taste buds haven't changed," Mike said, grinning and putting a bit of swagger into his voice. Oh, the man was a flirt when he wanted to be. "It's a good, sloppy, barbecue brisket sandwich."

For some reason, the way he described it made Gerty laugh. She tilted her head back and faced the heavens, feeling freer and lighter than she had since learning about her fiancé's misdeeds.

"You got it." She leveled her gaze at Mike. "Guess who put one on their menu, courtesy of my daddy?"

"Hilde?" he guessed.

Gerty nodded, feeling quite flirtatious herself. She took a step toward him and ran her fingers up the front of his shirt, bumping them over the straps of the sling. "Maybe we should go get one sometime."

"Yeah," he said, his voice somewhat hoarse. "Maybe we should."

She grinned at him, danced ahead of him, and turned around. "All right. I'm gonna go check the cupboards for some of those gross granola bars. You find us a shady spot to sit, and I'll come find you." They'd done this before, because Gerty could open cabinets and sneak through a house without leaving any evidence that she'd been there.

Gerty hurried off to do that while Mike laughed at her, and as she entered the cabin which had sat dormant for the winter and spring, she couldn't help feeling like a new door had just opened in her life. Sure, maybe she was like this cabin. Maybe she needed some TLC after a long season of darkness. Maybe she needed to be aired out and cleaned up. Maybe she needed to get a coat of fresh paint and some new curtains.

Maybe then, she'd be all fixed up to fall in love again.

As she searched through the empty cupboards, she wondered how many other women Mike had kissed. She wondered if he'd ever been in love. She wondered if God had really brought them back to this farm, at this time, so they could have their second chance.

Empty-handed, she left the cabin and started looking for Mike. There was only one thing to do—well, two really.

Heal. Gerty needed to heal first.

Then, she'd find out if she and Mike could take the fire between them and hold it in their hands without getting burned.

———

***Read it today by scanning the QR code below with your phone!***

**His First Love (Book 1):** She broke up with him a decade ago. He's back in town after finishing a degree at MIT, ready to start his job at the family company. Can Hunter and Molly find their way through their pasts to build a future together?

**His Second Chance (Book 2):** They broke up over twenty years ago. She's lost everything when she shows up at the farm in Ivory Peaks where he works. Can Matt and Gloria heal from their pasts to find a future happily-ever-after with each other?

**His Third Try (Book 3):** He moved to Ivory Peaks with his daughter to start over after a devastating break-up. She's never had a meaningful relationship with a man, especially a cowboy. Can Boone and Cosette help each other heal enough to build a happily-ever-after...and a family?

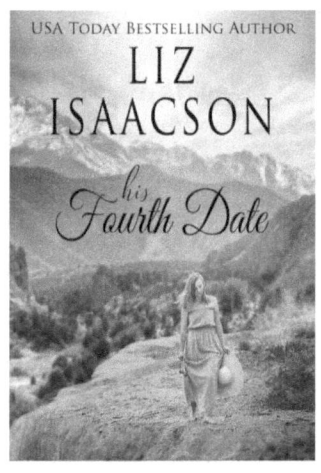

**His Fourth Date (Book 4):** Their relationship has been nothing but loose goats, a leaking roof, and her complete humiliation after he pays her mortgage so she won't lose her farm. Travis wants to go back in time and start over with Poppy, but he doesn't know how. Can a small town speed-dating event get their second chance off on the right foot?

**His Fifth Kiss (Book 5):** They once had a few summers together. Now, Michael Hammond is back in town after a devastating injury overseas. He's looking to reset and recover...not to fall in love. But with Gertrude Whettstein also back at the farm, can Gerty and Mike make their second chance romance into a happily-ever-after?

**His Sixth Sweetheart (Book 6):** She's had a crush on him for decades. He's finally in a place where he feels ready to date the boss's daughter. Can Cord and Jane take their relationship to the next level without getting burned?

**His Seventh Stop (Book 7):** He's a seasoned cowboy on a delivery mission. She's a resilient hobby farm owner braving the winter storm. Can Keith and Lindsay forge a bond in the heart of a tempest and find love in the calm that follows?

**His Eighth Ride (Book 8):** Tag has secretly admired Opal from afar. He even went so far as to ask her out, but the timing was all off, and now he's just awkward around his best friend's little sister. Then, she finds Tag in a precarious situation as he's breaking a horse. **Can their unexpected reunion mend the fences between them and finally lead them to the forever love they've been waiting for?**

**His Ninth Promise (Book 9):** At home on the Hammond Family Farm, where gypsy souls and rodeo dreams collide, Tucker's heart has been beating for Bobbie Jo. But with her heart set on a distant love and Tucker searching for something more, their paths seemed destined to cross but never converge. **Can he stick it out for another ride if the promise is coming home to Bobbie Jo?**

**His Tenth Dance (Book 10):** Mission has carried the weight of his past for a long time, and letting someone in feels like a risk. But maybe, just maybe, Kristie is worth it. When his granddad tells her about his secret crush, sparks fly between them, walls come down, and love might just get a second chance to take the lead... if Kristie and Mission are willing to take a leap of faith.

**Colton (Book 1):** All the maid at Whiskey Mountain Lodge wants for her birthday is a handsome cowboy billionaire. And Colton can make that wish come true—if only he hadn't escaped to Coral Canyon after being left at the altar...

**Wes (Book 2):** She broke up with him to date another man...who broke her heart. He's a former CEO with nothing to do who can't get her out of his head. Can Wes and Bree find a way toward happily-ever-after at Whiskey Mountain Lodge?

**Gray (Book 3):** She's best friends with the single dad cowboy's brother and has watched two friends find love with the sexy new cowboys in town. When Gray Hammond comes to Whiskey Mountain Lodge with his son, will Elise finally get her own happily-ever-after with one of the Hammond brothers?

**Cy (Book 4):** A cowboy billionaire beast, the woman he asks out in front of everyone, and the family traditions that softens his heart and bring Cy and Patsy together.

**Ames (Book 5):** A cowboy billionaire who's rough around the edges, the woman he ghosted last Christmas, and their second chance at happily-ever-after.

**Graham (Book 1):** A cowboy returning to his hometown—and the best friend he left a dozen years before. This Christmas, can Graham and Laney build a family and find their happily-ever-after?

**Eli (Book 2):** A man who's traded his power suits for cowboy boots has feelings for his nanny...can Eli and Meg find love this Christmas?

**Andrew (Book 3):** A public relations director who moonlights as a cowboy, the woman who dislikes him and his energy company, and the job that could bring Andrew and Becca together...

**Beau (Book 4):** A cowboy lawyer turned bodyguard...including the celebrity country singer looking for a quick and quiet resolution to her problems. Can opposites Beau and Lily really attract this Christmas?

**Todd (Book 5):** A billionaire bull rider and the pretty country music singer he's boarding with...Can Todd and VI make the best of a difficult situation and maybe even find love this Christmas?

**Liam (Book 6):** A holiday bachelor auction brings a cowboy billionaire doctor and a country music star together. Will Rose and Liam be able to navigate their opposites to find a future together?

**Finn (Book 7):** Her sons want her to be happy, but she's too old to be set up on a blind date...isn't she? Can Amanda and Finn make their blind date into lasting love?

**Zach (Book 8):** Celia is finally ready to date again—but not the man whose family has a century-old feud with hers... Can Celia and Zach really make their *Romeo and Juliet* love story end in love and not tragedy?

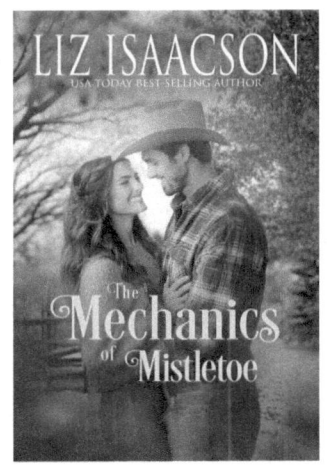

**The Mechanics of Mistletoe (Book 1):** Bear Glover can be a grizzly or a teddy, and he's always thought he'd be just fine working his generational family ranch and going back to the ancient homestead alone. But his crush on Samantha Benton won't go away. She's a genius with a wrench on Bear's tractors...and his heart. Can he tame his wild side and get the girl, or will he be left broken-hearted this Christmas season?

**The Horsepower of the Holiday (Book 2):** Ranger Glover has worked at Shiloh Ridge Ranch his entire life. The cowboys do everything from horseback there, but when he goes to town to trade in some trucks, somehow Oakley Hatch persuades him to take some ATVs back to the ranch. (Bear is NOT happy.)

She's a former race car driver who's got Ranger all revved up... Can he remember who he is and get Oakley to slow down enough to fall in love, or will there simply be too much horsepower in the holiday this year for a real relationship?

LIZ ISAACSON

USA TODAY BEST-SELLING AUTHOR

The
Construction
of Cheer

**The Construction of Cheer (Book 3):** Bishop Glover is the youngest brother, and he usually keeps his head down and gets the job done. When Montana Martin shows up at Shiloh Ridge Ranch looking for work, he finds himself inventing construction projects that need doing just to keep her coming around. (Again, Bear is NOT happy.) She wants to build her own construction firm, but she ends up carving a place for herself inside Bishop's heart. Can he convince her *he's* all she needs this Christmas season, or will her cheer rest solely on the success of her business?

**The Secret of Santa (Book 4):** He's a fun-loving cowboy with a heart of gold. She's the woman who keeps putting him on hold. Can Ace and Holly Ann make a relationship work this Christmas?

**The Gift of Gingerbread (Book 5):** She's the only daughter in the Glover family. He's got a secret that drove him out of town years ago. Can Arizona and Duke find common ground and their happily-ever-after this Christmas?

**The Harmony of Holly (Book 6):** He's as prickly as his name, but the new woman in town has caught his eye. Can Cactus shelve his temper and shed his cowboy hermit skin fast enough to make a relationship with Willa work?

**The Chemistry of Christmas (Book 7):** He's the black sheep of the family, and she's a chemist who understands formulas, not emotions. Can Preacher and Charlie take their quirks and turn them into a strong relationship this Christmas?

**The Delivery of Decor (Book 8):** When he falls, he falls hard and deep. She literally drives away from every relationship she's ever had. Can Ward somehow get Dot to stay this Christmas?

**The Blessing of Babies (Book 9):** Don't miss out on a single moment of the Glover family saga in this bridge story linking Ward and Judge's love stories!

The Glovers love God, country, dogs, horses, and family. Not necessarily in that order. ;)

Many of them are married now, with babies on the way, and there are lessons to be learned, forgiveness to be had and given, and new names coming to the family tree in southern Three Rivers!

**The Networking of the Nativity (Book 10):** He's had a crush on her for years. She doesn't want to date until her daughter is out of the house. Will June take a change on Judge when the success of his Christmas light display depends on her networking abilities?

**The Yes at Yuletide (Book 11):** If they can't find a way to bridge the gap between their aspirations and their love, this winter wedding could be the last holiday they spend side by side. Will Ollie and Aurora discover a path that keeps their hearts—and their dreams—together, or will this Christmas be the beginning of a new kind of goodbye?

**The Wrangling of the Wreath (Book 12):** He's been so busy trying to find Miss Right. She's been right in front of him the whole time. This Christmas, can Mister and Libby take their relationship out of the best friend zone?

**The Hope of Her Heart (Book 13):** She's the only Glover without a significant other. He's been searching for someone who can love him *and* his daughter. Can Etta and August make a meaningful connection this Christmas?

**Rhett (Book 1):** To save her business, she'll have to risk her heart. She needs a husband to be credible as a matchmaker. He wants to help a neighbor. **Will their fake marriage take them out of the friend zone?**

**Tripp (Book 2):** She needs a husband to keep her son. He's wanted to take their relationship to the next level, but she's always pushing him away. Will their trivial tie take them all the way to happily-ever-after?

**Liam (Book 3):** She's desperate to save her ranch. He wants to help her any way he can. Will their invented I-Do open doors that have previously been closed and lead to a happily-ever-after for both of them?

**Jeremiah (Book 4):** He wants to prove to his brothers that he's not broken. She just wants him. Will a fake marriage heal him or push her further away?

**Wyatt (Book 5):** To get her inheritance, she needs a husband. He's wanted to fly with her for ages. Can their pretend pledge turn into something real?

**Skyler (Book 6):** She needs a new last name to stay in school. He's willing to help a fellow student. Can this wanna-be wife show the playboy that some things should be taken seriously?

**Micah (Book 7):** They were just actors auditioning for a play. The marriage was just for the audition – until a clerical error results in a legal marriage. Can these two ex-lovers negotiate this new ground between them and achieve new roles in each other's lives?

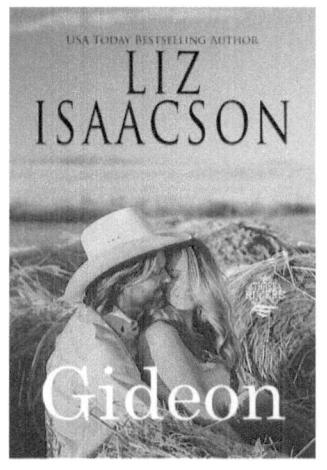

**Gideon (Book 8):** It's 1971, and Gideon Walker is on the cutting edge of all the technology coming out of Texas. He has big dreams and wants to make something of himself. Then he meets Penny Aarons, and everything changes. He only has eyes for her, but she's got plans and dreams of her own...

Read this origin romance for Momma and Daddy from the Seven Sons series today!

# About Liz

Liz Isaacson writes inspirational romance, usually set in Texas, or Wyoming, or anywhere else horses and cowboys exist. She lives in Utah, where she writes full-time, takes her two dogs to the park everyday, and eats a lot of veggies while writing. Find her on her website, along with all of her pen names, at feelgoodfictionbooks.com.

www.ingramcontent.com/pod-product-compliance
Lightning Source LLC
Chambersburg PA
CBHW050608110726
47899CB00001B/26